Curse of the Coral Bride

www.immanionpress.wox.org

Curse of the Coral Bride

Brian Stableford

IMMANION
PRESS
Stafford, England

Curse of the Coral Bride
By Brian Stableford
© 2005

Cover Design Ade Daniel
Art Direction and Typesetting by Gabriel Strange
Editor Donna Scott

Set in Minion Web 9pt

0 9 8 7 6 5 4 3 2 1

An Immanion Press Edition
http://www.immanionpress.wox.org/
info@immanionpress.wox.org

ISBN 1-9048-5313-7

Curse of the Coral Bride

Prologue

Brian Stableford

Lysariel, a King Unknown to Himself

1

Legend informs us that there was a time, unimaginably long ago, when human beings were far more intimately acquainted with their past than their future. Not only did they have the beginnings of a history, inscribed in books and other records of a more versatile kind, but they had only to look around them--or, at most, to dig shallow pits in the soil of their fields--in order to discover all manner of relics of the past. The past in question, being of exceedingly short duration, was easily reconstructed into a single story. The story was doubtless polluted by many myths and misconceptions, but it was within the grasp of the imagination in a way that our past is not.

Legend also informs us that a seed of truth lies at the root of all its manifold fabrications and fabulations, but that is a manifest lie. In this particular instance, however, logic agrees with legend in judging that there must indeed have been human beings at the dawn of the first civilization whose past could be measured in mere millennia while their future--unknown to them--was to be measured in billions of years.

The relics that littered the world in the infancy of that primal humankind must have given the first civilized humans a limited, but nevertheless intriguing, insight into those of their own ancestral societies which had left neither history nor legend behind. There may well have been relics even of the creatures that had lived in the world before the advent of humankind, since the very first creatures had crept out of the oceanic womb of the world to colonize the barren continents.

In those days, logic assures us, human beings could only have had the slightest inkling of the future that awaited them, as yet unmade. They must have calculated soon enough that the sun, whose fortunate light was the animator of their world, might continue to glow for thousands of millions of years. Being short-lived creatures, however--legend and logic

9

agree in insisting that they must have been almost as prone as common men of today to premature decease--they would have found it direly difficult to expand their hopes and dreams to encompass such a span. The majority among them probably had arrogance enough to think of their own brief prehistory as an epic of sorts, but only the tiniest minority could have glimpsed in their imagination the most infinitesimal fragment of the Epic of the Humankinds to come.

The Revelations of Suomynona, the Last Prophet

Lysariel took the deepest breath of which he was capable, and plunged his head beneath the surface for a fourth time. Irritated by Triasymon's anxiety and constant warnings against diving too deep, he was determined to show his uncle that he had no need of such tender and restrictive care. Before the water cut off the sound he heard the first syllable of yet another shouted instruction, but he did not want to hear what he was being told to do. He wanted to prove to Triasymon--and Manazzoryn too--that he was no longer a child, and was more than ready to surpass the limitations of childhood.

Lysariel was 2,179 days old--a boy's age, in the reckoning of most men, but a man's age in the reckoning of most boys.

He dived, determined this time to reach the bottom of the trench. This time, he would touch the sea-bed beyond the reef for the first time, and snatch up whatever came to hand as a trophy to prove his courage and his endurance.

Lysariel was confident, and full of pride, even though he had not the slightest notion that he was a king.

He swam down into the dark water, kicking his legs to drive himself ever deeper. When he had first dived in the water had been full of light, but the darkness waiting below him was already deepening from green to black. Lysariel knew that Triasymon had brought his two nephews out here in order to provide a lesson in fear. The old man had intended to demonstrate that the shallow and placid waters within the reef were unusually hospitable, and that the ocean beyond was a murderous monster to be treated with the utmost respect and discretion. Triasymon wanted to fill him with a healthy dread of rough water and dark depths-- but that was not the lesson Lysariel intended to take with him. Lysariel was determined to make it clear to his uncle and his brother alike that he was not a man to be intimidated by turbulent water or predatory fish, and that even the deepest darkness held no terrors for him.

Lysariel did not look back once as he propelled himself downwards. He refused to waste time and impetus in seeking reassurance that the faint glow of the sunlit surface was still there. He fixed his attention on the murk below. Within the reef, the sea-bed was always visible even from the surface, swarming with dainty and brightly-coloured fish; he and Manazzoryn had learned to swim in such placid waters almost before they could walk. This was very different; in the trench on the outer rim of the reef it was very easy to dive so deep that the turbid water all but eclipsed the sun's roseate light, without getting anywhere near the bottom, and the living creatures that lurked in the lower depths of the abyss were by no means dainty or colourful.

The fishermen of Harstpoint cast their drift-nets for surface-dwelling shoals, and they never used lines or trawling-nets that were capable of plumbing the trench, but they sometimes picked up trench-dwelling fish that had drifted closer to the surface than usual in pursuit of prey. Triasymon had occasionally taken the trouble to bring the uglier ones to the boys' attention, citing them as evidence of the monstrousness of the creatures that lived at the bottom of the underwater cliff. According to Triasymon, the predators that fed on the shoals--sharklongs and whirligigs--were meek by comparison with the predators of the lightless depths, but Lysariel was not easily intimidated. He had seen the scars carried by men bitten by sharklongs or stung by whirligigs, and knew such attacks to be rare. He could not imagine that the monsters of the deep were any more ready to attack a man, or that they would be any more deadly if they did. In any case, such fear as he had was counterbalanced by a curious kind of greed. It was in the dark depths, he had been assured by older men than Triasymon, of a more imaginative bent, that the most precious corals could be found.

Perhaps valuable corals had grown within the reef as well as without, in the distant past, but there were none to be found in shallow water nowadays. Lysariel could see the logic of that absence easily enough; their visibility must have made precious corals on the inner face of the reef easy to find and easy to harvest, by divers who had little or nothing to fear in cutting them loose. The precious corals that extended down the outer face of the reef, by contrast, would be far more difficult to locate and far more difficult to secure. Nowadays, the only treasures worthy of the name that were accessible from Harstpoint must be cloaked by darkness and danger, and thus reserved to the brave and the bold. Lysariel was just young enough to dream of finding some such treasure, and just old enough to believe that he might have sufficient strength, ingenuity and luck to take firm hold of it if he did. So he went further and further down, into thick black water whose avid chill gripped his body like a vice--but his outstretched hand met nothing solid.

He had no idea how far he still had to go, but he ignored the growing discomfort in his lungs. Triasymon, in the midst of all his careful warnings, had mentioned that it was possible for a man to touch the bottom of the trench, if only he were firm enough in his purpose and strong enough to hold his breath. His uncle had told him this in order to reassure him that he need not panic if things went badly wrong--but his uncle did not know him as well as he thought he did.

11

Brian Stableford

Lysariel knew that he had to conserve enough breath and enough strength to resurface, and that he must not come up too quickly, but he would not allow himself to be anxious about that. His younger brother Manazzoryn was the anxious one. Manazzoryn always stayed on the surface long enough to hear Triasymon's commands, and never disobeyed them, but Lysariel was very conscious of being the older of the two, the one destined by birth to be the leader, the adventurer, the pioneer. So Lysariel the adventurer went down into the gloom, glorying in the simplicity of it all.

The darkness seemed absolute now, as if it had no limit in any direction--but Lysariel knew that the appearance was treacherous. No more than forty armlengths to his right there was a wall of ancient rock: the natural rampart on which the reef was constructed. That rock-face could hurt him if he swam into a protruding spur, and it was not impossible, even if he stayed well clear of it, that something dangerous might emerge from it. Triasymon had told him--in yet another hopeless attempt to cultivate his anxieties--that the cliff was pitted with countless caves and burrows, some of them natural and others carefully excavated by living creatures. Such coverts were the lairs of a multitude of sea-creatures, most of them harmless but some few exceedingly dangerous. On the other hand, Lysariel thought, those same pits and cracks might also be host to rare corals, most of them worthless but some few very valuable indeed. Even so, Triasymon's injunction not to stray too close to the rock-face was one that Lysariel intended to obey, until he had good grounds to be confident that he could reach the bottom of the trench whenever he wished, and work there with as much comfort as any man alive.

It was because he still conserved this cautious intention that Lysariel was shocked to observe the red light filtering through the water from the direction of the underwater cliff. He knew immediately that the light could not be visible in these turbid depths unless it were very close at hand--perhaps no more than three or four armlengths away. Lysariel knew that he ought to kick away from the faint and fugitive light immediately. Perhaps he would have done so had his right hand not touched the sea-bottom at that very moment.

The sea-bed was barer than he had expected, given the thickness of the particles suspended in the water. There was nothing immediately to hand that would qualify as a trophy of his victory, so he let his body drift a little further down while he moved his outstretched hand in slow arcs, casting about for a pebble or a mobile shellfish--and in the meantime, he looked towards the light.

The glow was diffuse, like a fire obscured by fog, and there was no shape or shadow within it that Lysariel could actually see, but there was a strange allure in the fragile luminosity: something which acted upon his imagination and his mind. The suggestion it made to him could not be

12

formulated in words, but he knew that he was subject to a temptation...perhaps even a kind of invitation. The exotic light entered into his open eyes, unrivalled by that of the sun or the fugitive stars. It was, he reminded himself, the only light he had, and he was its only mindful observer--perhaps the only mindful observer it had attracted for a very long time.

Lysariel knew that the most precious coral of all was red. How much more precious, he wondered, would coral be that glowed red, with its own internal fire?

That was when he realised that he had lingered too long. Quite suddenly, he felt perfectly certain that he could no longer get back to the surface. He was convinced that his lungs would not hold his breath, and his legs would not keep their strength long enough to propel him all the way back to the surface.

I shall die, Lysariel thought. *Pride and ambition have carried me too far.*

He still had no trophy, but he abandoned his groping and turned himself around. Somewhere in the turn he lost sight of the light, and mere seconds afterwards he was overtaken by the inconvenient fear that he had lost his sense of direction entirely, to the extent that he did not even know which way the surface was.

Belatedly, Lysariel discovered the fear that Triasymon had brought him out beyond the reef to find and to face. He felt panic rise in his breast as his lungs began to protest at their ill-treatment. He felt light-headed, almost delirious--but then the panic died as he felt a renewed sense of certainty that was much more generous in its implications.

It was as if a voice speaking directly into his thoughts said to him: "You are safe with me. You will always be safe with me."

He felt certain, now, that he was safe. He knew, now, not merely where he was but what he could do.

He felt as if some kindly creature of the deep--some lustful mermaid, perhaps--had taken him in a subtle and tender embrace, and had pushed him in exactly the direction he needed to go.

He swam, not slowly but not too rapidly either, and he kept swimming very steadily until the green glow of the surface welcomed his eyes again. He knew that he ought to feel glad, but he was unable to muster the slightest delight or relief, partly because he no longer had the slightest doubt that he would be safe and partly because the green colour of filtered sunlight seemed so weak and so unhealthy by comparison with the power and virility of the red glow that had entered into his mind like a possessive passion. When his head burst through the surface again and his lungs let loose their toxic cargo in order to draw in fresh air, Lysariel wanted to shout out in exultation, to proclaim his manhood, but the impetus simply was not there, and he drifted in silence on the passing waves while the huge vermilion eye of the dying sun stared implacably down upon him. Several minutes passed before an angry and fearful Triasymon grabbed him around the waist, and steered him back towards the little boat where Manazzoryn was waiting for them both.

"You fool!" Triasymon cried, when he was sure that his nephew was breathing. "You might have drowned!"

Lysariel made no reply--not because he lacked the strength to form a coherent speech, but because he had nothing to say. For the first time in his life, he had a secret to keep.

Legend assures us that the great majority of the multitudinous humankinds who preceded us as dwellers on the surface of the Earth were united into global civilizations. So vast is our prehistory, and so vague our legendary lore, that we have no reliable means of estimating the number of the exceptions, but logic assures us that our remotest ancestors must have been among them. We may be sure, therefore, that one of the many things our ultimate humankind has in common with primal humankind is the unhappy and undignified distinction of being so fragmented that its petty nations are perpetually engaged in games of war and conquest. There is, however, one important difference between our conflicts and theirs, which is that they must have fought in order to win objectives that were at least attainable, if not actually worthwhile. We have no such privilege.

Our wars are as futile as every other action and project in which we engage. Their combatants know this as well as anyone, and probably better than men of a peaceful and scholarly disposition, but it is no disincentive. If anything, the reverse is the case; men who know that there is nothing to be gained by violence may draw the corollary conclusion that there is nothing to be lost by it. Our primal ancestors must have been more discreet in their calculations than those of us who are inclined to games of conquest. No one knows the true extent of the Epic of the Humankinds, but no matter how many tales and verses it contains it cannot contain very many warriors as easily-disposed to recklessness as ours.

The best breeding-grounds of such warriors are not, as might be expected, the nations clustered on the seven Ultimate Continents which have conveniently disputable borders; they are, in fact, those nations that

15

are islands challengingly demarcated by troublesome seas. The fertile plains where nomad herdsmen are locked in eternal conflict with settled agriculturalists cannot compete with island chains as arenas of empire-building, for the simple reason that the ocean is so overfull of fish that a man need only labour upon the sea for two days in ten to secure his living, whereas a tiller of the soil must labour at least twice as long. In addition to this fundamental reason, small islands are ready-packaged by nature as units of conquest, and there never was a broad sea that did not encourage the piratical temperament and its associated habits. In all the ultimate world, therefore, there is no milieu quite as conducive to violent recklessness as the archipelago of Ambriocyatha in the New Tethys Sea.

The maps I have consulted disagree, as maps are ever wont to do, as to the exact number of Ambriocyatha's constituent islands, but my own preferred total is seven hundred and thirty-nine. The prophetic estimate I deem to be the most trustworthy suggests that four hundred and three will still be inhabited by human beings when the sun consumes them all, and we might as well accept the figure as it is of no particular relevance or consequence. The empires that flourish in such regions as Ambriocyatha are always of short duration, and their decay always inspires their pirate predators with insane delusions of grandeur. The last of them all, the Empire of Yura--the only one to have fallen within living memory--was certainly no exception.

(When I employ the term "living memory" I refer, of course, to the span attainable by those who term themselves the Tithonian Elite, which is conventionally estimated at seven years, rather than the single year that tradition calculates as the average life-expectancy of a common man. Men who reach the fullest extent of their span may, of course, complete their second year and embark upon a third, but few can contrive such longevity in a world as plague-ridden and as inclined to violence as ours.)

The Revelations of Suomynona, the Last Prophet

Lysariel and Manazzoryn were the orphaned sons of a fisherman named Alveyadey. Alveyadey's father and grandfather had been fishermen before him; the family had always lived in a meagre cottage, situated close to the northernmost tip of the Harstpoint peninsula, which projected from the northern coast of the island of Scleracina, one of the northernmost islands in the Ambriocyathan archipelago. If a man were to sail due north from the extremity of Harstpoint, Triasymon had once told his nephews, he would not touch land again until he ran ashore on the barren strand of the polar continent--although he could find far more promising shores in the east, the west and the bountiful south.

Triasymon's voice had been tinged with regret when he said that, because he had no boat capable of making such a journey. His brother's fishing-boat, which had been handed down through a dozen generations--although hardly a spar of its original hull remained unreplaced--had been lost at sea in a savage storm, not long after Manazzoryn's birth. The boys' mother, Astroma, had looked to her unmarried brother-in-law for support when her husband died, and Triasymon had provided it willingly enough. Lysariel believed that Triasymon would have married Astroma had she not died soon afterwards herself, unable or unwilling to fight off the effects of some random infection. The fact that he had not married their mother had not prevented Triasymon from being a second father to Lysariel and his brother.

Lysariel had been convinced while he was still a child that he could remember his father's face and kindly manner as well as his mother's smile and the gentleness of her touch. Now that he was a child no longer, however, he knew that all such supposed memories had probably been manufactured from the fine fabric of regret. Triasymon was the only guardian and educator he had ever known.

Lysariel took it for granted that Triasymon had kept and educated Manazzoryn and himself as well as he could, even though he had no boat and could not fish the waters beyond the barrier reefs that formed a ragged protective wall around Scleracina's northern coast. Triasymon had taught him to cast lines from various vantage-points along the peninsula, and to collect shellfish as the tide retreated from its western shore in pursuit of the setting sun, but Lysariel had never valued such lessons nearly as much as he valued lessons in diving.

A good diver equipped with a sharp knife and a powerful lever could gather sedentary shellfish that a follower of the tide could never reach; he could also--if he were fortunate enough--find saleable specimens among the manifold species of coral that constituted the outlying reefs and clung to the walls of the crevices and sea-caves scattered along the shore. It was a diver that the young Lysariel was ambitious to be, and no ordinary plunderer of the quiet waters within the reef. Lysariel wanted to be a hero among divers: a man of universally-acknowledged prowess. He said as much to Triasymon more than once, but he was never convinced that Triasymon took him seriously--until the day that he first touched the sea-bed beside the Dark Cliff, and saw the red light that shone mysteriously within its depths.

When he had recovered his strength and composure, however, Lysariel found that his uncle was still angry with him.

"Are you an imbecile, to take such risks?" Triasymon demanded. "Are you so determined to kill yourself that you take no heed at all of my warnings?"

"I did not hear your warning, uncle," Lysariel said, resentfully, as he lay back in the stern of the boat, letting the heat of the ruddy sun dispel the deepwater chill that had crept almost unheeded into his flesh.

"More fool you," Triasymon said, standing over Lysariel while Manazzoryn plied the oars. "The one action more stupid than failing to heed a warning is refusing to wait long enough to hear it. You have no

17

idea how much danger there is in those dark depths, and you should not have gone down there. You should have listened to me, but you did not even wait to hear what I had to say."

Lysariel was not pleased to be scolded in this way. He believed that he deserved credit for his accomplishment. "I am a good diver," he said. "In time, I shall be a far better diver than you ever were. You give out too many warnings--so many that their force is lost on others, although they have made a coward out of you."

Lysariel heard Manazzoryn draw in his breath as that insult was voiced, and he half-expected to be slapped hard, but Triasymon seemed more hurt than offended by the slur.

"Perhaps you will be a better diver than I am, one day," Triasymon replied, tartly, "but you will have to live long enough to acquire the skill. You will not do that if you continue to behave as recklessly as you did today. A man who knows his limitations is no coward--and a man who thinks he has none issues daily invitations to disaster."

Lysariel looked to his brother for support, as was his habit, but Manazzoryn seemed more than usually reluctant to offer it. "You frightened me, Lysariel," his younger brother said. "I thought you would never come up--that you were lost."

"I was not in any difficulty," Lysariel retorted. "Since I cannot be a fisherman, I shall be a diver, and since I must be a diver, I shall be the best diver in all Scleracina. I shall train myself as hard as I can, and I shall be brave. If I invite disaster, I suppose I shall have to answer when it comes to call--but I shall invite good fortune too, and the means to make myself rich."

Triasymon sighed, but he did not seem entirely displeased with his nephew's boldness. "When men dive into the sea carrying knives with untrustworthy blades and shafts of fragile wood," he told Lysariel, not unkindly, "they put themselves at a severe disadvantage relative to the creatures that compete with them for prey. A man has nothing to fear, even from the most dreadful sharklongs, the deadliest whirligigs and the bulkiest chthuloids, if he has a good boat to carry him on the surface of their realm, from which he may lower sturdy nets and on whose deck he may wield strong gaffs and heavy hammers. Even if he is threatened by megatopes or leviathans he may set his craft a-dancing with clever use of sail, hurling fierce harpoons in the meantime. A man in a boat, with a crew to command, is master of the element--but a diver is a ready-made victim, a poorly-defended morsel for any one of a hundred horrid things. Are you really sure that you want to be a diver, Lysariel? Are you certain that you want to take such risks?"

"I suppose I would rather have a good strong boat," Lysariel conceded, sitting up and pulling on his shirt, "if there were any chance of getting one. Given that there is not, I must make what I can of myself."

"But we might get a boat, one day," Manazzoryn put in. "Might we not, uncle?"

Lysariel saw Triasymon frown then, as if that were a question whose implications he did not like to consider. "When I was your age," he said, "there were hundreds of boats in Harstpoint. There were three skilled boat-builders within half a day's walk. When successful men replaced their vessels, they often gave away the ones for which they had no further use, on the promise of a dividend of future catches. But that was in the days before Orlu and Viragan began to build their fleets. All the boat-builders in Scleracina are lodged in Clarassour nowadays, and there are barely three dozen vessels fishing from the point."

While Triasymon was speaking Manazzoryn had brought the boat to a narrow passage through which it could re-enter the calmer waters between the reef and the shore, and Triasymon took up a gaff from the belly of the boat in order to use it as a lever, helping Manazzoryn to steer the boat through the dangerous gap.

"Who are Orlu and Viragan, exactly?" Lysariel wanted to know, when he had digested the import of Triasymon's reply. "I've heard the names a hundred times, spoken with awe or disgust, but I have no idea how they came to be such a power in the land."

"The empire was much stronger in the old days," Triasymon told him. "The governor issued his orders knowing that any disobedience could and would be punished--but there has been trouble in Yura for thousands of days now, and its fleet is not the irresistible force it once was. The Yurans still reckon Orlu and Viragan common pirates, but those who live under the Yuran yoke have a different estimate of Yura's outlaws. I believe they prefer to term themselves merchant adventurers nowadays, and are treated with caution and respect in the neighbouring islands because no one expects the emperor to send a fleet to destroy them. They have been rivals in the past, but Yura has always been their common adversary and they have always helped one another against the more powerful foe. Now, if the rumours are to be trusted, Yura is becoming their common ally rather than their adversary. If so, their fortunes are made and they will be more inclined to act in concert."

"Why would the emperor become their ally?" Manazzoryn asked.

"What the empire cannot be bothered to crush, it adapts to its own purposes," Triasymon said. "If it has been decided in Yura that it would require too much effort to put an end to their adventures, the emperor's captains will probably try to make friends with Orlu and Viragan, taking a cut of their profits in return for allowing them to work unhindered. At any rate, they seem to have been free to conduct their affairs much as they wish for nearly a year now. Under the spur of their former rivalry their fleets have grown from a handful of vessels apiece to more than a hundred; neither one wishes to be outdone by the other, although they are too wise in their ambition to turn their competition into violent conflict.

19

They have set all the boat-builders in the realm to work for them, and the fishing-fleets hereabouts have suffered. They have been decreasing in numbers for some time, although their catches have improved for lack of competition."

Lysariel was already bored with this lesson in history, but his brother was still curious. Whenever a conversation turned to the folk who lived in distant Clarassour, Manazzoryn was always anxious to know more. Having recently attained two thousand days of age, the younger brother was beginning to take a keen interest in the configuration of his society and his world, and he had more patience than Lysariel.

"Will there be a rebellion, if Orlu and Viragan continue to grow more powerful?" Manazzoryn asked. "Will the governor be deposed, do you think?"

"I wouldn't know about that," Triasymon confessed. "I don't take much notice of political talk. But I doubt that Orlu and Viragan would go to war. What would be the point?"

"Because the world's about to end, you mean?" Manazzoryn said.

"I don't know about that, either," Triasymon replied. "What I mean is that somebody has to sit on the so-called throne in Clarassour's so-called palace, and it really doesn't matter much to ordinary folk who it is. If Orlu and Viragan can do what they like, and are as rich as anyone could reasonably want to be, why should they bother to go to war to get rid of the governor? Why should they take risks when they already have everything they need?"

"Because they can," Lysariel put in, moved by lingering resentment. "If they can do what they want, why shouldn't they take a few risks? You might be the kind of man who always leaves things as they are unless you can see a powerful reason for changing them--but that's not the only kind of man there is. You might be content to dive inside the reef for meagre harvests of shellfish, so long as you can keep starvation at bay--but I'm not. I want to be a real diver, and I will be, no matter what the risks might be."

Triasymon frowned, but made no reply; Lysariel was mildly surprised to have won the argument so easily, but congratulated himself on having made so powerful a case. The sun's heat had warmed him now, and he had begun to luxuriate in its ruddy glow. Why, he wondered, was the surface of the sea so palely green when seen from below? Why was it not as pinkly red as the sun's face, or as lushly crimson as the light he had glimpsed in the depths of the trench?

"If they have so many ships now," Manazzoryn said, pensively, "Orlu and Viragan must need men to crew them, and masters to command the crews. There must be opportunities for seamen in Clarassour."

"For seamen, yes," Triasymon told him. "But the likes of Orlu and Viragan don't hire fishermen, let alone the orphan sons of fishermen, who have never handled anything bigger than a rowing-boat. They hire ruthless hagglers, and fighting-men more ruthless still, so that they may buy what they condescend to buy and steal whatever else they care to take."

The boat bumped on the shore then, and the three of them leapt on to the sand, ready to haul it over the beach and past the tide-line. They took up their accustomed positions, and bent their backs to the work. For several minutes they had no breath to spare for idle talk--but when the boat was safe Lysariel was quick to retake his challenging attitude. "I could be a fighting-man, if I owned a sword," he told his uncle. "I might even be a merchant, had I a market in which to train. But all I have is the sea, and no fishing-boat to sail upon her, so the most I can hope to be is a diver. If I am to be a diver, I shall be a great diver. I shall not settle for anything less."

"I would not want you to settle for less, if that is your desire," his uncle assured him, soothingly. "All I ask is that you don't attempt more than you can achieve. Skills do not develop overnight, and great skills are the work of a lifetime. You must swim to strengthen your arms and legs, and you must discipline your lungs to hold as much air as possible for as long as possible. You must train yourself very carefully before you try anything as dangerous as the waters you tried to plumb today. It'll be some time before you can reach the bottom of that cliff."

"But I did reach the bottom!" Lysariel protested. He saw immediately that his uncle did not believe him. "I *did*," he insisted. "The sea-bed was bare, but I saw what was there. I saw a cave full of glowing coral."

Triasymon frowned at that. "There's no such thing," he said, firmly, "and if there were, it would be best to avoid it."

"Why?" Lysariel demanded, angrily. "If you think there's no such thing, why say that it's best avoided?"

"Everything strange is best avoided," Triasymon told him, sternly. "Nothing that glows in the depths of the sea can possibly be good-—it's most likely a lure to attract prey into the gape of monstrous jaws."

"It was coral," Lysariel said, stubbornly. "Precious coral."

"It was most likely an illusion, spawned by the dwindling of the air within your lungs," Triasymon insisted. "And if it was not, it was something accursed."

Lysariel was tempted to call his uncle a coward again, but he knew that the ready repetition of such an offence would not be easily forgiven. Triasymon might be a stubborn fool grown content with mediocre limitations, but it would only cause unnecessary trouble to keep on telling him so. For that reason, Lysariel stored the impulse away resentfully, where it might take root and grow--and deep within himself, where that seed was lodged, he already felt a curious kind of glow, like the heat of a newly-lit fire that was struggling to burn more brightly. It might only have been the spirit of his youth, impelling him to manhood, but in his mind's eye Lysariel saw that ambitious glimmer as an echo of the eerie light he had glimpsed at the bottom of the sea, like a new-born sun within the embers of the dying world.

By the time that the Yuran Empire was finally obliterated, by the great plague commonly called the Platinum Death, it held no more than thirty-seven other isles in thrall. Scleracina was the largest, which fact contributed considerably to the resentment of its subject status harboured by many of its people. Although most Scleracinians were as disinterested in politics as the majority of continent-dwellers, there as a substantial minority who believed--quite falsely--that their island had once been a proud and happy nation, in which everyone was better-fed and more comfortably housed than they were under Yuran rule. This nostalgic myth misinformed the dissatisfied Scleracinians that in the days when they had had kings of their own, those rulers had been unusually wise in the making of laws and unusually just in their administration of the laws they made.

Although there was not an atom of truth in this concatenation of idle fancies, its nourishment created in many of the people of Scleracina a peculiar avidity to be ruled once again before the world's end, however briefly, by men of their own myopic kind, who had been born and raised within their own narrow span. This strange desire ultimately came to fulfilment, although the consequences of that fulfilment were not at all what the dissatisfied folk of Scleracina had anticipated, and very far from what they desired.

The Revelations of Suomynona, the Last Prophet

"Teach us about precious coral, Uncle," Manazzoryn said, when they had finished their last meal of the day and sat in their chairs savouring the long twilight. "Shellfish we know well enough as a harvest for divers to bring in, but the nobler kinds of coral are a mystery to us still."

Lysariel understood that his brother was trying to help him, trying to
ease Triasymon's mind in respect of his new-found determination to be
something other than he was. He knew that he ought to be grateful, but he
could not help feeling that his dream and his ambition might be better
unsullied by such vulgar practicalities. For ten years he and his brother
had been hunting and eating shellfish, and Lysariel had cultivated a fine
contempt for them. He had never encountered gargantuaclams or
drillerwhelks, and he could not imagine that such creatures could really
be dangerous, let alone glamorous. On the other hand, he knew full well
how pitiful a price even the finest globesters fetched in the marketplace.
Mere shellfish would never provide him with an incentive to be a better
diver, and he could not believe that a man like Triasymon could possibly
know enough about valuable corals to provide a better one. Even so, he
listened as patiently as he could to what his uncle had to say, while
nursing secret fancies of his own.

"What we call coral is actually the collective tegument of a host of
tiny colonial organisms," Triasymon explained to the brothers, speaking
to them in his most pedestrian and pedagogical manner, as if they were no
more than five hundred days old. "It is like the shell of a moussel or an
eyester, but the proportion of the coral creatures' bodies to their
protective fortress is much smaller. The living elements of an edifice of
coral are invariably tiny, but they are prodigious builders. Although there
are multitudes alive at any one moment, and their generations are short-
lived, their collaborative effort is wondrously effective. A large tree of
coral is not merely the product of millions of makers, but of thousands of
years.

"Some corals, whose work has no value in the market, are left alone
to construct trees that are a hundred times as tall and broad as the largest
tree to be found in any of Scleracina's forests and orchards. It is
sometimes said that even noble coral may produce such giants in the
ocean depths, far beyond the reach of human divers, but that is probably a
lie, because most coral-making creatures cannot live too far from the
light, or under too much pressure. At any rate, noble coral is sufficiently
valuable as a medium of ornamentation that its trees are rarely allowed to
grow much beyond a handspan.

"As you've doubtless observed, not all corals build tree-like forms as
their generations live and die, expanding their tiny empires as they pass.
Some construct fans, others produce globes pockmarked with holes. Some
grow sideways like creeping carpets, especially in the hollows of caves
where the water is not as efficiently renewed by the ebb and flow of the
tides. Carpet-like corals increase in thickness with time, laying down
sheets of material that can be cut into building-blocks, and they often put
forth protrusions, like horns or fingers. Some of the oldest buildings in
Clarassour are partly made from sea-green coral blocks, and some of the
oldest monuments are faced with sculpted panels of black or blue coral,

24

but you'll see little enough of those species on this storm-racked peninsula, where builders must use stone of a sturdier kind. Carpet corals in blue or black must have had a substantial market value in the distant past, perhaps before the Yuran conquest, but there are no buyers to be found today. The only corals worth gathering are noble corals, especially those whose colour ranges from gold to brilliant red."

"Especially if they glow with their own inner light," Lysariel put in, moved by a spirit of perversity.

"Perhaps that would make them more valuable still," Triasymon conceded. "Always provided, of course, that they continue to glow when they are brought up into the air and the sunlight. Fish whose scales seem gloriously bright in the water sometimes lose their lustre when they are caught and landed."

During the next few days, Triasymon began to look out for unusual specimens of coral when he dived from the boat, and he also took to searching through the detritus trawled up by the local fishing boats or cast up on the shore. When he took his nephews out towards the reef so that they might practice their diving he took care to direct their attention to all the living corals to be found nearby, and he offered them occasional accounts of more exotic specimens he had seen in the past--but he would not take Lysariel back to the trench in which he had so nearly perished, and he would not agree to dive there himself in the hope of catching a glimpse of the red glow that Lysariel had seen.

Lysariel was impatient with his uncle's hesitation--all the more so when he realised that Triasymon really did believe that he had been the victim of a hallucination brought on by excessive strain. When they went out in the boat or strode along the shore in pursuit of food for their table Lysariel was content to do his work and hold his tongue, but when the twilight deepened and the fire was lit in the cottage, he made no secret of his restlessness.

"I saw what I saw, uncle," Lysariel told Triasymon defiantly, as the three of them huddled beside a slowly-dying fire one evening, reluctant to go to bed until they had wrung the last benefit from the dusty driftwood. "It was a cave set in the base of the underwater cliff--a grotto filled with glowing coral. Its walls were covered with coral, and there were projections extending from its roof and its floor, sometimes meeting in the middle to form pillars." He had convinced himself that this was, indeed, what he had seen, although he knew that he had not been close enough to make out any details. His memory was not only sharp and clear but charged with emotion of a curiously sensual kind.

"You could not possibly have seen so much, or so clearly," Triasymon insisted, his perspicacity annoying Lysariel even more than his stubbornness. "In any case, I never heard from anyone hereabouts that luminous red carpet-corals had ever been on display in Clarassour's marketplace, or within its finer houses. Trinkets made from noble coral are commonly worn by the wives and daughters of the rich, and you may be sure that if any were to be easily harvested that glowed in the dark, they would be proudly displayed. Such materials, if they exist, are not to be treated as ready sources of revenue."

"You only have to swim down as I did," Lysariel told him, "and you would see for yourself that the cave is real."

"But to do that," Triasymon told him, taking up a poker to stir more life from the charred embers, "I would have to swim far too close to the edge of the rock-face, into waters choked with black debris. Even if I were prepared to expose myself to all the vicious and venomous creatures that make their homes in the slits and crevices of the cliff, I would not be able to trust my eyes."

"Why not?" Manazzoryn asked, ducking back as the re-enlivened fire spat sparks and splinters on to the hearth.

"Because crevices in the sea-bed and caves let into its slopes are treacherous places in more ways than one," Triasymon answered, "and the kinds of light that are generated under the sea are always deceptive. There are fish in the ocean wilderness beyond the reefs that use light as a lure to attract the attention of their prey, and there may well be cave-creatures that do likewise. Cthulhoids, mersnakes and lumpreys all use caves as lairs, and would surely benefit from such lures if they could produce them, or exploit other creatures that can. Even a sea-cave whose mouth is as wide as the doorway of a house should not be entered casually by any sane man, no matter what might be glimpsed in its interior by means of internal light--indeed, my opinion is that the more alluring the interior seems, especially if it is brightly illuminated, the greater the danger will be that lurks therein."

"So you would never venture into a grotto furnished with noble coral, uncle?" Lysariel said. "No matter how brightly it glowed, you would resist the temptation, fearing that you might be seized and devoured."

"I would never enter such a place," Triasymon confirmed. "To the best of my knowledge, no man of Scleracina has ever brought such a peculiar harvest to any of its marketplaces during the seven thousand days that I have been alive, and no artefact of that sort survives from earlier times on any island I have visited. If glowing coral ever existed, its secret was obviously very well-guarded."

"Seven thousand days is not a great deal, if the world is as old as legend declares," Lysariel said, "and it is said that there are more than seven hundred islands in Ambriocyatha, of which you have visited exactly three. If the relics of a hundred thousand Earthly civilizations have crumbled into mere atoms, recirculated again and again and again in our bodies and our artefacts, and the relics of a hundred thousand more still lurk in the forgotten nooks and crannies of a world that would take a thousand days to sail around, the mere fact that you have heard no rumour of luminous noble coral can hardly be taken to prove that it has never existed, or that it still exists today."

"Is the world really so old?" Manazzoryn asked, sceptically. "Or have we invented a past replete with riches to make up for the fact that we have so few?" But the conversation was not to be turned so easily into a philosophical reverie.

"Lack of rumour is no proof of anything," Triasymon admitted to Lysariel, readily enough, "but it is evidence enough for me that if the unrumoured item does exist, it is best left alone."

Lysariel was more than ready to assume that his uncle's hesitation was a measure of his failure as a man of enterprise rather than the responsible exercise of sensible caution. He was also convinced that Triasymon's refusal to admit that Lysariel really had seen what he claimed to have seen was a mere excuse for his reluctance to dive in the same place--but he wondered whether Triasymon's determination to keep the argument going, in spite of Manazzoryn's attempt to end it, might be evidence of the fact that Triasymon was not yet as content with his own passivity and timidity as he wished to be.

"Would you not like to be the first man to bring some new produce to the marketplace in Clarassour, uncle?" Lysariel asked him. "Would you not like the chance to pit your wits against the expert hagglers to discover the appropriate price of something they had never seen before?"

"Perhaps," Triasymon admitted, after a slight pause. "But I would not like to be merely one more man who had died in an attempt to accomplish the impossible."

"I shall return to that cave one day," Lysariel told his uncle, "whether you sanction it or not."

Triasymon picked up the poker again, although the ailing fire did not seem to be in any condition to benefit from further agitation. Lysariel watched as the old man raked the blunt head of the crude instrument through the glowing ashes, rattling the grate, and knew that it was time to retire for the midnight. "First you must convince me that you are capable of returning safely, Lysariel," Triasymon said, eventually. "Only show me that you are a better diver than I am, and I shall be content to sit on the surface in my boat, waiting patiently for you to bring back your unprecedented treasure."

"I will," Lysariel assured him--and he would surely have tried, had Damozel Fate not intervened to prevent him, in a very sudden and unexpected fashion.

Brian Stableford

In the days of the Yuran conquest--which was as stupidly violent as such conquests usually are--the royal family of Scleracina, whose so-called palace was in the so-called city of Clarassour, had been slaughtered. Every last man, woman and child had been cut into little pieces, which were then cast into the sea to feed the fish and the crustaceans on whose bounty the islanders depended for their sustenance. But families are, by their nature, complex and sprawling organisms to which it is exceedingly difficult to set a limit. Moreover, genealogists are as renowned for their ingenuity as their stubbornness; the reconstitution of a royal lineage, no matter how widespread the massacre intended for its obliteration, only requires that its ancestral lines be traced far enough backwards to reveal forgotten sub-branches, which can then be extrapolated forwards again to disclose the existence of unsuspecting contemporaries.

Such contemporaries often live in humble, or even mean, surroundings, but blood is blood and when royal blood is required in living veins it can be found as easily as it can be shed. Although they had always been careful to keep the datum secret from the zealous officers of the Yuran government, the genealogists of Scleracina always knew the identity of the legitimate heir to the isle's ancient throne, and they preserved that knowledge carefully against the day when the legitimate monarchy might be restored, determined to do so even if their mission should extend to the last syllable of recordable time--which, as things turned out, it very nearly did.

The Revelations of Suomynona, the Last Prophet

Lysariel realised soon enough that he could not possibly match his uncle in the water until he was fully grown, and he judged that he still had several hundred days to grow before he reached the full extent of his mature stature. He realised, too, that he must practice hard even while he was still unready if he were ever to have the chance of overtaking Triasymon's mature strength and skill. It was in the determined and methodical pursuit of this cause that the rightful king of Scleracina began to learn the lesson of patience from the ever-patient corals that had hedged the intimate waters of Harstpoint since time immemorial.

He began to learn patience--but he only made a beginning, and perhaps it was not the best kind of patience, because it was generated and sustained by obsession and dissatisfaction. Triasymon seemed content with his nephew's attitude--doubtless he thought the lesson worth the price--but Lysariel was not entirely content with himself. Once he had seen the ruddy glow in the depths beyond the reef he could not shake the conviction that something had gone awry in his life, which becoming a diver might appease but would never fully assuage.

Although Triasymon would not take the brothers back into the waters outside the reef until he was confident that Lysariel had the skill to plumb their depths, he did show them caves that opened into calmer and clearer waters within the reef, including a grotto set in the base of an underwater crag, whose tip showed above the waves when the tide was at its lowest. This cave was far easier to reach than the one Lysariel had glimpsed, but its sprawling base extended numerous jags, like the arms of a brittlestar. These ragged extensions made convenient anchorages for corals and weeds, and the dense subaquatic forest that had grown up there was a convenient feeding-ground for fish and their predators.

By virtue of the local profusion of living creatures, the caves let into the rock at the junctions from which the jags extended were not easy to approach, and the way was filled with dangers. Lysariel and his brother made several unsuccessful attempts to pass into the entrance of the grotto, but they were forced back on two occasions by families of mersnakes and on three others by a huge cthulhoid. On the fifth attempt, however, they were able to get close enough to the grotto's mouth for Lysariel to look into it and see the extent of the carpet-corals lining its walls.

These corals patterned the walls of the cave in sullen greens, sombre blues and dull purples, and did not glow at all--but Lysariel was not at all dismayed by this prosaic discovery, and continued to use the spur of rock as a practice-ground, repeatedly swimming down to a depth from which he could see into the interior of the cave. Such descents took him deep into an undergrowth of weed, where he sometimes found his feet entangled by accident or design, and where any number of watchful predators were constantly ready to take a bite out of him, but he learned to be wary and to extricate himself immediately from such commonplace traps.

In the meantime, Lysariel's memory of the red-glowing cave outside the reef grew ever sharper, and increasingly detailed. Although he knew well enough that his memories must have been embroidered by imagination, as his early memories of his mother had been, he would not admit that there was anything unreal about the image of the cave's interior that was expanding by degrees within his mind.

"The shining coral is a marvel unparalleled," he told Triasymon and Manazzoryn, while they sat by their fire as yet another night darkened by degrees, having made a meal of shellfish they had gathered in the twilight, and vegetables from their kitchen garden. "It varies in hue between scarlet and gold. It does not merely cover the walls of the cave; it descends from the ceiling and ascends from the floor in formations akin to stalactites and stalagmites, which sometimes meet to form glistening towers whose sinuous shapes are like statues with upstretched arms. The whole place is alive, although it is entirely free of weed. Luminous creatures like great flat worms ooze over the surface, while cthulhoids have hollowed out a dozen nests and mersnakes perform acrobatics, glorying in the fabulous light. If only we could cut one of those columns at the base and the crown, and draw it up to the surface!"

"All you actually saw was a gleam in the murky distance," Triasymon reminded him. "The rest is fancy. At any rate, it would be impossible to do any extensive work at such a depth, even if you had some kind of breathing apparatus, and no one I know has a rope long enough to raise your prize to the surface. If there really is luminous coral in those unpromising depths, the best harvest you or I could hope to attain would be fragments dislodged by the burrowing cthulhoids and swept out of the entrance by their tentacles."

Lysariel noticed, as he was bound to do, that his uncle was now prepared to say "if" and "you or I". Little by little, his scepticism was being smoothed into a gentler form, massaged into a mere matter of rhetoric, while his imagination was drawing him into the game of speculation.

"When I have become the kind of diver I intend to be," Lysariel told his uncle, in a grandiose manner, "I will obtain a better harvest than you or I could ever have imagined a hundred days ago."

"If you ever become the kind of diver you intend to be," Triasymon replied, "you will have sense enough to know that if there is light in such an unlikely place, it must be generated for a purpose, as a trap. You will admit, then, that I know what I am talking about."

"It might be impossible for one man to do extensive work in such a place," Manazzoryn put in, trying to make his own contribution to the fantasy that they were building by firelight, "but a team of expert divers might do it, if they worked together cleverly enough. As for finding a thread long enough and strong enough to draw it up...well, there must be rope-makers in Clarassour who supply the rigging that Orlu and Viragan

31

Brian Stableford

require for their pirate ships, and iron-mongers who supply their anchor-chains."

"Experienced divers would be too wise to make up any such team," was Triasymon's judgment. "And no ship would lower its anchor into an abyss like that."

"I shall work alone, so that no man may dispute my prize," was Lysariel's response. "As for raising it....perhaps it will not be so very heavy."

"And I dare say that you'll fight cthulhoids with your right hand while your left plies a saw," Triasymon suggested, "and you'll use your toes, of course, to tie the mersnakes in knots."

"I shall do what I have to do," was Lysariel's reply to that. "Believe me, uncle, I shall do what I have to do. That is the kind of man I intend to be, now that I am no longer a boy."

At that moment there was a knock on their door: an imperious rapping, made by something far more solid than a set of bare knuckles. Lysariel had never heard such a knock before, and it sent shivers through him. His experience of visitors was far from vast, but there was something about the way the knocking echoed in the narrow cottage that filled him with a sense of foreboding. *It is the light that has entered into me,* he thought. *It is stirring, as though agitated by an insistent poker.*

Triasymon went to the door, moving warily. Although he kept no genuine weapons in the house, he always kept a gaff within arm's reach of the doorway that could double as a spear, and he laid his right hand upon its shaft as he called out: "Who's there? How many are you?"

"We are two, and friends," was the reply. "Captain Sharuman and Captain Akabar, come from Clarassour on horseback although we are seamen by vocation. We beg you to open the door, Master Triasymon, for we have news to delight you."

"Captains of what?" Triasymon asked. "What could any seamen, let alone captains, want with the likes of us? And what news could they possibly bring to delight us?"

"We are captains of the finest merchant vessels in Scleracina's fleet," was the tart reply to his first question, "and if you'll open the door to us we'll gladly tell you our news. We mean you no harm, sire, and the news we bring you is the best you'll ever hear."

The firelight within the cottage was not very bright, and the first thing Triasymon did when he let go of the gaff was to pluck a candle off the shelf and throw it to Manazzoryn so that he might light it. He waited until the wick flared before he unbarred the door, apparently determined that captains of fine merchant vessels should not think his home too dark. Lysariel studied the quizzical expression on his uncle's face, and took note of the anxiety that was written in his features. "We could not keep them out if we wanted to, uncle," he observed, "and there is surely no reason to think that anyone would wish us harm."

32

Triasymon scowled at his nephew, but not in an angry way. "You have led too quiet a life," the old man murmured. "No one has reason to wish us any harm, but that does not mean that no one will." When Manazzoryn had planted the soft candle in a tray, though, Triasymon unbolted the door. While the door was swinging open, Lysariel stood up and moved to a position a few paces behind his uncle, so that when the visitors came into view he and Triasymon could meet the strangers' curious stare together.

Lysariel saw two men, both powerfully built and richly dressed. One was wearing a sheathed sword, but it was obviously the other--the older and larger of the two--who had knocked. He still held the massive instrument whose heel he had used as a knocker: a double-headed axe, whose brightly-polished blades caught and concentrated the starlight so that they glittered like the surface of a calm sea. As to what the two visitors saw in their turn, Lysariel could only guess. Had he been asked, he would have said that they probably saw a fatherless boy on the threshold of manhood, wretchedly dressed but not without a certain pride...but their reaction to the sight of him would soon have given the lie to his automatic supposition.

Both men measured Triasymon with a long glance, then both looked past the man in the doorway to the younger one who stood behind. Then, deliberately and unhurriedly, both men bowed. They did so without any apparent irony or condescension. Their faces were perfectly steady as the older one said: "We seek Lysariel, son of Alveyadey, King of Scleracina. We were told that we could find him in the house of Triasymon."

When the man with the axe finished speaking, the silence that fell seemed tangible. Lysariel discovered a strange taste on his tongue, which must have come from the roof of his mouth, like a strange sweat.

"Lysariel, son of Alveyadey, is my name," Lysariel told the two men, "but my father was no king, and nor am I."

The two men bowed again, and they stepped past Triasymon into the candlelit room. "You are indeed a king, Lysariel, son of Alveyadey," the younger one said. "There is no doubt about it, Your Majesty. My name is Akabar, and my large companion is Sharuman. We are captains in your merchant navy, under the command of Prince Orlu and Prince Viragan. We have come to bring you to your throne. The Yuran occupation is ended at last, and Scleracina is free."

Lysariel could make no reply to this; he was utterly dazed. Manazzoryn had started to his feet, but he too was speechless. It was left to Triasymon to say: "If you really mean what you are saying, there has been some mistake."

This time it was the older messenger, Sharuman, who replied. He did not turn to look back at Triasymon, but kept his eyes fixed on Lysariel's face. He was holding his battle-axe in two hands, but not in a threatening manner. "We are entirely serious, Your Majesty, and there has been no mistake. You are the rightful king of Scleracina, and always have been. Your father was king before you, and his father before him--but the secret of their succession had to be kept, even from them. The Yuran conquerors had to be convinced that they had slaughtered every member of the ruling family--but the Yuran Empire is no more; it has collapsed in its very core, swept way by the ravages of the platinum death. Scleracina is free. The governor is dead. The truth can now be made manifest, and the rightful king set upon his throne. We have no power to command you, Your Majesty, but we humbly ask that you come with us. We have brought a carriage, and men-at-arms to serve as escort."

"Lysariel?" The quavering voice that framed the name was Manazzoryn's.

Lysariel swallowed, determined that when he spoke, his voice would not tremble at all--but Triasymon would not wait.

"My brother Alveyadey was a fisherman all his life," Triasymon said. "His father was a fisherman before him. Their boat had grown old, a patchwork of poor wood which fell apart under the harassment of one storm too many. They were as far from being kings as any man alive."

"How else could they have been securely hidden?" Sharuman said, gently, his eyes still measuring Lysariel. So far as Lysariel could tell, the captain was not displeased with what he saw.

"It is true, Your Majesty," Akabar added. "What possible reason could we have for lying?" But there was a slight hint of mischief in his tone, now. He was enjoying the spectacle of the rude discomfort and dizzying shock his news had generated. Lysariel judged that even though the two men meant what they said, they were by no means insensitive to the absurdity of the situation.

"Have you brought an army because you fear attack?" Lysariel asked, keeping his voice perfectly calm.

"Just a carriage, Your Majesty, and a few soldiers to serve as a guard-of-honour," Sharuman said. "There is no need for an army. Yura has fallen into desolation without the necessity of fighting a war. You will be safe--I can guarantee that. No one wishes you any harm. This is the happiest day in Scleracina's history; our only regret is that we had to wait for it until the world has almost ended."

"You called Orlu and Viragan princes," Lysariel observed. "I have never heard them called by that title before." It seemed to him that Akabar almost laughed, but Sharuman had better control of himself

"My master Prince Viragan is your most loyal and fervent supporter," the older of the two visitors replied, "with the sole exception of his very good friend, Prince Orlu. They hold the city and port of Clarassour in your name, and they are waiting at the palace to receive you. They are the joint commanders of your navy, who will defend your kingdom against any and all external threats, should any defence ever become necessary. Will you come with us, Your Majesty, and gladden the hearts of all your subjects?"

Lysariel looked sideways at his brother, and then looked back at his uncle. Neither of them seemed to have the least comprehension of what was happening, or the least resolution to move them to action.

A few minutes earlier, Lysariel had had no ambition but to be a diver, but even then he had had no intention of being anything less than the very best of divers, the fearless master of the darkest waters and the discoverer of the most precious treasures of the deep. Why should he not be a king instead, if the opportunity were there? Had he not always believed, in his heart of hearts, that he was misplaced in society, capable of far better than the future had seemingly laid out for him? Was it really so astonishing that Damozel Fate had kept this trick up her sleeve, ready to surprise and delight him?

This is what the light was trying to tell me, he thought. *This is why the passion entered into me, and why I felt that something was amiss with me. I am not to be a diver after all. I am to be a king. I have always been a king, even though I did not know it. How could I ever have guessed?*

"We shall come," he said to the man with the axe, keeping his voice perfectly steady. "My uncle, Triasymon, is my most trusted advisor. My brother, Manazzoryn, is my best-loved companion. We shall come to Clarassour as a company, ready to do what we must. This is the beginning of a new era, and we shall be glad to play our parts."

"Thank you, Your Majesty," said Captain Sharuman, raising his axe to his lips and kissing the double blade.

"We are pleased to do your bidding, Your Majesty," said Captain Akabar, bowing lower than he had bowed before.

"We shall need time to pack our things," said Triasymon, hesitantly.

"We shall not need much time for that," King Lysariel said, his voice already taking on a more imperious tone. "We have little in store, and little that fits us for the life that will now be ours."

"Long live the king!" said Sharuman and Akabar, together.

"Thank you," said Lysariel, whose only ambition, but a few moments earlier, had been to make himself a coral diver. "I feel that I am a king, after all. I think that I always felt it, but dared not quite believe it, and mistook my ambition for something else entirely. Now I see what my destiny is, and I cannot refuse it."

And when Lysariel looked into himself he found, much to his relief, that every word he had said was true--or true enough. The moment was indeed the beginning of a new era, and he was indeed glad to play his part, as were his trustworthy uncle and his beloved brother. He had indeed always felt that he was cut from better cloth than his fellows, although he had not dared to believe how fine a man he really was. Who could possibly hesitate in such a matter as this? In any case, what choice did he have, given that he really was the legitimate king of Scleracina? What choice did anyone have, in a dying world, whether he were the greatest of kings or the humblest of scavengers, but to do what was expected of him? What

Brian Stableford

sort of man could refuse the destiny that had been written by Damozel
Fate in his blood and bones?

Part One

Brian Stableford

Giraiazal, a Magician Fortunate in Exile

1

The Platinum Death was so-named by Petrichus, a physician resident in the city of Jeannerat, on the north-western coast of Ulvalu. Petrichus had long nursed a theory that the mythical metals of the ancient world had not been elementary substances at all but merely contagions afflicting humble iron after the fashion of ordinary rust, each of which had its counterpart in the contagions afflicting human beings.

"The Platinum Death is the penultimate plague, and the contagion will be removed by the etheric winds within a thousand days or so." this sage declared, as soon as the disease in question had devastated Jeannerat. "We shall have nothing further to fear from natural corrosions until the Titanium Death makes its appearance, in two or three years' time, to administer the final *coup de grâce* to our exhausted species."

Petrichus did not expect to live long enough to see whether his prediction would come true, for he was more than fourteen thousand days old when he uttered it, and this proved to be one of the few instances in which his expectations--or lack of them--proved correct. He fell downstairs and broke his neck while ascending by candlelight to his bedroom after a night's heavy drinking, a mere twelve days after making his unwelcome contribution to the world's vocabulary.

The Revelations of Suomynona, the Last Prophet

When Meronicos the Magnificent, the last emperor of Yura, sent forth a summons requiring every diviner and magician in the realm to report to his palace for a great conference, the royal messenger found Giraiazal of Natalarch relaxing in his bath.

Although the magician leapt out of the murky water with alacrity, and towelled himself dry with all possible expedition, he could not avoid feeling greatly embarrassed to have been found in such a state of unreadiness. Giraiazal was not the kind of prophet to waste overmuch time in peering into the petty details of his own future, because he knew

39

full well how resentful Damozel Fate was of such pettifogging self-indulgence, but he knew how important it is for a magician to conserve an image of total preparedness for the sake of his clients.

While he waited for his carriage to be brought to his door and his horses to be hitched, Giraiazal set about repairing the damage. "To tell the truth," he informed the messenger, having observed the sweat standing upon the man's excessively rubicund features, "I had not expected you for another hour. You must have made uncommon haste in getting here. Your zeal does you credit, and I shall be sure to mention it at the palace."

Ordinarily, praise such as this would have delighted an imperial herald of such meagre status, but on this occasion the man was content with an ironic sigh. "I can assure you, Master Magician," the messenger replied, "that it was not on your account that I hurried. To tell *you* the truth, I was exceedingly glad to get out of the capital--and you may say what you like at the palace, for now that my duty has been properly discharged, I shall take the liberty of not returning."

This was a remarkable speech in more ways than one, and might have been construed as treasonous by a lord of the realm--but Giraiazal was no nobleman, and was far more anxious to discover the cause of such insolence than punish the consequence. Where a common man might simply have asked a question, however, a magician was bound to divine the answer for himself.

It took Giraiazal a full twenty seconds to reach this conclusion, but at least half of that was due to his reluctance to face it rather than to the inherent difficulty of the logical process. "The Platinum Death has arrived on the island," he said, dully.

"So it has," said the messenger. "And I am gone, now that I need not fear being declared an outlaw for failing to discharge my duty. You, Master Magician, must make your own decision." The herald did not need to spell out the fact that now that Giraiazal had received the summons, he would be declared an outlaw himself if he failed to obey it.

Giraiazal immediately set aside the embarrassment he had felt at being found in the bath when the emperor's agent came to call. The real embarrassment was not in not having known why the messenger had come, but in having been present to receive him. Had he really been prepared he would not have been in his bath, or his house, or even his neighbourhood. He did consider the possibility of making his way to the nearest port and leaving Yura in spite of the emperor's command, but only briefly. He would never be able to obtain a passage, and his reputation as a wizard--though not inconsiderable--was insufficient to deter the local informers from betraying him to the authorities for a relatively meagre fee. "I will go to the palace immediately," he assured the herald. "The emperor will need me."

"Aye," said the messenger, "that he will. Be assured that he will not be the only one to hope that you--and a hundred others like you--might be adequate to answer his need. If you can brew a potion to stop the Platinum Death, you'll have the gratitude of every man, woman and child in Yura." The herald's voice was heavily laden with scepticism, but not of an aggressive or mocking kind; the man really did hope that Giraiazal--or another of the hundred like him--might be able to find a cure for the dread disease.

"The remedies of herbasacralism have their limitations," Giraiazal conceded, "as do the oracles contained in the ever-changing skies and skilfully shuffled cards. Even the greatest magicians remain subject to the whims of our unkind mistress, Damozel Fate--but if the emperor needs us, we must do what we can."

Giraiazal's groom came in then to inform him that the carriage was ready, and to tell the herald that his saddle had been put on a fresh horse. Giraiazal made no objection to this, not merely because he owed a duty to the emperor to answer the needs of imperial heralds but because he did not expect to have any further need of his own horses--save for those now harnessed to his carriage--for quite some time. Although he had not had the opportunity to put the question to the stars or the cards, he felt very confident that the conference of magicians and diviners summoned by Meronicos would not find a rapid solution to the realm's afflictions.

Giraiazal contemplated taking a number of ready-made potions in his luggage but decided against it. Anything the summoned magicians produced on their arrival would be put to the test immediately, and it would not be to anyone's advantage to be rapidly identified as a man whose medicines lacked efficacy. When the herald rode off to the east, therefore, and Giraiazal's coachman took the eastbound road, Giraiazal waved the other man a friendly farewell. Then he set himself to deep contemplation of the various strategies by which he might hope to survive the ordeal to come.

Giraiazal liked to think of himself as an eclectic magician, and one more deserving of the title than many others. He had been educated in no less than four of the arcane divinatory arts--astrology, cartomancy, rhabdomancy and hepatoscopy--although he considered himself truly expert only in the first two. Like all the empire's physicians, he had been intensively trained in the practical art of herbasacralism, but he had also devoted some time to the much less well-known and much less widely-practised art of morpheomorphism. He also claimed elementary skills in the arts of anathematization and exorcism, although he had wisely refrained from exercising these skills overmuch, on the perfectly valid grounds that curses of all sorts are apt to recoil upon their sender. Although Giraiazal was careful never to lay claim to any vast achievements in any of his areas of expertise, he was always ready to be admired for the breadth of his knowledge and the abundance of his accomplishments.

The Natalarch from which Giraiazal hailed was one of the least of Yura's subject islands. The time of his birth there he was careful never to reveal, in order that he might take advantage of the common assumption that magicians are much older than they seem, so no one in Yura know what age he had attained when he arrived in the empire's heart, having already completed his schooling in the Academy of Xeroth. Since that arrival, however, he had enjoyed a moderately prosperous career pandering to the supernatural needs of Yura's aristocracy, and had been careful to harbour no higher ambition than the indefinite extension of that moderately successful career. Now that the prospect of further extension had come to seem unlikely he did not waste time chiding himself for not having anticipated the imminent arrival of the Platinum Death. Even if he had had an accurate warning, he would have been reluctant to flee in a panic, not because he did not fear the plague but because it would have been extremely difficult to identify a safe destination without careful research. Given that he would be dependent in any case upon the whim of Damozel Fate, he thought, it would probably be better to deal with her in relatively familiar surroundings--and while the palace itself hardly qualified as 'familiar surroundings', he did have the slight advantage of knowing, at least by reputation, the great majority of the colleagues with whom he would be required to work.

"My first objective," Giraiazal told himself, by way of gathering and boosting his morale, "must be to hide myself away until I can measure the situation accurately and determine what strategies my rivals intend to follow. There is bound to come a time, sooner or later, when I am brought out of the crowd--or its remnant--to make my own judgment as to what might be done for the empire's, or at least the emperor's, salvation. I must be ready, when the ideal moment comes, to offer the advice that will serve me best and give me the best chance of surviving the emperor's wrath. It is possible that the safest course will be to add my voice to that of a company, but it is equally conceivable that there will be no safety at all in numbers. It will surely be reckless to offer a testable solution too hastily, but it might be equally reckless to delay too long, while the number of plague-victims increases exponentially. Whenever the moment comes, however, the vital question remains the same. What can I possibly say to the emperor that will buy me a chance to survive this disaster?"

This was not an easy puzzle to solve, and Giraiazal had made little or no progress with it when his carriage drew up in front of the lodge in the palace grounds that had been set aside for the use of Yura's magicians. He was not surprised, though far from delighted, to see that the lodge was heavily guarded--not, he presumed, for the purpose of keeping unwelcome visitors out.

Within the building Giraiazal found things much as he had expected--which is to say that the half of the magicians assembled there were engaged in fierce arguments over the relative merits of their oracular methods and practical arts, while the remainder were anxiously awaiting news from the hospital of the efficacy of measures they had already advertised. Only two-thirds of the intended company had been gathered thus far, and Giraiazal did not need to consult the heavens or lay out his trumps to anticipate that the disputes would become even fiercer as their number increased.

That evening, just as the sun's disc was halved by the black horizon, the emperor sent a demand to the lodge requiring the realm's diviners to communicate a definitive judgment on the fate of the island and the empire by the following noon, and a full-prioritized list of recommendations for preventative action. He might as well have demanded that they stop the sun in the sky. In the long hours of intense negotiation that followed, during which Giraiazal's hesitation passed almost entirely unnoticed, the members of the conference failed to reach agreement on any point whatsoever. It was not simply that the astrologers could not agree with the rhabdomancers, nor the cartomancers with the hepatoscopists; the adherents of each specialism could not agree with one another. The astrologers of Yura had been engaged in fierce theoretical disputes for thousands of days, and the first instinct of rivals who had grown used to treating one another with open contempt was to use the crisis as another opportunity for venting their spleen upon one another. Their tempers were not improved when they received reports, shortly after midnight, that the first cases of the Platinum Death had been reported within the court.

Such was the fervour of the disputes that raged in the lodge that when the time came for the report to be made to the emperor, numerous voices were raised to insist on being heard. Although Giraiazal knew how very unwise it would be to confront the emperor with a clamour of contending claims, he also knew how utterly impossible it would be to talk sense into the clamourers, so he had to be content to let their foolishness take its course, in the hope that their errors might win sufficient delay to help him find a viable strategy for himself. Although he would not be able to witness the consequences of their recklessness directly, he had no doubt that a reliable account of it would be carried back to the lodge in no time at all--and so it proved.

The largest group among the party who demanded to make their case before the emperor consisted of nineteen astrologers, whose members successfully argued that their number entitled them to be heard first. Their spokesman informed Meronicos the Magnificent that the only reason why no clear warning had been given of the advent of the Platinum Death was that members of the rival school had obtained too much influence in the court and had prevented the custodians of astrological truth from being heard. According to this spokesman, the coming of the Platinum Death had been clearly presaged in a brief flaring--unnoticed by common men who had no telescopes--of one of the sixty-eight red stars that kept the White Star company in the night sky. If only the science of astrology had retained the theoretical purity that it had possessed in former eras, this news could have been widely publicized in plenty of time for precautionary action to be taken, but the spread of heresy had confused the situation. The only unambiguous warnings that his followers had been able to issue had been delivered covertly to a handful of clients who had been wise enough to ignore the influential hypocrites and to pay the relevant fees to the honest traditionalists. In return, these fortunate individuals had received notice to flee the island, and a list of safe destinations. The spokesman for this party offered to provide the emperor and his noblemen with that list as soon as he and they were clear of the harbour in the fastest ship in his fleet.

Even though the nineteen practitioners refused to name the men to whom they had given warning--on the grounds that they always promised confidentiality to all their clients and always kept their word--their claims commanded a certain credibility by virtue of the number of claimants, which was suggestive of a reasonable level of agreement if not of orthodoxy, and the vehemence with which they put the blame for their own failures on their theoretical opponents. Meronicos the Magnificent, impressed by the weight of their arguments and their alacrity in demanding to be heard ahead of all their rivals, ordered the nineteen to be immediately removed to separate torture-chambers and sternly interrogated until they had disclosed their list of safe destinations--after which they were to be executed for treason, on the grounds that neither they nor any of their unnamed clients had taken the trouble to communicate the relevant information to him in good enough time.

This judgment, as might be expected, gave some pause to the other diviners who had been anxious to put their cases forward ahead of their fellows. The 'heretics' who had been so viciously attacked by the nineteen had always claimed that the White Star alone was useful for the prediction of events on Earth, and they had been ready to argue that the advent of the Platinum Death could only have been foreseeable by those supernaturally gifted with the ability to judge the White Star's shifting moods, but the treatment of their rivals forced them to rethink their strategy in a hurry. Thirteen of these theoreticians, who were very satisfied with the sentence passed on their enemies, while being exceedingly anxious to avoid a similar judgment, soon improvised a different argument.

The spokesman for this party told the emperor that they had been unable to give adequate warning to any of their own patrons, because the White Star had only communicated the awful truth to them mere minutes before they had been summoned to the conference, obviously having done so precisely in order that the first beneficiaries of the intelligence might be Meronicos and his closest confidants. Alas, he said, they had been prevented from making the truth known immediately upon their arrival by their nineteen arrogant rivals, who had arrived so full of wrath that they had been able to drown out wiser and more scrupulous voices. He and his followers were, however, perfectly ready to tell the emperor exactly where he ought to go in order to make himself safe, and just as ready to rely on his judgment and charity in deciding who ought to accompany him there.

It was well known at court that the theoretical pretensions of this fashionable party had never excited anything but derision from less well-placed astrologers, so the emperor was disposed to accept the claim that they had been prevented from making their discoveries known even though they were the more powerful company. As soon as he indicated that he was ready to lend them a sympathetic ear, however, a third and even smaller party of astrologers within the delegation--numbering only seven--immediately lodged a protest, accusing the thirteen of rank charlatanry. These slanderers, improvising hastily and perhaps none too wisely, suggested that the flagitious rays of the White Star were actually the source of the plague ravaging the empire, and that all the inhabitants of Earth would have been dead long ago were it not for the benign influence of the Motile Entities, which were the only trustworthy oracles to be found in the heavens and which laboured every night to undo the terrible work of their pale rival.

The thirteen who had been slandered immediately entered counterclaims of their own, to the effect that the Motile Entities were the source of the Platinum Death. The emperor, sorely confused by this undesirable dispute, delivered all twenty of these various claimants into the hands of his torturers, directing those worthy servants to go to any lengths necessary in order to find out which of them were lying.

At this point, the twenty-three remaining diviners who had demanded to be in the first company to have the emperor's ear--comprising seven cartomancers, six rhabdomancers and ten assorted adherents of more esoteric methods--all decided that they were far less certain than they had momentarily thought as to the source of the plague and the measures that the emperor ought to take in response, and that they needed more time to compete their researches. It did them no good; the impatient Meronicos handed them over to his executioners, so that they might serve as an example to other ditherers. Then he sent a message to the lodge saying that he would hold another audience an hour before sunset, at which time he expected to receive far better advice than he had so far been offered.

Brian Stableford

At the dawn of time, legend declares--with the particular solemnity that legend always reserves for its most fanciful assertions--the sun was yellow. Its disc, which was too bright to be regarded with the naked eye at any other time than the moment of its setting, could be eclipsed by the ball of a man's thumb held at an arm's full stretch. If this is true, our ancestors must have been giants--unless, of course, the sun was much smaller and fiercer then than it is now. Perhaps it was. Perhaps there really were nine worlds circling it instead of only one. Perhaps the year really was a mere few hundred days in length instead of a round ten thousand. Perhaps the days in question were measurably shorter than the ones we count. Perhaps their hours were shorter than ours, and their minutes longer. Perhaps the night sky really was filled with white fixed stars, instead of the sixty-eight red ones that--together with their single white companion-- now make a backcloth for the twelve Motile Entities.

Perhaps none of these assertions is true--but one thing we need not and cannot doubt is that the world is very, very old. It is old enough to have seen more kinds of human beings than we can now enumerate, and changes more drastic than we can now envisage. Having lost so much of our past, we know almost as little of the prospect that faced the first generations of primal humankind as the primal humans did. Did they ever imagine that their descendants would use the fabric of their neighbour worlds to build a shell around the sun? Did they ever imagine that their descendants would fly to the worlds of countless neighbour suns, and build shells around those too? Did they ever imagine that their descendants would move their world so that it would not be swallowed along with the shell they had built when the sun underwent its penultimate metamorphosis?

Brian Stableford

There are, of course, sceptics among us who will say that if the primal humans ever did imagine such things they were fools, and that we too are fools if we believe the legends which tell us that such things actually happened. Alas, we *are* fools, perhaps as foolish as our remotest ancestors and perhaps even more foolish than they; it is because we are fools that we have so little notion of the accomplishments of those of our ancestors who were not as foolish as we are. We find enormous difficulty in entertaining fancies of a different sun and different stars within our feeble dreams, no matter how deftly such notions might be fitted to our burden of regret, but if the manifold humankinds have preserved one item of learning within the wilderness of forgetfulness, it is this: the worlds in which our remoter ancestors lived were not merely stranger than we imagine, but stranger than we can imagine. We have no way to judge the limits of their possibilities, and may be sadly mistaken even as to the real possibilities of our own.

The Revelations of Suomynona, the Last Prophet

Although Giraiazal counted astrology among his most conspicuous talents, he had prudently refused to ally himself with any of the hastily-convened parties which had been first in line to make their excuses to the emperor. Insofar as he had taken any part at all in the debates raging in the lodge, he had been content to keep company with long-serving herbasacralists, who were busy comparing the merits of various recipes, and desperately hoping that one of their number might once have read, in some rare and half-forgotten book, of a rare and long-neglected herb whose one and only medical use--to cure the Platinum Death--had made it seem quite unnecessary to generations of their predecessors, who had never been confronted by that particular plague.

Those potions that had so far been tested by the emperor's civil servants had all been condemned as utterly ineffective, no matter how assiduously they had been crammed with opiates and euphorics as well as ingredients that might actually alleviate some few of the symptoms of the Platinum Death. Alas, the emperor's men were not concerned with such minor natters as whether the victims of the Platinum Death died painlessly or gladly; they had been instructed not to settle for anything less than a cure.

"We must present the emperor with a recipe whose ingredients are exceedingly difficult to obtain," one physician declared. "It is the only way to gain time. If we can all agree a formula, we can create a powerful impression of authority."

"This is Yura," a sceptic observed. "The emperor is ever enthusiastic to boast that anything known to man can be bought in the capital's marketplace. If we make him out to be a liar he will not be pleased with us."

48

"In that case," another suggested, "we might do better to select a few key ingredients that are often faked, so that we may shift the blame to the local apothecaries when the formula fails."

"It might be wiser to pass judgment on the ingredients before the potion is mixed," was the opinion of another. "If we can reject items repeatedly on the grounds that they are not what their suppliers claim, we might contrive a shortage of suppliers as well as goods."

"But if we are seen to be employing delaying tactics," the sceptic pointed out, "you can be sure that it will be held against us. If you are hoping to delay matters until the emperor himself is dead, you are fools. As soon as he falls ill he will issue orders to have us all killed. The astrologers let their spite run away with them, but they had the right idea in trying to persuade the emperor to flee aboard a ship, and to take them with him."

"I'd far rather he fled on a ship and left us behind," was the immediate counter to that argument. "I'd rather take my chances in a plague-ridden city than among the company of a ship, with or without Meronicos the Mercurial as its master."

While this whispered discussion was going on, the number of herbasacralists quartered in the lodge continued to decrease by slow degrees as recipes were tested--and while two hours still remained before the emperor's second deadline, three hepatoscopists fell ill, clearly exhibiting the early symptoms of the Platinum Death.

It was at this point that Giraiazal, for the first time in his life, made a decision to be bold. Rather than forsake the conspiracy of herbasacralists merely to join a conspiracy of rhabdomancers or numerologists, he decided that the time had come to make a pre-emptive strike. He asked the captain of the guard if he might see the emperor before the hour appointed for the next collective audience, in order to demonstrate his skill as a morpheomorphist. So esoteric was this art, even in Yura, that he had to explain to the guardsman that a morpheomorphist is a shaper of dreams. He was careful to swear the captain to secrecy, lest news of his offer reach any other herbasacralists who were also educated in the more esoteric art.

Fortunately, Meronicos the Magnificent immediately agreed to Giraiazal's request for a private hearing. Unfortunately, the emperor did not seem to be in a good mood. "So, Giraiazal of Natalarch," he said, when the magician was brought to stand before the throne, "you think that you can stop the plague in its tracks by giving us pleasant dreams. I hope that you are not intending to use the foolish tactic of blaming the plague's victims for their own failure to save themselves because they were not clever enough to avoid nightmares."

"I would not stoop so low, your magnificence," Giraiazal assured the emperor. "I cannot guarantee that I can force any man to dream pleasantly if nightmares are determined to afflict him--but I can and will undertake to provide armaments to ameliorate the afflictions of the flesh."

"Ameliorate?" Meronicos echoed. "I do not like that word. I prefer the words *prevention* and *cure*. I do not want you to tell me that you can make my death feel pleasant, or even welcome. I want you to assure me that I will not die."

It was at this point that Giraiazal took his gamble. "That, your magnificence, I cannot do--nor can any wizard whose power is inadequate to remove him from a dying world," he said. "All I can guarantee is to increase the probability that you will escape the plague, and to make you better able to fight it if it does infect you--but that much I can guarantee."

There was a moment when it seemed that the emperor might react badly to this speech, and on many another occasion he certainly would have done--but Giraiazal had chosen his moment wisely. Meronicos the Magnificent was finely poised between bilious wrath and nihilistic despair, still capable of forming a wry smile.

"Oh well," the emperor said. "I suppose there is a certain amusement to be found in honesty--and we all have the remainder of the long night ahead of us, in which it will be sorely difficult to sleep, let alone to dream. I shall summon what remains of my court, so that you may shape our last fugitive delusions."

"Alas, your magnificence," Giraiazal said, maintaining his pose, "I doubt that I have power enough to minister to the dreams of any significant proportion of your sons, daughters, concubines, judges, dukes, counts, barons, knights, governors, generals, manicurists and stewards, no matter how cruelly the Platinum Death has whittled down their numbers. I am only one man, and dreams are difficult to tame. If you command me to do it, I will gladly exert every fibre of my being to muster the dream-strength of a hundred of your loyal subjects, or a thousand--but I would stand a far greater chance of success if I were allowed to concentrate all my attention and skill on a single individual. It is not for me to say who that individual ought to be, and I readily acknowledge that the dreams of an emperor, being innately imperious themselves, might be the most resistant of all to my meagre influence, but I am a loyal and steadfast subject, and I stand ready to do whatever must be done."

The wry smile had vanished by now, but the emperor still seemed to be intrigued by Giraiazal's temerity. Giraiazal knew that Meronicos had always taken pride in his own ability to make a witty speech. "It is a difficult decision for an emperor to make," Meronicos said, sarcastically, "but when all is said and done, it cannot be denied there is one man more precious to any empire than all his subjects put together. As Emperor of Yura, I am bound to instruct you, Master Morpheomorphist, to concentrate the entirety of your effort and skill on the business of shaping my own dreams, and imbuing them with the power to resist the invasion of their fleshy host by the Platinum Death."

So generous was the emperor that the Master Morpheomorphist was permitted to approach a little closer to the throne, and to extend his arms towards the emperor's sacred person while he intoned his instructive suggestions.

Giraiazal was, of course, too diplomatic to mention that the even most elementary manuals recommended that the physician should actually lay his hands upon his patient, and that no suggestion was likely to be effective unless the patient were properly entranced. Even so, while he scribbled a recipe for a mildly hallucinogenic opiate, which would be made up by the emperor's personal physician and tested on his poison-taster, he took the opportunity to say: "There is a bond between us now, your magnificence, which will connect your dreams with mine no matter how far apart we are. We shall not share our dreams, of course, because it is unthinkable that an unworthy mind like mine should ever be privileged to glimpse the contents of such an intelligence as yours, but while I am able to dream my morpheomorphic energy will entirely be at your disposal, adding its force to yours."

Giraiazal retreated to the lodge before the members of the second company of diviners laid their various cases before the emperor, but he was glad to hear that they fared rather better than the first, only a dozen being handed over to the torturers and executioners without delay. He had great difficulty in going to sleep but he put on a convincing show, because he was sure that the emperor's agents were watching him and he knew that an insomniac morpheomorphist cannot inspire confidence in his clients. He was expert enough in his art to trade reality for sham in the end, but no sooner had he fallen into a genuine sleep than he was roughly awakened with the news that the emperor had had a terrible nightmare, and was demanding an account of it.

A lesser man might have considered himself lost, but Giraiazal was determined to overcome this difficulty. When he was thrown roughly down in front of the throne, with the emperor's red-rimmed eyes angrily upon him, he brought himself to his feet with ostentatious dignity, and politely asked Meronicos the Magnificent for a description of the nightmare he had experienced.

The emperor informed the magician, coldly, that he had been chased by giant flightless birds, and had been forced to take refuge in a termitary, whose loathsome inhabitants had crawled over every inch of his skin while he did not dare move a muscle for fear of being pecked to death.

"That is excellent, your magnificence," Giraiazal told him. "I hardly dared hope for anything quite as propitious so early in my course of treatment. The dream-birds were undoubtedly representations of the Platinum Death, and the walls of the termitary were the walls of the dream-fortress that my morpheomorphic art has constructed on your behalf. The termites themselves are the ultimate soldiers, innumerable and irresistible, steadfastly loyal and unhesitatingly self-sacrificing. If they

51

seem loathsome even to you, your magnificence, who stands in no danger from then, imagine what effect they have on their enemies! You have begun the work of making yourself safe, your magnificence; only continue to dream, under the benign influence of my prescription, and you will grow stronger still. I cannot tell you that the plague is impotent to hurt you at all, but I can assure you that you are better equipped to fight it now than you were a few hours ago--and I can assure you, too, that while I remain capable of dreaming, you will have the benefit of my dream-health as well as your own."

The emperor was gracious enough to accept this explanation, and he thanked Giraiazal for his efforts, although he still seemed somewhat distressed.

"I have decided to leave Yura, Master Morpheomorphist," the emperor said. "My torturers have now discovered a reasonable consensus among the astrologers and cartomancers committed to their care as to the safest refuge available. Would you like to come with me, Giraiazal of Natalarch, to soothe my dreams?"

Giraiazal had no difficulty at all in identifying this as a trick question.

"Your magnificence," the Master Morpheomorphist said, without the slightest hesitation, "I would gladly come with you to the ends of the Earth, if that were your wish. Should you desire me to stay here, however, I would be equally glad to obey your instruction. It will make no difference to the treatment I have administered, because my dream-strength is yours to draw upon wherever I might be, just as my body and intelligence are yours to dispose of as you please. All I ask is that you should consider your own interests, and the extent to which my safety figures in them."

"You are a clever man, Giraiazal," the emperor said, "and I admire you for that. I have a reputation to maintain as a paragon of justice, so I am bound to reward you for the service you have rendered, even though it seemed a little discomfiting. I would like to keep you close by me, but I am not certain that I could abide too many noons and nights in which nasty insects crawl over me for hours on end while I lie utterly helpless. On the other hand, I see that there is an argument to be made for not leaving you here to be summarily slain by the plague or the rioters who will doubtless storm the palace when news of my departure leaks out. I shall demonstrate my generosity by allowing you to take simultaneous passage on a ship bound for another port that is destined--according to the best information extracted by my loyal torturers--to remain free from the Platinum Death until the world ends. I shall go south, to the port of Havenheart on the warm and pleasant isle of Pernatura, while you shall go north, to the port of Clarassour on the island of Scleracina. I shall, of course, send a letter to the governor to tell him exactly how a man like you ought to be received."

"I am more grateful than I could ever communicate to you, your magnificence" Giraiazal answered, with perfect sincerity.

Giraiazal would, of course, have been more grateful still had he known that Pernatura would be depopulated by the Platinum Death within a tenday, while Scleracina was indeed appointed by Damozel Fate to remain free of the disease until the world ended. The magician never found out whether Meronicos the Magnificent blamed his own dire fate upon the inefficiency of Yura's torturers or the vengeful determination of Yura's astrologers. Nor was he ever reliably informed as to whether the emperor's last drug-assisted dreams were pleasant or not.

The most popular methods of divination that have survived the attrition of the ages are astrology and cartomancy. It is commonly argued that they owe their survival to their relative accuracy, although sceptics suggest that their popularity is entirely accountable in terms of the profusion and complexity of their indications. Fierce disputes still rage as to which of the two disciplines is preferable, although the disagreements between rival theorists within each tradition are even fiercer. So-called eclectic diviners invariably employ both of them, although they may cling hard to particular theories of interpretation within each tradition and often supplement their researches with such minor techniques as rhabdomancy, numerology and hepatoscopy, which offer much less scope in the range and complexity of their indications.

All schools of divination claim foundations in the remotest antiquity, but none of their claims can be taken seriously. The idea that primal humans might have practised astrology has a certain plausibility, by virtue of the fact the sky was already there, awaiting study, when the first glimmerings of self-consciousness stirred in their rapidly-evolving brains. If there is any truth at all in the legends that have been handed down to us, however, the objects of observation present in that sky must have been very different from those available to the contemporary observer. Adherents of astrology do not deny this, but their attempts to turn the assertion to their advantage are not entirely convincing.

The Revelations of Suomynona, the Last Prophet

The captain of the vessel which conveyed Giraiazal to Scleracina, whose name was Cardelier, insisted at first on referring to him as an exile, and treating him with the same scrupulous politeness as he would have afforded to a powerful nobleman suspected of unprovable treasons. Cardelier's officers followed his lead. In time, however, the captain warmed towards his passenger, and began to rely upon him for good conversation and amusement. The vessel's crew, on the other hand, were exceedingly grateful from the very beginning for the fact that they had been granted permission to sail away from doomed Yura, and they were unanimous in their recognition that Giraiazal was a far less troublesome passenger than some they might have been required to carry. Their goodwill soon matured into a healthy admiration. Giraiazal readily forgave Cardelier for his initial coolness, and made every effort to ingratiate himself further with the captain and his officers by casting optimistic horoscopes for them.

With every day that passed without the Platinum Death making an appearance on board, the mood of officers and crewmen alike improved dramatically. By the time the vessel was half way to Scleracina the prevailing mood was exceedingly cheerful--but Captain Cardelier would not let Giraiazal take a peek at the letter he bore, because it was addressed to the governor of the island.

"I am sworn to deliver it into the hands of the person to whom it is addressed," Cardelier told the magician, sternly, "and I am a man who knows how to do his duty. The confidentiality of official dispatches is one of the principles on which the Empire of Yura is founded, and no seed of corruption will take root therein aboard my ship. Anyway, my friend, what kind of a wizard are you, if you cannot discover what it says without looking? If your horoscopes are reliable, you must know exactly what awaits you on Scleracina."

Giraiazal knew that the captain, although he was by no means stupid, was not enough of an intellectual to understand the Principle of Paradoxicality, which usually confounded diviners' attempts to inquire into their own futures, so he let the matter drop. He also ceased to protest against the captain's error in regarding him as an exile, realising that it would probably do him no harm in his new home to be regarded as a troublesome dissident against the tyranny of Yura--and, even more significantly, as a man of sufficient importance to be punished by exile rather than summary execution.

This judgment proved to be a wise one, because the first news that came aboard the vessel when Cardelier eventually dropped anchor in Clarassour's harbour was that the governor had been deposed and executed on the previous day, and that Scleracina was now independent of the Yuran Empire. Giraiazal was glad to observe that Cardelier did not seem particularly astonished by this unwelcome development, even though it caused him some distress, and that the captain had a contingency plan ready.

"Those old rogues Orlu and Viragan have made their move at last," Cardelier told his officers, while Giraiazal hovered in the background.

"They'll confiscate our cargo, of course, but they won't move against us if we don't move against them. In fact, they'll be glad to welcome us if we're prepared to transfer our allegiance. Now, you all know that I'm an honourable man who would never dream of turning his coat, but I'm also an adaptable man who knows which way the wind is blowing. We all know what a state Yura was in when we left it, and we all know how lucky we were not to have brought the Platinum Death away with us. The Empire's a thing of the past, and we have a duty to its memory, and the principles for which it stood, to steer clear of plague-ridden ports for as long as we can. Our manifest duty to the values by which we've always lived is to help the good folk of Clarassour to keep their island safe, and they'll need good men and sound ships to make absolutely sure that no other vessel coming from our direction makes a landfall until the Platinum Death is a spent force. Are we agreed on our course of action?"

His fellows agreed readily enough--but when Giraiazal suggested that the emperor's letter could now be handed over to him, given that its addressee was dead, the captain refused.

"Our negotiations with Orlu and Viragan are bound to be a trifle awkward," Cardelier explained, "without a stray wizard entering into the equation. I need to make a demonstration of my good faith, so the letter has to go to them. I'm sure you understand--indeed, you must have anticipated it, being a diviner of such skill."

Giraiazal assured the captain that he understood perfectly. He was reasonably content, though not entirely free of trepidation, to be allowed to be present when the captain handed the letter over to the new masters of Scleracina on the bridge of his vessel.

Orlu and Viragan, although they now termed themselves merchant princes, had the appearance of common pirates to Giraiazal. They were both large and swarthy men, with impressive black beards, although Orlu was slightly taller, broader and bushier about the jaws. They both bore scars, seemingly inflicted by sword-cuts, about the cheeks and temples; it was difficult to tell whose were the longest and nastiest, because two of Viragan's were half-hidden by his long hair. The chief difference between them was in their eyes; Orlu's were as dark as might have been expected of a man of his complexion, while Viragan's were pale blue, like those of a newborn child. In a man of another kind this ameliorating feature might have been reckoned an advantage, but Giraiazal quickly formed the impression that Orlu was proud to seem the uglier and more brutal of the two.

Neither Orlu nor Viragan could read, but they had brought two companions with them, who were evidently better educated, in spite of the fact that they were powerfully-built and heavily-armed, one of them with an impressive double-headed axe. These two men, whose names were Akabar and Sharuman, scanned the letter together, each taking one side of the parchment sheet between a thumb and a forefinger.

"Well," said Orlu, when he saw his man smiling. "What does it say?"

"It informs the governor that this diviner and physician, Giraiazal of Natalarch, is a very clever and exceedingly dangerous man," Akabar replied. "It asks that if he should chance to arrive in good health, he should be kept well-fed, but under the tightest possible security--and that he should not be allowed to sleep. It instructs that he should be kept in a brightly lit cell without a bed, with a very uncomfortable floor, and that if ever he should seem to be on the point of falling asleep in spite of these precautions, he should be rudely prevented from so doing. This treatment is to be continued indefinitely."

"I don't understand," Orlu said. "What on Earth is the point of that?"

"I think that the treatment is intended to drive the man mad, Prince Orlu," Viragan put in. "Wouldn't you agree, Captain Sharuman?"

"I would," the second reader confirmed.

"Why?" Orlu wanted to know.

"It seems that the magician was the emperor's morpheomorphist," Akabar said. "It is written here that he had the temerity to claim that the emperor's dreams were linked to his in some mysterious way. It seems that the emperor resented the impertinence."

"He might have resented the impertinence" Sharuman observed, releasing his hold on the parchment and leaning insouciantly on his axe, "but he seems to have been cautious in exercising his disbelief."

Giraiazal was keenly aware of the fact that Orlu and Viragan were both staring at him, appraising him wonderingly. "The emperor is rather ungrateful," He said, adopting a negligent attitude. "I might have saved him, had he trusted me. He did not, and will probably die in consequence. I shall not mourn for him. I shall be glad to offer my services to more deserving masters."

"Will you, indeed?" murmured Viragan.

"Do we need a morpheomorphist?" Orlu asked.

"We need physicians of any sort," Viragan replied. "For generations, Scleracina has lost too many of its capable men to Yura. Now that our beloved king is about to be restored to his throne, he will need wise and clever men to assist him in the unfamiliar work of governance. What else can you do, Master Morpheomorphist. You know ordinary medicines, I presume?"

"Of course," Giraiazal told the merchant princes. "As well as being a highly competent herbasacralist I am also an eclectic magician, fully-trained in astrology, cartomancy, rhabdomancy and hepatoscopy, although I only claim practised expertise in astrology and cartomancy."

"Can you curse our enemies?" Orlu wanted to know.

"In a dire emergency, I could," Giraiazal replied. "But anathematization is a difficult and treacherous art, and I never use it lightly. My long experience has taught me that magic used for healing usually preserves its users too, while magic employed for destruction often exacts severe taxation from them."

"Wise words," murmured Viragan. "I begin to see how you beguiled Morenicos the Insignificant."

"You'll do, I suppose," was Orlu's verdict. "If the emperor wanted to hurt you, but didn't dare to have your head chopped off, you must be useful for something. We'll find you better quarters than the governor was ordered to provide--in the palace, no less. It's not as grand as Yura's palace, but it'll do."

"I shall be grateful for whatever shelter you care to offer a hapless exile, Your Highnesses," Giraiazal assured the merchant princes.

"You had better take a room in an inn for the time being," Viragan told him. "The palace is being made ready for the king and his family. We shall summon you when our preparatory work is done--you may be sure that we shall find an appropriate apartment for you. Look after him, Cardelier--we'll leave him in your charge for a little while longer, if you don't mind."

The Scleracinan navy's most recent recruit assured his new masters that he did not mind in the least. The captain took Giraiazal ashore with him, and guided him to the Outsiders Inn, where he always lodged himself, telling the landlord that the magician was a man of great power and influence. The result of this advertisement was that Cardelier ended up with the second-best room, while Giraiazal got the best, but there was too little difference for the insult to rankle.

Giraiazal immediately set about securing his reputation in conversation with the landlord and his other guests, all of whom were seamen and merchants. The magician let it be known that although it was difficult for him to be certain, given that the charges laid against him had been kept secret, he was entirely innocent of the particular unprovable treasons that had led to his banishment. On the other hand, he dropped hints to the effect that he had never been an admirer of Meronicos the Magnificent, and that it was only his scrupulous regard for the honour of his profession that had made him exert his powers on the emperor's behalf. He was careful not to suggest that he would require any favours from the embryonic elite of Clarassour, claiming that he would be perfectly content with whatever lonely garret might be assigned to him when the two merchant princes had completed their rearrangement of the palace. All that a true scholar required of life, he explained to anyone who cared to listen, was a good brass telescope to assist his patient observations of the sixty-nine stars, a handsome deck of silk-sheathed cards to shuffle, an embroidered table-cloth on which to lay them out, a plush carpet on which to cast his wands, and a few sharp knives of a kind ideal for the dissection of animal livers.

In spite of the chilliness of the nights he spent in the inn, and the fact that even the best bedroom had no fireplace, Giraiazal made haste to calculate the fortunes of a few enthusiastic consultants. He was able to assure them all that Damozel Fate was well-disposed towards them--as, indeed, she always seemed to be to merchants who had the common sense to seek and secure the protection of careful merchant princes. When a carrier-bird from one of Orlu's captains brought the news that Meronicos the Magnificent was dead, however, Giraiazal was not among those who cheered very loudly. Indeed, he professed to be sorry, and opined that if only the emperor had paid more heed to the advice provided by his faithful morpheomorphist instead of reacting with such cunning ingratitude, Meronicos might have survived the collapse of his empire.

"All empires pass, however tyrannical they might be," he observed to a group of his new friends, which included Captain Cardelier. "It will not matter in the slightest whether there is one less in the world when the sun finally decides to make a meal of the Earth. Meronicos would have been a happier man had he not striven so hard to attain and sustain his magnificence."

"How true!" the captain replied. "A wise man must adapt his ambitions to his prospects. I, for instance, am perfectly content to be master of a good ship, while my new masters are each perfectly content with a half-share in an island. We must all make the best of whatever time is left to us before the sun dies, and it is useless to aspire to more than we can sensibly use and consume."

The summons that Giraiazal had been expecting came that evening, politely delivered by Captain Akabar, who said that his master Prince Orlu would like the pleasure of Giraiazal's company at dinner.

"I shall be delighted to cast Prince Orlu's horoscope," Giraiazal said, "if you will only tell me his exact age and name his place of birth."

"That will not be necessary," Akabar assured him.

"Shall I bring my cards, then?" the magician asked. "I fear that my deck is old and its pictures are faded, but I have a good rapport with them."

"That will not be necessary either," Orlu's captain said. "Prince Orlu desires to welcome you to his table as a friend of Scleracina, not as a prophet. We all have confidence in our future, now."

Giraiazal was not unduly worried by the newly-elevated merchant prince's reluctance to provide the fundamental data of astrological calculation, because he knew that merchants were notoriously superstitious about the hazards of allowing potential rivals access to such delicate information. Nor was he dismayed by the injunction to leave his cards behind. He was more anxious about the fact that the invitation was to Orlu's house rather than the palace, and that no mention had been made of Viragan's attendance.

"Will Prince Viragan be present?" he asked, as if it were a matter of scant importance.

"Not on this occasion, alas," Akabar replied. "Scleracina's princes are busy men, and there is much to be done before the rightful king can be restored to his throne."

Given that the two merchant princes seemed to be equal partners, at least for the time being, Giraiazal did not want to offer any implication that he might favour one merchant prince over the other. On the other hand, he certainly could not refuse the invitation.

He set off boldly, determined to be careful.

Brian Stableford

Whatever the extent of the fugitive truth preserved in in legend's fancies might be, one thing of which we can be perfectly certain is that the nascent humans of immeasurably ancient days were blessed in the one respect that we are most atrociously cursed. *They did not know their future.* They could not see their imminent end written in the storms that trouble the face of our glowering sun. They were not oppressed by the certainty that their every achievement was fated soon to be annihilated and their every legacy expunged from the face of creation. They were not afflicted by the knowledge that any children they bore were gifts to oblivion, or by the certainty that any inheritance they cared to store up would require to be very rapidly spent if it were not to go entirely to waste.

We know our future now; it is doom, not long delayed. If we cannot name the day, or even the year, of the Earth's demise we can be more or less certain as to which generations that destruction will afflict. We have no need to make generous provision for our children, for the likelihood is that they will never grow old--and if a few of them contrive to do so, their own children certainly will not. Alone of all the humankinds which have populated the Earth, we know that any plans we make must be made for ourselves and our living offspring, because the overwhelming likelihood is that all but a meagre few of the presently-unborn never will be born.

The Revelations of Suomynona, the Last Prophet

While he pecked away at the relatively ungenerous fare set out on Prince Orlu's table, Giraiazal was asked to say what he knew about the power and influence of every named individual on a tediously long list of the noblemen of Yura and its various subject islands. Captains Cardelier and

Akabar, who were seated on either side of him, had already mentioned a few of these persons as known casualties of the plague, but Giraiazal had no way of telling whether the rest were alive or dead, so he was careful to be as honest as he could in his estimations of their character and the disposal of their inheritances. Fortunately, Orlu seemed quite satisfied with the information he received.

"I cannot believe that what is left of the Yuran aristocracy and their placemen on nearer isles will think it worth the effort to raise a fleet to attack Scleracina, now that news of our secession must have spread far and wide," the merchant prince told the magician, amiably. "Even if they did, I am perfectly certain that Viragan and I, acting in concert, could subvert any attempt to do so without overmuch expenditure--but we must be careful nevertheless. We must discover everything we can about the strength of our future enemies--and our future friends."

"A great many of Yura's captains will want to join forces with us, now that the empire has fallen," Cardelier kindly explained to Giraiazal, although the magician had already deduced as much. "Some we shall eventually accept into our own ranks, always provided that their vessels have been in quarantine long enough to prove that they are free of infection; others we shall pretend to accept, although we shall subsequently dispose of them, replacing them with our own men. We shall also have to make new business arrangements with the masters of all the islands with which we trade. Such negotiations can be delicate."

Such negotiations must be all the more delicate, Giraiazal thought, when the balance of power between Orlu and his erstwhile rival Viragan had yet to be precisely calculated and determined--but he did not voice the thought.

"I had never realised before how very complicated and troublesome the business of government is," Orlu admitted, blithely. "We have waited so long to be masters of our own destiny, and now that we are free we find ourselves drowning in a morass of petty detail. I am very glad indeed to have a friend like Viragan to share the burdens of organization and command. It is fortunate that we are so very similar, even in the make-up of our families. It would be better, I suppose, if we had more children than one apiece--but since we have not, it is as well that our daughters are nearly the same age."

"What age is that, Your Highness?" Giraiazal asked, ever able to recognise and respond to a prompt when he heard one. "I would be very glad to cast your daughter's horoscope for her, if you will permit it."

"That is very kind of you, Master Magician," Orlu said. "As it happens, I already have a strong feeling which suggests that my beloved Calia will marry into the royal family; I suppose the only issue for Damozel Fate to determine is whether she will marry King Lysariel or his younger brother Manazzoryn. I would, of course, be delighted with either match, provided that Calia and Zintrah are happy with their choices."

"I would be glad to cast the horoscopes of both young women, Your Highness," Giraiazal murmured, cautiously, "and to lay out my cards on behalf of both. I dare say that the king and his brother will be equally interested to know what I can discover of their own futures."

"I dare say that they will," Orlu agreed. "It so happens that while Viragan and I have been sorting through the effects of the old governor and his hangers-on, and rooting through the palace's ancient store-rooms, we have found an abundance of magical apparatus that a man like you would doubtless find very useful. We are agreed that you should have it all, as a gift, in order that you may use it to the best advantage of the nation and the king. We feel perfectly certain that any horoscopes you cast and any stories constructed by the cards you lay out will show all our endeavours in a very favourable light, and promise us all the kind of future that we deserve and desire."

"I am sure that your confidence is well-founded," Giraiazal said. "Your generosity is most welcome, and I shall do my utmost to be worthy of your trust."

Giraiazal had not needed the lesson of his lucky condemnation to exile to be thoroughly convinced that a popular prophet ought to be generous in his disposition of good news, miserly in hoarding the rest, and ever-ready to cultivate a useful dependence on his divinatory insight and practical assistance. In order to serve the last item of this agenda, he was careful to drop a few hints into his desultory conversations with Cardelier and Akabar to the effect that a few awkward reefs might still lie ahead of Orlu's merchant fleet, and Viragan's too, which might well require an expert pilot to make their avoidance certain. As he had anticipated, these hints were rapidly relayed to Orlu's ears, and when the dinner was over Orlu took him aside for a confidential consultation.

"What trouble have you foreseen, Master Astrologer?" Orlu asked, his tone a trifle ominous.

Giraiazal knew that he had to be very careful, but he also knew that Orlu had deliberately set certain matters before him for consideration. He lowered his voice, as he always did before continuing into hazardous waters. "Even the firmest alliance, built on the most secure foundations of mutual interest, Your Highness," he observed, "can sometimes be upset or eroded by the careless actions of children who have not yet learned to be wise. Daughters are, for the most part, considerably more sensible and more compliant than sons, and I am sure that your beloved Calia is a paragon of all the feminine virtues--even more so, were that possible, than Viragan's beloved Zintrah--but it might be wise to give scrupulous attention to the calculation of her future. You will doubtless make your own estimate of her potential, and the possibilities that now exist--given the sudden advancement of her station--of making the best possible marriage for her. If you would like me to add the produce of my divinatory arts to that of your practical acumen, I would be only too happy to oblige."

Orlu considered this carefully phrased offer for more than a minute before deciding that it met his requirements. "In that case," he said. "I shall be pleased to tell you the exact hour and place of her birth--and to save my dear friend Viragan the trouble, I shall also tell you the exact hour and place of Zintrah's birth. Nothing would give me greater pleasure, you see, than to know that Zintrah will be satisfied with her own destiny, and will not be jealous even if it should turn out that the king prefers Calia."

"I will be glad to do everything I can to ensure the happiness of both young women," Giraiazal promised. "I presume that Viragan will be as anxious as you are to ensure that his child will be happy in the near future, given that the sun may not permit any of her generation to enjoy the mellow fruits of old age."

Once Orlu had provided the relevant data, Giraiazal returned to his lodgings. He went up to his room immediately, and wasted no time in calculating the dispositions of the White Star, the sixty-eight red stars and the twelve Motile Entities at the birth-times of Orlu's daughter Calia and Viragan's daughter Zintrah. Knowing how delicately his own future prospects might be balanced on the satisfactory outcome of his calculations, he was fully prepared for promising outcomes, but he performed both tasks with all the scrupulousness of a true scholar.

Much to his dismay, alas, he discovered exceedingly ominous possibilities lurking in both charts. The evidence was both abundant and clear.

Giraiazal's first response to the discomfiting signs displayed by the two star-charts he had sketched was to reach for his careworn pack of cards and shuffle them contemplatively. When they felt right, he laid out two neat arrays.

His alarm was further compounded as the magician saw that the cross-shaped figures were crammed with picture-cards of a decidedly awkward nature, including such baleful figures as the Hanged Man, the Sullied Virgin, the Tower Struck by Lightning, the Blighted Herd, the Empty Throne, the Lost Treasure and the Ship Carried Aloft by a Waterspout. Even in close combination, such cards were not necessarily harbingers of disaster, and their interpretation was strongly dependent on the imagination of the observing magician, but Giraiazal found that his internal organs had been suddenly struck by a very inconvenient ache. Having no medicinal herbs ready to hand with which to make up a soothing potion and set his mood right, he had no way of calming the upset, and he began to regret the impatience that had set him to work on his task while he was still at the Outsiders Inn awaiting his summons to the palace.

Although Giraiazal prowled around the table on which the charts and the cards were set out for a full quarter of an hour, hoping to find a more favourable vantage point, neither instrument conveyed any image to his distressed intelligence but a prospect of tragedy not very long delayed. So far as the shorter term was concerned, admittedly, the magician's panic-threatened imagination was able to conjure up futuristic echoes of anticipatory delight, public pride, and even a certain amount of physical ecstasy in both sets of diagrams, but the overwhelming general impression was that all these good things flattered only to deceive, and that the culmination of the whole process would be almost as awful in Zintrah's case as in Calia's.

The magician had no wands with which to obtain a third opinion, and for the time being he was so short of hard currency that buying a brace of hares or a couple of chickens whose laying days were over--either of which would make several very tasty meals once their livers had been interrogated--was out of the question. In any case, reliable hepatoscopy, even to answer the questions posed by a common client, required a sheep or a working dog; to determine the fortune of a future queen would need an experienced fighting bull or a eagle slain by an arrow.

Giraiazal had to suppose that further consultation of the intentions of Damozel Fate would only annoy her if he were hasty and impatient; if he could not find adequate solace in the displays she had so far provided, he would not find them in any others he might now solicit. He cursed his cards as worn-out wrecks, incompetent even for cheating at whist, then took leave to wonder whether the midwives in attendance at Calia's and Zintrah's birthing-beds might have lied about their times of delivery for some reason connected with the local idiosyncrasies of witchcraft. Of this, however, he could not convince himself.

"Well," he said, in the end, "I suppose I shall have to be even more careful than usual in passing on the intelligence of the stars and the trumps. I have fetched up among strangers, in a foreign land that is in the midst of a political upheaval, not to mention the fact that the end of the world is imminent. Of course the stars are full of ominous possibilities--but the sky is always subject to change, and the Motile Entities have been uncertain in their courses of late. And what is the good of having a deck of cards if one cannot act upon its warnings? Yes, bad things are likely to happen here, as they are happening everywhere, but I am the magician who outwitted the whimsicality of Meronicos the Magnificent. If anyone can save these children from the future threats massing around them, I am the man. If I assure Orlu and Viragan that everything will be well, I will not be lying, but merely expressing confidence in my own powers as a seer, a sage and a saviour of situations. Anyway, once I am installed in the palace, with much better equipment at my disposal, I might be able to make more generous calculations and lay out kinder cards."

In spite of these self-reassurances, Giraiazal did not hurry off to Orlu's house to tell the merchant prince his news; he waited patiently for the inevitable summons.

This time, the message that Captain Akabar brought him was that he was to come to the council-chamber in the palace.

The palace of Clarassour was far less grand than the one Meronicos the Magnificent had occupied in Yura, even though its outer walls were handsomely decorated with sea-green blocks of some substance that Giraiazal had never seen before, with numerous carved panels in dark blue and jet black. The interior was clean and tidy; the floors gave every evidence of having recently been scrubbed, the pictures embroidered on the wall-hangings had been repaired with reasonably good thread, and the furniture had been polished.

The council-chamber, which had probably been designed as a banqueting-hall, was adjacent to the throne room; its conference-table was old enough to be venerable without being rickety, and most of the twenty-two chairs set around it comprised a set. When Akabar and Giraiazal arrived Orlu and Viragan were engrossed in discussion with a dozen of their captains, including Cardelier, but the merchant princes did not make their new guest wait. The magician was immediately offered a seat near the head of the table.

"Your new quarters are ready, Giraiazal," Prince Orlu informed him. "In order to facilitate your observations of the sky, we have placed you at the very top of the western tower. The apartment was formerly a set of attics, but we have made it comfortable for you."

"Thank you, Your Highness," Giraiazal said.

"You shall have a boy to assist you in your work," Orlu went on, "and a maid to carry food from the kitchens and waste to the cesspit. Now, what news do you have for us regarding the future of our newly-restored realm?"

"There will be celebrations, Your Highness," Giraiazal prophesied, confidently. "There will be much rejoicing at the new order. The king and his brother will be welcomed extravagantly. The merchant princes of Scleracina will be increasingly prosperous."

"Bravo," said Viragan. "But my dear friend Orlu tells me that he has provided you with the means to make some slightly more specific predictions. I understand that he has kindly provided you with the birth-times of both our daughters. I would love to know what Damozel Fate has in store for my beloved Zintrah."

"Your daughter, Prince Viragan, is destined to marry into the royal family," Giraiazal told the merchant prince, without hesitation. "Her wedding day will be the happiest day of her life. She will be loved with a fervour rarely found among kings and courtiers, because her husband will be a very exceptional man, so uxorious that no other privilege of royalty will mean more to him than the love of his destined bride."

"That is excellent news," said Orlu. "Do you see, Viragan, how fortunate we are to have such a seer in Scleracina now that we have regained our independence? But what of my beloved Calia, Master Magician? What is her destiny?"

"It is surprisingly similar, Your Highness," Giraiazal told him. "Indeed, Damozel Fate intends that your two daughters shall be sisters in law as well as in friendship. Both will marry into the royal family, and both will be loved as they deserve, each of them rapturously received by her husband."

"I am as glad to hear that as my dear friend Orlu was to hear good news of my daughter," Viragan said, "but your account is a little lacking in detail, is it not? Can you not tell us which of the two royal brothers each of our daughters will wed?"

"Alas," said Giraiazal, "that is not entirely a matter for Damozel Fate to settle. Mistress of causation she may be, but there is a certain quality in the human heart that is privileged to evade her strictness. Love, Your Highnesses, will play its part in determining whether Calia or Zintrah weds King Lysariel--but I can assure you that whichever fails to capture his heart will have Manazzoryn's instead."

The magician did not really expect to get away with this evasion, but thought it worth making in order to establish the extreme difficulty of coming down on one side or the other when any decision was to be made between the two merchant princes. He was right; the princes continued to press him, and he had to make the best judgment he could on the basis of what he already knew about the two men. He eventually condescended to suggest, under considerable pressure, that insofar as the stars and the cards could make any judgment their opinion was that Orlu's daughter Calia was the more likely to marry King Lysariel.

Both merchant princes smiled broadly at this news, and Giraiazal was delighted--if a trifle puzzled--to observe that Viragan's smile was actually a little wider than Orlu's, and had no obvious trace of insincerity about it. Indeed, Giraiazal felt a curious sensation in his gut, which informed him that Viragan actually preferred this outcome, and had let him alone while he was invited to dine at Orlu's table in the expectation that it would come about.

"It must be difficult even for the most clear-sighted prophet to look into the future nowadays, without being blinded by the glare of the exploding sun," Orlu said, generously. "We thank you for your heroic efforts, Master Magician, and look forward to seeing what you can do with all the new apparatus we have secured on your behalf."

"Even the glare of the sun's imminent death cannot obscure the quiet radiance of your two daughters' intricately-entangled fates, Your Highnesses," Giraiazal answered. "Calia and Zintrah will delight in being as much loved by their husbands as they are by their fathers, and I feel certain that the love which their husbands have for them will never fade in

Brian Stableford

that unfortunate fashion which is so commonly encountered in the
marriages of ordinary folk."

"We are pleased to hear it," Viragan said. "Orlu and I are agreed,
Master Magician, that you shall be the new king's Grand Vizier. Lysariel
has been raised in ignorance of his true station, and he will need all the
good advice he can obtain. Orlu and I will assist his uncle, Triasymon, to
guide him in practical matters, such as the revision of Scleracina's legal
code and the subsequent dispensation of justice, and also in the
assessment and collection of the new taxes that will need to be levied on
the population in order to restore the island to its former glory. You shall
be Lysariel's guide in matters intellectual and spiritual: his mentor and his
personal counsellor. Yours will be the responsibility of ensuring that he
recognises the propriety and inevitability of our practical advice."

"That is very generous, Your Highness," Giraiazal said, silently
congratulating himself on the apparent success of his diplomacy.

It is the duty of every magician to overstate his competence; after all, how can a client be expected to have faith in an astrologer's advice if the astrologer seems less than certain in his own mind? As every healer knows full well--and what is a diviner but a healer of ills to come?--there is nothing more vital to the success of a cure than the patient's faith that it will work; it is for this reason that modest magicians are as rare as temperate innkeepers and squeamish torturers. Great magicians must, however, be realists as well as egotists; even the greatest must occasionally nurture doubts as to the extent of his competence--or, at least, the competence of his instruments.

Common men are apt to assume, with the encouragement of astrologers, that the evidence of the stars is perfectly objective, and that the only uncertainty affecting a horoscope is the interpretative skill of its reader. It is only because the world is about to end that I am free to reveal this secret without being reckoned a traitor to my kind, but this is a misconception. The truth is that astrological data have no intrinsic meaning; they only serve as agents of provocation to the innate divinatory power contained within the minds of astrologers.

No astrologer worthy of the name ever doubts that he has the power in question, but every astrologer knows full well that he is only a little more than human, and thus not entirely invulnerable to the possibility of error. When a wise astrologer sees an ominous pattern in a star-chart, especially when he had been hoping and expecting to see glorious possibilities, he is duty-bound to wonder whether the flaw might be in himself--temporarily, of course--rather than the future. He is in honour bound, especially if cruel circumstance has forced him to a diet consisting largely of shellfish, to consider the possibility that he might be suffering

Brian Stableford

from a touch of dyspepsia brought on by a bad moussel, or a slight upsurge of black bile caused by climbing too many stairs.

On the other hand, the wise astrologer is also bound to consider the possibility that he might be right, and take all possible precautions against the materialization of his dark anxieties.

The Revelations of Suomynona, the Last Prophet

When King Lysariel and his brother were brought into Clarassour with their uncle and guardian Triasymon, Giraiazal was as pleased as Prince Orlu and Prince Viragan must have been to discover that they were unusually handsome youths of no conspicuous intelligence or explicit political ambition. Overawed by their new situation, Lysariel and Manazzoryn were rather subdued, scrupulously polite and extravagantly grateful to the two merchant princes who proposed to restore them to their rightful place in society. Lysariel did, however, give some indication of being more adaptable to his situation than might be entirely desirable; he was already so entranced with the idea of being a king that Giraiazal was a little anxious on his behalf. The magician knew that Orlu and Viragan would not allow the new king any opportunity to evolve into a tyrant, but he had lived long enough to know that kings who have no real authority often direct such power as they have into whimsical channels.

The position of Grand Vizier having already been filled, Giraiazal had suggested to Prince Orlu and Prince Viragan that they offer Triasymon the title of Lord Chancellor. Giraiazal confidently predicted that the old man would accept that post immediately, without having the least idea of what duties and privileges were attached to it--and that when Triasymon eventually discovered that there were no obvious duties at all, he would be so relieved that he would feel no resentment at the equal absence of any obvious privileges other than a generous stipend. The accuracy of these predictions further enhanced the Grand Vizier's standing in the eyes of the merchant princes.

In the meantime, Giraiazal's meagre possessions were moved from his narrow room at the Outsiders Inn to his remote but reasonably lavish apartment within the western tower of the palace. The stone stairway spiralling up to his door seemed likely to prove tiresome, but the fact that he had a boy and girl to fetch and carry for him offset the inconvenience. The boy, Burrel, was only thirteen hundred days old and not very sturdily built, but he did seem to have a ready wit and had potential as an apprentice. The girl, whose name was Mergin, was two hundred days Burrel's senior and considerably sturdier, so they made a useful pair.

Giraiazal's bedroom and sitting-room were lightly furnished, but the roof-space above them proved to be stuffed with the chattels of half a dozen earlier magical advisors, which must have been stored up by degrees as each one had excited the displeasure of his employers by failing to predict some arbitrary catastrophe. Giraiazal's delight at the inheritance of this richly eccentric treasure-trove was only slightly tempered by his awareness of the circumstances of its accumulation; he knew that the greater part of it would be as worn-out and useless as his own apparatus, but he was optimistic that a few items of real value must be lurking among such an abundance of dross.

At Giraiazal's suggestion, Triasymon was given quarters exactly equivalent to his own in the eastern tower, in an apartment whose uppermost element was far less cluttered but whose living-accommodation was decorated even more tastefully. The former scavenger thanked the magician profusely, seemingly delighted because the tapestries hung to conceal the bleakness of the grey stone walls were lavishly embroidered with marine imagery, and hence well-calculated to ward off home-sickness. These images included an extensive depiction of a reef that Triasymon declared to be marvellously accurate, save for the understandable licence that the embroiderer had taken in populating it with an impossible abundance of noble coral and other marketable excrescences.

"Lysariel loves coral," the Lord Chancellor confided to Giraiazal. "If there is one thing about being a king that will delight him more than any other, it is the opportunity to become a connoisseur of noble coral."

Giraiazal carefully filed this information away for deployment in his future prophecies.

The installation of the new king in the palace, and his subsequent coronation, passed without a hitch. As Giraiazal had promised, the celebrations throughout the island nation were enthusiastic and sincere. Orlu and Viragan gave every indication of being as closely united by brotherly love as Lysariel and Manazzoryn evidently were. Giraiazal was glad to observe that there was no apparent disagreement between Orlu and Viragan as to which of their daughters ought to marry which brother, and that Viragan continued to show not the slightest hint of resentment of Giraiazal's suggestion that Calia was more likely than Zintrah to marry the new king.

"Lysariel will make an excellent king, will he not, Master Magician?" Viragan said to Giraiazal after the coronation ceremony, while the two merchant princes and the king's faithful vizier were toasting their good fortune in rich red wine.

"I am sure that he will," Giraiazal replied. "He is handsome, and there is no malice in him. He has a certain ambitious pride, but that is no bad quality in a king, if he can be educated to direct it wisely. Triasymon has kindly furnished me with details of Lysariel's birth, and Manazzoryn's too, so I shall be able to try out my new equipment in casting their horoscopes and laying out their cards."

"Do you suppose that you will be able to obtain a clearer indication from these calculations as to the identity of Lysariel's destined queen?" Orlu put in. Giraiazal deduced from this insistence that Orlu did not believe in Viragan's seeming contentment with the situation as it was already defined, and that the larger of the two merchant princes suspected his friend and rival of hoping to take advantage of the residual uncertainty.

"It is certainly possible," Giraiazal said, judiciously, "but I dare not make any promises. The hearts of young men are often as capricious as those of young women, and equally apt to defy the prudent inclinations of Damozel Fate."

"Ah yes," said Viragan. "I had never quite understood why Damozel Fate exacts her worst punishments upon the young, but that might help to account for it. Still, if it is the lovely Calia's fate to marry the king, I doubt that the king will have the slightest chance of avoiding the capture of his heart."

"Zintrah and Calia would make equally excellent queens," Giraiazal said, carefully. "They are both possessed of the essential seriousness that a queen requires." Even as he spoke, however, he was prompted by Viragan's attitude to wonder whether the daughter who became queen really ought to be reckoned the more fortunate.

"And what of the king's brother?" Orlu asked. "What do you make of him, Master Magician?"

"I shall have to consult my instruments to make an accurate assessment of his future," Giraiazal replied, as he was bound to do, "but he seems very likeable. Manazzoryn is not quite as handsome as his brother, but I suspect that he is steadier, and that he has a greater capacity for laughter and amiability."

"Do you think so, Giraiazal?" Viragan murmured, rhetorically. "I had come to a similar conclusion myself. Manazzoryn is steadier, and more amiable--but amiability and the ability to laugh are not necessarily good things in a prince of the realm. Lysariel has an imperious quality, and perhaps a touch of impetuousness--no bad things in a king, as our Grand Vizier has wisely indicated."

Giraiazal was not at all sure what Viragan was trying to imply, so he remained silent. Orlu was, however, more than ready to respond. "You are right about that, Prince Viragan," he said. "Lysariel does seem a trifle headstrong, now that he is beginning to settle into his new role--but we shall all take care to educate him in his responsibilities. To rule well requires a company rather than an individual, and a rich variety of talents and skills. If only the world were not set to end so soon, I would unhesitatingly declare that the marriage of Lysariel would be the founding moment of a great dynasty; as things are, we must be content to be as happy and prosperous as we can while the sun lets us live. Shall we dare to hope, Prince Viragan, that you and I might live long into a third year, while our children and their husbands might attain their second?" The intoxicated prince raised his glass as he spoke, in a bold salute.

"I think we might," Viragan agreed, raising his glass in an identical fashion, "and we ought to wish continued good health to you, of course, Master Magician."

"Of course," Orlu added.

King Lysariel's nascent desire to be master in his own house was not made inconveniently manifest in the days that followed; he seemed well content to take advice from his richly talented team of advisors. For the first tenday of his reign he was furiously busy adding his mark to proclamations and decrees, all of which were drawn up and presented to him by his two guardian princes. Unable to understand the legalistic jargon in which these documents were composed--or, of course, to read them--the king was content to rely on the assurances of his wise vizier that the measures thus put in hand would all work to the advantage and glory of his kingdom.

Even Giraiazal found the details of these new laws and taxes exceedingly tedious to read and analyse, but he found no reason therein to doubt that the habits formed by the newly-elevated princes in the days when they had been reckoned notorious pirates by the residents of less happy isles were out of keeping with the designs they had now that they were merchant princes. Their authority and wealth seemed certain to increase by leaps and bounds as they reaped the just reward of their lifelong endeavours. Orlu and Viragan were careful to make sure that the king and his brother would also benefit handsomely from all Lysariel's hard work; it was intrinsic to the plans of the merchant princes that the new royal family should cultivate a healthy appetite for grandeur and glory.

In the second and third tendays of Lysariel's kingship the brothers hurled themselves into a career of hectic dissipation. They exhausted themselves daily with an abundance of meat and sweetmeats, wine and opium, and the delights of satisfied lust. For the duration of this interval Orlu and Viragan carefully kept their daughters at home, and made sure that the wenches recruited to assuage the brothers' carnal desires were considerably less beautiful as well as considerably less refined in etiquette and conversation.

It was not until the first enthusiasms of Lysariel and Manazzoryn had been properly sated that Giraiazal ventured to advise the brothers that they ought both to marry, not only to fulfil the duty of securing a clear line of succession but also to begin the cultivation of the domestic joy and satisfaction to which all royal persons are entitled. This suggestion won the enthusiastic support of Chancellor Triasymon, who had long since developed that contemptuous distaste for luxury and reckless self-indulgence which many poor men erect as a barrier against permanent dissatisfaction.

"But how shall we find suitable wives?" Lysariel asked his Grand Vizier. "Should we send ambassadors to scour the islands of the archipelago for nubile princesses?"

"It would be ridiculous to tackle the problem in such a haphazard fashion, Your Majesty," Giraiazal told them, "when you have a magician of my vast abilities as your adviser. I have already calculated your fortunes very accurately, and I am happy to tell you that the wives selected by the sixty-nine stars and the greater trumps as your perfect partners are already resident in the isle of Scleracina. The stars, the cards and I are mere advisers, of course, and in matters of the heart every man must make up his own mind, but if you order me to do it I will gladly have the candidates in question brought to the palace so that you may judge their suitability yourselves."

"Do it," said Lysariel, after the briefest pause to seek and receive Manazzoryn's approval.

Giraiazal did as he was ordered. Calia, the daughter of Orlu, and Zintrah, the daughter of Viragan, were brought to the palace without a moment's delay. Fortunately, they were looking their very best. They had been very carefully made up by their maids, and were clad in the finest gowns that had ever been seen in Scleracina. Orlu and Viragan had looted these gowns many years before from an Ondamanese vessel blown into the treacherous waters of the archipelago by a generous typhoon, and had carefully put them away until their daughters grew into them.

Giraiazal had not seen the two girls in the flesh before their presentation to the king and his brother. He saw immediately that Calia was slightly the more beautiful of the two, but he thought that she had a certain hardness about her. Zintrah seemed the more sensuous of the two, and might have been a trifle more attractive to an older man who valued pliability, but Giraiazal judged that Lysariel was more likely to elect, in the end, to yield his heart to gloss and glamour than to softness and sensuality.

This was something of a relief to the magician, given that he had already prophesied exactly that outcome, although he was glad to note that the margin of preference did not seem so great that it could not have been swayed by careful influence and judicious advice. Indeed, both brothers seemed at first to be quite infatuated with both sisters, and their twenty days of orgiastic indulgence had left them with a certain lingering affection for the notion that a powerful man need not be narrow in distributing his attentions.

The two girls had been secluded for so long that they were dazzled by the spectrum of opportunity that had suddenly opened up before them. They too seemed initially disinclined to focus their attentions narrowly, but this lack of spontaneous discrimination only made it easier for Giraiazal and their chaperones to ease them in the directions that they were destined to follow.

For the first few days of their managed courtship, the four young people met as a group, happy in their collective delight. By the time another tenday had elapsed, however, matters had been carefully contrived so that Calia and Lysariel were identified as a natural pair, while Manazzoryn and Zintrah were persuaded to think of themselves in a similar fashion. Even Triasymon, without knowing quite what he was doing or why, diligently added his own counsel to that of Giraiazal and the two merchant princes.

By the time that another tenday had elapsed, two firm engagements were contracted. Lysariel was betrothed to Calia, and Manazzoryn to Zintrah. This was, of course, occasion for even more celebration throughout the island, and everything seemed set fair for the kingdom of Scleracina to obtain more enjoyment from the sun's twilight than any other nation on the surface of the planet.

Only Giraiazal knew that this happy time was not destined to last for more than a tiny fraction of the world's dotage, and even he protested privately against his own suspicions. He assured himself continually that the ever-changing heavens might yet reverse their verdict, no matter how unlikely such reversals of fortune usually were. He also told himself that, as soon as the potions he had prescribed for his minor ailments had taken full effect, he would be far better able to see pleasant aspects in the various pictorial arrays he laid out on his table.

"I am growing old," the magician reminded himself, more than once. "It is only natural that I should not feel as well as I did when I was young. It is my duty as an honest magician to take my own physical deterioration into account when formulating my visions. In any case, it is my clear responsibility to err on the side of optimism--because, when all is said and done, I am calculating the fortunes of four young people who have every possible advantage. They are young, they are healthy, they are handsome, they are rich, and they have a company of advisors as clever as any in the world. If they are not favourites of Damozel Fate, who is?"

Giraiazal was not entirely convinced by these careful dissimulations, but he succeeded in pushing his doubts to the back of his mind, so that he could concentrate his thoughts on more immediate matters.

The teachers in our Academies of Magic are convinced that what has once been inscribed in the record of Futurity by Damozel Fate cannot, in its essence, be defied or defeated--but they are also enthusiastic to suggest that a seer generously forewarned by the Damozel as to the tricks she has in store is not merely permitted but expected to supply palliatives against their worst effects. Critics of academic magic sometimes argue that there is a logical inconsistency in making both these assertions, but one only has to consider the nature of the world to understand that they are right. Some eventualities are, indeed, inevitable; others are merely contingent. The greatest refinement in a magician's artistry lies in being able to tell the two kinds of eventuality apart.

Apprentice magicians are also encouraged by their teachers to hope that the Damozel's most dutiful seers might be permitted to draw a reasonable profit from their mistress's most piquant revelations. For this, too, they attract a certain criticism, but in this matter too they are right. Seers ought to delight in turning prophecy into profit, for that is their incentive to be diligent as well as the proof of their skill.

In addition to their validity, these two educational principles have long been a rich fountainhead of comedies and tragedies alike--for which reason even sceptics ought to be pleased with their respectability.

The Revelations of Suomynona, the Last Prophet

As soon as the matter of the royal marriages was settled, Giraiazal returned to his studies with a new fervour. Having given Damozel Fate a helping hand in setting the pattern of Scleracina's destiny--for which, he told himself, she would doubtless be grateful--he now felt obliged to do everything possible to counter any problems that Goodwife Chance might be inclined to throw into the pot. There were far too many shadows hanging over the future that his four young charges were now committed to share to allow him to believe that they could all be avoided, but he hoped that considerable amelioration might be possible, if he could only get a clearer idea of the exact forms the menaces might take.

The magician had not enjoyed a great deal of spare time of late, but what time he had been able to find he had wisely employed in making a rigorous search of the magical apparatus abandoned in his attics, determined to discover and deploy more reliable means of divination than he had brought with him from Yura.

There was no shortage of such apparatus to be found; in the course of his investigations Giraiazal had unearthed three telescopes (one refracting, two reflecting), five skrying-glasses (two globes, two mirrors and a kaleidoscope), seven decks of cards (three equipped with thirty trumps, three with thirty-six, and one with an absurdly optimistic forty-two), four pendulums (one bob being an iron ball, one an agate disc, one a jet image of a cthulhoid and one the shrunken head of an albino girl-child), three sets of rhabdomantic wands (one set of forty, one of sixty-four and one, which had presumably belonged to the same unsuccessful optimist as the forty-two trumps, of ninety-two) and two complete sets of instruments for the vivisection and analysis of animal entrails. Unfortunately, he had no very reliable way of identifying the relative virtue of each device, and he knew from bitter experience that majorities could never be wholly trusted in matters of divination, because divinatory instruments sometimes reacted resentfully to any contest or checking process.

Faced with this embarrassment of potential riches, Giraiazal found the business of selection very vexatious, but he knew that he had to play to his own strengths and concentrate on his best specialisms. When the royal engagements had been announced--thus clarifying a situation that had been fraught with an inconvenient uncertainty in his earlier calculations--he set out to make a new investigation of the now-firmly-linked fates of Lysariel-and-Calia, and of Manazzoryn-and-Zintrah.

Giraiazal thought it best to make his initial enquiries with the aid of the sturdiest and gaudiest of the newly discovered decks of cards. The choice was not determined merely by the fact that he was as well-schooled and well-practised in cartomancy as he was in astrology, but also by a peculiar tingle that this particular deck had imparted to his fingers when he had first riffled through it. Such tingles, he was convinced, were often useful and trustworthy intuitions when they were not mere manifestations of cramp.

Thirty-six trumps, Giraiazal told himself as he shuffled the deck, should be more than adequate to enable him to distinguish the most immediate of the threats that lay in wait for the king, his brother and their chosen brides.

No sooner had he begun turning the cards in the two sets of overlapping arrays, however, than he regretted his choice. Had Lady Death not made her appearance in the very centre of the pattern he would have been able to tell himself that her exclusion was definite, but there she was. And there, in her train, were the Hanged Man and the Sullied Virgin, the Blighted Herd and the Ship Carried Aloft by a Waterspout, not to mention the Tower Struck by Lightning, the Eternally-Bleeding Wound, the Pointing Spectre and the Long-Lost Moon. Even the Vampire Queen--a trump absent from every pack he had previously owned, and therefore quite unfamiliar to him--made a very bold appearance at the crux of Lysariel's array and the terminus of Calia's.

Perhaps, after all, he thought, rather belatedly, it might have been better to cast a set of wands, whose pattern could not have been nearly so definite in its balefulness.

Keenly aware of his responsibility as a master magician and a king's Grand Vizier, Giraiazal was sorely tempted to shuffle the remainder of the deck and lay out a new fortune on top of the first, which could hardly help displaying a plethora of good omens, but he resisted the impulse. He knew that fortune-tellers who took liberties in their relations with Damozel Fate were in clear violation of the protocols of their profession. The one unforgivable sin of cartomancy was the conscious use of a partial deck stacked in favour of a client--even a royal client.

"He who seeks to avoid the pitfalls in his own path," Giraiazal quoted, remembering the lessons of his youth, "does well to focus his mind on those that lie in wait for others. To protect myself, it is necessary to protect those put in my charge, so it is a very good thing that I have been given fair warning of the threats massed against them. Were I stupid enough to ignore what Damozel Fate has shown me, I would deserve to be caught up in these disasters and damned by their unwinding, but if I am clever enough to make full use of the revelations, I ought to be able to avert the worst consequences for others as well as myself."

When Giraiazal went from his cards to the best of his three telescopes, therefore, he did not go in the desperate hope that the stars and the Motile Entities might have a different story to tell him. He made his observations and calculations with the firm expectation that he would find dire threats, and with a solid determination to see those threats more clearly, so that he might be better able to oppose them. He knew that if Scleracina's royal family were indeed to be visited by catastrophe, he must be seen by his all patrons to have acted wisely in its anticipation and bravely in its counteraction. If he should fail to bring his charges through their time of trial, then it must be clear to all interested observers that he had failed valiantly, having struggled mightily against overwhelming odds.

Mercifully, the stars Giraiazal consulted on behalf of the royal family were not entirely devoid of hope. Some force as nebulous as it was nefandous seemed to be avid to consume all four of the founding members of the new royal house. Even so, it seemed to Giraiazal, once he had summoned every vestige of his skill and intelligence, that careful vigilance and clever response might defeat that force at almost every turn. If testimony of the stars could be trusted, the progress of the unfolding catastrophe could at least be interrupted--and there were definite signs of a happier time to come for the survivors, always provided that there were any survivors once Lady Death had done her worst.

While painstakingly drawing these conclusions, Giraiazal could not help recalling the fate of the astrologers who had allowed the spite of their theoretical differences to overwhelm their common sense when Meronicos the Formerly Magnificent had demanded their wisest counsel.

Giraiazal had never been able to excite himself overmuch with theoretical disputes, because he considered it his duty as an eclectic magician to be sympathetic to all points of view. The calculations he had made would have seemed more specific in their implications had he been more rigid in his theoretical affiliations, but he was glad that he was such a flexible man, because he valued the margin of uncertainty that left him abundant scope for measured interference.

"I must be adaptable," he told himself. "No matter how successful or unsuccessful I am in the early phases of my scheme, I must be adaptable. I must continue to be the man who confounded the worst inclinations of Meronicos the Murderous. I must work hard, but I must not work too hard, lest I fall victim to my own excessive zeal."

Despite his resolution not to work too hard, though, the magician worked ceaselessly through more than one noon and more than one midnight to find and collect all the crumbs of comfort contained in his analyses. It was a stressful task, because the potions he fed himself to keep him awake undid all the good work formerly done by the soothing potions he had used to quell his aches and ailments, but he drove himself relentlessly to its completion.

The whole tale told by Damozel Fate, when the magician had unravelled it to the best of his ability, seemed to be that the not-long-extended and probably misfortunate reign of King Lysariel--whose latter phases seemed likely to be overlaid for a while by the temporary Regency of Manazzoryn--would be followed by the reign of Lysariel's son.

There was more than a slight chance--indeed, considered in the right mood, and from the right perspective, it seemed almost a promise--that the son of Lysariel would live a long and prosperous life. Although a new plague was likely to descend on Scleracina within a few hundred days, perhaps in belated compensation for the negligence of the Platinum Death, Lysariel's son was fairly certain to survive it.

Fortunately, all the indications were that the plague that would visit Scleracina would be less murderously-inclined than the Platinum Death, and that the great majority of its victims would make a full recovery. Calia was seemingly fated to be among the new plague's earliest casualties, but there was more than a slight chance--again, considered in the right mood, and from the right perspective, it seemed almost a promise--that she would recover from its symptoms. Zintrah's prospects seemed better, but also more confused; Giraiazal took the relevant signs to imply that she too would suffer, but might grow stronger thereafter if she could withstand her various tribulations.

Although this tale seemed to be bad news for Lysariel, Manazzoryn and their wives, Giraiazal gratefully observed that it was not necessarily bad news for Orlu and Viragan. The merchant princes had no reason to care overmuch about which particular individual sat upon the throne of Scleracina, provided that he was tractable. A child-king might be even more convenient from their point of view than a boy-king. As for their much-beloved daughters, if either or both of them contrived to achieve a dignified widowhood, that might actually enhance their usefulness as instruments of state; and if they did not...well, they were, at the end of the day, only daughters, not sons.

"My course is clear," Giraiazal murmured, fighting hard to maintain some semblance of complacency, as much for his own private benefit as for the necessity of keeping up appearances as he moved about the court. "If I can only maintain the confidence of Orlu and Viragan long enough to become vizier to the next king of Scleracina, I shall not need to have my own horoscope cast in order to be sure that I shall have a good and restful life thereafter, which might extend even to the world's end if I can brew medicines potent enough to double my natural span. For the next thousand days, however, I must be extraordinarily vigilant, and ready to meet a long sequence of stern challenges. I am anxious, but that is only natural. How proud I shall be if I come through unscathed! What a magician I shall be if I can solve such problems as these! Anyhow, what choice do I have, now that I have been so unlucky as to win the trust and friendship of pirate princes like Orlu and Viragan?"

He did not intend to confide any of this to anyone, least of all his servants, but Burrel in particular seemed always to be hovering around, awaiting instruction. It was Burrel, in the end, who dared to suggest to him that his public statements were not an entirely accurate record of his beliefs.

Giraiazal knew better than to strike a servant, because he knew how fondly such inferior individuals nursed grudges, and how many opportunities they had to take sly revenge, so he took another course.

"You are absolutely right, my little friend," he said, warmly. "I can already see that you have the makings of a magician, even though you have a great deal yet to learn. You must trust me, Burrel, as I trust you. A good magician must be very careful, and discreet. Observe me closely, and guard your thoughts as closely as your words, and you shall be my successor, heir to all my knowledge as well as all my wealth."

"I shall be very pleased to learn from you, master," Burrel replied, "and I am anxious to help you in every way I can. You must tell me what you need from me, and help me to understand why you need it."

"You must not expect understanding to grow too swiftly," the magician told the boy. "I am no ordinary scholar, when all is said and done. I am the master of two practical arts as well as four divinatory skills--and although I have never been put to any severe test, I am sure that I have the makings of an unusually effective dispenser of anathemas and curses, should the need ever arise. As a morpheomorphist I have few equals; who was it, after all, who made a fortress of the dreams of the emperor of Yura, which would surely have sustained him for far longer had he not been so foolish as to banish me from his capital. My skill as a morpheomorphist delivered me from that predicament, and my many other skills will sustain me through any future danger I might encounter. All that you require in order to live long and prosper greatly is to put your trust in me, your appointed master. Understanding will come, with time; for now, you need only give me your utmost loyalty."

"I shall do that," Burrel promised, "but I cannot help being anxious for you. If a great man like you is afraid, a mite like me has every right to be terrified."

"Afraid?" queried Giraiazal. "Not I. I am sometimes serious, sometimes fretful, sometimes anxious--but never afraid. If I happen to find that those in my charge are to be teased and harassed by Damozel Fate and her sisters, then I assume that her purpose is to ascertain and prove my capacity as their defender. I shall not let her down; I shall do everything possible to make myself worthy of the position of Grand Vizier of Scleracina, which she has kindly allotted to me. I am not afraid, Giraiazal of Natalarch is never afraid!"

Having fired himself up with this rousing speech, whose loud declamation had almost convinced him of its absolute veracity, Giraiazal set out to search his newly-acquired stock for magical devices which might help the royal brothers and their brides to mount a defence against the various evils that threatened them. The results of his search were slightly disappointing, but he did not emerge from his labours with empty hands. Indeed, he firmly believed that he had contrived to discover four objects that might be uniquely useful to each of the young people in his charge, in being specifically suited to the predicaments that awaited them. While far from perfect as supernatural defences, he judged that they would make excellent wedding-gifts. If they had sufficient effect to demonstrate the power of his foresight and the determination of his will, he supposed that the fact of their provision might save his own life, even if the gifts could not save the lives of their recipients.

According to the testimony of the cards, the most urgent and immediate of Damozel Fate's threats was to Calia, whose near future was overshadowed by the symptoms of a horrid disease.

Although the Platinum Death had passed Scleracina by, Giraiazal knew that the world was still overfull of diseases. Some of them had doubtless been dark companions to many different humankinds, their ancestries traceable to the earliest days of life on Earth; others had presumably been brought to Earth in the days of the legendary starfarers. With diseases of the former kind, herbasacralist theory suggested, some accommodation had been reached and some immunity installed, with the result that although they were very commonly encountered they were rarely fatal to anyone but the newly-born and the very old. Contagions of the latter kind were far more mercurial; their patterns and processes of transmission were little understood, and most of them were rarely seen, but no truces had ever been made in the course of their battles with humankind. When they struck, they struck hard; their symptoms were often terrible, and very often fatal. The disposition of Giraiazal's arrays of cards informed him that Calia was destined to fall victim to a malady of the second kind, but his astrological calculations offered a more hopeful suggestion that the plague's consequent ravages in Scleracina would not result in a vast number of fatalities, however unpleasant its symptoms might be.

Giraiazal knew that there was no point in trying to buy or brew medicines to combat most alien sicknesses, because Mater Nature's pharmacopeia, though carefully stocked with antidotes against her own darts, had little or no armour against extraterrestrial scourges. If Calia's nemesis was to be fought, the magician decided, then she had to be strengthened in herself. Her flesh had to be equipped to throw off the most aggressive fevers, and to heal the ugliest lesions. In brief, she needed the most powerful amulet he could find--preferably one equipped with a crystal that was itself alien to Earth, forged by the fires of some extraterrestrial furnace.

He sorted through all the amulets his attic until he found the best silver mounting; it was a poor thing in itself, but he knew that its power would be dramatically enhanced once he had replaced its stone--a fake emerald--with a more appropriate crystal. According to the texts he had read during his own apprenticeship, the clear crystal he set in its face was of a kind that had not merely been formed outside the Earth, but in a world set at the juncture of overlapping dimensions, where time flowed at very different rates. The crystal should, in consequence, have become a richer repository of endurance than any Giraiazal had ever encountered before. With that advantage, the magician thought, Calia might well survive her sickness; and even if she did not survive long, the testimony of the cards and stars alike was that she ought to live long enough to bear a son.

After Calia, the darkest shadow seemed to be cast over King Lysariel himself, although it seemed to Giraiazal that many subsidiary misfortunes lay between the king and his final extinction. Calia's misfortunes were, of course, bound to resound in her husband; her suffering would generate suffering in him, and the more he loved her, the more extended and amplified his own pain would be.

Giraiazal carefully considered the possibility that Lysariel would suffer enough on Calia's behalf to account for all the darkness staining his own destiny, but decided in the end that there must be further afflictions involved. It seemed to the magician, as he caressed the cards exposed on his tablecloth and tried to draw out every last drop of inspiration, that Lysariel's worst trials would be afflicted upon him by debilitating delusions. If those could not be contained, he would quite possibly go mad--and Giraiazal knew full well how dangerous madness could be in a king.

Giraiazal knew that there was no point in trying to stave off delusions with an amulet. Durance was not a factor in matters of that sort; what was necessary was an agent that might turn nightmares into something less unpleasant, something that could soften a man's dreams by intruding hope and ecstasy to undermine dread and despair, and clarify his vision so as to dispel all mental nebulosity. Fortunately, the magician found among his inherited treasures a magnum of tonic wine whose bottle was of a kind exclusively made in ancient Yethlyreom.

The sealed vessel had survived the fall and ruination of more than one empire, and Giraiazal did not doubt that its contents still had power to infuse their drinker with self-confidence and zest. He would have been more confident still if he had known exactly what vintage the tonic was, and who had bottled it, but he told himself that he was lucky to find anything at all of that sort, and ought not to quibble over details. He could not taste the wine, of course, because its power would be greatly diluted if it were opened prematurely, but if there were a slight probability that it would prove less powerful than he hoped, there had to be an equally slight probability that it would promote a degree of mental clarity that had almost vanished from a world grown decrepit. All in all, Giraiazal thought, the virtue of the wine was a gamble well worth taking; it might well extend Lysariel's life for several hundred days, and even if it did not do that it might keep his head clear long enough for him to offer a fine example to his son.

The threats to Manazzoryn's welfare seemed somewhat less urgent than those overhanging his brother, but no less vague. The juxtaposition of Lady Death with the Hanged Man in his sector of the intricately-entwined pattern suggested a matter of revenge, and the most recent horoscope Giraiazal had calculated implied that he might either commit or fall victim to some reckless and horrible act for which the perpetrator would later feel very regretful--but as to exactly what that act might be, and exactly when it might be carried out, the occult texts had nothing to declare.

Giraiazal hesitated for a long time over the most appropriate way to counter this unclear threat, but in the end he settled on some fibres of hemp which--according to the parchment in which they had been wrapped--had been harvested from the "enriched" soil within the impact-crater of a meteorite that had strayed into the skies of Earth from some long-disintegrated galaxy. According to the author of the manuscript, similar fibres had been found to "still the guilt which feasts on sinners' hearts, and protect them from its penalties". The magician could have wished for more elaborate testimony, and some solid evidence of the reliability of the source, but it seemed the most hopeful resource he had, so he carefully wove the fibres into the fabric of a decorative girdle, along with ornamental threads of gold, silver and bronze.

The testimony of the oracles was that Zintrah would very probably survive her sister-in-law, her brother-in-law and her husband before giving up her own ghost--which seemed to offer her every opportunity to live for a long time, if Giraiazal could save even one of the others from imminent danger. Her prospects were shadowed, to be sure, but it was easy enough to believe that there was nothing further to what he had already discovered lying in wait for her. If, as he had already foretold, she and Calia were to become the best of friends, then Calia's death might wound her almost as deeply as it would wound Lysariel, and she was bound to partake of Manazzoryn's distress at his brother's suffering as well as the regret that was fated to harass him. At any rate, she seem to have less need than Calia of the endurance a powerful amulet would provide; the magician judged that an appropriate medicine might be adequate.

There were several concoctions that might have suited his purpose among the phials and packets heaped up in the corners of the attic, but most were perishable and Giraiazal could not to be certain that they were unspoiled. The safest, it seemed to him, was the desiccated pollen of a rare species of mandrake; the ultrafine dust had the property, when breathed, of numbing pain more effectively than any opiate, fostering courage in the face of disaster, and imparting endurance. It was not as powerful as the amulet he had set aside for Calia, but he hoped that it would answer Zintrah's seemingly limited requirements.

Thus forearmed, Giraiazal of Natalarch, Grand Vizier of Scleracina, began to feel a good deal better about himself and his prospects. He even began to relish the thought of a struggle that might allow him to make the fullest use of his talents, his skills and his cleverness.

Brian Stableford

Part Two

Brian Stableford

The Misfortunes of Queen Calia

1

There are those among us who ask why we are here at all, if previous humankinds had the powers credited to them by legend. If we have relatively near ancestors who were immortal, they ask, why are we so conspicuously mortal? If we have nearer ancestors who abandoned the Earth when it entered its planetary dotage, why are we not where they are? Why is anyone here, if the first prophets who foresaw our doom had opportunity a-plenty to strip the planet of everything alive as well as everything valuable, and transplant the whole of their society and environment to a new home orbiting a younger sun?

As usual, we have no guides in the quest for answers but logic and legend--a fact which is itself significant. If our ancestors had wanted us to know more, they could have made provision for our information by gifting us far more copies of a far greater number of imperishable texts than the stubbornly cryptic specimens said to be included among the books currently hoarded by our most learned magicians. The fact that they did not do so may only signify that they did not care, but as the trouble they would have needed to take was so slight, the likelier conclusion is that the omission was deliberate. Logic suggests that our ancestors condemned us to ignorance just as they condemned us to death. We are bound to wonder why--but the most probable answers to that question are more likely to add to our distress than to assuage it.

The Revelations of Suomynona, the Last Prophet

When Giraiazal, in his capacity of Grand Vizier of Scleracina, presented his wedding-gifts to King Lysariel, Prince Manazzoryn and their intended brides he was very discreet in summarising their properties. The accounts he gave of their power were deliberately vague, and he did not actively discourage the notion that their primary merits were ornamental. He was,

91

in consequence, not surprised that the recipients' expressions of gratitude were tokenistic--but he was convinced that he had done the right thing. The four young people were consumed by their new-found happiness and full of hope for the future; they would not have been grateful for ominous warnings from which they were not yet in a position to benefit.

The merchant princes had to be approached in a different way. Knowing that they would blame him for any unexpected development, Giraiazal was careful to explain to them that dangers lay ahead, and equally enthusiastic to tell them that he had taken all possible precautions against the relevant threats.

"I have done my very best to calculate the dangers which face your daughters and their husbands," he confided to Orlu and Viragan, during a private conference, "and in every case I have taken the best precautions I can. I know that you will both do your best to provide the rather different kinds of protection for which you are well-equipped. If we all stand together in the coming time of trouble, we shall surely prevail, no matter what stings and curses Damozel Fate might devise to test our mettle."

Fortunately, the merchant princes were in too good a mood to have it easily soured, so they took away from this speech the impression that Giraiazal had been most anxious to make: that he and they were fast partners, all three united in a single cause, and that they could rely on him to defend their interests as best he could.

It was only to his new-found friend Triasymon that Giraiazal gave any hint of the real extent of his anxieties. "The end of the world is nigh," he said, philosophically, when he visited the Lord Chancellor in his apartments to share a meal of fine fish, "and men who have already seen much suffering--among which company you and I are certainly to be counted--have every reason to hope that Dame Misfortune might relent in her persecutions while we prepare for our collective annihilation. Alas, I fear that our hopes might be dashed. The king and his queen will be happy for a while, but tribulations are in store for them. They are young, and very excited, so they will not remember anything I have said to them during this last tenday--but you must remember for them, Lord Chancellor. You must be alert in watching over them, and you must do what you can to make sure that they look after the gifts that I have bestowed upon them. Those items might be infinitely precious when the need arises for their use; they must be kept safe until the relevant moments arrive, one by one, and their recipients must be prepared to use them when I tell you that the time is ripe."

Triasymon looked at Giraiazal strangely, as if he were far from sure that he--or, indeed, any magician--could be trusted as far as a feather might be hurled into a headwind, but in the end he said: "I will be alert in watching over my nephews and their lovely wives, and I will do everything I can to see that they take appropriate action in the face of every threat."

"Good," said Giraiazal. "I am sorry that I have nothing for you. I fear that I have not yet taken the trouble to calculate what might befall you in times to come, although I will gladly try to do so if you will tell me the time and day of your birth."

Triasymon looked at him strangely. Giraiazal guessed that, like many an old man unpractised in arithmetic, the Lord Chancellor had long ago lost count of the number of his days, but that he would have been too proud to admit it even before his elevation to the nobility. "I would rather you did not inquire too closely into my fate and fortune," Triasymon told him, stiffly. "In my experience, it is better to have no expectations, thus to conserve the possibility of pleasant surprises."

"That is a wise choice for some men," Giraiazal conceded. He did not add the corollary to that opinion, which was that for others it would be a catastrophic foolishness. Instead, he said: "To tell you the truth, I am as grateful for your discretion as I am for Orlu's and Viragan's. When a seer tries to tell the fortunes of a large number of individuals whose fates are intricately linked, the multitudinous connections can create a tremendous confusion in his mind. I will get a clearer picture if I am able to concentrate on your nephews and their brides.

"I am glad to be of assistance, Lord Vizier," the scavenger said, with all due politeness.

Once the two engagements had been properly celebrated, Calia and Zintrah were removed to their homes and carefully secluded while preparations were made for the double marriage-ceremony. Orlu and Viragan reported to the impatient king and his princely brother that the two young women were delirious with excitement and thought of nothing else but their husbands-to-be. They would have said this in any case, but there was sufficient surprise and amusement in the manner of their reportage to suggest to Giraiazal that it might actually be true. As to the condition of Lysariel and Manazzoryn, there could be no doubt; everyone within the palace, or who had occasion to visit the palace, knew full well how delighted the two brothers were with the prospect of their approaching nuptials.

The more cynical members of the royal household were mildly astonished that the king and his brother should be so ready to forsake a multitude of mistresses for the restrictions of the marriage bed, for even kings have standards of discretion to observe--and, while bachelor kings may hire whores by the dozen, wedded ones are expected to confine their extramarital attentions to a handful of favourites. Giraiazal, on the other hand, was not in the least surprised.

The brothers had not been raised as noblemen, with aristocratic ideas of privilege and aristocratic expectations of excess; they had been raised as common folk, with an innate respect for moderation, and an inherent sensitivity to order and succession. They had been grateful for the opportunity of wild self-indulgence, but they were incapable of regarding it as anything more than a mere phase in a life-trajectory that would inevitably bear them towards settlement, stability and perpetual effort. For young men of their stripe, the desirability of marriage was governed entirely by the desirability of the marriage partner, and the promise of a beautiful and dutiful bride was so powerful a prospect as to stifle all other considerations.

Or, to put it another way, the fact that Lysariel had been told that he was now a king was still merely that: a fact. In order to *feel* like a king, he needed a queen: a queen who was capable of being everything that a queen ought to be, thus enabling her husband to become and be everything that a king ought to be. And the same argument applied to Manazzoryn, who needed a similar reinforcement of his role as the brother of a king.

At any rate, Giraiazal saw clearly enough how difficult Lysariel and Manazzoryn found it to think of anything but their weddings, and he sympathised with their difficulty. Mercifully, their preoccupation did not interfere in any measurable way with the smooth running of affairs of state; Lysariel continued to make his mark on the parchments that were set before him, and the orders thus signed were executed with remarkable precision by those multitudinous agents of Scleracina's merchant princes who now served the realm as its civil service.

Now that he finally had the leisure to leave the palace for short stretches of time, in order to wander the streets of Clarassour and drop in on his old friends at the Outsiders Inn, Giraiazal was able to observe that Lysariel's delighted willingness to fulfil his duties as a hereditary monarch had further increased his popularity among the ordinary people of Scleracina. Lysariel was popular in any case because he was the rightful king, who had emerged in the island's hour of need to replace the mere governor who was Yura's hated puppet. The common opinion admitted that his accession to the throne had been followed by a marked increase in taxation, but judged that such an increase was only to be expected, given that Scleracina was now a nation again, and must conduct its affairs as a nation should.

Giraiazal also had the opportunity to judge how easily Orlu and Viragan had taken command of the armed forces that had previously been under Yura's notional control. It would probably have been enough, he supposed, simply to continue paying their wages, but the merchant princes had prudently decided that a modest increase was in order. Nor had the merchant princes encountered any hindrance in discreetly swelling the ranks of the forces under their command. The conversion of their merchant fleets into a heavily-armed navy had posed no problems, given that they already employed a large number of skilled fighting men and owned very considerable personal arsenals.

The people of Scleracina were more than ready to thank Damozel Fate for all this good fortune, and to take it as an obvious sign that their newly restored nation enjoyed the favour of whatever gods still cared to associate themselves with the doomed world. Thus it was that things went well for everyone as the wedding-day of the king and his brother approached. The weather was mild, as befitted the vernal season--no one was still alive on the island who remembered the previous winter, and no one expected to live to see the summer--and the vast red eye of the sun seemed slightly less baleful in the sight of its beholders than was normally the case.

The double wedding was a splendid affair, with much feasting and a great many fireworks. The citizens of Clarassour did such a magnificent job of emptying their marketplace of fine produce that Orlu and Viragan easily exceeded all previous records for a single day's profit.

Manazzoryn and Zintrah spent their honeymoon in a beautiful villa on Scleracina's east coast, which had formerly been used by the governor for the entertainment of visiting dignitaries. Lysariel's responsibilities did not permit him to do likewise, but every effort was made by his servants to make the royal apartment into a worthy bridal suite, and to make sure that the king and queen had adequate time and space for love-making.

Lysariel and Calia were munificently joyful for tenday after tenday, and the whole palace shared in their joy. Orlu and Viragan made merry in their own homes, where the festivities were rumoured to last the clock around, uninterrupted by noon and night alike. Even Giraiazal contrived to bed Mergin once or twice in the western tower, in spite of his advanced age and the seriousness of his vocation.

A lesser magician might have taken the opportunity to forget that darker times would arrive soon enough, but Giraiazal was always careful not to let his more uplifting potions go to his head, and he remained alert to any news of disharmony. None came, but Burrel--who had a brother among the king's body-servants--did relay some slightly disquieting gossip about the king's state of mind.

Thanks to the success of his relationship with Queen Calia, the young king had apparently become fully conscious of the power that he had to determine his own happiness. For the first time since Akabar and Sharuman had fetched him from Harstpoint, Lysariel had acquired an authentic sense of entitlement to do the kinds of things that only kings could do. This was hardly unexpected, and hardly ruinous, but Giraiazal could not help feeling a slight tingling in his extremities while he waited to see exactly what expression this growing self-confidence might find.

Eventually--again for the first time--King Lysariel decided to make a decree that was entirely his own. Fortunately, the proposition he had formulated seemed quite harmless. Even more fortunately, he had confidence enough in his advisors to summon Giraiazal to a private conference before making any public pronouncement.

"I have decided to have an image made of my beautiful queen, Lord Vizier," the king declared, "so that her present perfection may be preserved for the delight of future generations."

Giraiazal's immediate reaction to this news was that it was hardly worth the bother, given that the number of human generations to come was extremely unlikely to exceed two and might well remain singular, but he could hardly say so. "An excellent notion, Your Majesty," was what he actually said. "I congratulate you on your enterprise, and your sensitivity. The representation will undoubtedly be an unsurpassable masterpiece. Shall I launch an investigation to identify the most skilful painter in the island?"

"I do not want a painting," King Lysariel said, firmly. "I want a proper image: life-sized and solid."

"That is a veritable inspiration, Your Majesty!" Giraiazal replied. "White marble is so much more dignified than vulgar oil-paint. I shall instead begin a search for the most skilful sculptor in all the land."

"And the most skilful divers," the king added.

"Divers, Your Majesty?" Giraiazal queried, uncertainly. "Do you not mean quarrymen?"

"No, Lord Vizier," the king said. "I mean divers. Since my queen is unique and perfect, her image must also be unique and perfect. It will be made of coral."

"Coral, Your Majesty?" was all Giraiazal could say to that. He remembered, belatedly, what Triasymon had told him about Lysariel's fascination with coral. Obviously, he should have anticipated this course of events, even without the assistance of the Greater Trumps and the Motile Entities--there seemed, however, to be no harm in the suggestion. The worst that could happen, so far as Giraiazal could see, was that it might prove impossible to gather enough coral to make a statue, or that the material might prove unworkable--neither of which could be reckoned his fault, by the king or the merchant princes.

"Don't worry, Lord Vizier," Lysariel said, evidently having leapt to his own conclusion about the reason for Giraiazal's hesitancy. "I know all there is to know about coral, thanks partly to my uncle's educational efforts and partly to my own explorations when I was a humble apprentice diver. I know perfectly well that noble coral is not the kind of material from which a full-sized statue could be made, even if we could gather or buy enough of it. I'm not such a fool as to ask a sculptor to make a solid mosaic out of fragments of tree coral--but there are other corals, every bit as wondrous, which grow in sheets on the walls of undersea caves, and in columns stretching from the floors of those caves to their ceilings. I am fortunate enough to have discovered the location of one particular cave whose beauty is unique; had I only known you then, you would doubtless have been able to tell me that I was fated to make that discovery precisely because I was soon to come into my legitimate inheritance."

"Yes, Your Majesty," Giraiazal murmured, reflexively, although this last statement had awakened a certain trepidation in him, in case it might be true that Damozel Fate had guided the king-to-be to his discovery. If so, there must have been a purpose in her suggestion--but what purpose could there possibly be, except to facilitate the making of a very special work of art?

"I want you to hire divers to cut the most generous column of coral that is contained in that cave, Lord Vizier," the king continued. "Then the column is to be brought here, so that a sculptor can be set to work in its fashioning. The Lord Chancellor can probably give you the names of the best divers in Harstpoint, although you'll have to bring in more from other parts of the island. The work of cutting the columns will have to be done in shifts, and the cave might have to be cleared of cthulhoids first...not to mention mersnakes and a few lumpreys."

Giraiazal was not a swimmer, but he had been in markets a-plenty. Yuran fishmongers were notorious for their habit of displaying the corpses of fearsome monsters--or little pieces of allegedly fearsome monsters--in order to demonstrate the fairness of the prices they advertised, which might otherwise have been considered extortionate. "Cthulhoids?" he queried. "Are they not rather horrible, and dangerous?"

"Horrible to look at, most certainly," King Lysariel agreed. "But their reputation for doing harm to swimmers is greatly exaggerated. Almost as greatly exaggerated, in fact, as the venomousness of mersnakes. Cutting the thickest column within the cave will be a challenge, I admit, but it can be done if the determination is there. My own determination is firm, and I expect no less from my loyal subjects."

"Yes, Your Majesty," Giraiazal said, bowing low before he retired from the royal presence.

The magician repeated the substance of this conversation to the Lord Chancellor at the first possible opportunity, when he chanced to meet him in a corridor.

Had Triasymon known Giraiazal better, and trusted him, his response would probably have been less wary, but the magician judged that although the boys' uncle was in a situation in which he had never expected to find himself, he was determinedly protective of his nephews.

"Lysariel is a good boy," the Lord Chancellor remarked, unhelpfully.

"I don't doubt it, my Lord," Giraiazal said. "But what I need to know is: can it be done? And if it can be done, should it be done?" He tried as best he could to read the true answers to those questions in Triasymon's eyes, but Triasymon had the advantage of his own innocence and confusion.

"Perhaps it could be done," the chancellor said, defensively, "if the determination were there. It would be very difficult--but it is true, I suppose, that cthulhoids are not quite as aggressive or as murderously competent as rumour declares, and mersnakes not quite as poisonous. I suppose the real question we ought to address is whether it is worth doing, given that the light within the cave might be a lure of some kind-- but I am reluctant to trust my own judgment in a matter such as this. Lysariel is the king, after all."

"A lure, you say?" Giraiazal said, picking out the key word. "Bait in a trap, you mean?"

"I don't know," Triasymon admitted. If he was unsure of the real depth of his anxiety, however, he had no doubts about the depth of his loyalty; he was quick to add: "But Lysariel is the only one who actually saw the cave, and the light within it."

Giraiazal toyed with the idea that a mysterious light within an underwater cave might have been laid out specifically to attract a king-to-be, but could not muster overmuch anxiety about such a seeming absurdity. He decided to consult Orlu and Viragan before proceeding any further, but found himself forestalled. Calia had already spoken to her father by the time Giraiazal next encountered them in the council-chamber.

"This cave sounds intriguing," Orlu said to him. "There have always been rumours of precious corals that were known in Scleracina before the Yuran invasion, knowledge of whose whereabouts was suppressed lest word of their nature should come to the conquerors' ears. I should like to see a specimen of this luminous variety, so that I can form a proper estimate of its marketability."

"What better motive could the island's divers have than to serve their beloved king?" Viragan said, when Giraiazal turned to solicit his opinion. "With such an incentive before them, they will surely laugh at the dangers and make what preparations they can with bold determination. The statue might indeed turn out to be a masterpiece--and that would be good for the reputation of Scleracina in the archipelago. We have been regarded as an outpost of barbarism for far too long."

"Very well, Your Highnesses," Giraiazal said, glad that he did not have to return to the king with conflicting advice ringing in his ears. "Shall I leave the hiring of the divers to you and Triasymon, while I try to locate the greatest sculptor on the island?"

"That will be easy enough," said Viragan. "I have never met the man, but his reputation declares that there is no one else to compare with Urbishek."

"If rumour can be trusted, Urbishek is your man," Orlu confirmed, when Giraiazal turned to him for confirmation. "He is rumoured to have magical interests, but you'd understand that well enough, wouldn't you? You might even have heard of him. Dabbler in sorcery or not, he is said to be a sculptor of exceptional quality."

Giraiazal had not heard of Urbishek before Viragan mentioned his name, but he was not unduly surprised to hear that a great sculptor had a subsidiary reputation as magical dilettante. All sculptors were occasionally asked to make images for use in the casting of sorcerous curses, and many were probably willing to fulfil such commissions whether they believed in the efficacy of curses or not. At any rate, Giraiazal sent a summoner to command Urbishek's presence in Clarassour at the earliest possible date, while the Lord Chancellor and the two merchant princes set about assembling a team of divers.

Once he had seen a few samples of the man's work King Lysariel freely expressed his pleasure at Giraiazal's choice of sculptor. "I want you to make a full-sized likeness of my queen," the king told the artist, when Giraiazal brought him to the royal apartment. "This must be no ordinary likeness, no common or garden statue; there must not be another image like it in the whole world."

Urbishek, for his part, was delighted to receive such a commission. "I have been waiting for this opportunity all my life, Your Majesty," he said. "I shall make you an image fit for the stuff of legend: the most glorious statue the world has seen for a thousand years, or will ever see again. I shall make you a work of art that would make the legions of the world's deserters deeply embittered, were they ever to discover that they had left too soon to see such a marvel forged. Only condescend to give me material worthy of my art--I have always yearned to work in pure gold."

"I will give you something better than that," King Lysariel promised. "I will give you living gold, alloyed with a crimson redder than blood and brighter than the sun."

"I do not understand, Your Majesty," Urbishek said, glancing sideways at Giraiazal to reproach the magician for not having given him warning of this.

"The image is to be made from coral," the king said.

Urbishek's face fell. "Coral is not a good medium for sculpture, Your Majesty," he said, hesitantly. "It may be carved into tiny effigies easily enough, but so far as I know, no one has ever made a full-sized human figure out of coral."

"That is why it is perfect for our purpose," Lysariel told him. "It will require unparalleled ingenuity--but so much the better."

Giraiazal could see that Urbishek knew better than to maintain the least display of reluctance in front of a novice in monarchy, but he was sensitive to the sculptor's underlying displeasure. "So much the better, Your Majesty," Urbishek agreed, in a very lukewarm tone. "Unparalleled ingenuity I have; I shall look forward to the opportunity to deploy it."

"The divers will begin work as soon as possible," King Lysariel told him. "Provided that the statue pleases me, you may name your own price, over and above the glory that will inevitably be attached to your name if you can make the most of your opportunity."

Urbishek obviously knew better than to take this offer at face value, given that it would have to be endorsed by Orlu and Viragan--who had a fearsome reputation as hagglers--but Giraiazal did his best to reassure him on that score. "You will have your due reward, my friend," he said. "Our two merchant princes are as enthusiastic to see this job done well as the king is himself.

"I am glad to hear that," was Urbishek's nakedly insincere reply. "It will be a great honour to please my king, if I can."

There are some among us, who nurture guilt and remorse after the fashion of addicts, who declare that ultimate mankind is being punished: that the humans abandoned on Earth when all who had the means of leaving departed for other worlds must have been criminals, madmen, beggars and other parasites of which they wanted to be rid. Fortunately, this is not really credible; whatever vices our better ancestors may have conserved, they must have been capable of making far better provision than we can for the least fortunate members of their society.

The punishment hypothesis may gain slightly in plausibility if we adopt the modified thesis that there was not one but a long sequence of abandonments, whose consequence was a long and slow descent into decadence by a hundred or a thousand degrees. In this view, each exodus of the world's most competent individuals left it to be repopulated by the most feeble, cretinous and unadventurous members of the relevant humankind. Even so, it still requires us to suspect our more capable ancestors of an appalling negligence, and I believe that we can be confident in rejecting it.

One preferable hypothesis, on emotional as well as rational grounds, is that the myriad tales told of the exploits of the better humankinds constitute a mere cacophony of myths and fancies, by which our nearer ancestors sought to explain and justify their sharp sense of their own woeful inadequacy. There are some who argue that even if this is not so, it is what we ought to choose to believe, for the sake of our own self-esteem. If even a tiny fraction of the Great Epic of the Many Humankinds is true, these sophists assert, then we are bound to recognise in ourselves the merest relics of a Golden Age, left to lie neglected on an abandoned and derelict shore, not merely forgotten but despised, everything we are and

Brian Stableford

everything we possess having been carefully weighed, and found to be not worth saving from the holocaust to come. Far better to believe that our ancestors were liars, who never left the Earth at all.

There is however, another possibility. Had our starfaring ancestors left nothing behind them when they departed, the sun that had nurtured them for thousands of millions of years--of whatever individual duration-- would have died unobserved. If, as legend assures us, the new worlds to which our distant cousins removed themselves are so far away that light takes centuries to reach them, the news of the sun's demise would be ridiculously belated by the time they received it. Is it possible, we are bound to wonder, that we were left here in order to bear witness to the death of the sun? Are we here to ensure that the Earth does not die uninhabited and unappreciated? Are we here to add a vital dimension of *meaning* to the inevitable event?

The Revelations of Suomynona, the Last Prophet

Things did not go smoothly on the reef off Harstpoint. Orlu and Viragan hired twelve of the best divers in Scleracina, and the team was supervised by the Lord Chancellor himself--while Giraiazal was content merely to observe--but three of the twelve were lost in the initial assaults on the cave. The first drowned in a cthulhoid's multitentacular clasp, the second was poisoned by multiple mersnake bites, and the third bled to death after his flesh was seared and scarified by a shoal of lumpreys. The third death was the most inconvenient, to begin with, because it attracted half a hundred sharklongs into the waters within the reef--but these attracted half a dozen fishing-smacks in their turn, and a company of harpooners. These human predators found an opportunity for further sport, if not for profit, in hunting down a few of the cthulhoids that had been forced out of the coral-lined cave.

The cave *was* lined with luminous coral; that, at least, was no illusion- -but confirmation of the fact left Giraiazal to wonder what it implied. Might the grotto be a carefully-baited trap, as Triasymon had suggested? If so, what kind of a trap might it be--and who, exactly, was it intended to ensnare? The magician tried to reassure himself with the assertion that if the trap had been made to capture the king-to-be, it had already failed. However many lives it might claim now, Lysariel's was perfectly safe.

Once the cave was free of dangerous creatures, the divers worked in shifts, three teams of three--one of whom plied a saw while the other two protected him from attack--taking turns of ten or twelve minutes each. It soon became obvious to Giraiazal, though, that three teams were not nearly enough; the rest-time between shifts was far too short and if the cave were left unguarded for any length of time the lumpreys and mersnakes were quick to begin a determined process of recolonization.

After three days Triasymon had to hire another dozen divers. These were not as skilled, and their attempts to match their predecessors soon

102

led to casualties; one man drowned after becoming tangled in weed; another was badly injured by a jellyfish sting and a third lost a foot to a marauding sharklong. When a fourth man was hurt by a mersnake bite Triasymon had to join that team himself in order to keep up the work rate.

It took two further days to saw through the top and bottom of the column that had been selected for the king's statue. When it was finally hauled to the surface in mid-afternoon the divers were ecstatic with triumph. The men waiting in the boats immediately saw, however, that the coral was not nearly as bright in daylight as it had been in the dark depths.

The divers were less enthusiastic when Viragan, who had come from Clarassour with Captain Sharuman to watch the task completed, asked them to continue work.

"Take another column, if you wish," the merchant prince instructed them, "or break lumps from the walls--whichever seems to you to be the most convenient way to obtain more samples. It will be easier now, while the cave is unoccupied, than it will be at any future time."

The Lord Chancellor protested that there would be plenty of chippings once Urbishek got to work, but Viragan was adamant that he needed more substantial blocks in order to make a proper investigation of the potential marketability of the material.

When Giraiazal interrogated the divers about the prize they had already claimed, they told him how disappointed they were that the light of day made the column look duller by far than it had seemed while it glowed in the magical cave. They suggested that it could not be as valuable as Viragan hoped. When Viragan heard them complaining, though, he was quick to argue that the cut coral would probably regain its luminosity and allure once night fell, or if it were placed in a dark room.

Giraiazal was not convinced of this at first, but when he made a superficial examination of the column he had to admit that the coral was highly unusual. It was softer and more even in texture than wood or horn, and its colour was magnificent; although it did not seem to him to be luminous, at least for the moment, it did seem to respond to the blood-coloured light of the sun, showing its own scarlet tints with increasing boldness while the amber through which the rosy streaks were sinuously extended seemed to flow like molten gold. He supervised the workmen who wrapped it up carefully and loaded it into a cart for transportation to Clarassour.

After some negotiation with the merchant prince, the divers agreed to return to their work, provided that they could operate in fours rather than threes, with two men simultaneously plying saws and levers while two more kept them safe from harm.

Alas, matters did not work out that way. Cthulhoids gathered outside the cave, almost as if they had grouped as an army, attacking *en masse* as the teams of divers struggled to fill the nets let down by the ship with their produce. Three more men died and two more were seriously injured before Viragan finally agreed to call off the quest in the following mid-morning.

"Seven men dead and five badly hurt is a high price to pay for coral," Triasymon said to Viragan, as they and Giraiazal were ferried in a small boat to a ship that Captain Sharuman had brought into the waters off the reef, to save them from having to ride back to Clarassour.

"They died for their king," Viragan told the Lord Chancellor. "They were fortunate to have the opportunity--and all their wages will be paid in full, to the widows and children of the men who could not collect their due."

"I wish now that the boy had never found out that the cave existed," Triasymon went on. "I wish, too, that I had not responded to his discovery by telling him all that I know about coral. I was wrong to feed his fancy. And I should have confessed my fears more frankly to Giraiazal, when he told me what Lysariel had asked him to do."

"You were absolutely right to tell the boy what he wanted to know," Viragan assured him. "You taught him more than you intended. He will be a better man--and a better king--because of it."

Will he, though? Giraiazal wondered. *Damozel Fate has confusion in store for him, and this business now seems more likely to add to that confusion than to ameliorate it.* He did not speak aloud, though; he knew that he had to consult his oracles before issuing any public warnings.

When Sharuman's ship docked in Clarassour its passengers found that the cart had beaten them to the capital. King Lysariel was delighted with the column of coral that had been hewn from the living walls of the undersea cave. On his orders, it had already been set up in the centre of a north-facing chamber on the ground floor of the palace, which had been newly fitted out as a studio for Urbishek. Giraiazal and Triasymon hastened to see it, while Viragan returned to his own house.

When the Grand Vizier and the Lord Chancellor arrived Lysariel and the sculptor were inspecting the column very closely, walking around and around it while caressing its surface with their right hands.

"It feels right," the king said to Urbishek, while his uncle and Giraiazal looked on. "It is warm to the touch, and yields slightly to pressure. It cannot be alive, I suppose, having been rudely severed from its roots above and below, and lifted out of its element, but I am not certain that it is yet entirely dead. Will that interfere with your work, sculptor?"

"I do not think so," Urbishek told him, sounding a little more confident now that he had examined the material with which he was expected to work. "I have scrutinized the surface of the coral with a magnifying glass, which allows me to see the cells of the organism, and they do indeed seem to have residual vestiges of life, but once I begin to shape the statue the detritus of those cells will be pared away. The substance within the heart of the column will doubtless be inert, and I shall be able to shape it exactly as I please."

"I'm not so sure of that," Triasymon put in, stepping forward to place his own hand on the crimson-and-gold surface. "Tree corals, I know, are alive only at the tips of their branches, and fan-corals only at the rim--but this is a creature of a different kind. I wonder if its whole substance might be alive. Is that possible, Master Magician?"

"It is possible," Giraiazal conceded, reluctant to admit that he had not the slightest knowledge of coral, and no way to assess the exact extent of the possibility. "I should like to have some specimens of it myself, so that I can conduct my own investigation."

This seemed to the magician to be a harmless enough request, but he noticed that Urbishek frowned, as if the sculptor's competence to analyse his own material were being insulted.

"Most corals are stony and brittle," Urbishek said, thoughtfully. "Chisels must be plied with the utmost care, and it is safer by far to work them with files and sandpaper, although they take a fine polish. This material seems to me to be more vitreous, quite different in nature and far more inviting to an artist."

"I do not understand what difference you mean," Giraiazal said. "Vitreous means glassy, and glass is brittle." Again, this seemed to him a harmless observation, but Urbishek scowled as if a challenge had been issued and a deliberate slur cast on his expertise.

"You are right, of course, Master Magician" Urbishek said, curling his lip to communicate the fact that he did not approve of Giraiazal's interruption, even though etiquette compelled him to reply politely, "but when I say that coral is stony I mean that it is crystalline: that it is a true solid that would become liquid by sudden melting, were the temperature to bring about the transformation attainable. Vitreous substances like glass are false solids, which soften by degrees as heat is applied to them; they have no melting point because they are not organized into crystalline lattices. They are still fluid, although they flow so very slowly that their deformations are invisible to the human eye."

Lysariel frowned as he tried to grapple with this nice distinction. "But what difference does it make to your work, Master Sculptor?" he demanded. "Will you be able to make the image or not?"

"I shall certainly be able to make the image, Your Majesty," Urbishek said, obviously having decided that it was safe to make the commitment. "The difference is a good one, which should work to our advantage. With your permission, I shall experiment with the chips and flakes removed from the surface, to see how they respond to heat. If they can be softened by relatively gentle flames, heat will become my assistant in shaping and smoothing the lines of the statue--and if the temperature required to soften them turns out to be inconveniently high, we shall be no worse off than we would have been if the material were as stony as other corals."

"Do what you must, Master Sculptor" King Lysariel said, airily, "but you will let us know, will you not, if the substance is too responsive to heat. I would not like to set the image on a pedestal only to see it melt in the course of an unusually hot noonday."

"It seemed solid enough while it lay in the cart that carried it away from Harstpoint," Triasymon observed, drily. "Last noonday was bright enough, but it failed to reduce the column to a puddle."

"Good," was the king's judgment. "I see no need for further delay-- you will begin immediately, Master Sculptor."

"In that case, Your Majesty," Urbishek said, "I should like to see the queen, dressed and posed as you require, set beside the column. I shall need to study the figure carefully."

King Lysariel immediately sent for Queen Calia. Triasymon withdrew but when Giraiazal signalled that he would like to remain the king gave him permission.

Lysariel and Giraiazal both watched carefully as the sculptor suggested poses, until one was found to which the king was prepared to give his consent. It was a relaxed pose, as befitted a female figure, but it did require a certain effort from the sitter. The column was not wide enough to permit overmuch extension of the arms, but it was agreed between king and artist that the right hand should be raised and placed modestly upon the bosom, while the left should rest upon the hip.

Lysariel and Giraiazal continued to watch while the sculptor moved around and around the upright column, until it was decided which part of its surface should serve as the front. Giraiazal had been careful to say no more lest he risk giving further offence to the sculptor, but it seemed that the damage had already been done. Urbishek asked to be left to continue with his work without the pressure of further observation, saying: "I cannot be disturbed while I work. I require an environment conducive to my creativity. If Your Majesty wishes to be present while I work, I shall of course be delighted to welcome you--but I must beg you to order that no one else enters the studio while I am here, and that the room should be locked when I am resting. I am sorry to ask this of you, but I find your vizier a particularly inconvenient presence."

Giraiazal opened his mouth to protest, but he did not get the chance. Lysariel was impatient to make progress with his project. "Go away, Giraiazal," the king said. "See to it that Master Urbishek's requirements are met. I shall remain." Giraiazal realised then that he might have done better to leave with Triasymon rather than wait until he received an explicit command to leave and stay away.

Urbishek did not seem inclined to crow over his victory. When Giraiazal looked back into the room before closing the door behind him he saw that the sculptor, apparently completely absorbed by his contemplation of the coral block, had already picked up his tools and was preparing to strike the first scarlet flake from the column. The king, meanwhile, had settled into a statue-like pose himself.

Giraiazal made sure that he was loitering in the corridor outside the studio when the sitting finally ended--apparently because Calia had begged for release--but there was to be no remission of his banishment. Lysariel led his wife away, promising Urbishek that she would return as soon as she was properly refreshed. When Urbishek eventually reported to the king that the application of moderate heat would not, after all, be a useful accessory to his customary skills, Giraiazal had to hear the news at second hand from Triasymon.

"Am I to be given any flakes of the coral, so that I might conduct my own experiments?" Giraiazal asked.

Triasymon only shrugged, which Giraiazal had no alternative but to regard as a negative answer. He dared not ask King Lysariel, although the young man seemed friendly enough when he condescended to give his vizier some further news. "The sculptor's work will be long, and rather tiring for my wife, Lord Vizier," he said. "Urbishek will not require her to maintain her pose continuously, so long as she is ready to resume it when he asks, but the work will be long and arduous. He has suggested that I have a sofa placed next to her station, and a decanter of water set on a table close at hand, with a little fruit. I asked him if a servant might be allowed to read to her, so that the hours would not weigh so heavily upon her but he begged me not to do that. I suppose I must consent to his wishes; I am the king, but he is the artist, and I dare not risk the slightest impairment of the quality of his work."

"Of course not, Your Majesty," Giraiazal said.

"Uncle Triasymon will see to it that the studio is properly equipped," Lysariel said. "Urbishek seems to find your presence especially irksome, perhaps because your magical abilities give you a greater presence than common men. It is ridiculous, I suppose, but I must ask you to humour him. You understand, do you not?"

"Of course, Your Majesty," Giraiazal said, concealing his annoyance. He watched from a distance while two well-upholstered sofas and a table were moved into the studio, followed by a huge fruit-bowl and several decanters. He stood by, too, while Triasymon--having been forbidden to organize a relay of musicians and lecters to provide amusement--made arrangements for the fruit-bowl and the decanters to be discreetly filled by noon and by night, while Urbishek was resting.

In consequence of Urbishek's artistic temperament, and Lysariel's insistence on the flattery thereof, the image of Queen Calia began to take shape in secret. The only observer of the work in progress was the king, and even he was not a constant observer, because he was sometimes required in his council-chamber and had to make occasional ceremonial appearances in the court. The servants charged with replenishing the water, wine and fruit, moved in and out of the studio very swiftly, and the statue was invariably draped when they were permitted to enter the room.

In spite of Urbishek's initial disappointment regarding the coral's responsiveness to mild heat, the sculptor's work made reasonably rapid progress. Giraiazal had to rely on Burrel to collect gossip and convey it to his turret, but he was only slightly dissatisfied with Burrel's reports, even though it was not altogether clear how the information they contained could have been reliably gathered. For one so young, Burrel obviously had an unusual aptitude for the collection of information.

During the first few days, allegedly, Urbishek required his model to take up her pose fifty or sixty times a day, sometimes for a minute and sometimes for an hour--but as time went by and the image began to emerge from the stone he required progressively less of her and worked at an increasingly furious pace. It was, Burrel told his master--presumably taking advantage of a certain poetic licence--as if the queen's image had been imprinted on the sculptor's mind by the combination of his fierce concentration and increasing familiarity.

"Does the coral glow in the dark?" Giraiazal asked his servant, although he felt a considerable humiliation at having to do so.

"Yes, master, it does," the boy replied. "It glowed very dimly, at first, but as the form of our beloved queen emerges from the block she grows brighter and brighter. Sometimes, they say, the glow can be seen even in the brightest daylight--and sometimes it shines through the cloth that is draped over the image." Burrel's insertion into his account of the words "they say" served to remind Giraiazal that this was gossip rather than testimony from reliable eye-witnesses, and not to be taken entirely seriously--but he could not doubt that it was common gossip, for the same news was given to him no less than half a dozen times, by informants as widely placed in society as Mergin, Captain Cardelier and Lord Chancellor Triasymon.

On the sixth day of Urbishek's labour, Burrel reported that the sculptor had declared that he was now able to release his sitter for two or three days, although she would have to return when he began to bring forth the fine detail of her face--but when Queen Calia had exchanged a glance with her doting husband, she had declined the opportunity. She had said that she would be happy to remain close at hand, in order to avoid interrupting the sculptor's creative flow should some need to consult her figure or her features suddenly arise.

"Urbishek said: *As you wish, Your Majesties,*" Burrel reported, "and continued his work with all due zeal. *This will undoubtedly be your masterpiece,* King Lysariel said."

"Was that remark an appreciation, a prophecy or a command?" Giraiazal wanted to know--but that the boy could not tell him.

"All seems to be going very well," the boy said.

"So it does," was Giraiazal's uneasy reply.

If we really are here merely to witness the end of the world, much else that is mysterious about our own particular nature may be more readily explicable. Why should we be mortal, we are inclined to wonder, if our ancestors were not? Perhaps it is because we were designed to die, not merely in order that we would lose less when our world was consumed, but also to ensure that we and our world should have something in common. Perhaps it is because we were designed to be capable of mourning--indeed, to be ready-made experts in that once-lost art.

The use of the word "art" in this context may seem frivolous, but it is not. If our ancestors had even a fraction of the abilities granted to them by legend then they were works of human artistry themselves, and everything they made--even their detritus--must also be reckoned a work of art. Any attempt to imagine and evaluate their arts by comparison with our own is presumptuous and vain, but it is at least arguable that the essential motive forces of our own story-mongering--passion and death--are universal rather than local.

If we were indeed put here in order to play our part in the drama of the sun's demise, rather than being merely abandoned as objects beneath contempt, then we must have been gifted with emotion and mortality in order to play our parts properly, without any undue artifice or dissimulation. Should we be proud of this? Perhaps not. Should we even be glad of it? Perhaps not. But we ought perhaps to be grateful for the fact that it is a more flattering explanation of our nature than its rivals.

The Revelations of Suomynona, the Last Prophet

On the morning of the eleventh day of Urbishek's labour, things ceased to go well. Giraiazal was making a fresh set of observations of the positions of the Motile Entities when Burrel tumbled breathlessly into the room, having raced up the stairway.

"You must come at once, Master," the boy said. "Something terrible has happened."

"Where?" Giraiazal demanded, as he hurried to the door.

"The sculptor's studio."

"The studio that I am not allowed to enter?" Giraiazal asked, as he began to descend the stone staircase.

"You are needed now," was the boy's answer to that--and as they went hastily on their way, Burrel gave him a more elaborate account of the disaster that had struck.

Urbishek had been working on the statue's face, and had required his model to hold her features in the same expression for some considerable time. Temporarily released from her demanding pose, Queen Calia had happened to take up a bunch of luscious grapes which had been placed in the fruit-bowl that morning. Her father Orlu had obtained them, by way of legitimate taxation, from a ship that had strayed too close to Scleracina's southern shore while on a westward course from Kalasperanza to Aztyrka.

When the queen held the grapes above her head, opening her mouth to welcome the most pendulous, two hairy spiders had fallen out of the bunch. One had fallen into her open mouth while the other had landed on her left breast.

Astonished and panic-stricken, Queen Calia had swatted the second spider with her free hand while trying to spit out the first. Neither attempt had been successful. The spider at the queen's breast had responded to the ill-treatment by biting her; the other had refused to be expelled from her throat.

When Giraiazal arrived in the studio King Lysariel was extremely anxious to complete the story, although he was trembling feverishly and his voice seemed to be on the brink of decaying into a helpless babble.

"I leapt up from my own sofa as soon as I saw the spiders fall," he told Giraiazal, who was now cast in the role of court physician rather than unwelcome presence. "I lent my own efforts to those of my wife. A single thrust of my more powerful hand succeeded in dislodging the spider from my beloved's breast, and I brought my bootheel down on it before it could run under the sofa, crushing it. My hand's power was of no use, however, when I put my fingers into Calia's mouth and tried to grasp the spider within. It has not come out. *It has not come out!*"

The effort of conveying this last item of information, combined with the horror of the climactic observation, was too much for the king, who immediately began sobbing.

Giraiazal was glad to find that the queen was not choking, although she was certainly very distressed. He asked her to open her mouth, but she was in no condition to comply with any mere request, and he had to tell

Lysariel to force her mouth open so that he might look into it. Lysariel was still weeping prodigiously, but he managed to obey the instruction.

There was no sign of the spider. Giraiazal inferred that the horrid creature must have scrambled so deeply into the queen's throat that a reflexive movement of her muscles had defied her most urgent will, leaving her no alternative but to swallow the monster. When the magician reported this conclusion to the king, Calia overheard him, and the shock caused her to faint--but this was no bad thing, as it put an end to her hysterical convulsions. She fell back on to the sofa, quite inert.

Urbishek was fluttering around the sofa, thrown into utter confusion by anxiety; Giraiazal judged that he would be no help at all. Fortunately, Lysariel had sent a summons to Triasymon as well as Giraiazal while he still had his presence of mind. The magician directed the Lord Chancellor to take the queen's body in his strong arms, carry it to the royal apartment, and lay it down on the bed. Triasymon did as he was asked while Giraiazal and the increasingly distressed Lysariel followed him. Giraiazal could not help feeling a slight vindictive thrill as Lysariel ordered Urbishek to stay where he was.

By the time Triasymon had set Queen Calia down on her bed she was very feverish, and the breast that had been bitten had turned hard and brittle. The superficial flesh was beginning to crack under pressure from within, and a viscous fluid quite unlike blood was leaking through the cracks. Lysariel's anguish had become extreme while he observed the progress of these awful symptoms. He begged the magician to help his bride, then turned away to issue the most terrible threats against the servants who had placed the grapes in the bowl without making sure that they were safe and brought it to the sculptor's studio. Unfortunately, the only servant present at the time was the entirely guiltless Burrel, who had come to help his master. After venting his spleen in this manner Lysariel returned to pleading pitiably with Giraiazal to save the queen's life.

The magician assured the king that he would do everything possible, but curses and promises continued to tumble recklessly from Lysariel's mouth as Triasymon pulled him away from the bedside to allow Giraiazal room to conduct a better examination. While the anxious Giraiazal shook his head in consternation and dismay at the sight of so many unfamiliar and horrible symptoms, the equally anxious Lord Chancellor shook his nephew in a determined attempt to restore his equilibrium--but the king would not be comforted.

"You are the king of Scleracina, Lysariel," Triasymon said. "You must conduct yourself as a king, not as a boy. Giraiazal will make a potion to neutralize the spider's poison."

Giraiazal did not need this prompting. He ordered Burrel to see that the remains of the spider on which Lysariel had stamped were collected and taken to his attic. "Have the grapes put into a sack, Burrel," he said.

"There may be other spiders still inside the bunch. If so, I do not want them hurt, although I certainly do not want anyone else to be bitten."

"Is my queen dead?" Lysariel wailed. "Will my beloved die?"

"She is not dead," Triasymon told him, firmly. "Giraiazal foresaw this danger; he told Orlu and Viragan, and warned me to be on my guard. He knows what must be done."

Giraiazal was touched by this demonstration of confidence, but he could only hope that the last statement might be true. In fact he had only the vaguest notion of what must be done, for he had no idea what the poison was to which he must provide an antidote. The first thing he must do, he decided, was to force his patient to imbibe a liberal dose of an emetic, in the hope that the spider she had swallowed might be expelled without leaving too much poison behind.

"I have to fetch some medicines," he told Triasymon. "Keep the king safe, and try to make him calm. Have you sent word to Orlu?"

"Yes," Triasymon said.

Giraiazal hurried back to his turret, and came back down with equal alacrity. He met Burrel on the stair; the boy confirmed that he had the dead spider, and the grapes.

The emetic was immediately effective, but nothing showed within the queen's vomit that might have been all or part of a spider.

"My beloved is doomed!" Lysariel cried. "Is my beloved doomed?"

"No," said Triasymon, who still had tight hold of his nephew. "She is not." Manazzoryn and Zintrah arrived then, and were soon able to assist Triasymon in trying to calm the king.

Giraiazal inspected the wound in the queen's breast more carefully, and the brittle flesh around it. He had never before seen anything resembling the cloudy fluid that was oozing from a gradually extending network of fissures.

"I fear, Your Majesties," the magician said, when he had completed this examination, "that this condition will not be easily treated. I shall need time to examine the dead spider and the grapes. Fortunately, as the Lord Chancellor has said, I have had some forewarning of this catastrophe, and I have made what provision I could to counter its effects. You must find the amulet that I gave to the queen as a wedding-present--I presume that it is in her jewel-box--and place it around her neck. Do not expect a rapid cure, I beg of you. We must hope that the amulet will give her the strength to endure her symptoms while I begin the search for a cure. First, I must examine the spider. If she wakes up, summon me immediately. I shall make up a potion to soothe any pain she may have when she wakes, and once she is able to listen to me I shall bring my abilities as a morpheomorphist to bear as well as my expertise in herbasacralism."

It was Zintrah who found the amulet, but Lysariel had steadied himself enough to take it from her hand and place it around his wife's neck, carefully setting the jewel between her breasts.

"Can you cure her, Master Magician?" the king asked, his voice much more carefully controlled than it had been before. He was obviously making every effort to play the king now, but his wild eyes revealed the depth of his anxiety, and the desperation of his love.

"I do not know," Giraiazal said, recognising that this was not a time for reckless optimism. "But I promise you that the amulet will increase her powers of endurance very considerably; it will not easily surrender her to Lady Death." Having said this, he returned to his apartment again. The effort of climbing the steps twice within a matter of minutes reduced him almost to helplessness, but he pulled himself together and set to work immediately.

Unfortunately, closer examination of the spider gave him no clue as to its species. There were no more spiders hiding in the grapes, which seemed quite ordinary--so Giraiazal had no explanation ready when Orlu came thumping at his door, demanding to know how his daughter had been poisoned, and by whom.

"The spiders must have been hiding in the grapes when you took the cargo from the ship," was the safest judgment the magician could offer. "If they are shy by nature, they would have clung to their hiding-place until they had no alternative but to quit it. Have you ever seen such a creature as this before, Prince Orlu? Is it native to Scleracina?"

Orlu peered at the squashed spider. "I never saw one like it," he said, "but I'm a seaman."

"I never saw one like it either," Giraiazal told him, "but Ambriocyatha has many islands. We ought to show the remains to Cardelier, and as many other captains as you care to consult. I cannot believe that this was done deliberately, Prince Orlu. I cannot imagine who would do such a thing, or why."

Orlu nodded in response to this, but it seemed that his own imagination was not quite as limited as Giraiazal's. "I shall interrogate the servant who took them to the artist's studio," the pirate said, grimly. "Indeed, I shall interrogate everyone who laid a hand on them from the moment I took them from the captive vessel's hold. I shall send a ship to search for the vessel itself, and another to wherever the cargo was loaded--but all my captains will look at the spider first, and Viragan's too, in case one of them can tell us where it came from. I will get to the bottom of this--but in the meantime, can you save her?"

"I shall do everything I can," Giraiazal promised.

"You knew this would happen," Orlu said, in an accusing tone. "How? And why did you not prevent it?"

"I feared that some misfortune might overtake the queen and make her ill, because the stars and my cards told me so," Giraiazal replied. "I did not know what--but if there is one man in Scleracina who can save your daughter's life, I am that man." He felt it necessary to make the last point as strongly as possible.

Fortunately, Orlu seemed to grasp the logic of the situation. "Do what you can, Giraiazal," was the merchant prince's modest instruction. "My daughter's life is in your hands."

Giraiazal collected the medicines he needed and returned to the queen's sickroom, leaving Orlu to take charge of the dead spider.

The queen's fever grew steadily worse through the noonday, the evening and the following night. She eventually woke from her faint, but that only made matters worse; she could not go back to sleep because her body was continually racked by violent paroxysms, and she had to be given copious draughts of water to compensate for the perspiration that poured from every part of her body that had not yet been infected by the brittle patina which was slowly extending from her wound.

Giraiazal gave her potion after potion, with no immediate effect. Even though he was certain that she could not attend to spoken instructions, he attempted to exert his morpheomorphic talents upon her, but she could not respond to the gentle pressure of his fingers upon her forehead. The one good sign was that she did not seem to be slipping away, or growing conspicuously weaker; indeed, she revealed herself a warrior in her sorest distress. When she finally fell asleep she continued to breathe insistently.

Orlu and Zintrah undertook to take turns with Giraiazal to watch over Calia, and the magician accepted the offers gratefully. He was reluctant to entrust a similar duty to Lysariel because he was not entirely convinced that the king was sufficiently in possession of himself to follow the instructions he left behind, but, Lysariel boldly declared that no matter who else was present, he would never desert his post by his beloved's pillow, not even to sleep. "I wish it had been me," the king moaned, when Giraiazal tried to persuade him that he would be more useful if he consented to rest for a while. "I wish that I could have swallowed both monsters, and digested all their poisons."

"Wishing will not help, Your Majesty," said Giraiazal, "but if you would consent to swallow a sleeping-draught, you might wake up a good deal stronger."

"Never!" was Lysariel's response to that prescription--after which he addressed himself directly to his stricken spouse. "I only wish that I could take the poison from you now, my beloved! Life would be worthless if I no longer had you, whether I were a king or a beggar, lord of all creation or scavenger of its bleakest shore!"

Giraiazal sighed, reconciling himself to the necessity of treating two difficult patients rather than one.

The abscess in Calia's left breast continued to grow through the hours of darkness, but the cracks in her brittle flesh no longer gave out the murky fluid. Giraiazal hoped at first that this might be a hopeful sign, but soon found out that it was not. Examination of the queen's bodily wastes suggested that when the hardening tegument of her flesh had become resistant to the pressure from within, the soft tissues beneath the tumour had been rent instead, and the nasty fluid had been discharged into her gut. Some of it was expelled in periodic series of coughing-fits, and the rest eventually passed out in the other direction. The bowls in which these noisome wastes were collected were inspected very carefully, but there was no sign therein of anything resembling part of a spider.

When Orlu came to relieve the magician he told him that his first enquiries had yielded no result. "No one has recognised the spider," he said, "The servants who took the bowl to the artist's room were always under observation. If the spiders were deliberately introduced into the fruit, it was done before they reached the palace, or by magic. Tell me, magician: is there magic in this?"

"I do not know," Giraiazal answered, wishing that he had a better reply to give. "But if there is, the amulet will counter it."

"There is not much time left to the world, so they say," Orlu said, in a sombre tone, "but my daughter has not yet had her share."

Giraiazal dared not make any promises, despite all that he had seen in the stars and the cards to suggest that Calia ought not to die before she had borne Lysariel a child, but Orlu was not looking for promises. The merchant prince was very downcast; his daughter's illness had affected him more than Giraiazal could have anticipated, and perhaps more than Orlu could have anticipated himself, having always thought of himself as a ruthless and piratical man.

"There is hope," Giraiazal said, placing a hand on the taller man's arm in a kindly gesture that the merchant prince would never have tolerated before. "She has her father's strength, and my magic. There is hope."

Brian Stableford

By comparison with the alleged achievements of herbasacralism, those of the branch of practical magic known as morpheomorphism seem very modest. Although there are many magicians who are proud to be specialists in herbasacralism, specialist morpheomorphists are rare. Eclectic magicians who combine treatments of both kinds are, however, inclined to see them as natural partners in the curative project. Illness, these multitalented individuals opine, affects the mind as well as the body, and a wholly effective treatment ought to address the needs of the whole human being rather than narrowing its focus to the merely chemical transactions of the flesh.

Specialist herbasacralists are, as might be expected, inclined to attack the presumptions of eclectic magicians by arguing that herbasacralist remedies, far from neglecting the mental and subjective aspects of illness, actually have their greatest effects in that arena. Sceptics agree, arguing that the only significant effects of the great majority of herbasacralist remedies are analgesic and psychotropic--but this is to take scepticism to an unreasonable extreme. However meagre the legacy may be that our better ancestors preserved for our use, the remedial agents they set to grow in our woodlands, wetlands and hedgerows are an undeniably precious casket of gifts.

The Revelations of Suomynona, the Last Prophet

By the time the rim of the red sun next extended its thousand-league bridge over the western horizon, Giraiazal was convinced that the amulet he had given to the queen was exerting a benign effect. If she grew no better, she grew no worse; her life hung in the balance, but that balance seemed quite stable.

117

Unfortunately, no such stability had forced itself upon her husband; King Lysariel had now become convinced that his wife was lost to him. He had not left her, nor had he slept, but his presence was doing no good. He was stretched out on the bed alongside her as if he lay upon a torturer's rack, weeping and wailing prodigiously.

Orlu was also distressed by the continuation of his daughter's awful appearance, but he was made of sterner stuff than the king. "Your nephew is not helping his wife, my lord," he said to the Lord Chancellor, when Triasymon, Manazzoryn and Zintrah came into Calia's room to see if there was any news. "He is only making matters worse."

Triasymon hastened to make his nephew's apologies. "He is exhausted from lack of sleep, Your Highness. It is because he loves your daughter so passionately that he is so distraught."

"He refuses to sleep," Orlu said, "and I am sick of his incessant weeping and moaning. If he will not consent to take Giraiazal's advice you must remove him to another room. Have him put to bed and set his brother to look after him. He may return to the royal apartments when he is in a more constructive frame of mind."

A Lord Chancellor who had come to the post by a more orthodox route might have reminded Orlu that it was not for a mere merchant prince to give orders for the forcible removal of a king from the royal apartments, but Triasymon was a realist, In any case, Giraiazal assured the old man that Orlu was right, and that it would be better for Lysariel if he could be forced to rest. Triasymon agreed to do as he was asked, and asked Manazzoryn to help him remove Lysariel to his own rooms high in the eastern tower.

Lysariel put up some resistance, but he had grown weak while wallowing in his grief and eventually consented to be led away. Orlu and Zintrah remained by Calia's bedside while Giraiazal made up more potions. The magician sent a bottle containing a powerful opiate to Triasymon, urging the Lord Chancellor to make certain that Lysariel took it. When he brought his remaining bottles to Calia's bedroom, Giraiazal found the queen awake again, and more coherent than before. He immediately resumed the work of trying to minister to her dreams.

While he stroked his patient's forehead Giraiazal murmured instructions to her mind, telling her as precisely as he could what visions she ought to experience when she slipped into the world beyond the world, and how she should make shift to combat the images of her illness.

An hour passed while the magician exerted himself thus, and when the queen fell asleep again her face immediately became peaceful. The spasms that had racked her body for so long seemed to have ceased, and she gave no sign of any discomfort.

"Is it over?" Orlu asked. He had been prowling restlessly around the room while Giraiazal worked; like many men of action, he could hardly bear to be still when caught in an awkward situation.

"By no means," Giraiazal answered, bluntly. "This is an intermission, a temporary truce. The fight will not be concluded for a long time--but she is fighting, and that is a very good sign."

"Is there anything I can do to help her?" Orlu asked, emphasizing the word *do*.

"We are all doing what we can," Giraiazal told him.

At that moment, Prince Viragan came into the sickroom for the first time, and interrupted Orlu in his restless pacing so that he might pour out his condolences.

"If I can do anything else, my friend," Viragan concluded. "You have only to ask. I wish that one of my captains could have put a name to the spider, and told us whence it came, but every one who is in port has seen it now, and none of them recognised it. I have a report from one of my captains, delivered by carrier-bird this morning, to say that there is trouble in Kalasperanza which threatens our holdings there, but I will not go if there is anything I can do here."

"Trouble?" said Orlu. "What kind of trouble?"

"Assassination and sorcery. It was always a possibility that our efforts on behalf of Scleracina would inspire others. It was inevitable, I suppose, that some would not consent to have Yura's tyranny replaced even by such benign governance as ours.

"Who has been assassinated--and how?" Orlu asked.

"My steward, one of my captains and several local administrators who were in our pay. Poisoned, it is said."

"How?" Orlu persisted. "What poison, and how was it delivered?"

"Messages carried by birds are necessarily brief," Viragan told him. "The word *sorcery* probably signifies that the venom and method are stubbornly mysterious. Why? Can you possibly think...? I shall set sail without delay, my friend. If there is any connection between events in Kalasperanza and the injury to your daughter I shall certainly discover it."

"Cardelier is already on his way there," Orlu said. "He is a good man, but he was the empire's man less than a hundred days ago. Perhaps I should have sent Akabar to the plundered ship's port of origin. This cannot be coincidence. If there is anything to be discovered, it must be done with expedition. Birds can only fly home, so I cannot get word to Cardelier, but...yes, I will go myself. It was my ship that brought the lethal cargo. I will have my revenge on those who tricked me. If the secret of this business is to be found in Kalasperanza I'll turn the whole island upside-down."

Giraiazal wondered whether Prince Orlu might be taking far too much for granted, but he certainly did not want to say so. He knew how enthusiastic the merchant was to assist his daughter, and he suspected that if Orlu were forced to remain in the palace, or even on the island, his restlessness and impatience might make him an extremely inconvenient presence. For the moment, Orlu seemed well-disposed towards his daughter's physician, but the time might come when that benevolence would wear exceedingly thin. If Orlu had some mission to undertake more suited to his temperament, Giraiazal thought, that might work to everyone's advantage.

"What have the stars to say, Master Magician?" Viragan asked. "Is there sorcery in the queen's misfortune? Is there hope of finding an answer in Kalasperanza?"

"If there is sorcery involved," Giraiazal was quick to say, "that would account for the unfamiliarity of the queen's symptoms, and the fact that nothing seems to help but the magical properties of the amulet. If Captain Akabar can find the ship from which Orlu claimed those grapes in tax, or if Captain Cardelier can locate the cultivator of the grapes, they might recover information of great value. Cardelier is, as you say, a good man-- but he must be careful, if the man he seeks is a magician. What a pity I was not able to give him wards against sorcery before he sailed!"

"Give me whatever wards you can muster!" Orlu demanded. "I will find this mischievous fruit-grower, and tell him that I will destroy his lands, his crops and his entire family unless he provides an effective remedy for the evil his produce has wrought."

"Let me do it, my friend," Viragan said. "You should remain here, with your daughter. You can trust me to be as thorough and as brutal as you would yourself."

Giraiazal did not suppose that Orlu had any doubt on that score, but now that there was something to be done that was more exactly fitted to his talents and inclinations, the pirate prince was not about to be forced to exercise patience.

"I will go," Orlu said, in a voice that forbade any contradiction. "I will set sail immediately. I shall send a bird back as soon as I have any news-- and I will have news, if I have to burn every house and field on Kalasperanza to get it."

Giraiazal ran to his turret then, to find an amulet or two that might help to protect Orlu in a contest against a magician. In truth, he had no confidence in any of those he had discovered among his inherited treasure save for the one he had given Calia, but he thought them better than nothing and he had every confidence in Orlu's ability to overcome any but the most powerful sorcerer by sheer brute strength. He was a little ashamed of his own relief at bidding Orlu a fond farewell, but he could not be sorry to be rid--at least for a while--of the man most likely to rip his guts out and tear away his flesh with hot pincers if Calia should happen to die. He multiplied his excuses by assuring himself that Orlu might have been driven mad if he had been forced to sit helplessly beside his daughter's bed, impotently waiting for a recovery that might never come, and that a journey to Kalasperanza ought to be reckoned a clever prescription, which would assist a difficult patient to translate his anxious frustration into grimly purposive determination.

Orlu set sail on the afternoon tide. Viragan had urged him to take three or four of the most heavily armed vessels in his fleet to support his own ship, but Orlu refused, saying that speed was the essence of the mission.

Meanwhile, Triasymon came to tell Giraiazal that Lysariel had woken up in a much better state of mind, apparently quite recovered from his excessive anguish.

"Where is he?" Giraiazal enquired.

"He has gone to see Urbishek," Triasymon replied.

Giraiazal was mildly surprised that Lysariel had not rushed to find out how his wife was, but he was too busy with his patient to worry about the king's negligence. As the hours went by, however, and Lysariel still did not appear, he sent Burrel to find out what had become of him.

Burrel came back with the news that the king had instructed the sculptor to resume work on the statue and to redouble his efforts to complete the image. Giraiazal did not have to ask whether Urbishek had obeyed this command--to do otherwise would have been unthinkable. Apparently, Lysariel had decided to remain in the sculptor's studio to oversee the work rather than returning to his wife's bedside. Giraiazal could not imagine that Urbishek was happy about that decision, but the sculptor was in no position to object.

The horrors afflicting Calia's body had not yet spread to her lovely face, but Giraiazal was by no means sure that her features would remain unravaged for long. He knew that there was a strong possibility that she would never recover her former beauty, even if she survived the disease that had her in its grip.

The abscess within the queen's stony breast swelled again that evening. Secondary lesions were now beginning to form in her belly and her lower back. The flesh overlaying her abdominal cavity had hardened in the same way that her breasts had hardened, but it remained sufficiently flexible not to crack in the same manner; unfortunately, the consequence of this failure was that the abdominal abscesses did not leak, and came much faster to the point of bursting, presumably expelling some of their pus into her body-cavity.

The remaining pus was expelled over the next two days from both apertures of the queen's churning gut, but the expulsion was obviously not so complete as to leave no residues. These residues caused the surrounding tissues to suffer a necrosis whose blue-black colour was clearly visible through Calia's increasingly-translucent outer flesh; the multitudinous worms which bred in the necrotic organs could also be seen wriggling beneath the skin as they migrated into her limbs. When they reached the limits of their exodus, in her hands and feet, their movements grew more urgent, as if they were seething in frustration.

Giraiazal had no alternative but to slice the palms of Queen Calia's hands and the soles of her feet with razors, so that the worms might escape from her flesh. Like the pus that still spurted from her mouth and anus, the worms were collected in bowls by servants, then killed by plunging them into boiling water. Giraiazal had compresses made from cream and mustard, which were applied to Calia's glassy skin in the hope of easing its continuing transition, and they did indeed bring some relief to the beleaguered queen.

Giraiazal's skill as a morpheomorphist still had the upper hand of the queen's delirium, and he continued to dose her with opiates whenever she complained of excessive pain. This combination of treatments permitted her to endure the worst spasms of vomiting stoically. The magician assumed that there would be an opportunity to obtain her report on the nature of her dreams as soon as her condition was a little more settled, and so it proved. No further worms were generated in her flesh, and she became much calmer.

When Calia awoke was in the following midnight, she seemed perfectly lucid and did not complain of being in pain. Zintrah, who was watching over her, had immediately dispatched servants to wake Giraiazal and Lysariel--but when Giraiazal arrived, the king had not put in an appearance.

"She is asking for Lysariel!" Zintrah said. "She has told me that she loves her husband very dearly, and is determined to be well in order to bear him a child."

"That is good," the magician said. "Are you able to tell me what dreams you have had, Your Majesty, while you have been unconscious?"

"Yes," the queen replied. "I am not accustomed to remember my dreams for more than a moment or two after I wake, but the dream that has occupied me recently has extended for such a very long time that it is with me still."

"Tell me what you dreamed," Giraiazal said.

After exchanging a glance with her sister-in-law, the queen began to speak in a murmurous voice. "I went into a darkness deeper than any I have known before," she said. "No stars were shining in the sky, and there was no light to be seen near to the ground on which I walked. I walked for a very long way, unable at first to see where I was going, but in the end I saw a glimmer of red light ahead of me. I thought to begin with that it was a star, but its redness was tinged with gold and it grew as I approached. As I came closer I saw that it was a female figure, naked and all aglow. Her body was red and gold, the two colours swirling around one another as they described the contours of her form.

"I did not recognise her face, but I took her to be Lady Death, and although she was surrounded by shadows I sensed that she was standing in an open doorway. She stood aside to let me go through. As I stepped across the threshold my eyes acquired the ability to see in that darkness, and to perceive colours that I had never known to exist before. I was inside a tomb, and within the tomb was a sarcophagus hewn from a mineral darker than jet, but vividly colourful with the new hues that I had recently learned to see.

"I knew that if I pushed aside the lid of the sarcophagus, and climbed in to it so that I might lie down, time would stand still. Although the world was doomed, its destruction and dissolution would be impotent to reach me, because I would be lost in a moment that would never lapse. But I did not want to climb into the sarcophagus.

"I turned my head to look back at Lady Death, and saw that she was not solid at all, but something between a flame and a drop of water, all a-flicker with red and gold. She moved forward, more gracefully than any human dancer could contrive, and poured herself into the sarcophagus, which drank her as if she were a draught of vintage wine. I tasted her in my own mouth, and savoured her; neither her light nor her fire flowed into my body, but I felt a faint hint of a delicious intoxication. I wanted more, but there was no more to be had. Within the sarcophagus the liquid body of Lady Death had been engulfed and digested--but I did not want to follow her. I imagined that I too might be consumed, surrendering to the eternal moment of my alimentation, but I did not want to be preserved in that way, by becoming a part of some alien flesh immune from the scarifications of time and the eclipse of the sun.

"I wanted so desperately to live, in order to bear the child of my husband Lysariel. I did not want to be the bride of darkness, no matter how colourful darkness really is. So I crossed the threshold again, sacrificing my new eyesight, and strode into the darkness, searching for a new and more generous light.

"I walked for a very long time, always limping and often stumbling, but I would not give up. I knew that I had to keep going, and so I did, though it seemed an eternity before I saw light again. This time, it was candlelight. I had opened my eyes. Then I saw my sister's face, and knew that I was home. Where is my husband Lysariel?"

"You did very well, Your Highness," Giraiazal said, reaching out to touch her forehead with his fingertips. "But I fear that you might meet Lady Death again, on the far side of sleep, and will need all your strength to resist her temptations. The contagion carried by the spider is continuing its diabolical work within the temple of your flesh, and it will not be easily defeated--but I shall shape your sleep as best I can, and give you power over your dreams, in order that you might resist. It will not be easy, but you are not alone."

"No," said Zintrah. "You are not alone."

"Tell Lysariel that I love him," Calia said, before she slipped away into sleep again. Silence fell then, for a little while. Giraiazal felt very tired, but also hopeful. He reminded himself that his abilities as a morpheomorphist had saved his life in Yura, and might increase even more with further practice.

"Was that really Lady Death that my sister saw?" Zintrah asked, eventually.

"It was her own image of Lady Death," Giraiazal told her. "It is a good thing that she was able to confront that image explicitly, and bravely. The battle is not over, but I think she will live." He went out then to find the servant Zintrah had sent to fetch King Lysariel, to ask her why she had not brought him.

"He is with the sculptor Urbishek, my lord," the servant said. "He would not let me in and told me to go away."

"Is the image still not finished?" Giraiazal asked.

"I do not know, my lord," the servant said. "The king would only open the door by the merest crack. All I could see was a strange red-gold light that seemed to fill the room."

Giraiazal wondered whether he should go in search of Lysariel himself, but he decided against it. He had not been allowed into the sculptor's studio while the work was in progress before, and he did not suppose that he would be allowed in now. When he went back to Zintrah he said: "Perhaps it is as well that Lysariel cannot see his wife as she is now. He would be distressed to see the extent of the calcination of her flesh, and her mutilated fingers."

"Indeed he would," Zintrah agreed.

Calia's fingers and her toes had hardened around the slits the magician had made, and a fine blood-coloured dust had begun to trickle from them. Giraiazal collected some of the dust with a fine brush, and carefully transferred it to a phial, but he did not take it back to his turret or return to his bed. He waited patiently for Calia to wake up again, and tell him another dream.

Morpheomorphists disagree among themselves regarding the extent to which practitioners of the art can actually create dream-images in the mind of a patient--or, if they can, whether the relevant creative process involves the transmission of specific items of imagery or the subtle metamorphosis of images spontaneously generated by the dreaming patient. They also disagree as to whether differing degrees of success are primarily associated with different levels of skill on the part the practitioner or with variations in the suggestibility of the patient.

Such mild disputes pale into insignificance, however, by comparison with the arguments in which morpheomorphists routinely engage as to the manner in which the dream-imagery of sick individuals ought to be interpreted. It is with respect to this issue that rival schools of theory have developed over time, gradually hardening--as such schools always do-- into fiercely jealous orthodoxies. A wise practitioner always retains his flexibility, but wisdom is always easier to exercise when the pressure to obtain a good result is relatively gentle. When situations become desperate, narrow theories become the kind of straws at which men in fear of drowning may clutch.

The Revelations of Suomynona, the Last Prophet

"I was thirsty," Queen Calia told her devoted physician, "but there was no water to be had. I had thirsted so long that my flesh had become desiccated, and my tongue had turned to bone. I tried hard to weep in order that I might drink my tears, but only managed to produce a trickle of pure salt. I thought that I too might be made of salt, and might disperse into a mere heap, but when I looked down at my whiteness I found that I was a cloud adrift on an insistent breeze, which built into a gale and then became a thunderhead in a great storm.

"Then Lady Death appeared, as what my father calls a corposant: a creature of electric radiance. She began to whisper in my ear, saying to me that the life of a human is nothing compared to the life of the lightning. What we call a bolt, she said, is actually thousands upon thousands of individual pulses, and the split second for which the lightning seems to last is an eternity of sorts. I knew that she was telling the truth, because I knew that only the lightning truly comprehends the rapture of wrath and the exultation of rage. I wanted to howl with glee as only lightning can, to burn with ecstasy.

"But when I turned to look at Lady Death again, I saw myself mirrored in her radiant body, and I saw that my face was an eyeless skull, and my body a blanched skeleton. The only colour left in me was a flickering blue flame, like the one that dances in a glass of brandy to which a match has been set. There was a bone in my mouth, clicking and clattering against my teeth, and my hands were claws, the fingers tipped with talons. And then I knew that I did not want to be lightning, but only to bear my husband's child. And I hastened to wake up."

Giraiazal frowned when he heard this, partly because it did not seem to be encouraging news, and partly because it was the most bizarre dream he had ever been required to interpret. When Queen Calia had begun to tell him her dreams he had been glad to obtain any report at all, but now that the tale of her adventures in the world beyond the world was becoming increasingly complicated he felt bound to pay more attention to the vexed question of what it might mean--and the more attention he paid to that question, the less inspiration he felt.

Zintrah must have seen him frown, for she said: "You must help her, Master Magician."

"I will do what I can, Your Highness," Giraiazal promised. "But there seems to be another force within her, which is opposing my efforts to shape her sleep. I am trying as hard as I can to reformulate her dreams so that they have a curative effect, but I seem to be meeting an unnatural resistance. I cannot feel the thread of sense that might guide me through the labyrinth of her nightmares."

"Will she die, then, for lack of your guidance?"

Giraiazal wished that he could make a confident answer to that question, but the mystery of Calia's dreams had begun to weigh upon him, undermining his self-confidence. "For the moment," he answered, more honestly than he could have wished, "I cannot tell whether she will live or die--but if she dies, it will be the result of magic more powerful than my own."

"My father has said as much," Zintrah told him. "He is convinced, as Orlu is, that what my sister swallowed was no ordinary spider. She has been cursed. You must fight magic with magic, Giraiazal, lest evil triumph."

"That is exactly what I am doing," Giraiazal told her, "for exactly that reason." He could not help recalling the scant thanks he had received for cleverly shaping the sleep and interpreting the dreams of an emperor. He wondered what Lysariel would say and do if his wife were to die. He had been relieved to see Orlu removed from the scene, but the merchant prince would return soon enough, and it would be greatly to everyone's advantage if good news were awaiting him. Lysariel might be vengefully inclined too, if Calia was no better when he finally condescended to return to her bedside--and the king's erratic behaviour was causing Giraiazal some anxiety.

Calia had already fallen asleep again, with the magician's fingertips resting on her brow.

"This will be my final effort for tonight, Your Highness," Giraiazal told Zintrah. "If I should happen to fall into a trance, you must not wake me. I shall be fighting by her side in the wilderness of her nightmare. Pray that we might prevail."

The magician tried hard to give the impression of having fallen into a trance after issuing this warning, but he had only voiced that prediction and its associated instruction because he felt so very tired that he did not want to be woken up if he should fall asleep. In spite of his exhaustion, he could not let go of anxious consciousness. He kept repeating the details of Calia's latest dream to himself, wondering what they could possibly mean, and how he ought to respond. He had never been very assiduous in studying the different theories of morpheomorphism because he had always preferred to rely on his own instincts and improvisations, but he felt that he had now reached the limit of what instinct and improvisation could provide. He needed more, and he had no further reserves on which to draw.

Although he never actually went to sleep the magician kept his eyes closed and his body still, and he did not change his stance even when he heard someone else come into the room. Indeed, he maintained his position even more carefully, eager to maintain the pretence of being unconscious.

He heard Zintrah say: "Don't wake him! His sleep is magical. He has gone into Calia's dream to help her fight the curse that has laid her low."

"Has he indeed?" Giraiazal recognised the answering voice as Viragan's. "Well, I wish him the very best of luck. Where is your husband?"

"Asleep," Zintrah replied.

"And the other one--the king, that is?"

"With Urbishek."

"I do not like this Urbishek," Viragan said, in what seemed to Giraiazal to be a pensive tone. "I do not like his mysterious glowing statue.

127

It is a complication we could do without. Lysariel is becoming wilful, and unpredictable besides."

"He is grief-stricken," Zintrah said. "He loves Calia very much, as we all do."

"I see that," Viragan replied, with a hint of contempt in his voice. "Who could have imagined that black-hearted Orlu was capable of such affection? I had thought that I was the only man of our stripe with the sensitivity to love a daughter as much as that. Well, we learn as we live, or what would be the point of living at all, in a world damned to destruction? If we could not be surprised, we might as well die now as later. What triumph is there in a scheme that runs smoothly to its conclusion, without a single confusing hitch?"

"What scheme?" asked Zintrah. The puzzlement in her voice seemed authentic, although Giraiazal could not be absolutely sure without being able to measure her expression.

"Any scheme or none at all, my precious," the merchant prince said, indulgently. "I am waxing philosophical, as I sometimes like to do. I am no barbarian, you see. Orlu and I are very different, no matter how similar we may seem to common men."

"I don't understand," Zintrah said.

"No," Viragan replied, contentedly, "you don't. So Giraiazal is playing the morpheomorphist, sharing your dear sister's dream and fighting side by side with her against the subtle temptations of Lady Death." It occurred to Giraiazal that this speech might be intended for his ears rather than Zintrah's, and that the prince was by no means convinced that he was really asleep.

"Yes," said Zintrah. "I only wish that I could be there with him."

"I am sure that Calia knows that you are with her in spirit, my darling," Viragan said. "If she survives, she will doubtless be grateful. Perhaps she will--I had expected her to be dead by now, but I might have underestimated the magician's skill. I shall not do so again. We are very fortunate to have a man of his quality in Scleracina."

Calia stirred then, and moved her arm so that the elbow collided with Giraiazal's face. He opened his eyes immediately, and pretended to be surprised to see Viragan standing over him--but he said nothing, because Calia had opened her eyes too, and was searching with them for her loyal physician. Giraiazal sat up and looked down at her. It seemed to him that she was trying to smile, although her lips would not obey her sovereign will.

Giraiazal took the queen's hand in his and said: "Tell me your dream, Your Highness. Tell me what you did, and why."

"But you were there," the queen whispered. "Were you not? I wanted you to be there. I needed you. I thought you were there."

"I was there," Giraiazal assured her, slightly surprised by the extent of his own success, "but I was not the only shaper of your sleep. Tell me how the struggle went."

"I dreamed I was an insect," the queen murmured. "A jewelled beetle, which hummed as I flew, black and glossy in my brittle coat. I was flying by night, above a great cemetery with a million tombs. There were no stars shining, but the sky was not black; it was purple, as it is by day, but instead of the crimson disc of the sun there was a huge flower whose petals were coloured scarlet and gold. The style in the centre of the flower was black, and its anthers were tipped with crystal clusters. The whole world was filled with the scent of nectar, which I perceived in my insect form more sweetly and distinctly than any scent my human self had ever encountered.

"As I ascended into the bell of the flower, the sound of my humming wings was reflected from the petals, striking a chord that was as soothing as it was sublime. Every fibre of my being vibrated in sympathy, and I wanted to become that chord in order to take my place in the song of the cosmos. The scent of the nectar was overpowering, and I felt that I was turning into a delirium, a hallucination of the dreaming flower. But I heard another note too, whose pitch was more plaintive than my own, and I could not help but wonder whether there were other flowers more distant than the sky, and other songs more beautiful than mine.

"I landed on a petal, which trembled beneath my weight, and I knew that I was supposed to fly deeper, in search of the nectar's source, but I felt lost and troubled.

"I knew that if I fell out of the flower I would fall into the infinite cemetery, breaking my wing-cases upon the unforgiving tombstones, and that I would be condemned to crawl for the rest of my life--but I knew, too, that if I fled into the blossom's heart then I would never bear a child. I would be one with the song, one with the light, but I would never bear a child.

"A shadow fell upon me then, and when I turned I saw a spider flowing across the carpet of red and amber. I knew that she was Lady Death, and that she meant me no harm, but I did not want to go to her just yet. I told her that I could hear another note, another insect--perhaps not a wasp, or a dragonfly, or even a moth, perhaps no more than a fly or a gnat, but something troublesome nevertheless, something anxious and busy and not altogether despicable.

"It seemed to me that Lady Death hesitated then, in the way that Lady Death often does, even though she knows that you are hers, because everyone is hers in the end, and that hesitation is only foolishness. But she did hesitate, and I fell out of my beetle self. Wingless, I fell towards the grave, but I opened my mouth as if to sing, and made a noise that was more than a word but less than a note--and it brought me here."

"Remarkable!" Viragan murmured. "Truly remarkable!"

"She is getting better!" Zintrah said, exultantly, before Giraiazal could say anything. "My sister will live!"

But Calia still seemed unable to contrive a smile, and her body was stiil full of abscesses and lesions, and the red dust was still trickling from the open wounds in her alabaster flesh.

"Will she really live?" Viragan asked the magician.

"I fear that I cannot tell, Your Highness," Giraiazal told him. "The progress of her symptoms appears to have been arrested, but there is no sign of healing as yet. I have shaped her sleep as best I can, but my resources are all but exhausted, and my own head is spinning with the dream-force that flows between us. How long she can endure in this state I cannot tell, but I wish that Orlu would soon return from his quest, having been successful. Unless and until he comes, we shall simply have to hope that the queen can endure her trials."

"Shall we?" said Viragan. "Well, if you can do no more, I suppose we must. What did her dream signify, do you think?"

Giraiazal looked back at Calia then, who seemed just as curious to know what her experience had meant. His heart shrank momentarily, convulsed by the awareness of his ignorance, but he knew that he had to respond to the challenge. He summoned every last vestige of his strength and intelligence.

"Lady Death has come close to the queen on three occasions now," Giraiazal said, "but the queen is not ready to yield to her just yet. She is drawing on the power of the amulet, and the resilience of my own dream-force, which I am pleased to lend to her. The world beyond the world is full of mystery, but Lady Death cannot disguise herself well enough to delude Queen Calia, let alone seduce her. Our fight will go on for a while yet, but I hope and pray that your daughter is right, Your Highness, and that victory will be ours."

Then, at last, Calia contrived a smile. Outside, the darkness of night was yielding to another crimson dawn.

"You are a remarkable man, Lord Vizier," said Viragan. "But I can see that you are growing weak. Be careful that you do not destroy yourself in the fight to save the queen."

"I shall do my best," Giraiazal said. "I can do no more. Orlu expects no less. So does the king."

"But the king is not here," Viragan observed. "He should be here, but he is not. I shall go to see him, to find out what is amiss."

"That is very kind of you, Your Highness," Giraiazal said.

Throughout that day, Calia's fight for life seemed evenly balanced. The abscesses did not increase in number or size, and although a few more worms were generated, the queen was able to take sufficient nourishment to fuel their reproduction without further depletion of her own inner being. That inner being had been so extensively ravaged as to bring her to the brink of extinction, but with the assistance of the amulet that Giraiazal had provided, and the power of shaping that he had lent to her dreaming, she remained in a state of suspension.

She remained in that state for several days more--but Orlu did not return, and Lysariel did not come to her bedside. In the meantime, Urbishek continued to work on her image. Manazzoryn and Zintrah continued to take turns with Giraiazal to sit with Calia and minister to her needs.

According to the rumours that Burrel occasionally brought to his master, Urbishek had now abandoned his chisels and paring knives, having removed all but the last vestiges of surplus material from his image. He was using files, gougers and sandpapers now. The coral was yielding meekly enough to those instruments and the statue was shining ever more brightly. Triasymon, having heard the same rumours--he too was forbidden to enter the studio--told Giraiazal that Lysariel's coral must be very different from more familiar species.

"I had not expected the sculpture to progress so smoothly," the Lord Chancellor confessed, with a slight hint of resentment in his voice. "I suspected was that the coral's glowing colours might be a superficial phenomenon, associated with the activity of living cells, and that the interior of the column, being the detritus of generations long past, might be as white and as dull as bone. If recent reportage can be trusted, the material making up the core of the column is not only more pliable but even brighter than the surface layers. I do not understand that. How can it be that although the radiance of the outer layers seemed muted in daylight, the statue's luminosity has increased as the sculptor's excavations have been more profound?"

"I cannot tell," Giraiazal admitted.

Viragan was curious too, and he had the authority to demand an explanation. Lysariel would not respond to the summons he sent, but Urbishek had no alternative.

Somewhat to his surprise, Giraiazal was invited to be present when the merchant prince interviewed the sculptor Urbishek in the council-chamber. Triasymon was also there.

"I am astonished," the sculptor confessed. "I too had expected the faint luminosity of the coral to be a surface phenomenon. I am glad that I was wrong. When the image of Queen Calia has reached its final perfection--and I am very close to achieving that perfection now--it will be glorious to behold. It will not only be my masterpiece but the greatest masterpiece of our era. I am very grateful indeed that Mater Nature has seen fit to provide me with this opportunity, in furnishing such a uniquely precious material."

Triasymon could hardly wait to interrupt him. "In my experience," the Lord Chancellor said, "luminosity in creatures of the sea is a product of living cells. Is the coral within the column still alive, do you think? Is it possible that the inner layers of the formation had more life in them than the outer layers?"

"I cannot answer that," Urbishek confessed.

"Nor can I, having been refused material to examine," Giraiazal murmured.

"Refused?" Urbishek echoed. "Surely not. I shall be glad to give you a sack full of shavings, if you wish. I had assumed that Prince Viragan--who obtained a supply of his own from the cave--could have given you all the coral you required."

"My lapidarists have been making their own investigations," Viragan was quick to say, "but they have not found that the deeper layers of the fragments I gave them glow more fervently than the surfaces. That is odd, is it not?"

"Yes," Urbishek admitted, "It is."

Viragan turned to Giraiazal then, and said: "It is magic, is it not, Master Magician? There is no other explanation."

"How can I tell, Your Highness?" Giraiazal countered. "Even if I had been allowed to have specimens for examination, my time has been entirely taken up of late by tending the queen's illness."

"So it has," Viragan agreed. "Is she any better? Have you succeeded in vanquishing the evil force that appeared to be opposing your dominion over her dreams?"

"She is no worse," Giraiazal answered, cautiously. "I am still hopeful."

"Of course you are," was Viragan's reply to that. "Prince Orlu might return at any moment with good news, or even a remedy. I cannot help but wonder, though, why he has not sent a carrier-bird to let us know why he has been delayed."

"Perhaps he sent one out which did not reach us," Triasymon suggested. "It might have been taken by a hawk."

"Perhaps," Viragan agreed.

Giraiazal was careful to say nothing more. It did not seem to him to be a good time to be expressing opinions about any other matter than his patient's health.

The most influential school of morpheomorphist thought holds that a skilful practitioner ought to be able--and certainly ought to be willing--to interpret any and every dream a patient experiences as an allegory of the healing process. Theorists of this persuasion usually add the corollary that the morpheomorphist should also be able, and more than willing, to reserve a role within the reported dream-narrative for his own helpful insertions, whether these be creations or modifications.

The most extreme dissenters from this orthodoxy point out, with justification, that if every dream experienced by a patient is to be interpreted in terms of a healing process, the fact that many patients die in spite of the best efforts of their physicians is bound to seem embarrassing, and prejudicial to the good name of morpheomorphism. Adherents of this latter philosophy are convinced that there must be a reliable way of divining the probable fate of patients from the imagery of their dreams, and that the real work of the morpheomorphist ought to be the patient investigation of such correlations for the benefit of future practitioners.

This is, of course, arrant nonsense. Given that the world is about to end, there is no point whatsoever in conducting empirical enquiries of this kind. The simple fact is that if morpheomorphists cannot function effectively without reaping the rewards of further investigation, they are impotent to deal effectively with any of the problems experienced by their patients.

The Revelations of Suomynona, the Last Prophet

Now that Queen Calia's condition had stabilized Giraiazal was able to spend more time in his own rooms, updating his astrological charts and pursuing other investigations. When Urbishek sent him a sack full of coral shards from the statue, therefore, he immediately set about examining them with a magnifying glass.

Had he not been told that the emergent statue was more radiant than the lumpen block from which it had been hewn Giraiazal would have had difficulty sorting the pieces, but this information enabled him to judge the depth from which each fragment had come according to its native effulgence. He was able to see that the striations of the surface colouration had quickly given way to a near-uniformity of hue, but one that was strangely unstable.

Had the reds and yellows manifest on the outside of the column been thoroughly mixed as common pigments they would have produced the colour conventionally associated with the long-extinct and probably legendary orange, but that was not the effect obtained by their combination in the flakes of coral chipped from the layer proximate to the "skin" of Calia's image. By daylight the fragments from that layer seemed blood red, but in the dark--when their innate luminosity seemed to increase--the red softened to an ochreous amber tint.

Although Lysariel still refused to allow Giraiazal, or anyone else, into the room where the statue stood, Urbishek was now more than willing to boast about his achievements; indeed, the sculptor seemed to relish every opportunity to compliment himself on his unparalleled artistry. When Giraiazal stopped him in a corridor to ask him how the changes in colouration he had observed in the fragments were extrapolated on the surface of the image itself, Urbishek was only too happy to wax lyrical on the subject.

"Although the incarnadine glare of noon never strikes the image directly through the north-facing window of the studio," the sculptor explained, "the image attains her darkest and strangest hue at that hour. As an expert pigmentist, I deem that nuance to be true magenta, although you might prefer the herbasacralist's designation of strong damask. In the darkest midnight, however, when the White Star is invisible from the window and the great majority of its sixty-eight companions are similarly eclipsed, she shines almost as if she were a star herself."

"The colour then being a dark amber," Giraiazal prompted, thinking it better not to comment on the sculptor's use of a personal pronoun rather than an impersonal one in referring to the statue.

"By no means," Urbishek said. "She is brighter than that now. I would identify her fundamental shade as chrome yellow, although your different education might disposed you to think of it as luteous xanthin. Have you formed an opinion as to whether the substance is dead or alive?"

"I can find no signs of active protoplasm," Giraiazal told him, "but I have only been looking at flakes and shards; if the image retains a bolder luminosity, I suppose it is possible that it has properties that are lost to its wastes."

"That is true," the sculptor said, "I have examined her surface with a magnifying lens myself but I am not sure how to evaluate what I see. Had the coral been similar to other species I would have expected to find dead material left porous by the natural increase and outward migration of the living individuals. In fact, I could make little or no differentiation between what might be assumed to be living tissue and what appear to be mineral deposits. I admit that I am confused--all I am sure of is that she is hewn from no ordinary coral."

"If it were ordinary," Giraiazal pointed out, "King Lysariel would hardly have commanded you to derive an image from it. It may not be native to this world, but if the wisdom of lore and legend can be trusted, there are so many things now living on the Earth that were not here in the days before our ancestors travelled to the stars that the word *ordinary* has all but lost its meaning."

"We live in a world in which the extraordinary is commonplace," Urbishek agreed. "Even the imminent end of the world has become a trivial matter, accepted by everyone as a mere brute fact. My skills were honed by dealing with ordinary materials, whose properties are more-or-less consistent, but I am glad that they have been more than equal to this extraordinary task. Everything that is extraordinary is extraordinary in its own perverse way, whether it is native to the Earth or not, and poses a stern challenge to an artist--but I have met the challenge of capturing Queen Calia in living coral, and I have triumphed. I only wish that King Lysariel would allow me to display my work to the world."

"Will he not?" Giraiazal asked. "I have been so fully occupied with my other patient that I had almost forgotten that the king was exceedingly distressed, after his own fashion. I should have asked you long ago how he is."

"He seems to be fully recovered now," Urbishek replied. "He was laid low by grief for a while, but the fervent interest he has taken in my work has given time the opportunity to heal his spiritual wounds. I cannot say that he is cheerful, and I have been very careful not to remind him that the model of his coral bride is still abed, ravaged by disfiguring disease, but he has long since ceased to weep and moan. He is calm, though very fixed in his opinions and very sensitive to the slightest alteration in his surroundings."

"I wish that the king had allowed me to minister to his dreams," Giraiazal said, chewing his lip fretfully, "or at least to prescribe a useful combination of soothing medicines. I do not like to think of him fighting his ills without proper help and support--but if a patient will not yield to treatment, what is a physician to do?"

Urbishek bowed, rather ironically, to acknowledge this crucial limitation of Giraiazal's benevolence.

Brian Stableford

"I a glad that you have helped him, if only a little," Giraiazal was prompted to add. "You have made him a masterpiece, and he must be grateful for that."

Urbishek smiled, sardonically. "A true artist not only makes his masterpiece," he said, "he is also made by it. He is but a midwife to something far more wonderful than his own clumsy fingers. I suppose that magicians are prouder men by far than mere sculptors, and wiser too, but I dare say that shapers of dreams may still serve as midwives to visions not their own, which are determined to spill over into the world of flesh and metal." After firing this parting shot, the sculptor returned to his work.

Giraiazal assumed that Urbishek must be putting the final touches to his image now, and bringing it to perfection. In Urbishek's memory, Giraiazal supposed--and in his dreams, too--Calia must still be perfectly healthy, and perfectly beautiful. The sculptor undoubtedly had as much confidence in the accuracy of his memory as he had in the willingness of his material to be shaped in conformity with it. *If only I could harness the energy of that creative process and feed it to her dreams*, Giraiazal thought, *the queen would surely win her war*. Alas, he knew that even if the war were won, Calia would never recover the beauty she had possessed when Urbishek had begun his work--and still possessed in the artist's memory and Lysariel's obsessive eye. Although the lower part of her body--the legs, at least, with the exception of her mutilated toes--retained their form reasonably well, the upper part of her body had been permanently changed by her malady. Her face was less frequently contorted by pain now that his talents as a morpheomorphist were regularly brought to bear on her predicament, but her features were irrecoverably etched by the legacy of her struggles. Although her cheeks and temples never hardened as her breasts had done, nor erupted in boils or blisters, and had not been blurred by the writhing of multitudinous worms, they had been irredeemably rewrought by the early intensity of her torment. By the dawn of the thirteenth day of her illness, Calia no longer had the slightest claim to be reckoned one of the most beautiful women in Scleracina, let alone the world. It seemed impossible that she could ever recover the bloom of her youth, even if she were eventually to win her struggle for life--but she stubbornly refused to die. Even in her dreams, where all things seemed possible and distinctions between life and death were difficult to define, she refused to give up her struggle.

It was, apparently, on that thirteenth day that Urbishek applied the last finishing touches to the face of her coral counterpart. Always the perfectionist, the sculptor spent the hours of daylight--refusing to sleep at noonday--refining her eyes and her lips, while King Lysariel watched as if he were entranced. That, at least, was what Burrel reported to his master, on the basis of kitchen gossip. It was probably true, because Lysariel's first communication with the Lord Chancellor for some considerable time was an instruction that Urbishek's fee should be paid in full.

Having collected that fee, the ever-vigilant Burrel informed Giraiazal, Urbishek left the palace, muttering muted complaints about banishment and the loss of the opportunity to display his genius to the world. As soon as Urbishek had vanished into the night, the king had summoned a team of servants and told them that he had decided to move into a new apartment on an upper floor of the northern tower of the palace. He had commanded them to make up a bed for him, and then to move the image that Urbishek had made into his new bedchamber, where it was to be set by the window. When the image was transported, carefully draped in protective blankets, the king followed behind it, never more than two paces behind. When the statue had been unwrapped again, Lysariel had sent the servants away and had barred his door, giving orders that he was not to be disturbed.

"The statue is magical," Burrel told his master, with the blithe confidence of the ignorant. "It has bewitched the king."

"I must go to see him," Giraiazal muttered, in response to this dubious intelligence. "No matter what Urbishek says, he is not yet well. I must help him." But he could not go directly, because it was time for him to murmur suggestions to the queen as to what dreams she ought to have, if only she could resist the inner voice that bade her dance with Lady Death, and the intention lapsed yet again.

When Triasymon came to Giraiazal to complain bitterly about this new departure in the king's awkward behaviour, the magician felt moved to come to Lysariel's defence. "This catastrophe has been a little too much for him to bear," the magician said. "He is only a boy, who has recently been snatched out of one life and thrust into another that could hardly be more different. He was hurried into marriage as hectically as he was hurried into riches and responsibility. He has secluded himself with the queen's image because that image represents everything that has happened to him: not just the woman with whom he fell in love, but the first independent exercise of his new-found power. Even though he cannot bear to wait by her bedside, he is clinging to her life with all the fervour he can muster. When the queen recovers, he will surely rejoice with everyone else, and I do not doubt that he will be more than happy to resume his proper relationship with her, so that she may provide him with an heir. In the meantime, we must understand and forgive the form that his anguish has taken. I shall go to him as soon as I can, and I will persuade him to take the medicines he needs."

These judgments were, in the main, mere guesswork. Although Giraiazal had updated his star-charts with new observations of the mercurial movements of the Motile Entities, he had had no time to calculate a new horoscope for anyone but the queen, nor had he found an opportunity to lay out his prophetic cards on anyone's behalf but hers. He took what comfort he could from the analyses he did carry out, whose results were stubbornly ambiguous. He told himself that if Calia were close to death, the exact date of her demise ought to be clearly manifest in any competent prophetic investigation, and since it was not, she must be reckoned likely to survive. Alas, he did not know whether her chances of survival depended on some further protective action that he might take in response to his divinations--or, if so, what that action might be. As her physician and Scleracina's Grand Vizier, it was obviously his responsibility to labour unstintingly on her behalf, whatever the eventual outcome of his travails might be, and he felt in his heart that if he were to hope for favourable future treatment by his own adamantine mistress, Damozel Fate, then he must continue to offer proof of his capacity as an exceptionally loyal servant. The fact that he did not know how to bring matters to a successful conclusion continued to weigh very heavily upon him, and forced him more than once to take liberal doses of his own euphoric potions.

Fortunately, Giraiazal was not forced to bear this burden alone. From the very beginning, Zintrah had been a faithful assistant, and in recent days Manazzoryn had become equally anxious to help in every way he could. Giraiazal was grateful for this assistance; indeed, he was convinced that, notwithstanding the power of the amulet he had provided and his own talents as a physician, the queen's resistance to the forces of destruction working within her owed as much to the companionship provided by Zintrah and Manazzoryn as to his magic. When Lysariel removed himself to his new apartment, however--preferring a likeness of his wife to her actual company, as the kitchen rumour-mongers put it-- Zintrah became afraid of what might happen if ever she too were to fall ill. She confessed this anxiety to Giraiazal, who suggested that she should demand reassurances from Manazzoryn that he would never treat her thus.

Giraiazal guessed that Manazzoryn--who was secretly desperate, as all younger brothers are, to prove that he was a better man than the elder brother in whose shadow he had always lived--would not be in the least reluctant to offer the reassurance Zintrah sought. He was right; indeed, Manazzoryn went a little too far, openly criticising Lysariel as a weaker man than he had formerly been supposed to be, and a weaker king than his queen or Scleracina deserved. The younger brother even took leave to praise himself for stepping into the breach that the elder had vacated and labouring alongside Giraiazal to provide the relief that his sister-in-law required. Fortunately, Giraiazal and Zintrah were the only witnesses to these indiscretions, so they did not affect the admiration that Manazzoryn had won in the court and in the city by virtue of his earlier conduct.

Gradually, the collective efforts of Giraiazal and his assistants began to reap their just reward. No new abscesses formed in the queen's flesh, and those already established ceased to renew themselves. Calia's occasional vomitings became much less hectic, and she began to eat and drink more heartily during periods of wakefulness that became progressively longer and livelier. The cracked skin on her breasts began to fuse again, and the cuts on her hands and feet began to knit into scars.

Perhaps paradoxically, the queen's sleep became more disordered as her periods of consciousness became more composed; despite Giraiazal's shaping efforts her dreams were racked by nightmarish inclusions for a further tenday. The Grand Vizier was puzzled by this development, for which his training as a morpheomorphist had by no means prepared him, but he was glad to see its ultimate result.

The climax of Queen Calia's ordeal came in the hour before daybreak on the twenty-sixth day of her illness, when she opened her mouth to cry out in her troubled sleep. A living spider emerged therefrom, huge, bloated and seemingly intoxicated.

Brian Stableford

7

Evolutionist astrologers are content to suppose that legend is correct in its contention that there were a vast number of fixed stars making up the celestial backcloth when the Epic of the Humankinds began, which were sorted for conceptual convenience into a series of "constellations". They are similarly content to suppose that the Motile Entities of primitive astrology--the so-called "planets"--have been superseded in the interim, although they disagree as to the exact number of the originals; most estimates lie between five and thirteen, with the median at eight. The third major tenet of evolutionary astrology is that the original Motile Entities all moved in a single plane--the "ecliptic"--which took them all through the same sequence of twelve, or sometimes thirteen, constellations. There is, however, a significant minority even within the evolutionist ranks which dissents from this last opinion.

Even in this unimaginably distant era, the evolutionists argue, primal humans were able to intuit the knowledge that their destinies were dictated by the heavens. Primal astrology cannot have been effective, of course, because its practitioners had no opportunity to compare different skyscapes and correlate their displays with countless different historical sequences, but it must have been useful nevertheless in preparing the starfaring races who came after them to undertake the empirical researches necessary to put the science on a sound footing--with the eventual result that every subsequent change in the patterns visible from the Earth could be used as a means of anticipating the historical changes that would follow. Most evolutionists agree that astrological lore has suffered a progressive degradation during the aeons of Earth's decadence, with the result that its former certainty has been severely prejudiced, but

141

Brian Stableford

they insist that it retains enough of its former utility to be reckoned the best available guide to purposive conduct.

The Revelations of Suomynona, the Last Prophet

Manazzoryn, who was in attendance at the queen's bedside with Giraiazal, reacted more rapidly than the Grand Vizier to the spider's emergence from her mouth; he immediately brushed the creature on to the carpet and crushed it beneath his heel. After that, Calia slept and breathed more easily, and the lines etched by agony upon her face began to ease. Manazzoryn and Zintrah were rapturous with joy. Giraiazal, wary of what still might lie in store, was more cautious, but the improvement was sustained.

Giraiazal asked Manazzoryn to take the news to his brother that the queen was on the mend, thinking that Manazzoryn had a better chance than anyone else of persuading Lysariel to come down from his new apartment. When Manazzoryn came back, however, he was sorely puzzled. "He would not let me in," he reported. "I had to shout the good news outside his door. He laughed, and I thought at first that he was delighted-- but it seems that he was only amused, for he said his wife had been quite well for a full thirteen days, and that he and she were exceedingly happy in their new home."

This dereliction of duty was slightly less hurtful to the queen than it might have been, because it was not her husband that she first asked for when she recovered full consciousness of herself--it was her father.

"He set sail more than twenty days ago for Kalasperanza in search of the source of the grapes in which the poisonous spiders were lodged," Giraiazal told her. "He has not yet returned."

"But Kalasperanza is not much more than five days away--four with a fair wind, seven at the very most!" Calia objected. "Has he sent no word?"

Giraiazal was no seaman, and no geographer either, but it had occurred to him more than once to wonder why Orlu had not returned from his reckless expedition. While more urgent matters taxed his brain, though, he had not worried overmuch about what Orlu's failure to return might signify. He remembered now what Viragan had said about the possibility of a carrier-bird being taken by a hawk, but that no longer seemed adequate to explain the lack of any news. With Akabar and Cardelier also at sea, and also considerably delayed, there was no one in Orlu's organization with whom Giraiazal was in regular contact, and neither Viragan nor Captain Sharuman had raised the matter of Orlu's protracted absence again during the magician's brief excursions to the council chamber.

"It is a mystery, Your Majesty," Giraiazal confessed. "I will try to find out what has happened."

"My father will know," Zintrah put in. Anxious to stress the better part of the story, Zintrah told her friend how boldly and determinedly

Orlu had set off on his mission, refusing to let anyone else go in his stead even though Viragan had generously offered to do so.

"And did Lysariel go with him?" Calia asked, clearly having some vague recollection of the time that had passed since she was last aware of his presence. "Has he gone questing with my father, equally determined to find a cure for me?"

Zintrah turned away rather than attempt to answer these questions, and Calia did not press her, perhaps assuming that they had been treated as rhetorical enquiries. When Giraiazal left the room, however, Zintrah followed him and tugged at his sleeve.

"Lysariel must come down now," she said. "Whether he wishes it or not, he must come down."

"He is the king," Giraiazal pointed out. "We have no power to command him."

"You told Triasymon that he would rejoice with everyone else when the queen recovered," Zintrah reminded him. "You said that he was too distressed to continue seeing his wife while she lay at death's door--but she is better now, and he must be happy for her. She needs him by her side."

"I will do what I can," Giraiazal promised--but when he finally went up to the king's new apartment he found the door locked against him as it had been locked against Manazzoryn, and Lysariel would not open it. Giraiazal immediately began to regret his failure to carry through his earlier resolutions.

"You are ill, Your Majesty," he called, certain that Lysariel could hear him. "I wish that you would let me examine you."

"Nonsense, Lord Vizier," Lysariel replied. "I have never been healthier, nor happier, than I am now."

Giraiazal sighed deeply, wishing that he did not feel so poorly himself. He went to fetch Triasymon, convinced that the king's uncle would have better luck--but even though Triasymon hammered on the door until his knuckles bled, Lysariel would not open it.

"My wife and I are very happy," the king called through the closed door. "We need nothing but one another."

"He must have gone mad," Triasymon opined, "or else the kitchen gossip is true, and the living coral has bewitched him."

"Perhaps he is a little off-balance," Giraiazal said, painfully aware of the depth of the understatement, "but that makes it all the more necessary that we should help him."

"Shall we break the door down?" Triasymon asked.

Giraiazal studied the closed door carefully, estimating its strength. He could not see the bar holding it in place, but he had seen others of a similar kind. "I doubt that we can," he said. "We'd need half a dozen of Viragan's sailors, and a heavy ram."

They went away, and summoned Viragan to a conference.

143

"I hear that the news is good," said the smiling merchant prince, as soon as he arrived in the conference-chamber. "The queen is better. The city will rejoice."

"Alas," said Giraiazal, "it seems that the king is not. I should have taken care to shape his dreams as well as his wife's, but I exhausted all my strength in answering the more urgent need. I did not realise what the king's isolation signified."

"There is not a man in the world who could have saved Queen Calia's life while also ministering to her husband's grief," Triasymon assured him. "I should have seen to the boy. He is my nephew--the son that I never had."

"No one is at fault here," Viragan said, diplomatically. "It is obvious that the king cannot help himself, and that we cannot supply the help he needs until he is willing to receive it. Mercifully, the ship of state is proceeding very smoothly; what had to be done to set its course was done before the king went into seclusion. News of this kind is exceedingly difficult to contain--awkward rumours of bewitchment can already be heard along the waterfront--but the damage is by no means irredeemable. Recriminations will not help us; what we need is a plan of action."

"Break down his door," was Triasymon's advice.

"That might do more harm than good," Giraiazal said, anxiously. "But Your Highness is right--we need to take action. My main fear is that Calia will grow worse if she hears that Lysariel has gone mad. I do not like to deceive her, but it might be best to let Calia preserve her illusion that Lysariel is with Orlu. If we are clever, we need not lie to her, but our answers to any questions she may raise must be carefully elliptical."

"That is of no consequence," Triasymon said. "Lysariel is the problem, not Calia."

"Perhaps the time has come, Master Magician," Viragan said, judiciously, "for you to seek further advice from your oracles. Surely you can divine the best way of persuading him to open his door."

"The stars are rarely disposed to offer such specific advice," Giraiazal demurred--but he quickly took up the thread of the discussion lest his competence to hold his post might come to seem doubtful. "It seems to me that the person best fitted to the task of persuading the king to be reasonable--I mean his brother Manazzoryn--must devote himself entirely to that task, taking what advice he can from the three of us. Above all else, Manazzoryn must persuade the king to drink the wine that I gave him as a betrothal present; if anything can clear his head, that clever vintage will do the trick. If Manazzoryn succeeds soon enough in that task, with or without the aid of my divinations, we can put a stop to inconvenient rumours."

"Very clever," said Viragan, admiringly. "I think I can see the next stage in your argument. Even if the delay should prove protracted, we would only need to manufacture a rumour of our own sufficiently dramatic to overtake and diminish the one that is already abroad. I know I can rely on you, Master Magician, to discover the most useful formulation, so that it will be ready if we are forced to use it."

This suggestion took Giraiazal by surprise, but he saw no alternative but to agree to the proposition

"Rumours be damned," Triasymon said. "It's Lysariel we should be worried about.

"We are," Viragan assured him. "Lord Chancellor, you must speak to Manazzoryn immediately--and find this magical bottle of wine, if the king does not have it stored in his new apartment. While you go to your work, Noble Vizier, I shall see to my daughter--and then I shall return to my own responsibilities, which have become uncomfortably heavy by virtue of Orlu's long absence."

"Have you no word of him?" Giraiazal asked. "You and he have an entire merchant fleet moving ceaselessly back and forth, linking all the islands in the northern part of the archipelago. Surely someone must have heard news of Orlu?"

"Alas, no," Viragan said. "I can only hope that nothing terrible has happened to him. There have been a number of violent storms in the last ten days, although Scleracina has been spared the worst of their hectic wind and weather."

"What about Akabar?" Triasymon asked. "And the first captain who went to Kalasperanza--was it Cardelier?"

"I have no recent news of either of them," Viragan said. "I have sent captains of my own to search for them, but they have not yet returned. The only carrier birds to arrive in Clarassour within the last twenty days have brought routine reports of prices, shortages and cargoes successfully landed."

Giraiazal took leave to wonder whether this was the whole truth, or even an entire tissue of lies, but he certainly was not about to voice any such suspicion. He had other things to occupy his overstrained mind. While Manazzoryn was posted at his brother's door, charged with talking some sense into him, Giraiazal went to his attic and set to work on his horoscopes.

Such work had often seemed laborious, but Giraiazal had never found it as testing as he found it now. His powers of intuition, usually so active, appeared to have dwindled considerably, and he found himself dithering over matters of theory that had never preoccupied him before. No matter how hard he concentrated he was continually sidetracked by worries that he had previously disdained to entertain. Whenever a sceptical client had challenged him to explain why it was that the fates of men should be written in the heavens, where all but a few would remain unheeded and many of the remainder wrongly interpreted, Giraiazal had dismissed the question as a trivial item fit for armchair philosophers but not for practical prophets. Now, however, he could not shake off a creeping unease as to the whole basis of prophetic endeavour.

I must work harder, he told himself, sternly. *I have met one challenge successfully, but others still remain. I must maintain my composure, or Lysariel will never recover his.*

When he had analysed the king's chart as best he could, therefore, Giraiazal dealt out his cards, focusing his concentration with all the fervour he could muster, very hopeful of obtaining some additional enlightenment therefrom. Alas, the advice of all his oracles was that Lysariel would remain in dire danger so long as he continued to harbour his delusions, and that they would not easily yield to clarification. Giraiazal congratulated himself on his foresight in giving the king the wine of Yethlyreom for a wedding-present, but he knew only too well that the wine would be of no use unless Lysariel could be persuaded to drink it.

Turning from Lysariel's chart to Calia's, Giraiazal was disappointed-- but not unduly surprised--to find that the ominous signs continued to show almost as darkly as before. He took this to imply that the queen was still in danger of a relapse. Unless and until the king's delusions were dispelled, he decided, the queen could not be deemed to be safe--but the same ray of hope that had shone through before was evident still; although Lysariel's reign in Scleracina appeared likely to be short, the reign of his son seemed likely to be long. Surely, the magician thought, the strength of that sign must signify that Lysariel would recover from his present madness, at least for a while--but he could not shake off a worrisome suspicion that there was something amiss with his conclusions.

Tired as he was, with his wits more scattered than they had ever been before, he wrestled with the enigma long after the realization was forced upon him that he was incapable of making any further progress until his present debilitation relented. He dosed himself with one of his own potions, and went to bed.

When he awoke, Giraiazal was told by his faithful apprentice that Lysariel had not yet shown any evidence of an imminent recovery. Manazzoryn had pleaded with his brother for hours on end, and then berated him for several hours more, without any result. Lysariel's door remained firmly shut. Burrel reported, with an altogether unwarranted relish, that Manazzoryn had finally been reduced to sobbing and pleading. "*If you love me, brother,* he said, *if you love the memory of our father Alveyadey and our mother Astroma, I beg you to do us one small favour. I beg you to open the bottle of wine from far Yethlyreom which Giraiazal gave you on the day of your betrothal, and drink to the health and happiness of your bride. Though you will do nothing else for me, I implore you to do that. Is it to much to ask?*"

"And what did Lysariel say to that?" Giraiazal asked, not altogether pleased with the detailed nature of Burrel's reportage.

"That I cannot tell you," the servant said, glumly. "Prince Manazzoryn was the only one with his ear glued to the door."

So Giraiazal got up, and went in search of Manazzoryn, eventually finding him alone in his own apartment.

"He said: *No, brother, that is not too much to ask*." Manazzoryn informed the magician. "He said: *That I will do, and gladly. I have the flask in my hand, and I am breaking the seal....I have removed the stopper. The wine smells sweet, brother, sweeter than any I have ever encountered before. I am pouring it now, brother.....and lifting the goblet to my lips. Are you listening, brother? I drink to my bride, to her health and happiness. My life is henceforth dedicated entirely to her; it is nothing without her. With this wine, I offer her the blood of my veins and the fluid of my soul.* Those were his exact words, Lord Vizier, but I cannot be certain that he actually did drink the wine, or even that he actually had it with him in the room--although the bottle has not been found in the royal apartment. I thanked him, of course, and raced downstairs to tell my wife that I had been successful--but she pointed out, as I did just now, that I could not be certain that he was really doing what he said that he was doing. Then Zintrah went to Calia's room, leaving me to think it over. I suppose she is right--but I did my best, did I not?"

"You did," Giraiazal assured him. Then he went to Calia's room himself, but was astonished to find it empty, save for a servant who was refreshing the queen's bedlinen.

"Where is the queen?" Giraiazal asked.

"She felt better," the servant said. "She asked Princess Zintrah to take her for a walk in the open air."

Even as she spoke, however, Princess Zintrah came into the room.

"Where is the queen, Your Highness?" Giraiazal asked, again.

"She is feeling a great deal better," Zintrah said. "I left her sitting in the courtyard, near the entrance to the southern tower. She is shaded from the sun, and the air is cool. I came to fetch her a shawl."

The southern tower was some distance away from the royal apartments, and the palace was not unduly quiet, but the moment Giraiazal heard the faint sound of a distant scream he guessed whose voice it was, and cursed his various oracles for the lack of urgency with which they had communicated all their veiled warnings.

Brian Stableford

The principal schism between the leading schools of astrology relates to the nature of the Motile Entities. The "coincidentalist school" is so called because its adherents hold that they are artifacts abandoned by spacefaring civilizations whose utility as indicators in a horoscope is entirely fortuitous. The "teleological school" holds that they were built expressly to serve as indicators, and never had any other purpose.

Although this dispute may seem trivial it touches on much deeper philosophical issues. The coincidentalist thesis tends to assume, tacitly if not explicitly, that the correspondence which exists between events on Earth and events in the heavens arises out of the fact that both sets of epiphenomena are aspects of a much vaster implicate order which binds the universe together into a coherent whole. The teleological thesis, on the other hand, covertly imagines a much more direct causal connection between the two sets of phenomena, usually--though not invariably--supposing that there is a downward causal flow from sky to surface.

Some teleologists argue that the current in question is a straightforward magical determinism, akin to a constant stream of curses, geases and epiphanies, while others--who term themselves Esoteric Creationists--believe that whichever of the forerunner races engineered the Earth's ultimate inhabitants contrived to implant within our genetic material an innate tendency to orient our behaviour in anticipation of heavenly configurations to come. There is, of course, no purely logical reason why Esoteric Creationists should not also be coincidentalists, but in fact none are; Creationism is itself a teleological philosophy of sorts, and its adherents tend to favour teleological arguments at every level and in all areas of philosophical enquiry.

The Revelations of Suomynona, the Last Prophet

When Giraiazal arrived in the courtyard, having run at such an unaccustomed pace that his heart was hammering, a crowd had already gathered about the foot of the tower that stood at the southern corner of the palace. He shouldered his way through the crowd with a determination that gave his somewhat cadaverous frame a force that must have surprised the servants and men-at-arms who were thrust aside. Zintrah followed the path he cut, already in tears.

Queen Calia lay sprawled upon the ground, her limbs broken. At first glance, it seemed that she must have been set upon with astonishing fury by some monster that had snapped her arms and legs like dry reeds, but the people gathered around were already pointing upwards and asking one another whether anyone had seen her fall. Giraiazal knelt down beside the body to make sure that no vestige of life remained in it, but as soon as he was sure that the queen was really dead his eyes were drawn upwards, to the broad sill of a window letting light into an attic parallel to his own.

Giraiazal came to his feet, seized one of the guardsmen by the elbow and said: "Who is lodged in that room?"

"No one, my lord," the guardsman said. "It's naught but a dusty attic used for storage."

"What is it that is stored there?"

"I don't know, my lord. The steward has the key--one of them, at least."

Giraiazal did not bother to ask how many other keys there were. The guardsman would not know. Nor would it be any use to ask whether anyone present knew why the queen had gone up the staircase. If anyone did know, they would not admit it for fear of being held to blame. No one could have prevented the queen from doing as she wished, of course, but servants and soldiers would be equally well aware of the fact that whenever anything terrible happened scapegoats were in great demand and low supply.

It was not until Giraiazal looked down again at Calia's corpse that he noticed another discomfiting detail. The amulet he had given the queen as a wedding-present--which had been strung around her neck for the entire duration of her illness--was no longer there. Either she had removed it, or someone else had taken it from her.

"She must have been looking for Lysariel," Zintrah said. "She must have realised that he had moved into a new apartment, and decided that she would seek him out. Perhaps she asked which tower he was in, and became confused as to which direction is north and which is south. Perhaps she went to the window to get her bearings, dizzy with the exertion of climbing the stairs, and then was dazzled by the light of the sun...."

That was one perhaps too many, even for someone desperate to find an explanation, and Zintrah's voice trailed off. Giraiazal wondered

150

whether the imagined sequence of events was really credible--but he knew that this was not a matter to be determined by calculations of probability. Calia was the queen of Scleracina, wife to a king whose sanity had already been called into question. This was a situation of the utmost delicacy, an occasion for heroic diplomacy.

"Organise your men and get everyone else out of here," Giraiazal instructed the guardsmen. "Have the queen's body carried back to her room. Summon the Lord Chancellor and Prince Manazzoryn to the council-chamber, and send someone to fetch Prince Viragan from his house. There will have to be an inquiry into this unfortunate accident." He stressed the word *accident*, hoping that the guardsman would take the hint.

Having issued these commands, Giraiazal bowed to Princess Zintrah. "We must go inside, Your Highness," he said. "There is much to be decided, and it is all very urgent."

The most urgent thing of all, it now seemed, was to tackle the problem of Lysariel's recalcitrance. Giraiazal sent Manazzoryn back to his brother's door to relay the news that Queen Calia was dead, although he already knew what the king's answer would be.

Lysariel had refused to emerge from his seclusion to see his queen while she was alive; he was equally firm in his refusal to look at her corpse. Indeed, he refused to acknowledge that his wife was dead, assuring his brother that she was not only alive and well but perfectly happy. On being pressed, first by Manazzoryn and then by Triasymon, the king went even further, assuring them that his wife was not only as lively and lovely as ever, but was now beyond the reach of any conceivable corruption. Manazzoryn and Triasymon were forced to return to the council-chamber to admit defeat. Viragan had arrived by this time, but he was slumped in a chair, seemingly lost in thought.

"Your wine proved a dire disappointment," Triasymon told Giraiazal, his failure to talk sense into his nephew having left him a trifle resentful. "We were fools to trust in magic, which is ever apt to misfire."

"It is possible, I suppose," Giraiazal admitted, "that the vintage was not what I took it to be. It is even possible that it had been spoiled by poor keeping--but we must remember what it was supposed to accomplish. It was not supposed to preserve the queen from harm; it was supposed to clear the king's head."

"Which it most definitely has not done," Triasymon claimed. "He is more deluded now than he was before."

"If the core of his delusion is that the statue is actually his wife," Giraiazal countered, "then it has not altered in its quality, nor even in its intensity. If, however...."

"This is getting us nowhere," Viragan said, abruptly coming to his feet. "What the enchanted wine has done or not done is of no importance. The point at issue is what *we* must do. We had a plan, which went awry.

We were supposed, were we not, to have a contingency plan ready for implementation in that event. The queen's death was, admittedly, a complication we had ceased to anticipate--but with luck, our contingency plan should still be workable. The rumour of the king's madness is bound to be amplified by the queen's sudden death, but our own counter-rumour will benefit from a similar amplification if we can only distribute it with sufficient expedition and skill. What tale have you composed, Lord Vizier, to save our situation?"

This question took Giraiazal as much by surprise as Viragan's previous instruction to exercise his ingenuity on the manufacture of a story capable of overtaking and overwhelming the rumour of the king's madness. He had no alternative but to improvise hurriedly. Fortunately, because he was still rather distressed by Triasymon's unjustified criticism of his betrothal gift, his train of thought was already headed in a profitable direction.

"Well, Your Highness," he said, "I must confess that it seems to me that what the wine has or has not done is of considerable importance, precisely because the point at issue is what we ought to do next. It seems to me, in fact, that if the wine *was* good, but failed in its purpose, then its effect must have been countered by another agent. It seems to me that our good and noble king must have fallen victim to some vile sorcery at least thirteen days ago. To that extent, at least, the rumours circulating in the palace are probably true. Rather than countering them, it might be more politic to refine them."

"What do you mean?" Viragan prompted.

"I would undoubtedly have realised much sooner that Lysariel had been bewitched, had I not been concentrating all my attention and power on more urgent matters," Giraiazal said. "What we must do now, Your Highness, it seems to me, is to identify the source of that sorcery in order that it might be nullified."

"And in order to do that," Viragan said, "it might be useful, if not actually necessary, to seek the help of the populace at large."

"I suppose so," Giraiazal agreed. "They will doubtless be appalled to learn that their beloved king has been the object of a magical attack so soon after his restoration, and enthusiastic to render what assistance they can."

"Indeed," said Viragan. "I see now why Orlu was so impressed by your skills when he first met you, Master Magician. You are, indeed, a very cunning wizard. I see exactly where your argument is headed. When we beheaded the former governor, we were overly optimistic to think that the stroke would put an immediate end to Yura's malign influence on our sovereign affairs. Hope made us naive. Yura's oppression was not merely political, but magical. The governor was the horrid figurehead of Yura's manifest tyranny, but the insidious sinews of magical manipulation were concealed, and therefore uncut. No sooner had the rightful king been restored to his throne than he became the victim of cruel anathematization, and his beloved queen with him. While you laboured heroically to preserve Queen Calia from one nefandous enchantment, King Lysariel was more subtly victimized by another--and no sooner had you turned your attention to his relief than our enemies struck at their first target for a second time, more brutally than before. I see it all, now! Now that our beloved queen is dead, the enemy magicians are free to concentrate all their attentions on the king. He is in direr danger than we knew, and we shall need all the help we can get in the attempt to save him. You are absolutely right, Master Magician: this is not a time to be proud. We must ask Lysariel's loyal subjects to rally behind him. They must become hunters, every one. They must be ceaselessly vigilant, until we have identified the source of his monstrous sorcery."

Giraiazal was astonished to hear his vague suggestion made so elaborately concrete, and was forced to wonder whether he had been cleverly manipulated into making it in the first place--but that thought needed to be stored away for more careful consideration at a quieter time.

"Can this be true?" Triasymon asked, in the meantime--but the question only called forth a withering glance from the merchant prince.

"Do you have another explanation?" Viragan asked the Lord Chancellor. "It seems to me that it is the only one possible--do you not agree, Master Magician?"

"I do, Your Highness," Giraiazal agreed, setting aside his reservations. "It is, therefore, all the more urgent that we should bring the king back to his senses without further delay."

"The hunt for the sorcerers responsible for this outrage may be a long and difficult one," Viragan continued, after a brief pause for thought. "It will undoubtedly be successful, as such hunts always are--for no evil magician has cunning enough to remain concealed when an entire nation is set to search him out--but I fear that its successful conclusion might not be enough in itself to restore the king to sanity. There will be an uncomfortable interval, in any case. We may need further contingency plans. Do you not agree, Master Magician?"

"Yes indeed, Your Highness," Giraiazal was forced to say. "I shall measure the positions of the Motile Entities again, and make what haste I can to calculate...."

"You have done so much already, dear Giraiazal," Viragan interrupted him, smoothly, "that you must be quite exhausted. Perhaps it is my turn to make a calculation or two--purely in the interests of sparing your tired brain."

"What do you suggest, Your Highness?" Giraiazal asked, uncertainly.

"Well," said Viragan, "I am only a humble merchant, and my meagre intelligence cannot compete with your advanced and esoteric kind of wisdom, but it seems to me that we must make provision for the smooth running of our government while we track down the evil men who have temporarily deranged the king's senses. We need a regent who can step into his shoes--on a strictly temporary basis, for the time being, although we ought to bear in mind the slim but awful possibility that King Lysariel might never fully recover."

"What regent?" Triasymon said, suspiciously. "You want the job for yourself, I suppose."

"Certainly not," Prince Viragan was quick to reply. "I, for one, could not countenance any name being put forward but that of the king's loyal brother Manazzoryn, who has worked so tirelessly during the period of Lysariel's indisposition."

"That seems a wise decision, Your Highness," Giraiazal was quick to add. It was obvious to the magician that Viragan had had this scheme ready for some time, ready to unfold if--or when--Queen Calia died, and he had no alternative but to support it, at least until he could figure out what its future phases might involve.

"And I am perfectly certain," Viragan added, "that if my great friend Prince Orlu were here--even though he would be prostrate with desolation at the loss of his dear daughter--he would unhesitatingly add his voice to ours."

"I suppose Manazzoryn would be the natural choice," Triasymon conceded.

"Then yours must be the duty of notifying him of your decision, Lord Chancellor," Viragan said. "But before we go our separate ways, it might be as well if we were to bend our collective intelligence to the matter of identifying suspects whose names might be mentioned to the people should their search for fugitive magicians prove frustrating. After all, we would not want them to waste their time suspecting someone we know to be innocent, merely because of certain coincidental circumstances that are bound to seem odd to them."

"What's that supposed to mean?" Triasymon demanded.

"Merely that our good and loyal friend Giraiazal is a recent arrival on the island, having previously been resident in Yura," Viragan went on, "and he is undoubtedly a magician of unusual quality. You and I know that he is entirely trustworthy, Lord Chancellor, but the common people have not the advantage of our close acquaintance with him, nor our powers of insight."

"I take your point, Your Highness," Giraiazal said, hastily. "I had some opportunity to observe witch-hunts while I was in Yura. That experience did indeed suggest that, although the common people are by no means unenthusiastic in identifying suspects, they sometimes get carried away and become too profuse in their accusations. Your Highness is the possessor of invaluable local knowledge to which I, as a newcomer, am not party. Do you, perchance, have any theory as to who might have visited this atrocious curse upon our beloved ruler?"

"I hesitate to mention it" said Viragan, "and it may be as well to wait a while before the suspicion goes any further than this room, but I cannot help wondering about the character of this man Urbishek. He was, after all, the architect and maker of this foul homunculus which appears to have lured Lysariel away from the sickbed of his dear wife."

"That is true," Triasymon acknowledged. "Why else would my nephew, who had formerly been the most devoted of husbands, have deserted his wife in her hour of greatest need? The statue must indeed be accursed--why did I not see it before?"

"No blame can be attached to you," Viragan hastened to reassure the Lord Chancellor. "Nor to the Grand Vizier, who did not have time to investigate the shards and flakes chipped from the column when the sculptor began his nefarious work, and probably has not had time to give them more than a cursory glance since then. But now that we are forced to reflect upon what has happened...."

"We must not jump to conclusions," Giraiazal put in, "before I have made a proper investigation of the matter. I shall need to make very scrupulous inquiries of the stars, and lay out my cards with the utmost care. If Urbishek is indeed as powerful and ingenious a sorcerer as you have hypothesized, it would be direly dangerous for anyone unaccomplished in magic to uncover and evaluate his role in this tragedy."

"That is your prerogative, of course," said Viragan, graciously. "I shall leave the investigation entirely to you."

In response to this commission Giraiazal hastened back to his attic, and threw himself into his work yet again, with the zeal of a man desperate to find answers to exceedingly vexatious questions. Desperation is a poor ally in such circumstances, though, and Giraiazal had been taught at the very beginning of his schooling that oracles often exhibit a marked reluctance to reveal the future to a seer whose mind is not calm, and whose mood is not disinterested. Disinterest, in this instance, was something Giraiazal could not hope to attain; he knew now that he was caught in a web of deceit, spun by a spider of far greater ingenuity than the sculptor Urbishek--and he knew, too, that if he hoped to secure a comfortable future for himself, he would do far better to assist the spider in its weaving than to make the slightest attempt to break the expanding web.

The questions the magician asked of his oracles were, in consequence, not the ones that most excited his curiosity. He cast new horoscopes for King Lysariel, Prince Manazzoryn and Princess Zintrah, and found them all clouded by confusion as well as menace, but since the queen's death he had lost confidence in his own ability to form an accurate idea of the nature of the threats surrounding them. He did not come down from his turret again until he was summoned to attend Queen Calia's funeral.

155

Those who wept longest and loudest at the funeral ceremony were Zintrah and Manazzoryn, although Giraiazal condescended to shed a few fugitive tears himself. King Lysariel was not present, and his absence certainly did not go unnoticed among the crowds who followed the queen's coffin to its burial-ground. It was common knowledge by now that the king had fallen victim to malicious sorcery, and that Scleracina's hard-won independence from the Yuran yoke was under threat. When Manazzoryn's regency was announced by the Lord Chancellor, immediately after the moving funeral oration delivered by the Grand Vizier, it was greeted with near-universal approval.

As soon as the funeral was over the witch-hunt began. Although reliable news was sparse, Giraiazal presumed that it was carried forward as zealously as witch-hunts usually are--which is to say that it quickly dissolved into chaos as wild accusations were flung in any and every direction, however unlikely. The one thing upon which the common people seemed to be agreed, if Burrel's accounts could be trusted, was that it was as well that Prince Orlu had not yet returned from his mission to Kalasperanza, given that he was the kind of man who was wont to give expression to grief and wrath in an extremely violent manner, without caring overmuch how many innocent people might get hurt. Mercifully, Prince Viragan was a more judicious man, whose daughter was still alive and very well, so his influence upon the conduct of the witch-hunt was generally considered to be calm, fair and benign.

After the funeral Giraiazal returned to his labours in a slightly more determined mood. There was a great deal still to be done; he had to make what analysis he could of the spider that had crawled out of Calia's mouth, as well as re-examining the shards of coral chipped from the column that Urbishek had fashioned into an image of the queen. He also had to focus his mind and his divinatory talents on a proper analysis of the various dangers looming over Scleracina's royal household.

He did make progress, but it was slow and uncertain. He decided, albeit a little reluctantly, that there was substantial evidence to suggest that Urbishek might indeed have magical powers, perhaps resultant from some kind of demonic possession. These may have been derived independently of whatever uncanny force possessed the miraculous coral, in which case they might have entered into a synergistic collaboration with it; on the other hand, it was not impossible that the alien force had actually expanded out of the coral to possess the sculptor and make him a secondary instrument of its will. The disease-carrying spider had undoubtedly been independent of the coral when it fell into the queen's mouth, but Giraiazal felt free to wonder whether it might have been subsequently co-opted into some synergistic conspiracy of enchantments; if so, that made it more easily explicable that he was having such difficulty finding consistent reports of the future of the royal household.

The one thing that still seemed clear, in the testimony of his cards as in the evidence of the stars, was that the last king of Scleracina would be Lysariel's son. Calia could not now be the mother of that child, but the identity of her replacement was a datum that no apparatus would deign to reveal. Perhaps, Giraiazal thought, the matter had not yet been settled by Damozel Fate, who always liked to keep a few of her options open in order to tease and tantalise her many admirers.

Brian Stableford

Part Three

Brian Stableford

The Madness of King Lysariel

1

To the lay reader, the academic disagreements of astrologers are bound to seem confusing, and of no practical relevance. If a horoscope is accurate, ordinary men are wont to say, what does it matter whether the accuracy arises from coincidence or teleology? Given that every available method and theory indicates that the world is due to end within a few years--whether the exact figure turns out to be one, two, three or even four--why should anyone bother trying to figure out which of them produces that result by the cleverest means, or precisely what kind of cleverness is involved? A true prophet is, however, bound to take a different view.

My judgment--it would be false modesty to call it an opinion--is that the coincidentalist thesis is the correct one. To hold either version of the teleological thesis is to suspect our forerunners of taking far more trouble on our behalf than could ever have seemed reasonable. On the one hand, our forerunners must be supposed to have stocked the Mobile Entities with a vast supply of magical influences and to have set in place an enormously complicated mechanism to govern their gradual release; on the other, it is supposed to have done something similar to our remote ancestors, with the additional complication of extrapolating the release-mechanism across thousands, if not millions, of generations. That they had the power to do this we need not doubt--however long the Earth's decadence has been, we only need to continue backtracking to be certain of finding a forerunner race with the appropriate technical capability--but to assume that they would ever have bothered is to be guilty of an appalling arrogance. We know little or nothing about our remoter ancestors, but the one thing of which we may certain is that they had far too much business of their own to occupy themselves in making such minutely intricate provision for their successors.

The Revelations of Suomynona, the Last Prophet

While Clarassour was set abuzz with the noise of the hunt for evil magicians the palace became quieter. Manazzoryn, in his capacity as regent, ordered that Lysariel's door should not be forced until every possible effort had been made to persuade him to open it voluntarily. The regent made further efforts to accomplish this himself, as did his uncle Triasymon and his wife Zintrah--but to everyone's surprise, the king, having refused admission to all of them, eventually sent an urgent message requiring the immediate attendance of his Grand Vizier and Court Magician, Giraiazal of Natalarch.

Giraiazal had recovered sufficient presence of mind to conceal his astonishment at the receipt of this summons, and even contrived a plausible pretence of having expected it. When he presented himself at the closed door and announced his presence, though, the king insisted that he must send everyone else away and enter alone--terms to which the magician reluctantly agreed. Nor did Giraiazal make any objection when the door was closed behind him and three heavy bolts slammed into their pits. His gaze was immediately captured by the golden form of the coral image, but he tore it away in order to study the king's distraught expression.

"What is troubling you, Your Majesty?" Giraiazal asked, wondering whether the news of Calia's death had finally penetrated the fog of Lysariel's confusion. The king would not speak to him in the room where the coral statue stood, though; the magician was taken through a curtained doorway on to a high balcony overlooking the plaza and the harbour. Although the sun was only half-set--Giraiazal judged that its disc would not vanish for at least an hour--a dozen stars shone ominously bright in the evening sky, the White Star the most vivid of them all.

"Faithful Giraiazal," the king said, in a hoarse whisper, "I am in dire need of magical assistance. I need you to provide me with a love potion."

Giraiazal was thunderstruck, but he made every effort to conceal his amazement. "A love potion, Your Majesty?" he echoed. "How can Your Majesty possibly be in need of a love potion?"

"For the usual reason," was Lysariel's reply. "I fear that my wife no longer loves me as she should."

"What makes you think so, Your Majesty?" Giraiazal inquired, solicitously.

"There is a new hardness in her gaze, Giraiazal," the king replied. "For three days now she has looked at me as if I had disappointed her in some way. I swear that it is not so, and I have begged her to explain, but she continues to show me the same expression. Her passion is fading, and my need to reignite it is becoming desperate. I need an aphrodisiac, and you are the only man I know who can obtain or make it for me. Help me, Master Magician, I beg of you."

"I fear that your wife might not condescend to drink such a potion were I able to devise one," Giraiazal replied, after a moment's hesitation.

Lysariel's face fell. "You are right, Giraiazal," he said. "She refuses to share my food or my wine. I thought it was because she needed no nourishment but the benign light of the sun, but it is probably a matter of suspicion. I have to have all my meals sent up from the kitchens, you know, and left on a tray outside my door. My food could easily be poisoned, or otherwise doctored. But she will fade away if I cannot persuade her to take nourishment! Does it not seem to you that her light is weakening? Her strength has begun to fade, and it is all my fault!"

Giraiazal peeped through the curtains at the radiant statue, which seemed more than bright enough to him. His attention was, however, distracted when he noticed there was a familiar bottle standing on the table beside the statue. The seal had been broken, but the vessel was still more than three-quarters full. One measure had been drunk, but seven still remained. Was it possible, Giraiazal thought, that Lysariel simply had not consumed a dose of the wine of Yethlyreom sufficient to bring him to his senses? Was there still hope for his sanity?

"The situation may not be as bleak as Your Majesty assumes," the magician was quick to say. "There are two parties to every love-match, and more than one way to approach any difficulty that might arise therein. It is not necessary that your beloved should drink a potion, if you can be transformed in her eyes. That is the more roundabout way, and the more problematic, which is why it is less often attempted, but there is a happy coincidence here. Do you, perchance, remember the wine of Yethlyreom that was my wedding-present to you? You need only dose yourself thoroughly with the contents of that bottle to be restored in the sight of your beloved to the most glorious manhood imaginable--ah! but I had forgotten. Your brother asked you to drink a toast to your wife, and you have doubtless drained the bottle already--but no; had you done that, there would be no problem! I am confused, Your Majesty."

Lysariel seemed for a moment to be as confused as Giraiazal was pretending to be--but then his expression cleared. "You are right!" He said. "When I toasted her, she did seem very pleased."

Giraiazal started at this revelation, but concealed his shock of surprise. He realised, very belatedly, that Manazzoryn's assumption of triumph had been premature, by virtue of a false assumption. Lysariel had drunk to the health of the wrong bride. No wonder the radiant succubus had seemed pleased!

"Have you any of the wine left, Your Majesty?" Giraiazal asked, disingenuously.

"Yes," King Lysariel answered. It sits on the table, right there. It was sweet, I admit--very sweet--but I did not like it very much. My beloved seemed pleased that I had drunk to her health, but I felt a little strange thereafter, as if I were on the brink of some terrible hallucination. I do not

163

mind intoxication, as a rule, but there was something cold about the quality of that particular effect. Alas, the wine will be spoiled by now, will it not?"

That, Giraiazal thought, was the vital question. Alas, he did not know the answer. "We can only try, Your Majesty," he said, softly.

Lysariel seemed slightly unsure as to whether this advice was sound, but he had not been a king for long, and he had not yet cultivated the habit that all kings eventually acquire of ignoring all the best advice and heeding only the worst. He went back into the room, removed the cork from the bottle, and put his nose to the aperture.

"It smells sweet enough," he conceded. He poured the merest drop into a goblet and raised it to his lips. When that had gone down he poured a fuller measure, and drank it down. Six measures still remained, but he laid the goblet down very firmly. He whirled around to face the likeness of his dead wife, his face wreathed in smiles.

"How could I have doubted you, good Giraiazal!" he said, warmly. "See how her eyes light up again! There can be no greater magician than you in all Ambriocyatha! You have the gratitude of your king--and I do not need to tell you how precious a gift that is."

"If only you would take a little more, Your Majesty...."

Giraiazal was not allowed to finish the sentence. "Oh no!" the king replied. "This is powerful medicine, and I shall eke it out. You have done me a great service, but I am in command of myself now. I see now that the fault was in me, not in my bride. Go now--I have much to do."

"There is much to be done down below, Your Majesty," Giraiazal said, stubbornly. "There is a kingdom to be ruled."

"Yes, yes," Lysariel replied, impatiently. "See to it, man. You are my Grand Vizier, are you not? Get my lazy uncle to help you, and those scoundrel princes. Go! go!"

"Yes, Your Majesty," Giraiazal murmured, wearily, as he made his exit.

Had Viragan been in the palace Giraiazal would have felt obliged to make an immediate report of his failure to bring Lysariel to his senses, but the merchant prince was attending to matters of business, so the magician made his report to Manazzoryn instead.

"There is hope, then?" Manazzoryn said, when Giraiazal told him about the bottle that was still more than half-full.

"There is hope, Your Highness. Let us give him a little more time. If he will only consume the rest of the wine, he may yet come to his senses."

Having delivered this advice, Giraiazal returned to his lofty attic, where he immediately began laying out his cards yet again, to see if the omens had changed in any wise--and, if so, whether for the better or the worse. His hands were trembling so badly that he had to take a liberal dose of medicine, but he persisted nevertheless.

He persuaded himself, after an hour's steady perusal, that the outlook was a little more hopeful. When he consulted the positions of the Motile Entities relative to the sixty-nine stars, they too seemed to be more hopeful than his former calculations had predicted. Alas, when he tried to boost his confidence further by casting his best wands, they fell into a very ugly pattern, which reminded him very strongly of the spider that had crawled out of Calia's mouth. One question to which he did not want an unambiguous answer was the question of whether Queen Calia had been murdered--and, if so, by whom. He concentrated his mind on the matter of King Lysariel and his coral bride. He tried to remember exactly how the statue had appeared during the brief glimpses he had stolen. His mind's eye reproduced the image readily enough, but his attention was immediately drawn to her pose: the manner in which her right hand was positioned between her breasts, and the way her legs were subtly braced, as if she were about to take a step forward.

Can she possibly be alive? Giraiazal found himself thinking, using a personal pronoun instead of an impersonal one, just as Urbishek had. But he immediately found another voice with which to oppose himself. "It is a statue," he said, aloud. "Cursed or not, it is certainly inanimate." But he, of all people, knew how little even his most secure assumptions, and hence his best advice, were to be trusted.

The next day, Manazzoryn summoned the Grand Vizier to a conference of state. Giraiazal found the regent deep in conversation with his father-in-law and his uncle.

"I have been driven unwillingly to the conclusion that my brother is irredeemably mad, Giraiazal," Manazzoryn said, although there was something in his voice which suggested that he was repeating words spoken to him by another. "I fear that he needs to be put away, for his own good. Prince Viragan has generously offered to provide asylum for the king in his own house, and I am minded to accept. I am already appointed regent, but I shall find it a good deal easier to discharge my duties if Lysariel is no longer in the palace."

Giraiazal looked at the Lord Chancellor, then at the Merchant Prince. "But, Your Highness," he protested. "Only yesterday you agreed...."

"The regent is right, Master Magician," Viragan said, carelessly interrupting the magician. "While the king remains in his quarters, rumour runs riot. We have succeeded in deflecting the attention of the mob, but the underlying problem persists and we must take some action."

"If that image really is cursed," Triasymon said, dolefully, "then I suppose he ought to be separated from it, forcibly if necessary. If that brings him to his senses...."

"But there is still the wine!" Giraiazal said.

"Ah yes," said Viragan. "The magical wine. I hear that you visited the king yesterday, Lord Vizier. Did it really seem to you that he might come to his senses, if he could only finish the bottle?"

Giraiazal frowned. He realised that he had unwittingly interfered with Viragan's plan for a second time. The merchant prince had been patient while he fought for Calia's life, but that patience appeared to have worn thin now. He recalled Viragan's remarks about the suspicions of the people of Clarassour, and knew that the threat of accusation still hung over him, but he was reluctant to give up an opportunity he had so cleverly won.

"Your concern does you all credit, Your Highnesses," the magician said, carefully addressing all three men simultaneously, "but I did persuade the king to take a little more of the medicine that might yet clear his head. It is possible, in my opinion, that he might recover from the unhinged state of mind into which he has been cast sooner rather than later."

"But you can make no promises," Viragan pointed out.

"No," Giraiazal admitted. "I can make no promises. Is the possibility not enough? Should we not give King Lysariel every possible chance to recover? Do we not owe that to Scleracina, as well as to Lysariel?"

"That's true," Triasymon put in.

"I'm not so sure," was Manazzoryn's querulous judgment.

"In any case," Giraiazal said, hurriedly, "it might be impolitic to take any final decision about the king's future in the absence of one of the nation's two merchant princes."

Viragan's pale eyes became even harder then, although that was the only indication he gave that Giraiazal had struck a nerve. The magician realised that the news which Viragan had been patiently awaiting was some definite confirmation of Orlu's death--and it was the fact that this news had failed to arrive that was making Viragan anxious for the future of his schemes.

"Perhaps we should allow a few days more to pass before taking any precipitate action," Triasymon said, "in order to give the king every chance to come to his senses, and to allow Orlu more time to return from his futile errand of mercy."

Manazzoryn seemed to Giraiazal to be less grateful than he might have been for this intervention--which was, after all, an opportunity to postpone a course of action that must have seemed to him uncomfortably akin to a betrayal of his brother. Viragan, on the other hand, was quick to suggest a compromise.

"Surely the Lord Chancellor was right the first time," the merchant prince said, judiciously. "The longer we leave the king locked up with that monster, the less likely he is to recover. He opens his door twice a day to take in supplies, and Manazzoryn has suggested that it might be worth introducing a sleeping-draught into his food--but he has made a habit of ordering twice as much as a man requires, and I suspect that he is being very careful. Now that you have gained his confidence, Lord Vizier, I wonder whether you might be able to discover a way to facilitate the separation without a struggle? It would be a pity, would it not, if we were forced to adopt violent methods in order to subdue our legitimate ruler?"

Giraiazal took his time before replying. He knew that it would be dangerous to set himself against Viragan, but he also wanted to give his own instrument time to take effect. "The king has been ordering food for two because he thinks himself in company," he said, eventually. "On the other hand, he now believes that his coral bride has been refusing to eat because she is fearful. I am sure that now I have regained his confidence I can gain entry to his room again, and I believe that I could persuade him to drink a sleeping-draught by telling him that it was something else--but I still think that he might yet come out of his own accord, if he will only drink the rest of the wine of Yethlyreom quickly enough. I have given him a motive to do that, but his mind is still unclear. I am not working unopposed in this matter, any more than I was unopposed in trying to save the queen. Give me three more days; if the king has not come to his senses by then, I give you my word that I will help you take him unawares."

Viragan hesitated, but eventually nodded his head. "Have you made your magical inquiries regarding the sculptor Urbishek?" he asked. "Is he the one opposing your design?"

"One of them," Giraiazal said, deciding to take his courage in both hands. "There is another agent at work, I fear, which might be more dangerous by far."

"The coral monster," Viragan was quick to guess. "But that is Urbishek's work, is it not?"

"Perhaps it is," Giraiazal agreed. "But it may be that he too is a victim. It is quite possible that he had no ambitions beyond the aesthetic until he began working the coral, and that his willingness to venture anything for art's sake has been his undoing.

The ghost of a frown crossed Viragan's face, but then he seemed to realise the merit of the argument. "Ah," he said. "I see. But King Lysariel asked for the coral to be cut from that particular grotto, did he not? And he was first acquainted with its existence by the Lord Chancellor."

"I regretted that," Triasymon was quick to say. "I warned the boys about the dangers of temptation time and time again--did I not, Manazzoryn? I told them that cave was an evil place."

Manazzoryn confirmed that this was true. "I would never have sent divers into such danger myself," the regent said, firmly. "I can only think that my brother must have been under some vile enchantment before he thought of having the image made--before he ever learned that he was to be king."

"That is a shrewd hypothesis, well worthy of investigation," Giraiazal said, quick to seize upon it. "If the coral within the cave extended its powers of fascination while Lysariel still thought himself a fisherman's son, it must have known him better than he knew himself. The roots of this mystery may lie deeper than we have dared to suppose."

"Are you suggesting that the coral might have *intended* to be made into an image of the Queen of Scleracina?" Triasymon asked.

"No, my lord" said Viragan, thoughtfully. "It seems to me that what the magician is suggesting, if I might be so bold as to hazard a guess about such strange and esoteric matters, is that the coral might have intended to *become* the queen of Scleracina. Calia died soon after Manazzoryn implored him to drink to his queen, his wife and his beloved....and Lysariel certainly seems to believe that the statue is now his wife. It is indeed possible that all of our misfortunes have been the result of the coral bride's curse--and that any future misfortunes we may suffer might be attributable to the same cause. I can see the logic in Giraiazal's desire to shift the ultimate blame in this manner." His pale blue eyes were staring at Giraiazal with a quizzical expression that might even have been tinged with reluctant respect.

"There might not be any future misfortunes," Giraiazal said, "if Lysariel can only be brought to his senses. Urbishek, even if we think the very worst of him, is merely one one petty sorcerer among a host. The coral bride is something else: something unique. And we know, do we not, that she can be cut and chipped, if not abruptly shattered?" *What more could one ask of a scapegoat than that?* he added, silently.

"And even if the king cannot be restored to his senses soon enough," Viragan said, taking up the thread of the argument readily enough now that he had begun to appreciate its ramifications, "he will surely get better once the monster has been delivered up to justice."

"It sounds like the truth to me," the Lord Chancellor said.

That seemed to be enough for Viragan. "Well, my lord," he said, "if it can convince a man like you, it will surely convince the common folk. But it makes the matter of removing the king from the monster's clutches even more urgent, do you not think?"

"If only he can be persuaded to see the truth," Giraiazal declared, "all might yet be well." Discretion forbade him to add that this was was the only means he could envisage by which the way could be cleared for Lysariel to be succeeded, peacefully and naturally, by his son--but he wondered whether he had been wise to risk so much in the cause of a prophecy that he had kept secret, which surely could not require his help to come true, if Damozel Fate had already decided the matter.

Cartomancers are, as is only to be expected, every bit as avid as astrologers to equip themselves with an incredibly elaborate prehistory. They do not have the option of claiming that decks of cards already existed before the primal humans cultivated active intelligence and elementary technology, but they can and do assert that the ominous significance of the images depicted in the major arcana was recognised long before their prototypes were first painted.

Although many of the "greater trumps" refer to technological devices that can hardly have been possessed by the earliest cultures of all--the Tower Struck by Lightning and the Ship Carried Aloft by a Waterspout, for instance--and only a handful, including Lady Death and the Long-Lost Moon, are entirely divorced from technological considerations it is certainly conceivable that the mechanical devices were intrusions designed to update earlier schemes of ominous calculation. Indeed, many cartomancers believe that the decks of cards currently in use have actually undergone a kind of retrograde evolution, recovering the imagistic apparatus of an early post-primal society as our own society has regressed to a similar technological stage. It is presumed that during the middle phases of the Epic of the Humankinds, the images of the major arcana must have depicted devices of much greater capability.

One corollary of this scheme of cartomantic evolution is that the wide variety of the sets of trumps contained in modern decks of cards is easily explicable in terms of slightly different degrees of regression. There are, of course, numerous different schools of cartomancy, each of which claims to know which of the many kinds of packs is the most perfectly accommodated to the needs and demands of the End Time, but the schools are rarely exclusive; most cartomancers will use any deck that happens to fall into their hands, and the best-endowed usually possess half a dozen slightly variant decks.

A similar flexibility usually extends to more basic theoretical issues, and relatively few cartomancers take the trouble to classify themselves, or one another, as coincidentalists or teleologists. Many of them, however, tend to fall prey to a delusion that rarely affects astrological theoreticians: the delusion that in laying out their displays they are actually creating the future rather than than merely inquiring into it. The delusion is harmless, unless it is retranslated into action as a desire to cheat--but once a diviner begins to cheat, the convolutions of his self-delusion are apt to become much more intricate.

The Revelations of Suomynona, the Last Prophet

Those divers who had survived the process of extracting the luminous coral from the undersea cave on Lysariel's behalf were summoned to the palace by Prince Viragan and interrogated, with Giraiazal in attendance to aid assessment of the merits of their evidence. They needed little prompting to wax very eloquent on the subject of the bad reputation that luminous coral had always had. They were also unanimous in declaring that the grotto was no natural sea-cave; in their expert opinion, it gave every indication of having been hollowed out with considerable deliberation, though certainly not by human hands.

The diver who rose most enthusiastically to the occasion told Viragan and Giraiazal that the deep trenches lying some way beyond the reefs protecting that part of Scleracina's shore were well-known to be the habitat of monstrous burrowing creatures which had come from outside the Earth. Perhaps, he suggested, many such species had been motivated to new activity by the imminent end of the world. What they might hope to gain by expeditionary forays on to land he could not begin to guess, but he was sure that something of the sort must be happening--or, if not, that the unusual coral must be some unnatural excrescence of parasites that had travelled with the patient monsters of the deep from their own far-distant world.

"It is my belief," the enterprising diver concluded, when Giraiazal and Viragan had shown themselves willing to entertain such fancies, "that while King Lysariel and his brother Prince Manazzoryn were living in seclusion on the wild northern shore, awaiting the day of their restoration, they must have fallen under the influence of a diabolical intelligence innate within the coral. The king was probably commanded to give it a form in which it might walk the land. Perhaps it had no desire but to enjoy a measure of freedom while the opportunity still remained, but we dare not ignore the possibility that it has a far more terrible purpose, beyond the imagination of common folk like me."

When Prince Viragan suggested that such opinions might sound a trifle treasonous to less educated ears than his own, the diver was quick to assure him that no criticism of the king was intended. He and his fellows promised faithfully that anything they said outside the palace would be very carefully phrased so as to put all the blame where it belonged--on the maleficent coral--and to emphasize very strongly that the king was an innocent victim.

Afterwards, Giraiazal decided that he ought to go to see the king again, in order to make a closer inspection of the statue.

"If he will only admit you to his rooms," Viragan said, "that is certainly what you must do."

The merchant prince's scepticism proved unfounded. Lysariel admitted the magician without any procrastination or prevarication, apparently very glad to see him.

"How are you feeling today, Your Majesty?" Giraiazal asked, taking note of the fact that there was only one measure left in the bottle that had contained the wine of Yethlyreom.

"Very well indeed," Lysariel assured him. "My wife is of the same opinion; her eyes are full of love when she looks at me. I am delighted that I trusted your advice, and to have the opportunity to thank you."

Giraiazal had to pretend that this was excellent news, although he had hoped for a very different effect. Perhaps, he thought, the wine that the king had drunk had not been strong enough to force Lysariel to see the statue for what it was. If so, there was little hope now that the last draught would succeed in completing his disillusionment. Giraiazal did not like to consider the alternative hypotheses that the wine might have been spoiled, or mislabelled, or even deliberately adulterated.

"May I be permitted to examine your wife, Your Majesty?" Giraiazal asked. "Although I am optimistic that the problem has been conclusively solved, there remains a possibility that the effect of the wine will not be permanent. Given that there is only a single dose left, I may need to have another treatment in reserve."

"You fear a relapse?" Lysariel said, anxiously. "You think that she may become cold again?"

"It is merely a possibility, Your Majesty," the magician said, soothingly. "But we need to be ready for any contingency, do we not?"

"Yes, most certainly," the king replied. "I am depending on you, Lord Vizier, to prevent any such occurrence."

Lysariel was watching, at first with intense concentration, while Giraiazal made a close examination of the coral statue, but the magician was not to be put off. He carefully tested the statue's texture, which was softer than he had anticipated, and its luminosity, which was brighter. He also took note of the fact that the image was warmer than he had expected. He studied its features with minute care; they duplicated Queen Calia's former beauty very well. There seemed to be an exceptional hardness in the opaque stare which met his own when he peered into the eyes, but he was not intimidated. Giraiazal could not suppress a nagging

171

doubt as to whether the figure's pose was exactly the same as it had been last time he had seen it, but when he tried to work out exactly what had shifted he could not find a specific cause for the suspicion.

Is it really alive? he wondered. *If it is alive, is it capable of movement?* But both thoughts seemed absurd, unworthy of a man of his education, and he thrust them aside. The question he was here to address was: is it magical? And the answer he was obliged to find was *yes.* The statue's luminosity and unnatural warmth could both be cited as evidence supporting that conclusion, although a man in search of a different answer might have been tempted to argue that it was only warm because it had placed so that the sun's rays fell directly upon it for several hours before and after noon.

Giraiazal had to remind himself that there was good evidence, given the stories that Viragan had coaxed out of the fanciful diver, that the coral had been actively malevolent from the very beginning, long before Lysariel had first glimpsed the sea-cave. In any case, it would make a far better scapegoat than Urbishek, given that a scapegoat still seemed to be required. Perhaps, he thought, the statue had even been responsible for Queen Calia's death. If it *could* move about...but that was nonsense. It could not have left the room where Lysariel kept it captive.

"Well?" said the king. "What is your conclusion?"

"Your wife seems reasonably well, Your Majesty," Giraiazal said, "but I am not sure that the problem has been conclusively solved. I cannot help wondering whether this close and constant proximity is good for either of you. She might love you even more enthusiastically were temporary absence allowed to let her heart grow fonder."

"Nonsense," was Lysariel's prompt verdict on that suggestion. "We are inseparable."

"Will you not come down to the council chamber even for a little while, Your Majesty?" Giraiazal said, although he was already convinced that it was hopeless. "If only you would resume your monarchical duties, everything might still be well. You might maintain whatever relationship you please with your wife, in private, if only you will maintain your relationship with your people."

"I cannot imagine what you mean," was Lysariel's disappointing answer. "The whole world knows that I am recently married, and very much in love. May I not be allowed to enjoy my honeymoon while the ship of state is steered by my faithful advisors? I am all the more determined to make the most of her now that you have warned me that my beloved's affection might waver again."

"I wish you would reconsider, Your Majesty," Giraiazal said.

"I will not," was Lysariel's firm answer. "If further measures are necessary to ensure my wife's continuing love, I rely upon you to provide me with more wine."

In that case, Giraiazal thought, bitterly, *I might be forced to let Viragan have you, and make whatever provision I still can against the possibility of further disasters. But I am not finished yet.*

The magician returned to Viragan, and admitted that the king seemed unlikely to leave his apartments of his own accord before nightfall. He conceded that it might eventually be necessary for Viragan to fetch him out and place him in safe custody, but he did not say that the king had asked for more wine. Instead, he pleaded for three more days in which to use his powers of persuasion. "If I fail, Your Highness, I will gladly give you a sleeping-draught to put in his food," Giraiazal said, "but I have one more strategy to try."

"Very well," Viragan agreed, having apparently recovered the patience that he had briefly lost since Giraiazal had persuaded him that the coral bride would make a better scapegoat than Urbishek. "In the meantime, of course, you will doubtless take whatever measures you can to nullify the statue's occult powers, and render it vulnerable to our righteous vengeance?"

Giraiazal did not suppose for a moment that Viragan was an excessively superstitious man, but he was a magician, with the honour of his profession to uphold and a *quid pro quo* to provide. "While I remain safe and well, Prince Viragan," he assured his lord and master, "you have nothing whatsoever to fear from my rivals in magic. I shall cast the most powerful spells I can to ensure that the coral sorceress cannot harm you."

"And you will also protect me against Urbishek?"

"Urbishek?" Giraiazal was surprised by the additional demand. "I thought we had agreed that the coral bride is our enemy, and that the sculptor was a mere instrument of her malevolent will?"

"Indeed we had," Viragan agreed. "But it would surely be irresponsible to leave an instrument of such evil as this at liberty. As soon as you assure me that his magic can do me no harm, I shall take measures to ensure that he will not harm anyone else."

Giraiazal knew that he was being mocked. He judged from the expression in the merchant prince's eye that Viragan had decided to relish the challenge of dealing with the awkward knot that the commissioning of the statue had introduced into his plans. The former pirate was obviously capable of revelling in his own ingenuity, and was not entirely displeased to have it challenged. The magician was in no doubt as to where his own best interests lay, but he could not help feeling a certain frustration at being so easily manipulated.

"You may torture Urbishek as extensively as you desire, Your Highness," Giraiazal said, wearily, "and if the whim takes you while so amusing yourself to obtain a confession of various foul crimes, by all means do so. He cannot hurt you, with magic or by any other means. I shall be discreet in expressing my opinion that he is as much a victim in this as the king. I shall continue to hope that the curse that has been put

173

upon the king might be lifted, and that no similar misfortune will befall his brother. But I do recognise that it may not be easy to counter the awful curse of the coral bride."

"Your assiduousness does you great credit, Lord Vizier," Viragan said. "The king might recover his senses once he is safe in my house, especially if you can persuade him to come to me of his own free will--and if he does not recover, he will be carefully protected from any further harm. In the meantime, we shall doubtless have cause to be grateful that we have an excellent regent in Manazzoryn--and to hope with all our hearts that, with your aid, he will remain immune to the effects of the curse."

"Indeed we shall, Your Highness," Giraiazal said.

The merchant prince left the palace, in order to make sure that the sculptor Urbishek was seized and confined. Giraiazal knew that while Viragan was engaged in the leisurely business of shaping the sorcerer's confession, he was free to busy himself with his own plans, so he sought out Zintrah, without informing or asking permission from Manazzoryn. He pleaded for her assistance in winning Lysariel back from his sinister captor.

"Had I only known earlier what kind of material this coral is," Giraiazal told her, plaintively, "I might even have saved Calia. So distressed was I by her illness that I paid too little attention to other matters, and thus gave the evil statue the opportunity to beguile Lysariel. Had her husband been by her side when Calia emerged from her ordeal, he would surely have been delighted, and he would have kept close enough company with her thereafter to prevent her from suffering any kind of accident. I feel that this is all my fault, and I suspect that if Manazzoryn realises the extent of my failure he will probably have me beheaded. You are the only person who might be able to help me, and the only one who might be able to help poor Lysariel."

"What can I possibly do?" Zintrah asked.

"Lysariel must be distracted from his obsession, whatever the cost. You are the only one who can compete with the coral bride for his attention. I would not ask it of you if I were not desperate, but I am perfectly certain that there is no one else in Scleracina with sufficient natural charm combined with such abundant intelligence. If there is any mere human being equal to the task, you are the one--but it will require considerable patience and great courage, for our adversary is more than human, and also worse."

"No one else with sufficient charm and intelligence?" Zintrah echoed, pensively.

"No one," Giraiazal assured her. "This is the supreme test of human strength of character, and the only woman who can do it is a marvel among her own kind. There is no one in the entire world but you."

Experience had taught him that in dealing with women, whether young or old, it is never wise to be economical with flattery.

"The entire world?" Zintrah repeated.

"Will you help me, Your Highness?" Giraiazal begged.

"Calia was always my dearest friend," Zintrah declared, bravely. "We were sisters in spirit even before we married two brothers. I owe it to her to try. But I shall not tell Manazzoryn, in case I should fail. He would blame me then, as well as you, for being too weak to save his beloved brother."

"That is very wise," said Giraiazal. "This shall be our quest and our secret. Together, we shall prevail."

Later that day, when Giraiazal returned to Lysariel's quarters, he took Zintrah with him. He also had a sealed bottle not dissimilar to the one that had held the wine of Yethlyreom, although its contents were far less magical and somewhat more alcoholic.

When Lysariel saw that Giraiazal was not alone he made as if to close the door again but when the magician showed him the bottle, and signified by his body-language that he would not come in by himself, the king relented and allowed both his visitors to enter.

Giraiazal saw immediately that the king had taken the last measure of the authentic wine, and that the seeds of suggestion he had planted were taking effect. Lysariel's fear that the ardour of radiant wife might be cooling had returned.

Giraiazal took the king out on to the balcony, leaving Zintrah and the likeness of her sister-in-law to study one another. The magician whispered in the king's ear, saying: "I have found another flask of wine, Your Majesty, but it is not as powerful as the one I gave you as a wedding-present. It may need assistance to take effect. In the meantime, there is another way in which you might rekindle your wife's affections. It is a universally acknowledged fact that the fervour of a wife's love can always be increased by a modest dose of jealousy. It seems to me, therefore, that while you discreetly sup the wine, you might increase your own desirability in your beloved's eyes by making flirtatious conversation with your sister-in-law."

"You are not suggesting that I should mislead my wife, or cause her any anxiety, I hope?" Lysariel said. "I could not possibly stoop so low."

"Indeed not, Your Majesty," Giraiazal said. "That would be a terrible thing to do. I merely suggest that you permit her to observe that she does not have a monopoly on your attention. She is the queen, and will know that she has not the least cause for anxiety, but it will help to focus her mind. Do you not agree?"

The king did agree, albeit with a certain polite reluctance.

"Then I shall leave Zintrah here with the wine, Your Majesty," the magician said. "Drink as much as you please; I will ask her to bring more to you when you need it."

Brian Stableford

Giraiazal was pleased to observe that Lysariel permitted Zintrah to remain in his quarters for several hours thereafter--and when she emerged, she said that he had asked her to return the following morning with another bottle of wine. This she did. She returned for a second visit in the afternoon, once the blaze of noonday had abated sufficiently to make the room more comfortable.

This time, she did not emerge until dusk.

"I think the king is a great deal better, Lord Vizier," she told Giraiazal, when she reported her progress. "I think he might be ready to come out, were it not for the way the statue's unblinking eyes are always upon us. No matter how we arrange the furniture her gaze is always upon us. Even if we close curtains to exclude her from our sight Lysariel seems perpetually anxious about her observation. I have told him time and time again that she is my beloved sister as well as his wife, and that she wishes no harm to either of us, but his expressions of agreement lack force."

"That is not necessarily harmful to our cause," Giraiazal said. "If he is happy to talk to you--and he has been so utterly starved of authentic human intercourse of late that he must find the opportunity very welcome--even though he is fearful that his intentions might be misunderstood, he might be willing to remove himself from his golden leman in order to do it more comfortably. If only we can draw him outside the range of her evil influence, he might recover his sanity entirely. Do you think you might be able to persuade him to go with you to his old apartment, where you could talk in private?"

"I will try tomorrow morning," Zintrah promised. "Only supply me with one more bottle of enchanted wine."

That seemed a sensible notion, so Giraiazal spent the night employing his powers as a herbasacralist to import a little magic into a wine whose potency was considerable even without such assistance. When he gave it to Zintrah the next morning he said: "You have kept our secret, have you not? Manazzoryn has not been disturbed by your absence?"

"Not in the least," she told him. "My husband is the regent and he has many new duties to perform. His faithful merchant prince and Lord Chancellor are keeping him busy."

"Excellent," said the magician. "This is our last chance to save the king from a forceful separation that would undoubtedly be painful and difficult for all concerned. We must make the most of it."

When Zintrah next went into the king's apartment, Giraiazal waited outside, keeping watch from a shaded alcove. After an hour or so he saw the king and his brother's sister come out quietly, and make their way down the stairway.

The door to the apartment could not be locked from the outside, so there was nothing to prevent Giraiazal going in. He went immediately to where the statue stood, and began studying its contours with the utmost care.

176

The magician could not help wondering whether the statue might have changed its position yet again, albeit to a minuscule extent. Its right arm seemed to have relaxed a little more, while the left might have been slightly raised, and the attitude of the legs seemed more suggestive of an intention to walk.

After some consideration, Giraiazal dismissed these suspicions from his mind. The statue's features, at least, were quite unchanged. The eyes were as hard as adamant, as if they had been tempered by some hot emotion that Giraiazal could not quite identify.

"You are mine now," the magician said to the statue, "I have the measure of you. From now on, your curses will do *my* work." Then he left, in search of a team of servants who could carry the statue to his own apartment.

Brian Stableford

178

Cartomantic theory is, in general, far less preoccupied than astrological theory with the nature of the connection between indicators and consequent events, and far more concerned with the relationship between indicators and their interpreters. Very few astrologers would actually deny that their reading involves a subjective element--how, otherwise, would one be able to distinguish between two similarly-trained practitioners?-- but it is unusual for astrologers to stress the intuitive aspects of their art and those aspects do not figure large in rival theoretical accounts. Cartomantic theory, by contrast, usually devotes a great deal of attention to matters of "epistemological creativity", and rival accounts of that creative process are a major factor in distinguishing mutually-hostile schools of cartomancy.

The most readily identifiable field of dispute between cartomancers is between "inspirationists" and "methodologists". Inspirationists believe that the cartomancer's ability to extract meaning from an array of cards is largely dependent on subconscious processes whose access is necessarily indirect, while methodologists believe that meaning is best extrapolated by wholly conscious processes of deduction and association. What this means in practice is that inspirationists will often try to empty their minds of connected trains of thought while overlooking an array, aspiring to a mental state akin to a waking dream, while methodologists will concentrate intently, attempting to bring their consciousness into a strictly disciplined focus. Given the general flexibility of cartomantic theory, it is not surprising that there are many practitioners who shun both extremes, some of whom deliberately alternate between the contrasted states of mind, hoping to benefit from a metaphorical species of "binocular vision". Those cartomancers who fall prey to temptation are, of course, doubly assisted in their self-delusion by the cultivation of an ambiguous state of mind.

The Revelations of Suomynona, the Last Prophet

No sooner had Giraiazal begun congratulating himself for his success in separating King Lysariel from the coral bride than his plans went badly awry. When he reached the bottom of the staircase leading up to Lysariel's apartment he found Viragan waiting for him.

"Excellent work, Master Magician," the merchant prince said. "Everything is as it should be. Manazzoryn and Triasymon are waiting for us in the council-chamber.

Giraiazal could only hope that he gave no outward sign of surprise before saying: "I never doubted that I could do it, Your Highness. Where is the king now, if I might ask?"

"Your judgment was perfect, Master Magician. He agreed to go with my daughter to my house, where the two of them could be alone and undisturbed. She will guide him to his new residence, and turn the key the lock with her own fair hand. He will now be perfectly safe from all evil magic--and you have my solemn word that he will remain so."

"That is good news," Giraiazal said, numbly, while Viragan steered him through the corridors towards the council-chamber. "I see that everything has gone smoothly, as you doubtless knew it would."

"Yes I did," said Viragan. "I had every confidence in you, you see. Every confidence."

Triasymon did not seem so sure that everything was as it should be when Giraiazal, at Viragan's polite request, explained to the Lord Chancellor, the Prince Regent and three other councillors what he had done. "I wish I could have spoken to him as one man to another," Triasymon said. "I don't like to think of the boy being tricked like that, or imprisoned--even for his own protection. He's the legitimate king of Scleracina, when all is said and done."

"He hasn't been *imprisoned*, uncle," Manazzoryn put in. "He's been *taken to a place of safety*." Then his voice changed, his diction and pronunciation becoming more formal as he remembered who he now was: "I am assured that my brother had begun to show considerable improvement, with the aid of my loyal wife, but that further action was desperately necessary. We have firm proof of his enchantment, thanks to my father-in-law's enthusiastic pursuit of the truth. He has secured a confession which testifies to an astonishing depth and breadth of depravity on the part of the sorcerer Urbishek. We must not cease or slacken in our attempts to save my brother's sanity, and the first real step on the road to his recovery for his own sake is his separation from that terrible statue. I had no alternative but to accept Viragan's kind offer of safe asylum. I am more than ready to do my duty as my brother's regent until such time as he is fully recovered."

"More than ready," Giraiazal echoed, pensively. "Your loyalty does you credit, Your Highness." Then, moved by a resentful whim, he turned to Viragan again. "Is there any news of Prince Orlu, Your Highness? Surely you have heard something, after all this time? If some fatal misfortune had overtaken him, we would know it, would we not?"

Viragan immediately turned to one of the councillors who were dancing attendance on the regent: the ever-faithful Captain Sharuman. Sharuman no longer carried his double-headed axe when he strode around the palace, but his tread never seemed any less confident for his lack of conspicuous arms.

"Disturbing rumours have reached my ears," Sharuman said. "Orlu never reached Kalasperanza. His ship appears to have been lost, sunk without trace. Akabar and Cardelier are searching for any sign of him, but we fear the worst. He was a great seaman, and the common opinion is that he must have been the victim of evil magic. It is, I suppose, most likely that the sorcerers active in Kalasperanza acted to prevent his arrival in their midst, but there is much talk in Clarassour of the curse of the coral bride. There is sickness in the port, and although it is certainly nothing as virulent as the Platinum Death, people are understandably anxious. It is said that the symptoms are not unlike those which Queen Calia suffered. We fear that Prince Orlu has fallen victim to the curse."

Giraiazal found this assortment of data more than a little confusing, but he knew that the most important item was the suggestion--albeit uttered without any firm evidence--that Orlu's flagship must have been lost, and the merchant prince with it. In other circumstances, some suspicion might have looked in Viragan's direction, but with so much sorcery about, there was a veritable abundance of alternatives.

"If Prince Orlu does not return, it will be a terrible loss to Scleracina," Manazzoryn opined, "but that possibility makes it imperative that we offer firm proof to the world that Scleracina remains strong, and has a ruler with his wits about him."

Giraiazal had no difficulty whatsoever in recognising the strong influence of Prince Viragan on both the content and the manner of this speech. While the magician had been busy flattering Zintrah, Viragan had obviously not been idle. "You are absolutely right, Your Highness," Giraiazal said, humbly. "I can see that you have the situation well in hand. King Lysariel had to be put away, given that the opportunity presented itself. We all owe a great debt to his clever sister-in-law. Zintrah has given as much time and care to the king during these last few days as you, faithful Manazzoryn, gave to the queen in her darkest hours."

"It is all for the best," Manazzoryn said, with evident satisfaction.

"It would all have been so much simpler," Triasymon muttered, "if Lysariel had never hit upon the idea of making that accursed image."

"That is certainly true," Prince Viragan agreed.

181

"We cannot turn back time," said Giraiazal. "We must live in the present, and make such plans as we may for the narrow future that still separates us from our inevitable doom."

"Well put, Master Magician," said the merchant prince. "Given the circumstances in which we find ourselves--through no fault of our own--I believe that we have all made the best of a difficult situation. We must see to it that the notorious sorcerer Urbishek is burned alive in the plaza this very night, and that his flagitious statue is smashed to smithereens while he burns--but when that is done, all will be as it should be."

"Excellent," said Manazzoryn.

"I suppose it will," Triasymon admitted, grudgingly.

Giraiazal had already opened his mouth to agree when he was spared the sour necessity. Two of Viragan's men came through the door, tripping over their feet in their haste to beg the pardon of the regent and his councillors.

"What's wrong?" Viragan demanded, unceremoniously.

The newcomers were evidently too timid to address the entire company, and one came forward as if to whisper in the merchant prince's ear--but the man was out of breath and his hoarse voice had force enough to be overheard by everyone.

What he whispered was: "It's gone."

"Gone?" Viragan echoed, incredulously. "What do you mean, *gone*?"

Giraiazal knew that everyone present had to be aware that "gone" was synonymous with "not there", but as an expert diviner he was quick to deduce which particular absence had given rise to the hireling's anguish. "It was there not twenty minutes ago, Your Highness," he was quick to say. "I left it standing exactly where it has stood these last twenty days." He felt obliged to make this point lest any hint of suspicion be carelessly cast in his direction. He was, after all, the last person to have seen the coral statue, except for the persons who had removed it, and he had intended to have it removed to his own apartment at the earliest opportunity.

Viragan immediately fixed the magician with a sharp stare. "You went in to look at the coral monster when Zintrah lured Lysariel away from the apartment?" he asked, coldly.

It occurred to Giraiazal, a little belatedly, that he might have done better not to make that confession--but Viragan had met him at the bottom of the stair, and would surely have made the assumption. In any case, his course was fixed now. "I most certainly did," he reported. "I had to make sure of its condition. I already suspected that it was capable of movement, and I was determined to make sure that it did not follow Lysariel and Zintrah. It seemed to me, though, that it must be very slow, for it had only changed position slightly since Urbishek completed it. When I was sure that they were safely away, I left it alone. If it has shifted since then its powers of movement must have been very dramatically enhanced...."

Giraiazal was delighted to observe that Viragan did not know how to respond to this. For the first time, the merchant prince was undecided as to whether it would suit him best to encourage the rumour that the coral bride could walk, or to pour scorn on the notion.

Captain Sharuman was a little more down-to-earth than his master. "Either that," he said, flatly, "or it has been stolen."

"Stolen?" Triasymon said. "By whom? Giraiazal?" He was not accusing the magician, but merely asking for advice--but Giraiazal felt pressured nevertheless.

"How can I tell who might have stolen it, given that I was here when the theft happened?" the magician asked, placing the need to establish his alibi ahead of the need to conserve his reputation as a great diviner--but only momentarily. "As soon as I return to my apartment, however," he added, "I shall make every effort to find out."

Viragan had recovered his composure now. "There are always thieves about," the merchant prince said, philosophically. "The statue is precious, after all. My captains have been trading other pieces of the luminous coral in the neighbouring islands. They undoubtedly used tales of the wonderful image to bid up the price--and may thereby have offered an incentive to pirates. Under normal circumstances, no one would have dared...but with my dear friend Orlu away, perhaps never to return, and so many of my own men entangled in the meshes of affairs of state...."

Giraiazal did not suppose for a moment that Viragan was serious in suggesting that pirates might have raided the palace, but he knew that he was not the only one who had an interest in clouding the issue with confusion. "You might be right, Your Highness," he said. "But I am puzzled. Whether the statue became fully animate and walked away of its own accord, or whether it was captured by audacious thieves, its departure must surely have been witnessed. It is hardly unobtrusive, glowing as it does even in broad daylight."

"That is true," Viragan conceded, pensively. "Someone must have seen something. I shall make enquiries. If I find that thieves are responsible, I shall give them abundant cause to regret their temerity."

"But if it did walk away...." Manazzoryn said, uneasily.

Giraiazal saw an opportunity to take charge of the speculation, and could not resist the temptation to take it, even though he had no more idea than Viragan what account might eventually work to his best advantage. "I have seen a good deal of the statue in these last few days," he said, "and even though it never moved--at least not perceptibly--I always had the impression that it might. The thing is accursed, after all, shot through with some arcane witchcraft. The divers who harvested the coral on Urbishek's behalf may be correct in their assumption that it is animated by some alien intelligence that was always intent on finding a

183

new life in the open air. If the statue were merely tired of serving as an object of adoration for a besotted monarch, then its animation may be no cause for alarm--but if it has another scheme in mind...." He stopped there, determined to recover at least some of the initiative that Viragan had so casually usurped.

The merchant prince lasted five seconds before his curiosity got the better of him. "What scheme might that be, Master Magician?" he asked, politely.

"Well," Giraiazal said, carefully, "I can testify that the statue made no immediate response to Lysariel's departure with Zintrah. If something inspired it to move, another event provided the vital stimulus. I suppose it is possible that the statue has not tired of its human admirer at all. If it still relished its role as a substitute queen, and retained some psychic connection with its lover, it might conceivably have been brought to life by the king's distress when Zintrah secured him in his present accommodation. I suppose you have taken steps to ensure that poor Lysariel is well enough guarded against any ordinary attempt to release him or to do him harm--but who can tell what a living statue might be able to accomplish, if it were so minded?"

Viragan frowned when he heard this, but his expression cleared again soon enough. He obviously liked to keep a straight face when his plans were subject to awkward complications. He stroked one of his scars pensively, while his pale eyes stared into infinity.

Manazzoryn took the magician's suggestion far more seriously. "Who can tell what mission an animated image might have in mind?" he said, quietly--before adding, even more quietly: "If it has indeed absorbed the spirit of poor dead Calia, a reunion with its mad lover might not be the first object in its regretful mind."

No one else seemed to have taken any notice of what the regent had said, but Giraiazal was sure that Viragan had made a mental note of it, and he was very interested to hear it himself. It was the first time, so far as he knew, that anyone had made the suggestion that dead Calia's spirit might have entered into the coral statue. It was, he thought, a possibility worth careful consideration.

Giraiazal was also interested to observe that as the king's brother had voiced this original hypothesis, the nervous fingers of Manazzoryn's right hand had plucked nervously at his chemise. The loosened chemise now fell open at the front, and Giraiazal immediately observed that the girdle Manazzoryn had received as a wedding-present was tightly wound about his waist, disposed in such a manner that it would usually be invisible beneath his clothing.

How long, the magician wondered, had Manazzoryn been wearing the girdle? What had put the idea in the young man's mind that he might be in need of its protection?

184

"Whatever the situation is," Giraiazal said to the assembled company, by way of bringing the confused conference towards a conclusion, "it is obvious that we ought to locate the statue quickly, if we can. If thieves have stolen it, we must recover it--but we must be circumspect. Although it might eventually become necessary to publicize the object's loss and offer a reward for its return, it might be prudent in the shorter term to commission trusted men to make more discreet enquiries."

"I will do that," Viragan said. "My men are very discreet when they need to be." That was true--they knew that they might lose their tongues if they were not. "And in the meantime," the merchant prince added, in a tone that was all the more menacing for its conspicuous softness, "we must win what advantage we can from the execution of the sorcerer Urbishek."

Brian Stableford

Although the disputes between rival schools of cartomancy may seem philosophically uninteresting by comparison with the disagreement between astrological coincidentalists and teleologists, it is worth noting that they do have deeper correlates. The inspirationist thesis assumes, tacitly if not explicitly, that a greater sympathy between human individuals exists at a subconscious level than a conscious one, while a methodological approach implies the opposite. While this may seem to the lay reader to be a distinction of no particular consequence or interest, it has an important bearing on the fundamental nature of prophecy.

My judgment--again, I must insist that it is more than a mere opinion--is that the methodological approach is the correct one. Although we often find it convenient to deny that we are entirely responsible for our own actions, to do so is petty intellectual treason. The inspirationist approach to cartomancy implies that the objects of the inquiry, the indicators and the inquirers are all best understood as pawns of subconscious impulse--Ships Borne Aloft by Waterspouts, as it were-- rather than shrewd calculators of opportunity and advantage who move with as much precision as determination, like the Lightning that unerringly picks out a Tower within a hectic landscape.

The Revelations of Suomynona, the Last Prophet

Viragan was presumably correct in his estimation of the integrity of his servants, but Giraiazal knew that discreet enquiries about the whereabouts of missing property inevitably generate a momentum of their own. Before the ashes of Urbishek's pyre had cooled the news was all around the island that the statue of Calia forged out of ensorcelled coral by the black magician Urbishek had come to life and gone to ground, with

187

the undoubted intention of planning mischief. By the time that Manazzoryn, in his capacity as regent, had issued a proclamation to the effect that the statue had been stolen and that a lavish reward was offered for information leading to its recovery, the stratagem was widely seen for what it was: a belated attempt to quash the uglier rumour.

Giraiazal apologised profusely for his error of judgment, and was forgiven; Manazzoryn and Viragan were both intelligent enough to know that if only they had acquired definite news of the statue during the night--as they were certainly entitled to expect that they might--the problem would never have developed. Furthermore, Viragan had by now formed the judgment that the rumour could not possibly do the national interest--by which, of course, he meant himself--any real harm. "It does no harm to a newly-appointed regent to have the taverns and marketplaces preoccupied by harmless gossip about matters supernatural, rather than the discussion of practical politics," the merchant prince observed, when he next addressed the inner circle of the regent's councillors.

Giraiazal was mildly surprised to hear such cynicism openly expressed,but took it as evidence of Viragan's mood. The merchant prince was apparently not unduly disconcerted by the fact that his plans had stumbled over a second unanticipated obstacle. Indeed, it was not obvious that the merchant prince had any need to be concerned. The island and its regent, as well as the king, were secure in his control, and would certainly remain so unless Orlu should happen to return. That seemed less likely with every day that passed--and the more probable it became that Orlu would not return at all, the more probable it had to be that steps had been taken long ago to ensure that he never would.

It seemed to Giraiazal that Viragan was correct in the estimation that it was better for him that popular speculation about Orlu's possible fate should concentrate on supernatural agencies rather than mundane ones. Giraiazal strongly suspected, however, that Viragan would have been far happier if he had been certain that Orlu was dead. Given that so many other unexpected turns had confused his scheme, the pirate prince could hardly help wondering whether Orlu might have escaped whatever trap had been set for him--assuming, as Giraiazal was now prepared to do, that a trap *had* been set for him.

Giraiazal was not at all sure where his own interests lay in the matter. He had conceived a resentful dislike of Viragan, but it would be foolish to invite Viragan's wrath if Orlu were indeed dead, and might well be foolish even if Orlu lived. If Orlu ever did return, he would be bound to suspect that Giraiazal and Viragan had conspired against him, given the part Giraiazal had played in sending him away. Rational self-interest therefore demanded that Giraiazal should suppress his ill-feeling against Viragan, and do everything he could to make himself useful to the effective master of Scleracina--but Giraiazal was awkwardly conscious of the fact that he did not want to do that.

Giraiazal knew that an ordinary man possessed by such an irrational whim would do very well indeed to ignore it and to listen to the voice of reason--but he was also very conscious of the fact that he was not an ordinary man. He was a diviner, a magician and a physician. In fact, he was a wizard of no common competence. Had he not outwitted Meronicos the Malevolent in the final crisis of that evil emperor's reign? Had he not saved Queen Calia from the terrible disease communicated to her flesh by the monstrous spider? Had he not succeeded in freeing King Lysariel from the curse of the coral bride? It was true, of course, that some of these victories had proved less enduring than he could have wished, but the fact remained that he was a man of considerable occult intelligence. Did he not, therefore, have a responsibility to pay particular heed to his irrational impulses, on the rounds that their seeming irrationality might be evidence of their supernatural acuity?

Nor was this the only reason the magician found, when he searched his soul, for refusing to commit himself entirely to Prince Viragan's cause. For all Viragan's cleverness and manifest power, the scheme that he had hatched kept running into trouble. The coral bride had proved a more vexatious complication than anyone--even an experienced diviner like Giraiazal--could possibly have anticipated. Was that not clear evidence that Damozel Fate was working against Viragan, intent on frustrating his ambition? If Orlu had survived Viragan's trap, then Damozel Fate must have enlisted the support of Goodwife Chance to secure his escape--and if that were the case, it would be a foolish magician who would side with Viragan against his dark-eyed rival.

On the other hand, Giraiazal thought, Orlu--if he ever did return-- might not be kindly disposed towards anyone closely involved in his daughter's death, and even though Giraiazal had worked a near-miracle in curing her of her disease, the fact that she had died so soon after recovering might be construed by someone not fully cognisant of all the circumstances as *his* failure.

In addition to all these problematic considerations, Giraiazal had to grapple with the significance of the one explicit fact that the stars and the cards had condescended to reveal to him: that Lysariel's son would reign in Scleracina for a long time. Given Lysariel's present circumstances, it now seemed most likely that the mother of that as-yet-unborn son would be Zintrah. If that turned out to be the case, Manazzoryn would presumably assume--at least to begin with--that the child was his, although he would be bound to suspect the truth, and there would always be a danger that he might find out, in which case....

There was, of course, another possibility, but Giraiazal was initially inclined to reject as absurd the notion that a coral statue could ever become pregnant with a human child, no matter how cleverly it had been formed to represent a nubile woman. On the other hand, when he gave the matter more thought, he could not help but wonder whether all the mischievous suggestions he had made about the coral bride's ability to move might, after all, have been inspired by the same occult genius that might have inspired his determination not to take sides with Viragan while there was still a possibility that all the merchant prince's scheming would come to naught. In any case, if Viragan intended that Zintrah should bear Lysariel's son, so that he could be grandfather and regent to the heir to Scleracina's throne, the likelihood was that Lysariel, Manazzoryn and Triasymon would have to be cleared out of the way, one by one. Giraiazal could not be enthusiastic about being party to such a programme of murders, even if he were certain--and he was not--that his own name had been omitted from Viragan's schedule of victims.

As his suspicions grew regarding the plan that Viragan seemed to be following, Giraiazal was puzzled as to why the merchant would go to so much trouble, when the only real necessity of securing his dominion over Scleracina had been the disposal of his old rival Orlu. He was puzzled, too, as to why Viragan had allowed Orlu to make sure that Calia would marry Lysariel, rather than trying to place Zintrah as queen. Once he had considered the matter more carefully, however, the magician gained a better appreciation of the character of the merchant prince.

Giraiazal realised that Viragan must have planned from the very beginning to murder everyone who might conceivably become his rival, not merely for political power, but also for the good opinion of the people of Scleracina.

Viragan wanted to be a hero rather than a tyrant: a man admired for strength and virtue rather than brutality and cunning. He also wanted to be able to think of himself as a man of great subtlety and intelligence--that was why he relished the challenges posed by the unexpected intrusion and subsequent vanishment of the coral bride. Although the pirate prince was not the same sort of man as Meronicos of Yura, Giraiazal realised, he was just as whimsical in his monstrousness, and just as proud of his whimsicality.

Giraiazal thought himself a better man by far than that--he was a healer, after all--but he was conscious of the fact that not without a certain whimsicality of temperament himself. He did not want to lend his own talents to a man like Viragan. On the other hand, he did not want Viragan to have the slightest reason to suspect him of any disloyalty. He did not want to be manipulated by Viragan to any greater extent than he had already been manipulated, but nor did he want Viragan to think that he was not manipulable.

This cacophony of thoughts, speculations, feelings and ambitions would have added up to an exceedingly awkward predicament, had not Giraiazal had the stars and the cards to help him in his hour of need. He knew the limitations of his magic, but he also had faith in it. Damozel Fate was a fickle mistress, but he felt sure that if it came to a choice between her faithful servant Giraiazal and a murderous pirate, she would do the right thing. So Giraiazal continued to consult the stars, and deal out his trumps--keeping careful watch over the appearances of the Vampire Queen, which was the picture-card he had now come to associate with the coral bride--waiting patiently the while for news that he could turn to his advantage.

In the meantime, Burrel brought him a daily dose of gossip from the kitchens and the corridors, relishing every opportunity to serve his kindly master.

Try as they might, Viragan's agents could not find any evidence that the coral bride had been stolen, or any indication as to who might have dared. A handful of servants within and without the palace claimed to have glimpsed an unidentifiable figure swathed in a generous robe of grey wool, with a voluminous hood, which had moved stealthily out of the palace before disappearing from Clarassour's waterfront without any further trace, but Giraiazal was as sceptical about these reports as Viragan must have been. The magician was, of course prepared to suspect that the merchant prince might have had the statue stolen and by his own men, while establishing his own alibi by pretending astonishment when the news was brought to the council-chamber, but he did not think it likely because it would have served the merchant's interests far better to have the image smashed up in the plaza while Urbishek was burning.

As time went by, the rumours circulating in Clarassour regarding the missing statue grew more fanciful, as rumours circulating in a vacuum of real information invariably do. The idea that had occurred to Manazzoryn--that the force animating the missing likeness might be the unquiet spirit of dead Calia--was reproduced by other speculative voices.

The notion that the queen had been recalled from beyond the grave by the power of her husband's love had an intrinsic melodramatic appeal, as did the fancy that the separation of the two lovers had driven the entrapped spirit to such an extreme of grief that it had contrived to vivify its coral doppelganger. The supposition that the ensouled work of art might now be wandering the peninsula of Harstpoint in search of her lost love exerted such an influence on the popular imagination that occasional sightings of the peripatetic statue were reported from that region, each alleged witness asserting that the statue seemed to be searching for something, weeping as it went. All of these sightings were discounted as delusions by Viragan's assiduous agents.

On the thirtieth day of his regency, Manazzoryn summoned Giraiazal to his private apartment in order to consult him in his capacity as a physician.

"I need a potion to help me sleep," the regent said. "My new responsibilities weigh heavily upon me. I need help, too, in shaping my dreams, for whenever I do contrive to sleep I am troubled by nightmares."

"What sort of nightmares, Your Highness?" Giraiazal asked.

"Nightmares in which I am confronted and pursued by the fiery image of my brother's wife. I flee from her, when I can, but I can never escape, Sometimes, I cannot even flee, because my body is too heavy and no effort I make is sufficient to shift my leaden limbs. I am accursed, you see. The coral bride has fixed her evil attentions upon me as she fixed them upon my brother, but in a more malevolent fashion. You must help me as you helped poor Calia. You must soothe my dreams, and lend the force of your own dream-energy to my protection."

"I can certainly try, Your Highness," Giraiazal said, judiciously. "I can easily make a potion that will help you to sleep. The other problem requires greater artistry. If I can demystify your bad dreams I can begin to reshape them, but I must decipher them before I can change them. It may seem very strange to you that your dreams should become obsessed with the coral image that formerly obsessed your brother's waking hours, but it is not inexplicable, given that you have recently stepped into his shoes. He is still the king, of course, just as he is still the elder brother, but you have taken his responsibilities upon your own shoulders--where, as you have observed, they weigh heavily upon you. In order to have better dreams, you must reconcile yourself to the idea that you are not at fault in this matter. If you will consent to let me lay my hands on your head, and listen to my voice, I believe that I can help you do that. The girdle that I gave you as a wedding-present ought to assist in securing that effect--indeed, I am surprised that it has not been adequate to the task."

"You are kind, Giraiazal," Manazzoryn said, "and I will of course be grateful for your touch and your healing words. I admit that I have been wearing the girdle you gave me, in the hope that it would help me, and I am sorry that it has not been adequate to my need. Tell me, though--is it really possible that the rumours are true, and that the spirit of my brother's wife really has returned from the afterlife to possess the coral statue?"

It would have been undiplomatic to point out that Manazzoryn was the one who had started that particular rumour, so Giraiazal answered very carefully. "I have certainly heard tell of statues rendered ambulatory by such questing spirits," he said, "and love is, in essence, a supernatural force--all the more so when it is allied with conspicuous insanity. Unless and until I can make a close examination of the entity in question, however, I shall be unable to determine whether some kind of larva has taken possession of the image--and, if so, exactly what kind it might be."

"But you did examine it," Manazzoryn pointed out. "You were, in fact, the last person to see it before it disappeared."

"True," Giraiazal admitted. "But my examination was unguided by any particular hypothesis. I was alert to signs of life and intelligence, of which I took due note, but not to any indications there might have been of the identity of that intelligence."

"But you have consulted your various instruments of divination, have you not?" Manazzoryn persisted. "Given that you have so many, surely they can give you some indication of the statue's nature."

"I cannot calculate the horoscope of a statue, Your Highness," Giraiazal protested. "Nor can I tell the fortune of a dead person. You may be sure that I am keeping a careful watch over your own fate, and that of your beloved wife, but the future is never entirely clear no matter what resources one brings to the business of reading it--for which we should, of course, be grateful."

"How so?" Manazzoryn objected. "I, for one, would be very grateful for some plain news of tomorrow, unadorned with the customary ifs, buts and maybes."

"The only items of prediction which stand out clear and unambiguous are inevitabilities, Your Highness," Giraiazal told him. "It does us no good to know that certain things are inevitable, for their inevitability means that we are powerless to influence them. The only useful information recoverable from any instrument of divination is that which comes seasoned with ifs, buts and maybes, because it is within that margin of uncertainty that we may act to produce the results we desire and to prevent those that we loathe. My long experience as an eclectic diviner has taught me that there is far too much of the inevitable in the world's tomorrows, and far too few ifs, buts and maybes."

Manazzoryn was in no mood to discuss the finer points of esoteric philosophy. "Can the spirit be dispossessed?" he asked, abruptly. "Can the statue be made inanimate again and destroyed, as we all agreed that it should be?" As the regent spoke, Giraiazal noticed that his right hand had slipped unthinkingly inside his chemise, the fingers reaching out as if to touch the girdle that he wore beneath.

"Almost certainly," said Giraiazal, "but not, I fear, until it has been found and examined. The wisdom of lore and legend instructs us that an exorcist must not only know the name of the spirit he seeks to banish but must also do his work at close quarters. While the image remains in hiding, all that we can sensibly do is to keep searching for it."

"You are supposed to be skilled in the art of making curses," Manazzoryn protested.

"So I am, Your Highness," Giraiazal replied, in a dignified manner. "Should you desire me to pronounce an anathema against the rats infesting the warehouses on the waterfront, or the mice in the inland cornfields, I could do it collectively, and without actually confronting them, but a human or demonic spirit is a different matter, for humans and demons can only be cursed by name. Individual curses can only take full effect if they are pronounced while the administering magician is looking directly at the object of his ire, preferably eye to eye. Shall I make up the sleeping potion now, Your Highness?"

"I suppose so," said Manazzoryn, dismissively.

193

"I will bring it here within the hour," Giraiazal promised. "When you have drunk it, I shall lay my hands on your head and exert my best efforts to the shaping of your dreams. You must give me a more detailed account of your dreams, so that I may begin the work of shaping them."

"Thank you, Giraiazal," the regent said. "You are a better advisor than I deserve."

It might have been polite to deny that, but Giraiazal only bowed his head before he turned away and went to do as he was bid. When he returned, Manazzoryn told him exactly how the coral bride confronted him in her dreams, burning bright with anger, as if she were fury made flame, and Giraiazal suggested to him that he ought to watch that flame burn itself out, and become a harmless ember.

The following morning, Manazzoryn--after consultation with his Lord Chancellor--doubled the reward he had offered for information leading to the recovery of the statue of Queen Calia. Giraiazal thought it a pointless gesture, given that the information in question was by no means price-sensitive.

That same morning, Zintrah announced that she was with child.

This latter news was cause for considerable celebration in the palace and the city--and eventually, as the news spread, throughout Scleracina. Although Manazzoryn was only the regent, he was also the king's brother, so his first-born son would be the heir presumptive to the throne. Because it seemed improbable that the widowed and deluded Lysariel would be able to sire an heir apparent in the foreseeable future, the likelihood was that Zintrah's child would one day be king of Scleracina--always provided that it turned out to be a boy.

"Will my child be a son?" Zintrah asked Giraiazal, anxiously, as soon as his instruments of divination had confirmed her pregnancy and offered a good estimate of the child's day of birth.

"Almost certainly," the magician replied, having already compiled a hypothetical horoscope based on the most likely day of the child's delivery.

"Will he be as handsome as his father?" Zintrah demanded. "Will he be king of Scleracina? Will he be one of those rare and lucky men who live long and prosper, in spite of the fact that the world is due to end?"

Those were more difficult questions, which required more careful answers. Giraiazal had pored over his cards and charts for hours, trying to discover the most accurate account that Damozel Fate was yet prepared to concede to his intuition.

"Your son will certainly be as handsome as his father," Giraiazal was able to inform the mother-to-be, "and he will almost certainly live long and prosper, even though his future path is strewn with potential obstacles. With the aid of good advisors he might clear them all, but he will need the very best advice to make the most of his opportunities. I shall, of course, be able to make a more detailed and far more accurate calculation when I know the precise moment of his birth."

In fact, Giraiazal had been able to determine a good deal more than he was prepared to tell Zintrah. He had never quite forgiven her for letting out the secret he had asked her to keep while she was helping him to bring Lysariel to his senses, although he ought to have anticipated that her father had had a hand in the matter from the start. For this reason, he would have been inclined to hold something back in any case, and there were other reasons for discretion. Given that the cards stubbornly insisted that the next king of Scleracina--who would also, in all likelihood, be the last king of Scleracina--would be Lysariel's son and not Manazzoryn's, Giraiazal felt obliged to employ certain circumlocutions in talking about him. The oracles had also suggested that Lysariel might still have an important role to play in deciding the fate of his realm, although they were not inclined to specify exactly what he would do in order to make that effect certain, or when.

Having committed himself from the outset to the cause of bringing Lysariel to his senses, Giraiazal continued to make every effort to minister to the king, but Viragan obstructed him at every turn. The merchant prince insisted that the king was in no condition to receive visitors, and remained resolute even when Giraiazal pointed out that it was precisely because the king was in such dire straits that he needed the careful attention of a skilled physician.

The magician tried to persuade Manazzoryn to add leverage to his claims, even venturing to intrude such suggestions into his morpheomorphic ministrations, but the regent was very reluctant to do or say anything that might annoy Viragan. Even Triasymon was too hesitant to be of any practical use. "We ought to help Lysariel," Giraiazal told them both, when Viragan had absented himself from the palace in order to made plans for a lavish feast in celebration of his daughter's good fortune. "We owe it to him to renew our efforts, now that he is no longer under the sway of the image."

"We must be realistic," Manazzoryn replied. "If he is truly beyond help, we must look forward."

"Even if he is not beyond help," Triasymon added, "there are questions of priority. Manazzoryn will soon have a son, and your primary duty as Grand Vizier is to make sure that Zintrah is safe and well. Until Lysariel's condition improves, there seems little point in your trying to influence his dreams."

Giraiazal knew that these opinions were Viragan's, parroted by victims of cunning persuasion. Any magician worthy of the name ought to be able to exert far greater influence than a mere merchant, but Giraiazal feared that he would not be able to make much headway while he could not subdue Manazzoryn's horrid dreams--and that he had so far failed to do, despite exerting all the force of his morpheomorphic art. The problem

195

was not that he could not determine what was troubling Manazzoryn--he believed that he understood that very well--but rather that he dared not let Manazzoryn know exactly how much he did understand.

The plans Viragan made for the feast in honour of his daughter's pregnancy were soon revealed in all their ostentation. It appeared that the festival would be every bit as munificent as the one he and Orlu had mounted jointly to celebrate the double wedding of their daughters, if not more so. The dubious propriety of this decision went unchallenged. For the next two tendays Viragan's ships were more active than ever before, sailing in every direction in pursuit of rich cargoes--including a few that were eventually bought with honest coin, out of the necessity for haste.

All the captains of Viragan's navy had been instructed to seek out further news of Orlu, but none came back with any reliable information. There had been violent storms around Kalasperanza at the time when Orlu should have arrived there, which might have blown his ship into the remoter regions of the archipelago, and perhaps far out into the ocean wilderness, but there had been plenty of time for him to make his way back again had he not been overcome by some further disaster. Since the devastation of Yura and a hundred other islands by the Platinum Death there were many regions of the archipelago that were shunned by traders and looters alike, and the suggestion was often made that Orlu's storm-battered ship might have had no alternative but to make its landfall on a plague-infested shore from which there was no escape, but this was only a hypothesis--no one had actually seen the stranded ship.

For his part, the regent Manazzoryn gave his father-in-law free use of the palace, its apartments and its servants, so that the magnificence of the occasion would not be constrained by the narrower confines of Viragan's own house. The ceilings were bleached; the marble floors were repaired and polished; the wall-hangings were renewed with fine and elaborate fabrics. Jugglers and fire-eaters were hired, dwarfs and dancers recruited, and every musician on the island was ordered to tune his instrument to the best of his ability. A huge supply of white fish and giant lobsters was packed in ice, and birds of gaudy plumage collected in pens for plucking and roasting.

These elaborate preparations were not in vain. The feast was undoubtedly the most fabulous ever celebrated in Scleracina, eclipsing the double wedding, and it was declared to be a great success by everyone--except, presumably, the two men-at-arms who drew black chips in the lottery held to determine who would stand guard outside Lysariel's prison while all their fellows were busy at the palace.

When the rest of Viragan's servants returned home shortly after dawn, however, they found these two unfortunates lying dead, their necks cleanly broken. One man's half-pike was missing and the other had not a trace of blood upon its blade. The lock on the door had been shattered, and Lysariel had vanished.

It is always useful, in a royal family, to have a few heirs in reserve. Lady Death being the casual predator she is, no boy-child can ever be certain of growing to manhood, no matter how strong he might be, and there are certain advantages in maintaining a healthy stock of sons and younger brothers. On the other hand, there is nothing like a profusion of potential heirs to provoke insidious plots and dastardly murders. It is not merely those hapless unfortunates who are in line to inherit thrones who are inevitably tempted to consider the potential rewards of patricide and fratricide, but the infinitely more dangerous and instinctively mischievous individuals who are ambitious to be powers behind thrones.

The Revelations of Suomynona, the Last Prophet

Scleracina's rumour-mongers, whose narrative skills had been honed to perfection by their recent exercise, went to work with a will when the news got out that mad King Lysariel had been carelessly mislaid by his keepers. On the following day, the ever-vigilant Burrel reported to his master that the tale was being told all over the island of how Queen Calia had returned, in the fiery body of her coralline image, to reclaim her lost lover. Having murdered his guards without the slightest difficulty, the coral bride had trumphantly borne the deranged king away.

When Giraiazal interrogated Burrel further, however, he had a distinct impression that the boy was holding something back. It was not the first time he had suspected that Burrel's reportage was a trifle selective, but on previous occasions he had dismissed the matter from his mind, considering kitchen gossip too trivial a matter to be worth pursuit. This time, he had other reasons for wondering whether it might not be useful to collect his own intelligence from without the palace walls--so he

197

took himself off that evening to his one-time abode, the Outsiders Inn, with the intention of renewing a few old acquaintances.

At first, the conversation in the hostel's tap room followed the same paths that Burrel had already mapped out for the magician, issuing increasingly wild speculations as to where Lysariel might have been taken by his coral bride. Seamen on shore leave favoured the grotto from which the coral had been hewn, where Lysariel was believed to have been transformed into a column of living coral next to that of his beloved. Farmers who had come to buy and sell in the marketplace, on the other hand, favoured an inland hermitage where the two lovers were busily exchanging and homogenising their substance, so that the mad king was becoming harder and more golden while his queen was becoming softer and less luminous. A third party declared that the two must have sailed away on a magical ship, bound for an enchanted isle far beyond the limits of Ambriocyatha, where a whole population of gemlike houris served as incorruptible love-slaves to their fleshy husbands.

It was not until wine and ale had been flowing for some time that these gaudy fancies began to decay like over-ripe fruit, and not until the greater number of the casual drinkers had drifted away--leaving a population almost entirely composed of seamen--that the general conversation split into half a dozen fractions and the whispers drifting to Giraiazal's eager ears began to take on a more conspiratorial tone.

It was at this point that a man whose face was muffled by a hood sat down on a bench next to Giraiazal and whispered: "You are not safe here, my lord. If you value good advice, return to the palace now, before the lingering twilight fades to darkness."

The voice was disguised, but not cleverly enough to fool Giraiazal. "Cardelier?" he said. "Is that you?"

The captain groaned. "Don't speak my name aloud!" he said. "Would you answer a good turn with a bad one?"

"I don't know what you mean," Giraiazal answered, lowering his voice. "I had no idea you were in Clarassour. Why haven't I seen you in the council-chamber?"

"Leave now!" said the hooded man. "I'll follow you--we'll find a place where we can talk, if you must, but we can't stay here. Too many hired spies, and far too many erstwhile honest men waiting their chance to turn rogue. Go!"

Giraiazal did as he was bid, walking out of the inn without another word--but he did not head back up the hill towards the palace, whose battlements and ornamented flagstaffs stood proud against the dimming clouds. Instead, he went down to the quay and along the shore, conscious all the while that he was being followed at a not-so-discreet distance by Captain Cardelier.

The magician walked past half a dozen docked ships, whose sentries kept their eyes on him all the while, until he eventually came to a series of empty berths facing a seemingly-deserted warehouse whose loading-doors were wide open. He slipped inside the warehouse, and made his way to a shadowed corner where there was no shelter nearby for the advantage of hidden eavesdroppers.

When he turned to meet Cardelier, the magician saw that the captain's dagger was unsheathed--but he also saw that the captain had no immediate intention of committing murder.

"Tell me that you were not sent to look for me," Cardelier said.

"I had not the slightest expectation of finding you at the inn," Giraiazal told him. "I thought you were still at sea, searching for Orlu."

"Did you? Well, I thought that you could not be a spy, given that every man on the island knows your name and rank--but I also know that there are too many men about who would not trouble to make that deduction. I had formed the impression when we were neighbours that you were a tolerably honest man, within the limits of your ludicrously dishonest profession, and I am reluctant to revise my opinion without proof--so tell me frankly, are you Viragan's agent or not?"

"Ah!" Giraiazal said. "No, I am not--at least, no more than I have to be, to save my own skin. My servant is, I think--and almost everyone else I meet by day--but I am my own man. I might ask you the same question, might I not? Can there be anyone left in Clarassour who is aught else but Viragan's man, given that poor Orlu has been given up for lost?"

Cardelier's face was not clearly visible, thanks to the lowered hood, so it was impossible for the magician to judge whether the captain smiled, or how wryly. "The matter's not so simple," the seaman replied, eventually. "Even if Orlu were really dead, there's many who'd far rather follow Akabar--or, for that matter, any Demon Lord from the Empire of the Dead--than Viragan. Old grudges die hard in a place like this. We're not in the empire any longer."

"Are you sure that Orlu is alive?" Giraiazal asked.

"As sure as I can be, given that I haven't seen him for more than a tenday. But I've taken a terrible risk in telling you that, for we're all hoping that Viragan doesn't know quite what to believe. It will work to our advantage if he thinks that Orlu's survival might be a mere rumour, spread by Akabar for his own sly purposes."

It immediately occurred to Giraiazal that Cardelier might be telling him this in order to create exactly that uncertainty, and it also occurred to him that Cardelier might have an interest in creating an illusion that Orlu were alive, even if he were in fact dead. What interested him more, though, was the implication that Scleracina was on the brink of civil war because too many men had too many reasons for refusing to knuckle under to Viragan...and might tremble on that brink for a while yet.

"I am a fool, am I not?" the magician said, softly. "I have spent so much time measuring the positions of the Motile Entities in the night sky, and poring over my stubbornly enigmatic trumps, that I have forgotten to attend to what is going on around me, but a few paces distant. I have been content to receive my news through carefully angled channels, and have not even made careful observations of the crowd in the council-chamber. It is, I suppose, made up entirely of Viragan's placemen now--so far as he can judge their loyalties, that is."

"We have all been fools," Cardelier told him. "When Calia married the king, Orlu really thought that he had won the contest--that he had stolen a march on Viragan. So did we all. We really believed that Viragan might be content with half a kingdom and a peaceful dotage. It was not as if he had not given ample evidence in the past to prove him incapable of any such compromise...or so, at least, I am assured. I am as new to this as you are, of course, and I am not at all certain that I am doing the right thing in remaining loyal to Orlu--who, seen from an objective point of view, is probably no better than Viragan--merely because I happened to be placed under his command when I transferred my allegiance from Yura to Scleracina. We have both been thrown into a pool of crafty sharklongs, without the knowledge we need to judge our own best interests. Do you know any more than I do, Master Magician?"

"A good deal," Giraiazal said, as he was bound to do. "I have the stars to guide me, after all."

"I'm a seaman," Cardelier reminded him. "I've always steered by the stars--but I don't want to get into an argument as to which of us has received the most reliable advice. It certainly seems to be the case that I know things that you did not--until I told you. Are you willing and able to return the favour?"

Giraiazal was chastened by this rebuke. "I know now that Viragan always planned to concede the first advantage to Orlu," he said. "He never intended for a moment that Calia would live to bear Lysariel's child--but his plans were confused, not merely by the king's instruction that the coral statue be made, but by the amulet I gave the queen and the assistance I lent to her dreams. I have been a fool, Cardelier, as you say, even in my capacity as a prophet. I failed to divine the most essential detail of all. But I was not entirely a fool. My magic defeated the magic that was set to destroy the queen, forcing a reversion to brute force. Alas, I collaborated unwittingly in despatching Orlu on what was doubtless intended to be his last voyage--but he escaped the trap, did he not? Now it is Viragan whose position is exposed, and he must wait for his enemy to strike from the shadows. That campaign has begun, has it not? It was you who freed Lysariel!"

"I only wish it were," Cardelier said. "We intended to--but when we got there, the cupboard was bare."

Giraiazal was astounded by this news, having been very proud of himself for working out so rapidly that Orlu's men must have released the king by way of a counterstroke against Viragan's machinations. "Who, then...?" he began.

"Whoever stole the coral courtesan, if Viragan did not," Cardelier opined. "Triasymon's name has been mentioned."

"Triasymon!" Giraiazal did not attempt to conceal his scepticism. "Do you really think he has the subtlety of mind for games like this?"

"Frankly, no," Cardelier admitted, tapping the point of his dagger against his chin. "But there are some among us who believe that he has the benefit of a subtle adviser."

Giraiazal immediately recognised this as a scarcely veiled accusation, and did not know whether to be flattered or frightened. "If it had been me," he pointed out, "I certainly would not have been so foolish as to come to the Outsiders Inn in search of fresher gossip than the stale stuff that is delivered to my door. If I had taken Lysariel, or knew who had...believe me, Captain Cardelier, I do not."

"You have told me twice over what a fool you are," Cardelier reminded him. "Fortunately or unfortunately, I did not believe you--but I cannot believe that you have the king, or that you gave instructions for his capture. Alas, I find it just as hard to believe that Viragan staged the king's abduction--not because two of his men were killed, but because I cannot see what he might hope to gain by it. Can you? Please don't tell me that you will need to consult your oracles; I need the judgment of your intelligence, not your educated illusions."

Giraiazal refused to be offended by the slight. He *had* been a fool, in spite of his education and his magical skills. Cardelier had every right to mock him. "I can't see why anyone would want to free the king," he said, slowly, "except to use him against Viragan."

"Nor can I," said the captain. "Which rather makes it look as if Orlu's right hand has no idea what his left is about, doesn't it?"

"Is Akabar the right hand or the left?" Giraiazal countered, having recovered his wits. "Are you a thumb, a forefinger or an eye--or perhaps a mere toe?"

"You're a brave man, Master Magician, if you are a spy," Cardelier observed, waving his blade suggestively. "But as I say, I'm reluctant to alter my first judgment--and if there's one thing on which everyone's agreed, it's your sincerity in trying to save Queen Calia's life. No one in this city ever knew of a physician who did as much in a seemingly lost cause, or worked as effectively. As you pointed out, when Viragan had to order that she be cast down from a high window he showed his brutal hand too soon, and no amount of slanders whispered abroad by his men will succeed in putting the blame on a sorcerously-inclined sculptor or a demon-infested statue. We may laugh about such stuff in the taverns and the public baths, but that's because we dare not declare too plainly what we know in our hearts."

"Don't underestimate the superstitions of your underlings, Captain," Giraiazal warned him, "or even your peers. In the course of my pursuit of what you call a ludicrously dishonest profession, I've scratched many a hardened sceptic and found a credulous imbecile beneath."

"My new peers are old pirates," Cardelier told him, "who have to provide for themselves and know the way to do it. Yura, on the other hand, was full of men whose fortunes--though considerable--depended entirely upon the emperor's whim. Such men are easy prey to superstition....and thus to men like you."

"I could take that as a compliment, coming from a self-confessed pirate," Giraiazal observed.

"As it was intended," Captain Cardelier conceded. "If you want to come with me now, I might be willing to take you. I dare say Orlu might be pleased to have you by his side."

Giraiazal was mildly surprised to be asked, but he shook his head-- and then in case the darkness was too deep for the gesture to be clear, said: "Thank you for the invitation, but I must refuse. Orlu might have better reason to be pleased if I am close by Viragan's side."

"He might, if he could trust you." Cardelier agreed. "Personally, I doubt whether you can even trust yourself to that extent. While you're by Viragan's side, it will be far too easy for Damozel Fate to dictate that you should also be *on* his side. On the other hand, it'll be a lot easier for him to kill you while you're within arm's reach. Remember that, if you decide to work against him within the palace--but I certainly won't try to stop you, if that's your intention."

"I have other work to do in the palace too," Giraiazal told him, his voice devoid of any emotional colour. "You might care to remember, though, that while some pirates are in their element at sea, and perfectly comfortable in hammocks, others require a different milieu, and relish the opportunity to sleep in wider beds."

"Well, old friend," Cardelier said, with a slight sigh, "I suppose we'll just have to hope that you're too selfish a man to be a true friend to Viragan, and that your beloved Damozel Fate will give you the opportunity as well as the motive to play him false. Remember, though-- Orlu knows what you did for his daughter. He is grateful, even though you could not save her. Viragan knows it too, and he knows how to bear a grudge while wearing a seductive smile." And with that, the captain stepped back and turned away. His boots were muffled, so the sound of his footfalls died away almost as soon as he had glided away into the night.

Giraiazal gathered his cloak about him to hide his beard, and bowed his head before emerging from the warehouse and hurrying back towards the palace. So far as he could tell, no one was following him--but he would not have been unduly worried if they had. From now on, he intended to conduct himself as if he were always discreetly followed, always carefully watched, and always under suspicion.

Because Clarassour was a port it was the seamen's fantasies that gradually gained the upper hand in the story-telling stakes. A more elaborate tale was eventually formulated, in which the coral bride had carried her unconscious husband into the wave-tossed and tempestuous sea--the evening of the abduction had been unusually calm, but breakers make such a fine detail that they intrude into every tale of mighty passion--and kept him alive while she transported him across the sea-bed by breathing warm air from her mouth to his, having manufactured it within the alchemical furnace of her soul. She had carried him thus until they attained the sunken palace where they were destined to live as happy merfolk, until the day when the sun's spasmic demise would cause the oceans to boil away.

This tale might have attained sufficient authority to become the stuff of legend had its plausibility not been rudely shattered by an inconvenient fact--to wit, that King Lysariel returned to his palace five days after his disappearance, quite alone.

6

Competent prophets are often feared, sometimes admired, almost always envied, and almost never pitied. In times past, prophets have been well content with this division of attitudes, and have been anxious to keep the secret that even a half-way competent prophet, let alone a great one, deserves nothing but pity. There is no very good reason why this truth should be a secret, given that an ounce of logic suffices to the deduction thereof, but if ever there were humankinds capable of powerful logic, ours is not one of them.

A great prophet--and I say this as the greatest of my generation--ought to be pitied because his every discovery is an agony. Whenever he foresees something that is certain to come about, he knows that there is nothing he can do about it--for if there were, it could not be certain. Whenever he sees something that is likely to come about, but not entirely certain, he knows that something can be done about it but he cannot know what; for if he did know what could be done, the event would not be likely at all, but either unlikely, if it were undesirable to him, or certain, if it were desirable. Whenever he foresees that something is unlikely to come about, but possible, he is in exactly the same predicament--he knows that its occurrence is contingent upon some action, but he cannot know whose or what.

The worse situation of all in which a prophet might find himself, however, is this: that he foresees some event that might or might not come about, *and also knows what actions might increase or decrease its probability.* In a circumstance of that kind, he is unable to remain a passive observer but must instead become a warrior in the wilderness of if, knowing all the while that his success cannot possibly be certain, or

205

even very likely, and that even his failure is fated to be in some wise paradoxical.

The Revelations of Suomynona, the Last Prophet

Giraiazal was subsequently able to ascertain that no one had tried to interrupt Lysariel as he walked through the streets of Clarassour, although thousands saw him pass by, and he was quickly recognised in spite of the ragged state of his clothing. There were undoubtedly many of Viragan's men among the crowds, who must have been under orders to report any sighting of the king and to apprehend him if at all possible, but every one of them had decided on the spur of the moment that a cautious approach to the second part of the injunction was in order.

Viragan was, in consequence, informed without delay that the king had returned--but not one of those who hastened to bring him that information attempted to bring him anything else. The pirate prince was later to ask them why, in a very angry fashion, but all he heard by way of reply was a string of excuses and pretexts, first among which was that Lysariel was, after all, the king of Scleracina and not a common felon.

When further pressed, the men who had decided not to step into the king's path reported that Lysariel had been carrying a sharp half-pike in his right hand and a pointed dagger almost long enough to qualify as a sword in his left, in a fashion which suggested that he was more than ready to use them both. They also reported that he had a very strange gleam in his eyes, golden in colour and fiery in kind, which reminded them of rumours of the coral bride's ability to cast nasty curses.

Although there had ben no sign of the statue itself, the merest suggestion that the dead queen might be present in spirit was enough to intimidate any ordinarily superstitious man. Giraiazal understood readily enough, therefore, when he came to weight this testimony for himself, how it was that Lysariel had reached the palace gates unheeded--and how it was that when he commanded that the gates be opened to let him in, the order was obeyed. The palace servants must have melted from his path with even greater alacrity than the crowds in the streets of Clarassour, so he strode through the newly-decorated corridors unchallenged and unhindered.

It was not until Lysariel drew near the council-chamber that Giraiazal was alerted to what was happening--and the magician considered himself fortunate to be close enough to run to see what was happening.

Had Lysariel been in a hurry Giraiazal would not have arrived in time, but he must have moved with calm deliberation. It was not until the king came in sight of the council-chamber's double door--by which time Giraiazal could see him--that he began to move a little more urgently, crying out at the top of his voice.

The word he cried was: "Murderer!"

206

It so happened that the regent was meeting with his Lord Chancellor and half a dozen other noble citizens at the time, and it could not have been at all clear at the moment when Lysariel burst into the room exactly who the target of his accusation might be. Many of them must, in fact, have jumped to the same conclusion as Giraiazal--which was that Lysariel had judged his moment badly and had arrived while his intended target was absent. Giraiazal knew, even before he hurried through the doorway after King Lysariel, that Prince Viragan was not in the chamber.

The councillors who made this presumption were not, of course disposed to take any chances. Although the majority had almost contrived to forget that they had ever been anything else but courtiers, the sight of a madman wielding a half-pike was exactly the kind of trigger required to remind them that there was not one among their company who had not been party to at least a few piratical exploits.

So far as these citizen-counsellors were aware, the only men in the room who were unlikely ever to have done anything that might be regarded--if only technically--as murder, were Manazzoryn and Triasymon. It was doubtless for this reason, Giraiazal thought, that Scleracina's ministers of state scattered in every possible direction when Lysariel made his dramatic entrance. Two who obviously judged that they could not reach the side or rear doors quickly enough hurled themselves head-first through the nearest windows.

This mass desertion left a clear path between the king and the capacious chair on which his younger brother sat, at the head of the long table. The two men-at-arms stationed behind the seat did not move around it to block the king's way. They were later to claim, when their turn came to be interrogated, that their own paths were blocked because Triasymon was standing to the right of his nephew's position and Giraiazal to the left, but this was a blatant lie which cost both of them their heads.

Triasymon was, however, the first person to recover his wits sufficiently to speak. "Lysariel!" he cried. "The departed gods be thanked! You are safe!"

Manazzoryn's reaction was far less understandable. The regent leapt to his feet as soon as the door burst open, and cast a desperate look behind him at the chamber's rear door, which opened to the adjacent throne room. One glance must have assured him that the crowd escaping by that route was too dense to be easily overtaken, but he moved in that direction anyhow, trying to shove his uncle out of the way.

Had Triasymon been better prepared he would certainly have stepped back out of the regent's way, but as it was he stumbled and fell to his knees, leaving his feet behind for the scrambling regent to trip over.

Manazzoryn picked himself up immediately, just as the blade of the half-pike came down upon the seat he had recently vacated. Had he still been in it the blow would have cleaved him in two from the top of his head to the vessels of his heart; because he was not, the blade became firmly embedded in the wood.

Lysariel howled in frustration.

Manazzoryn, obviously cognisant of the fact that he had no chance of escaping his pursuer, grabbed a half-pike from the nearer of the two men-at-arms, who surrendered it without the least resistance.

Triasymon, presumably moved more by amazement than strategic intent, tried to grab the half-pike that the second man-at-arms held out to him, but he was still on his knees and not in a good position to wield it effectively. In any case, Triasymon did not seem to have any very clear idea which of his nephews he was supposed to side with, nor any evident skill that might allow him to use the clumsy weapon as an efficient means of defence.

In the end, the Lord Chancellor looked helplessly on as Manazzoryn took advantage of Lysariel's failure to release his half-pike from the clutch of the seat to launch his own weapon in a horizontal sweep. The stroke would have plucked Lysariel's head from his shoulders had the king not been able to duck under it.

The momentum of the half-pike pulled the regent off-balance, and the weapon's continuing arc dipped dangerously low, forcing the rapidly-approaching Giraiazal to stop, and then to hurl himself backwards into a supine position while the blade sped past.

Lysariel immediately gave up the unequal struggle to release his own weapon, and abandoned the half-pike in favour of his poniard. This time he thrust forwards like a fencer instead of chopping down like a woodcutter, and would have skewered Manazzoryn's liver had the regent not been forced to follow the weight of his own carelessly-flung half-pike, which drew him out of the way in the nick of time.

This time, it was Giraiazal's feet that Manazzoryn tripped over--but he kept hold of the half-pike nevertheless, and when he came back to his own feet again he was able to bring the haft around just in time to intercept Lysariel's second dagger-thrust.

The regent found his voice at last, crying: "Brother!"

The only reply he received was another cry of "Murderer!"

Triasymon, realising that he ought to do something, extended the butt of the half-pike he held in an attempt to trip Lysariel, but the king demonstrated an unexpected agility by dancing over the clumsily-interposed shaft in order to launch yet another fierce thrust of his pointed dagger.

This one struck home, but not deeply. Manazzoryn was moving backwards, leaning back as far as he could, and the point of the blade scored his flesh without penetrating his rib-cage. He had to use his half-pike for support, preventing him from launching any retaliatory blow, but Lysariel was off-balance too and both brothers had to scramble to regain a proper fighting posture. Once they had done that, though, they were squared off in an exceedingly aggressive manner, and it was obvious to Giraiazal, even from his horizontal position, that the next blow was likely to be the last.

Had the two combatants been a hand's-breadth further apart, Lysariel's next thrust would have drawn as little blood as the previous one, and Manazzoryn's half-pike would have bisected him. Because they were closer together by that margin, Lysariel was able to strike first with his lighter weapon, and he drove the blade between Manazzoryn's ribs, straight into the chamber that held the lungs and heart.

Manazzoryn dropped his weapon and crumpled, with the dagger still in him. He had barely enough breath left to form what was presumably intended to be the initial syllable of the word *brother.*

Then, it seemed to the horrorstruck onlookers, time slowed almost to a standstill. The moments oozed by while nobody moved or spoke.

Eventually, King Lysariel raised his open hands to his face and looked at them, as if he were surprised to discover them empty.

Triasymon hesitated, but then passed the half-pike back to the man who had given it to him, came to his feet, and stepped forward to seize his surviving nephew by the forearms. "What have you done, Lysariel?" he moaned. "What have you done?"

"Why," said Lysariel, "I have avenged my wife's murder, as I am bound to do. I have slain her murderer, and my own usurper, as justice clearly required."

The Lord Chancellor stared at his nephew with utter horror, apparently convinced that he was utterly and irredeemably insane. Giraiazal, however, was not so sure. Although he had seen no detailed record of this atrocity written in the heavens or pictured in his overworked cards, he had certainly been aware of an intricate knot of dark and ominous threats overhanging both brothers, and he was now beginning to understand the true nature and full extent of that peculiar entanglement.

The magician hoped that Manazzoryn might not be dead, in spite of the interruption of his final utterance, but when he sat up and leaned over to inspect the body he soon ascertained that there was no life left in it at all. The dagger was deeply embedded; even if its point had contrived to pass below the heart, the stomach must have been punctured and burst. Arterial blood and chyme were leaking from the wound; only the presence of the blade was inhibiting the scarlet fountain. Manazzoryn had already expired, but the residual air rushing from his lungs made a brief whistling sound like the ghost of a scream.

Triasymon, meanwhile, had loosed his grip on one of Lysariel's arms in order to strike him across the face with his open palm. Giraiazal was not sure whether the old man's motive was to punish Lysariel for the murder he had committed, or for the slander he had voiced.

Lysariel seemed surprised to be slapped, but his resentment seemed to be that of a child unfairly treated rather than a monarch betrayed. "Uncle!" he said, angrily. "You have no right to do that!" His eyes were blazing, and for a moment they really did seem to emit an eerie yellow light, the like of which Giraiazal had never seen before.

"Right!" Triasymon retorted. "I have every right! Your mother gave me the right, and I thank the departed gods that she did not live to see this day. Murderer!"

The use of his own taunt against him startled Lysariel more than anything else his uncle had said. He looked down at Manazzoryn's corpse as if he were seeing it in a new way. The amber glow had gone from his gaze, and he seemed more frightened than angry.

"Manazzoryn?" he said. "Manazzoryn, is that you?"

It as as well that Triasymon was still holding on to one of his nephew's arms, because Lysariel lapsed into a swoon then, and would have fallen had the chancellor not taken his weight. Triasymon clung on until Giraiazal stood up and took Lysariel's other arm. Then the magician ordered the two men-at-arms to take the king and carry him to his bedroom.

"Which one, sire?" asked the soldier whose half-pike Manazzoryn had used to defend himself, his voice all a-tremble.

"His old bedroom," Giraiazal said, taking the trouble to add, by way of making a point: "not the apartment in which the coral bride enchanted him."

The king was carried away, leaving Triasymon and Giraiazal alone with the regent's body.

"Tell me that it was a lie," Triasymon said, as doubt finally caught up with him.

"Alas, I do not know that for sure," Giraiazal murmured. "If Calia *was* carried to that high window and thrown out, there are only three individuals likely to have done it."

"The coral monster!" Triasymon said. "It must have been."

"Must it?" Giraiazal riposted, keeping his voice very low. "I hope you are right." He did not say that the principal motive for this hope was not the desperate desire to believe Manazzoryn innocent, but anxiety as to what it might imply had Viragan done the deed and Lysariel been bewitched into thinking otherwise. It was not until this thought had preoccupied his mind for several seconds, however, that the magician reminded himself of what he had been firmly resolved to keep telling himself only a few minutes earlier: that Calia's death really might have been an accident.

"If Viragan is not already on his way here," Giraiazal said, speaking now as the Grand Vizier of Scleracina, "you must send for him, Triasymon. Tell him exactly what has happened, and don't try to stop him if he decides to take Lysariel back to his own house."

"And what will you do?" Triasymon asked, intemperately.

"I must consult my oracles," Giraiazal said, "to see whether Damozel Fate has urgent intelligence to deliver now which she has been careful to hide from me before." When Triasymon had left the room, however, Giraiazal knelt down beside the corpse again. Before he left in his turn he unfastened the girdle that he had given to Manazzoryn as a wedding-present, but which had not provided the protection he needed in spite of the desperation with which its owner had clung to it.

It was not until he got the girdle back to his rooms that Giraiazal was able to examine it with sufficient care to detect that it was a fake. He wondered briefly whether the active part might always have been a fake, and that he simply had not looked at it closely enough before--but he dismissed the possibility as an absurdity. What he held was not the girdle he had made for Manazzoryn; that one had been replaced by a profoundly unmagical duplicate, perhaps while its owner slept.

Giraiazal did not make any attempt to consult his oracles. Instead, he went swiftly downstairs again. He found Triasymon alone in the bloodstained council-chamber, in a very mournful mood. The Lord Chancellor informed him that Lysariel had indeed been taken back to Viragan's house, where he was to be placed in the same room as before. "Viragan has promised that the lock on the door will be repaired and reinforced," Triasymon told him, "and Viragan will order four guards to remain on duty outside the door at all times. Will that be enough, do you think, if the coral bride comes to reclaim him a second time?"

"I doubt it," Giraiazal said, glumly.

"What news is there from the stars, Master Astrologer?" Triasymon asked him, obviously feeling an entitlement to be both bold and rude. "Doubtless they have now adjusted themselves to predict what happened here today, although they did not see fit to let you in on the secret yesterday."

"The fault was mine," Giraiazal said, forthrightly. "I misread the signs."

"Now we have neither a sane king nor a competent regent," Triasymon pointed out. "Unless, of course, you have ambitions in that regard yourself."

"No more than you," Giraiazal retorted, "although you would be a more logical choice. Make sure you have your answer ready if Viragan raises the possibility."

"My answer is that I ought to return to Harstpoint," Triasymon said, bitterly. "I have a living there that I can understand, and scope for the only skills I own."

"That would probably be the wisest choice, Lord Chancellor," Giraiazal agreed, although he did not really care one way or the other. "But you might care to bear it in mind that once a man has stepped up in rank, it can be very difficult to step down again. No matter how little ambition you have on your own behalf, others may seek to use you--and if you decline, you might not long survive your apology."

"Are you threatening me, Master Magician?" Triasymon demanded, hotly.

"Certainly not, Lord Chancellor," Giraiazal assured him. "You are the only man in Clarassour that I trust wholeheartedly, and I would rather you did not depart."

Slightly mollified by this answer, and in a state of total confusion, Triasymon was moved to say: "What happens now, Master Magician?"

"I wish I knew," Giraiazal replied, more frankly than was his habit. "The fact that the king is still very obviously mad will not prevent speculation that there is method--or motive, at least--in his madness. Scleracina's rumour-mongers have become so confident in the exercise of their dubious art that it will require no more than a minute for them to work out that if Manazzoryn was a murderer, then Calia's fatal fall could not have been an accident. They will feel free to suggest reasons why Manazzoryn might have cast her down."

"What reasons?" Triasymon demanded.

"The one that will leap most readily to mind is that she must have tumbled over the sill while trying to avoid his illicit amorous advances."

"Ridiculous!" was Triasymon's judgment on that.

"I agree," Giraiazal said. "But that is the way that rumour works. They will say, too, that Manazzoryn was making advances to the queen because Zintrah was amorously involved with Lysariel."

"A foul lie!" Triasymon exclaimed.

"No doubt. But Zintrah had gone to see Lysariel, at my request, and it was Zintrah who contrived to part him from the coral bride. If she had only kept the secret, as I asked...but she told her father. Her motives were doubtless virtuous, but a secret shared is no longer a secret. It is already widely believed that Calia has returned from the grave to possess her likeness, and the rumour-mongers will now be able to supply a motive. No gossip in the world could resist the temptation to cast her in the role of an avenger from beyond, come to demand the settlement of a score and the punishment of her would-be rapist."

"I was under the impression that you were the rumour-monger-in-chief in these parts," Triasymon observed, sarcastically, "And that Viragan's agents were your mouthpieces."

"Rumour is a difficult horse to tame," Giraiazal told him. "But you are right--we must try. We must at least try to put it about that Queen Calia will now be able to rest in peace. The statue must already be dispirited, else it would surely have come to the palace with Lysariel. People ought to be persuaded easily enough that it rests in the quiet of its grotto, and will not be seen again."

"Is that true?" Triasymon asked.

"I have no good reason to doubt it," Giraiazal said, choosing his words with great care, "but if it will calm the fever of speculation, we should certainly hope that people will be willing to believe it. Perhaps we should summon that bold diver who appointed himself the spokesman of the crew, and ask him to swim down to the grotto so that he may count the columns connecting its roof to its floor--but that sort of ploy can wait. For now...."

"For now," said a new voice, cutting him off as sharply as the blade of a half-pike, "we must ensure that there is a strong hand in charge of Scleracina. We must demonstrate that order has been restored, and will be maintained." The voice was Viragan's. He had come to the palace as quickly as he could, having commanded his men to put Lysariel away again and make sure that he was safe.

"You are absolutely right, Your Highness," Giraiazal was quick to say, "and you shall have my unswerving loyalty in your capacity as regent."

Triasymon raised an eyebrow, but he had been warned to expect that the matter would be raised, and to make a decision in advance as to where he would stand. He was quick enough on the uptake to say: "And mine, Your Highness."

Viragan smiled at them both. "I had not looked for any such responsibility," he said, lying outrageously. "But since you have both asked me to take on the burden, I feel that I cannot refuse. If Damozel Fate insists, who am I to refuse her instruction? She does insist, I suppose? I have your assurance of that, Master Magician, do I not?"

"You have, sire," Giraiazal informed him. "Now that the king's madness has been proven beyond the shadow of a doubt to be irredeemable, the sole inheritor of the true royal blood of Scleracina is Zintrah's unborn son--your grandson. It will be perfectly obvious to everyone that the only man who can rule in his stead is you."

"I had not thought of it like that," Viragan said, proving himself a veritable prodigy among liars, "but you are a wise man, Giraiazal...a very wise man. Has anyone informed my daughter that her husband is dead?"

"Not yet," said Triasymon. "We thought that you..."

"I thank you for the thought," Viragan said. "But I fear that she might take the news badly--in which case, it might be better delivered by Giraiazal.

"I thank you for the compliment, my lord Regent," Giraiazal murmured, "but I feel certain that she will know by now what has happened, even though no one was sent to inform her."

"All the more reason to provide wise counsel and a healing hand," said Viragan. "Please go to her, my friend, and do what you can to ease her nightmares, as you eased Manazzoryn's."

Giraiazal knew that this last remark was not meant kindly, but he was careful to offer no sign of his resentment. He obeyed the order he had been given--but in the privacy of his own thoughts, as he went to Zintrah's

Brian Stableford

room, he was wondering what would become of Scleracina if Orlu should happen to return today--to discover not merely that his daughter was dead and her husband incarcerated, but that his former friend and colleague Viragan was king in all-but-name, exercising authority on behalf of an unborn child. Would he be too late to make his own bid for power, or would he be just in time to catch a useful surge of anxiety on the part of the populace as to the desirability of Viragan's regency?

7

The most valuable lesson that my long experience as a prophet has taught me is this: it is never a good idea to tempt Damozel Fate by trusting to her generosity. She is undoubtedly the best-beloved of the several sisters of Lady Death, and also the most perverse; she usually flatters only to deceive, and is most to be feared when she seems to be benevolently inclined. This is, however, merely an observation, not a moral; in the ultimate analysis, Damozel Fate's whims and responses are as irrelevant in our doomed world as those of any mortal creature.

The Revelations of Suomynona, the Last Prophet

Giraiazal soon found that he had been quite wrong to assume that rumour would run ahead of him to Zintrah's apartment; this was one item of news that her ladies-in-waiting had not been in any hurry to pass on. Rather than competing to be the first to convey the information to Her Highness's ears, they had all found excuses to be somewhere else. When Giraiazal arrived in Zintrah's room, therefore, he found her fast asleep on a sofa, her lovely face entirely unclouded by any nightmarish anxiety.

He did not need to shake her; although his entrance was by no means noisy she opened her eyes as he approached the sofa.

"Giraiazal--is that you?" she said, surprised to see him. Although he had not been avoiding her, the magician had not been much in her company since she had let her father in on their conspiracy to bring Lysariel to his senses.

"Yes, Your Highness," the Grand Vizier said, using a formal tone of voice to inform her that his was no casual visit.

She was not yet alarmed. "Did Manazzoryn send you?" she asked. The question was natural enough.

215

"No, Your Highness. Your father sent me. I fear that I am the bearer of terrible news."

The shadow that crossed her features before she straightened them again was a mere flicker. Zintrah had clearly been practising the skills necessary to the maintenance of a queenly aplomb. "Is it Manazzoryn?" she asked.

"Yes, Your Highness."

"Is he dead?"

"Yes, Your Highness."

This time the shadow lasted a little longer, but the magician was impressed nevertheless by the manner in which Zintrah maintained her composure. For a moment or two, Giraiazal almost believed that she had expected the news--but that impression did not last. Her composure collapsed abruptly, and she burst into tears. Giraiazal immediately repented of his suspicion. Zintrah could not possibly have had the slightest inkling that Manazzoryn was in danger; she was not party to her father's machinations, and even the multitalented Giraiazal had not been able to obtain any detailed forewarning of the tragedy.

"What happened?" Zintrah asked, as she fought to control the sobs convulsing her body.

"Lysariel came to the palace, carrying weapons stolen from the men set to guard him on the night of the feast. He attacked his brother. The soldiers on duty in the council chamber were old men and slow of wit-- and Lysariel is, after all, their king. Triasymon made a valiant attempt to stop the fight, but he is an old man too, and he did not want to hurt either of his nephews. I, alas, was knocked down. Although I did my best to trip Lysariel I was unable to prevent him carrying through his purpose. I doubt that anyone could have stopped him--Lysariel is, I fear, one of those madmen who can acquire the strength of ten for brief periods of violent action. At any rate, your husband made a very brave attempt to defend himself and to disarm his unfortunate brother without injuring him, but it was all in vain. Lysariel stabbed him in the heart. He must have died instantly, without feeling any pain. Your father was obliged to assume the regency."

"I am devastated," Zintrah declared. "Utterly devastated. This is not merely my tragedy, but Scleracina's. For Scleracina's sake, and the sake of my unborn son, I must be brave." She was not weeping quite as copiously now.

"I could not have put it better myself, Your Highness," Giraiazal said, glad that he had no necessity to lie but slightly surprised to find such a speech rising effortlessly to Zintrah's lips. "Your fortitude is very admirable; grief is the supreme test for a loyal wife, but I see that you will be equal to the challenge."

"I shall need help, of course, Giraiazal" she told him, "but I am sure that you will be able to meet that need. You must help me to shape my dreams, Master Magician, so that they will not undermine my strength and my courage. You will help me, will you not?" For a moment, she seemed to be an echo of her father, her will a faint and forlorn copy of his.

"I will do everything I can," Giraiazal promised. He sat down beside her, and comforted her as best he could. He placed his sensitive fingers on her forehead, and spoke to her in a soft voice, telling her to go back to sleep--but her agitation was too great to permit her to sleep, and she swatted his fingers away after suffering their pressure for a few moments. She would not let him send for a sleeping-draught, but she did become calmer when he took his hand away. He would have left the room, but she called him back. Although she would not let him place his hands on her head, she nevertheless kept him by her side for several hours.

"We are living in confused times, Giraiazal," Zintrah told the magician, when she had recovered her equilibrium. "One would have thought that everything would be simplified as the world's end approaches, but the opposite appears to be the case. I want you to know that I bear you no grudge on account of your failure to anticipate the threat to my beloved husband, or to provide adequate means to prevent the disaster. How can any oracle calculate the actions of a madman? Nor do I hold it against you that you once assured me--falsely, it now seems-- that I might save the sanity of the king. How could you estimate the true extent of the power that the evil statue had? No woman in the world could have had charm enough to win Lysariel's affections away from the coral courtesan, but you were right to ask me to try. I still have every confidence in your abilities and your judgment."

"Thank you, Your Highness," Giraiazal, said, a little drily. He knew that it would be pointless to remind her that what he had actually said to her was that she alone in all the world had charm enough to *distract* Lysariel from his fetish, and that she had succeeded in that aim. Nor did he point out that if only she had followed his plan to the very end, instead of collaborating with her father to have the king seized and imprisoned, Lysariel might have recovered enough of his sanity to prevent the tragedy that had overtaken her husband. Instead, he said: "Will you let me send for a potion now, to help you sleep?"

"Will you exert your powers to the full in making sure that my dreams are pleasant?" she countered. "It is not for myself that I ask, but for my unborn son. I believe that the unborn, incapable of dreaming for themselves, are party to their mothers' nightmares, and I do not want my son to be born with phantoms shadowing his mind."

"I will do what I can, Your Highness," Giraiazal, promised, wondering how Zintrah had come by such an odd, but not implausible, belief. "If you will only permit me to lay my hands on your forehead, I will gladly exert what influence I can upon your dreams--but I must warn you, in all fairness, that even a skilled morpheomorphist cannot always set aside the effects of such powerful emotions as grief."

217

She frowned at that, and almost seemed inclined to swat his hand away again, but she thought better of it.

"It seems, alas, that Lysariel was faithful to his statuesque hussy to the bitter end," Zintrah mused, as she reluctantly offered her forehead to the magician's comforting caress. "She released him from his prison only to send him back here as a fratricide. On her instruction, he killed his own brother--his *innocent* brother. She is a malevolent demon and monster of mendacity, is she not? This foolish rumour which says that she is Calia reincarnate is the merest gossip?"

Giraiazal had carefully omitted to tell Zintrah that Lysariel had twice cried "Murderer!" before stabbing his brother to death, so he was intrigued by the emphasis she placed on the word *innocent*, but he did not want to read too much into it. "Your judgment is impeccable, Your Highness" the magician assured her, in a scrupulously low voice. "There is not the slightest evidence to support the absurd claim that the statue is animated by the spirit of Queen Calia, and every reason to believe that the process of animation began while Calia was still alive. Assuming, that is, that the figure was ever animated at all." He knew that the last statement was a risk, but he was curious to know how Zintrah would react to it.

"Why, what do you mean?" she asked. "Was it not you who assured us all that the image was and is animate?"

Giraiazal did not bother to object to the word *assured*, even though it was far too strong a term to describe his tentative suggestion. "The possibility still remains," he whispered, "that it was merely stolen. There is no proof that anyone assisted Lysariel in his escape from your father's custody, but even if he did have assistance, it is perfectly possible that the assistance was rendered by a human being. As to what Lysariel might have been told or persuaded to believe, and by whom, we can only speculate."

"No, no, Giraiazal," Zintrah told him, although her own voice was softening now as the gentle pressure of his hands took effect. "What has happened today is the firmest possible proof that the sorcerer's statue is alive, and that it intends to exact revenge for the death of its maker. Lysariel is undoubtedly bewitched, and there is no one else in all Scleracina--with the exception of yourself--who has magical power enough to do that. The coral monster must be responsible, must it not?"

Giraiazal was sure that Zintrah believed what she was saying; now that his hands had relaxed her she was half-entranced, and would not find it easy to lie.

"Your logic is impeccable, Your Highness," Giraiazal agreed. "One would be foolish to entertain any rival hypothesis for a moment." And yet, he thought, Lysariel had called her husband *murderer*. Why would the coral monster have told Lysariel that Manazzoryn was a murderer--and why would he have believed it?

He had not spoken this question aloud, and would not have done so even if he had not refrained from telling Zintrah what Lysariel had shouted as he slew her husband--but it was almost as if the idea had communicated itself to her brain by way of his magical hands. "The coral monster is a liar," Zintrah said, in a voice that was becoming sleepy. "And Lysariel is mad. You know that it is not true, do you not, Giraiazal?"

Giraiazal was not even certain what it was whose lack of truth he was supposed to know, so he said nothing. His hands had been at work for some minutes now, and whatever else Zintrah might have had in mind, her desire to benefit from his skill as a morpheomorphist seemed sincere. There was no further resistance in her; she had relaxed into a receptive state. After a long moment's pause, though, Giraiazal picked up the thread of the conversation, speaking to himself but putting the thoughts into whispered words. "On the other hand," he murmured, very softly indeed, "it is possible that Lysariel had some other reason to wish his brother dead--a motive that was transformed by his madness because his conscious mind could not have borne it."

Zintrah gave no evidence of having heard what he had said, and her lips did not move. Even so, he heard a voice that did not seem to be his own speak directly into his mind, saying: *But what other reason could he possibly have had?*

"We live, as Your Highness has wisely observed, in confused times," Giraiazal whispered, having almost slipped into a trance himself. "I have always been a scholarly man, preoccupied by my studies of the ever-changing firmament and the symbolism of my cards and wands. It is the penalty of those who strive too hard to decipher mysteries that they sometimes give too much thought to the unlikely, and not enough to the obvious. It did not occur to me to wonder whether Lysariel might be jealous of the comfort Manazzoryn gave to Calia while she lay ill, sometimes staying by her bedside for half the night, while you and I went exhausted to our rooms. Nor did it occur to me to wonder whether Manazzoryn might be jealous of the attention you paid to Lysariel while he was in the throes of his own very different illness. What a fool I have been! But I understand my errors now. I am mortified by the fact that I failed to protect Manazzoryn from the madness of Lysariel, just as I failed to protect Calia from the aftermath of her sickness--but I beg you never to doubt my loyalty or my sincerity, Your Highness. You know better than anyone else how long and hard I laboured to snatch Calia from the jaws of death, and how cunningly I attempted to pluck Lysariel from the clutches of obsession."

Zintrah started suddenly, and a reflexive response made him snatch his hands away from her forehead. He felt startled himself, and was momentarily confused as to who had said what, and to whom.

Zintrah sat up, and looked at him curiously. "I feel much better now," she said, "Thank you, Giraiazal. I think I can safely be let alone now. I am sure that my dreams will be untroubled, thanks to you."

Giraiazal did not move, although he muttered; "Yes, Your Highness."

"You may be assured that I shall continue to treasure your healing powers, Giraiazal, as I treasure your friendship," Zintrah said. "All will be well now, will it not? You have already promised me that my son will live long and prosper. I must be similarly armoured against disaster, must I not?"

This was a question to which Giraiazal could not give a definite reply. "I have seen no indication that any human hand will do you harm, Your Highness," he told her, phrasing the reply very carefully. "You may await the birth of your son without fear that any injury will come to you before his birth. He will be king--I am as sure of that as I am of anything. The storm-clouds that are gathering about Scleracina as we speak will not launch their fateful lightning against him."

He stood up, intending to depart, but the mercurial Zintrah seemed to have changed her mind yet again. "What storm-clouds?" she asked, sharply.

Giraiazal was in no hurry to return to the tedious business of calming her. "Don't be concerned, Your Highness," he said, soothingly. "Your father knows everything that he needs to know. Indeed, he knows a great deal more than I do about many important matters. He is a clever man, and you are fortunate to have him for a father. He will continue to take care of you to the very best of his ability--you may depend on that. Let him into your dreams, Your Highness. Let his dreams be yours, and you shall sleep as peacefully as any well-beloved daughter." With that admonition the magician decided that his spell was definitely concluded. He went swiftly to the door, and went out before she could interrupt him.

The magician returned to his turret, his mind alive once again with speculations and possibilities. So far as he could judge, Viragan must indeed know everything that he needed to know. He must, for instance, have known for some time that his grandson was Lysariel's son rather than Manazzoryn's. He must also be able to judge how much trouble there would be if or when Orlu made a belated reappearance in Scleracina. He must, in fact, know exactly what he was up against, and exactly what he would have to do to make his mastery secure--but that did not mean that the task would be easy, while Orlu had men like Cardelier ready to fight for him.

Giraiazal could not cast Orlu's or Viragan's horoscope, and there seemed little to be gained by further calculations relating to Lysariel and Zintrah, so he directed his attention to more general estimations. Instead of turning immediately to his telescope or his playing-cards he cast a set of wands and attempt to rouse his rhabdomantic powers to see into the future of the whole island, paying particular attention to the possible consequences of Orlu's return. His imagination was sluggish, but he eventually gained the definite impression that Orlu's return was inevitable and would not be long delayed. He dealt out his cards then, laying out a circular array that represented Scleracina rather than a cross representative of an individual. The baleful sign of the Long-lost Moon, coupled with that of the Eternal Wound in his cartomantic array, suggested to him that copious bloodshed might easily follow, but the disposition of the other trumps gave the magician no hint as to how this eventuality might be avoided, or its violence minimized.

The signs of impending conflict were equally clear in his star-charts, without any clear indication of which side might be victorious or how costly the victory might be. Finally, the magician instructed Burrel to bring him a cat, whose evisceration he promptly set about--but the pattern formed by the animal's entrails imposed no sympathetic echo on his tired brain at all. So far as he could read the bloody display, it was authentically chaotic. There was certainly nothing so definite as to suggest a decisive course of action. The magician was so wound up by these endeavours that he had to dose himself with opiates to send himself to sleep.

When he awoke, Giraiazal immediately attempted to collect his dreams for analysis, but they fled from his memory before he could mine the least inspiration from their imagery. To make matters worse, he found that he did not feel at all well, and had to wonder whether his groaning stomach might be the first symptom of some debilitating disease. He dosed himself with a judicious mixture of specifics against various fevers, throwing in a few more opiates as a precaution against his aches becoming agonies.

Thus fortified, he set himself to work again.

"You ought to go downstairs for a while, Master," Mergin advised him, when she saw how little he had eaten from the tray she had brought. "You are making yourself ill."

"Not I," Giraiazal told her. "I am a scholar and a prophet. Deep thought never harmed a true scholar, nor hard work a true prophet."

"The saying I know is that they never hurt anyone else," Mergin retorted--but he forgave her the impertinence.

"What do you see, Master?" Burrel asked him, though he ought to have known better.

"Nothing that concerns you, scantling," was Giraiazal's automatic reply to that question. He meant it, although Burrel might have had a very different notion of what concerned him.

"King Lysariel called Prince Manazzoryn a murderer," Burrel said, clearly unwilling to take the rebuke meekly. "Prince Manazzoryn must have killed Queen Calia. Will Queen Calia return to her grave now, or has she other business yet to conclude?"

"Lysariel is mad," Giraiazal replied, dully. "He may have been deluded into thinking his brother guilty. Queen Calia has never left her grave."

"The coral bride, then," Burrel said, stubbornly. "Is her business concluded, or has she more to do?"

Brian Stableford

Giraiazal did not know, but could not confess his ignorance to a raw apprentice. Alas, he did not seem to have the strength to contrive a convincing evasion. Fortunately he was spared the necessity by a loud rapping on his door. The summons was unwelcome, but he would have to meet it.

"We live, as Her Highness Princess Zintrah has so wisely observed, in confused times," Giraiazal whispered to himself, as Burrel went, with an ill grace, to open the door. "Damozel Fate is clearly in one of her less temperate moods. But who is more capable than I of dealing with her, even at her most recalcitrant?" Alas, he could not muster enough conviction to believe that the answer could possibly be "no one".

Prophets always prosper when things go well. It does not matter in the least whether they actually promised beforehand that things would go well--although wise prophets always give more weight to good news than to bad in making their reports--because they will get the credit anyway. The common mind is ever ready to fall into the trap of assuming that those who claim the power to anticipate the future must be responsible for the shape it assumes as the mists of uncertainty are precipitated into the dew of actuality. This misapprehension has its dark corollary, however, which is that when things go badly, prophets always reap more than their fair share of the blame, No matter how clear-sighted they have been in anticipating trouble, nor how liberal they have been in issuing their warnings, resentment of the unkindness of Damozel Fate will always rebound upon them.

For this reason, anyone who elects to follow the profession of prophecy, no matter how clever or well-educated he may be, must beware of the ingratitude and injustice that flourish in times of trouble. Such tendencies affect all men to some degree, but they are at their most dangerous in men whose dreams of power and glory are trembling on the brink of frustration and failure.

The Revelations of Suomynona, the Last Prophet

The summoner sent to Giraiazal's door took him to the council-chamber, where Viragan and Sharuman were waiting for him.

"My daughter is much better," Viragan told him. "The Lord Chancellor is making the arrangements for the funeral of his nephew, the former regent. Lysariel is safe. The whereabouts of the coral statue are still unknown."

It was obvious from the pirate's laconic tone that none of these items of news had anything to do with the reason Giraiazal had been summoned--but it was equally apparent that something was troubling him.

"You are anxious about Orlu," Giraiazal guessed. "You have news of him at last."

Viragan smiled bloodlessly. "The stars have kept you informed, I see," he said. "Have they told you whether Orlu's return will be a joyous one?"

"Strangely enough," Giraiazal said, "they incline to an opposite opinion. There will be trouble, and bloodshed."

"I wonder why you did not see fit to mention this earlier," Sharuman said, coldly--but Viragan raised a hand to silence him.

"Giraiazal has had other matters to occupy him," the regent said. "Even a great magician has only one pair of hands, and cannot think of everything at once. He might have warned us of the impending trouble, had we only taken the trouble to consult him with the right questions."

The magician did not feel well enough to engage in a verbal duel "What has happened, Your Highness?" he asked, flatly. "What news do you have?"

Viragan told him that a dozen of Orlu's captains had put to sea in the night, having crammed their ships with armed men. "I have told my men that we cannot be certain whether they are going to meet Orlu or Akabar," the regent said, "but I am certain in my own mind that it is Orlu. In any case, their intention seems clear enough: when they return, they will do so as an invasion-force."

"Why did they sail away at all?" Giraiazal asked. "It will surely be a great deal harder for them to return to port than it was to leave."

"A good question," Viragan said. "I can only presume that they intend to land elsewhere on the island--probably in the north, and that they will try to raise an army there to assault Clarassour from the landward side. They could not hope to win a sea-battle against my forces, and I do not think they can defeat us on land either, but the latter choice must seem the preferable option."

"They may not attack at all, of course," Sharuman put in. "They may think better of their madness once they understand that they cannot win. They might set themselves up as pirates, operating from a base on some other isle. It is what they know best, after all."

"The survivors will attempt to do that when they have been beaten," Viragan said, "but not until then. Orlu will attack."

"How can you be so sure, Your Highness?" Giraiazal asked.

"Why, Master Magician." said Viragan, sarcastically, "I can be sure because you have just told me so, having read the news in the stars. It seems that Orlu is angry. He has suffered misfortunes, for which he thinks me responsible. I am innocent, of course, but he always did have a suspicious mind and a hasty manner. Unlike you and I, he was not a man for careful calculation. It was my friendship that turned him into a successful merchant and helped him prosper, but he has forgotten that. I hate to fight him, but if I cannot make him see sense...."

"I see," Giraiazal said, mildly. "I suppose, Highness, you must have increased your own fleet considerably while Orlu was away--but perhaps not as considerably as you had hoped."

"I had hoped to forge a greater spirit of solidarity in Scleracina's navy," Viragan agreed. "It is a terrible tragedy that ancient rivalries should have spoiled my good intentions. I fear that the rebels have been sadly misled--but they have done what they have done, and I could not prevent it. I have no alternative now but to defend the realm against those who have turned traitor against it. They cannot win, of course--I dare say that the stars have assured you of that."

"I would need to consult them more closely to be sure of the ultimate outcome, Your Highness," Giraiazal said. "But I have the utmost confidence in your judgment of military matters, and if you assure me that your victory is inevitable, I cannot imagine that my oracles will disagree."

"*Our* victory, Giraiazal," Viragan said. "We are both committed, body and soul, to the cause of Scleracina."

"Body and soul," Giraiazal echoed, wishing that his voice did not sound so weak as he pronounced the words. "We are, as you say, steadfast in our loyalty to King Lysariel, however ill he might be."

Viragan frowned at hat. "Even a king must be held responsible for his crimes, Giraiazal," he said. "Lysariel is a slanderer and a fratricide--you witnessed that yourself. But that is a matter which must be put aside for now, while the kingdom is in danger. Our loyalty is to Scleracina, and it is for Scleracina that we must fight, if a fight is to be forced upon us."

"Let us hope that we might avoid it" Giraiazal said, wishing that he felt well enough to conduct the conversation more cleverly. "Traders like you and Orlu know far better than other men how valuable peace and stability are. Surely men who were merchants before they were princes will not be so foolish as to cast a newly-liberated island into the throes of a civil war."

"You are absolutely right, Master Magician," Viragan said. "But what choice do I have? I know as well as any man, alas, how awkward and violent my old friend Orlu can be."

Giraiazal knew that Viragan was playing with him contemptuously, having taken note of how tired and ill he was. "What is it that you want from me, Your Highness?" he asked.

Viragan smiled mirthlessly. "Two things, Lord Vizier. First, I want the assurance of the stars, and every other oracle at your disposal, that my position is invulnerable, and that I am certain to be the winner of any contest of arms fought on or around the island. I want that declaration formally proclaimed and loudly cried in every port, village and hamlet in the island. Secondly, I want the assurance of the stars, and of every other oracle you can enlist in their support, that although Lysariel's reign has been short and unhappy, the reign of Zintrah's as-yet-unborn son will be long and happy, and will bring great prosperity to the nation of Scleracina. I know that you have already made these promises in private, but they must now be made public, without further delay, for the sake of Scleracina. I know that you will help me in this, as you have helped me in so much else, because I know that you are an honest prophet and a good man. I leave the exact wording to you, of course, but I want you to draw up a declaration that can be proclaimed in the plaza before noon--with you in personal attendance, of course. Captain Sharuman can read and write, and he will be pleased to assist you in drawing up the document."

Giraiazal had not even energy enough to be resentful, let alone to resist. "Yes, Your Highness," he said, meekly.

"And when you have done that," Viragan said, taking obvious relish in his unchallengeable authority, "you had best go to see my daughter again. I think she may be in need of someone to interpret and shape her dreams. She has a good head on her shoulders, but she is very young, and is sometimes prone to slight confusion."

"Yes, Your Highness," Giraiazal said, again. He would far rather have gone to Zintrah's room immediately, but he had to sit down at the table first, with Sharuman and a blank parchment, while Viragan went to supervise the raising of his army. As Viragan had promised, however, Sharuman was perfectly happy to assist him in making a succinct explanation of exactly what the stars and their supplementary oracles had revealed concerning Scleracina's imminent time of troubles. Indeed, Sharuman seemed to have a better understanding of exactly what the stars had to say, and how, than his commander--which seemed a little odd, given that he had been manifestly sceptical of Giraiazal's ability to read and interpret oracles only a few minutes earlier.

"If I were to die now," Giraiazal said, softly, when Sharuman had finished writing down the proclamation, "the rumour might easily get around that I was not such a great magician after all, and that all my prophecies might have been badly mistaken, if not a mere tissue of lies."

"You needn't worry about that, old man," Sharuman said, brusquely. "I never had much use for magicians myself, but my master takes a different view. He's not the kind of man to use you once and throw you away. He'll keep on using you, for as long as you care to be used."

Even in his depleted state, Giraiazal mustered enough resentment to scowl at that. "I am no mere mouthpiece," he said. "Meronicos of Yura was wise enough to treat me with respect, and you would be wise to do the same."

"I read the letter Meronicos sent with Cardelier," Sharuman reminded him. "I know exactly how much respect you won from

Meronicos the Minuscule, and exactly how much you deserved. Let's get this over with."

They went out into the plaza together, where a crowd was already gathered in expectation of hearing a proclamation of some importance. The crowd was bigger than any Giraiazal had ever seen before--proving, if he had needed proof, the old adage that nothing makes men hungrier for news than the possibility of war.

Fortunately, Giraiazal did not have to read his own words; that task was given to the owner of a far more powerful voice. All the magician had to do was stand by, signalling by his presence that the words were indeed his, issued on behalf of Damozel Fate, the stars in the sky, the major arcana, the wands of doom and the entrails of every animal that had ever walked upon or flown above the surface of the Earth.

After it was done, the magician was allowed to return to the palace, to visit his anxious patient, Princess Zintrah.

Zintrah was no longer as anxious as she had seemed to be on the previous evening. Indeed, she hardly seemed anxious at all now that her own troubles had been diminished by comparison with the threat to her beloved Scleracina.

"We must mourn Manazzoryn, of course," she said, "but we must not allow mourning to distract us from the threat of rebellion. Above all else, we must make sure that my unborn child is safe, and that he will be successfully delivered to his due destiny--which is to rule a peaceful, happy and well-defended nation for many glorious years. If that is what Damozel Fate desires, we must not let her down."

"Indeed we must not, Your Highness," Giraiazal agreed. "Will you tell me your dreams, so that I may work upon their substance?"

"Actually," she said, "I slept quite well. I cannot remember what I dreamed, if I dreamed anything at all. You are a great healer, Giraiazal, a great healer, but I fear that you have been neglecting yourself while you have worked so hard on my behalf. You had better go to back your own bed--my father would never forgive me if I let you perish from neglect. Shall I summon your servants?"

"Thank you, Your Highness," was all Giraiazal could say in reply to that. Fortunately Burrel and Mergin came quickly in response to the princess's request for help. Between the two of them they managed to carry him up the stairway in the western tower and put him to bed.

"Don't worry, Master," Burrel said. "I'll keep my ears open, and bring you all the news. Sleep now"

The boy was as good as his word. No further news of Orlu's fleet arrived in Clarassour that morning, but as soon as the noonday was over hasty messengers descended in some profusion from the farmlands inland of the capital. Orlu was indeed alive, it seemed, and had taken command of a fleet of ships comprised of fourteen of his vessels that had been

227

engaged in trade among the islands and thirteen more that had sneaked out of the harbour on the previous night.

At dusk, more messengers arrived to say that Orlu had disembarked his men on the Harstpoint peninsula, leaving his ships anchored outside the reef. Before midnight, all Clarassour knew that the pirate had summoned thousands more of his former followers to meet him at the neck of the peninsula, but hardly anyone had dared to answer the summons because of the prophecy that Orlu's was a cause already lost.

After the midnight, the news was amended very slightly to concede that some few of the men in question *were* on the move, with horses and carts and considerable stocks of arms, although the vast majority of Orlu's one-time employees had declared their loyalty to Zintrah's unborn son, and his duly-appointed regent Viragan. No one else, it was confidently said, would dare to join the doomed rebellion.

Giraiazal had not the slightest intention of rising from his bed again until the crisis had passed, even to consult his oracles, but he was not left in peace for long. Before the noonday there was a hammering at his door, which Burrel rushed to answer. Viragan and Triasymon came in together. Triasymon had been in the room before but Viragan never had, and Giraiazal watched the regent's eyes as they traced a path across the tables where his divinatory devices and potion-mixing apparatus was carefully set out, terminating their journey by dwelling for a few seconds on the low table bedside his bedhead, where Giraiazal had set his own medicine, and from which Mergin had not yet removed the unconsumed detritus of his last meal. Triasymon seemed very agitated, but Viragan was quite calm.

"I am sorry that you are ill, Lord Vizier," the regent said. "It is as well for the kingdom that you managed to divine the outcome of the impending conflict before you had to take to your bed." He had come to stand over Giraiazal while he spoke, and he took up the medicine-bottle from the bedside table. After removing the stopper he sniffed its contents judiciously. "Ah!" he said. "I see that you are not so proud as to refuse yourself the benefit of the sovereign remedy. I dare say that you feel much better now that you have slept the whole night through. After all, if a physician cannot heal himself, he can hardly expect trust from those in his charge."

Giraiazal sat up. Several hours had passed since he had taken his last dose of opium, and he would have drained the contents of the bottle had Viragan only consented to replace it on the table--but the regent kept his fist closed around it.

"I am a little better, Your Highness," Giraiazal said. "I believe that I could shuffle a deck of cards and lay it out, if your need for further advice is urgent."

"You have told us often enough about the dark shadows that lie across the future of our lovely realm," Viragan said. "I have been very grateful for all the trouble you have taken. My faithful Captain Sharuman, who thinks himself an educated man, assures me that you are a charlatan and a rumour-monger, but I am confident that the understanding I have gained in a lifetime of trade and enterprise is as good as any I might have obtained in a school. I have faith in you, Giraiazal. So has Triasymon."

"The situation is bad, Giraiazal," Triasymon said, responding to his cue. "Things have happened too quickly to allow any of us adequate time to think and plan. I cannot believe that Prince Orlu had any intention to attack his homeland when he first sailed away from it, and I cannot see why he should have reacted in this way to the news of his daughter's death and his son-in-law's madness. There is obviously some kind of misunderstanding here, which needs to be quickly disentangled. There has been tragedy enough in Scleracina without any further bloodshed, and Prince Orlu will surely grant that, if only it is properly explained to him."

Giraiazal did not like the sound of the words "properly explained", but he held his tongue, waiting for Viragan to elaborate.

"I cannot imagine why," Viragan said, his tone and manner mimicking the innocent puzzlement with which Triasymon's speech had been saturated, "but it seems that the declaration you made yesterday has not had as much effect as we had hoped. Your reputation in Scleracina is not as great as it ought to be, and it seems that many foolish individuals have chosen to ignore the warning contained in your prophecies. I am very sorry to have to ask you for a further effort, but I must."

"You want me to write another declaration?" Giraiazal said, disingenuously.

"No, Giraiazal," the Lord Chancellor said, when the Prince Regent graciously left him the opportunity to take over the burden of explanation. "We believe that Prince Orlu and his captains need to be persuaded that the stars are set against them. They need to be told that they cannot possibly win this war, and that a far better future awaits them elsewhere in Ambriocyatha, if only they will sail away to claim their proper destiny."

Giraiazal knew that there was nothing to be gained by challenging Triasymon's use of the word *we*, or questioning the source of his conviction as to what the stars had in store for Orlu, Akabar, Cardelier and more than twenty other captains. The only avenue of escape that was open to him was to plead that his illness made it impossible for him to rise from his bed, let alone to undertake a journey across the island. There was a possibility that Viragan might accept that excuse, and it was one that Giraiazal could have made without feeling in the least dishonest--but he had his reputation as a healer and magician to think of. If he pleaded impotence now, he might as well declare himself useless--and he remembered what Sharuman had said about having nothing to fear from Viragan while he could still demonstrate his usefulness.

"I can understand your concern, Your Highnesses," the magician said, "but I fear there is one thing you have forgotten."

229

"What's that?" Triasymon asked, quite innocently.

"What Giraiazal means," Viragan said, "is that he has already seen a time of troubles--that it is already written in the stars that there will be fighting, and bloodshed. He is telling us that it would be futile for him to try to prevent something that is fated to happen. But I remember his exact words when he spoke to Captain Sharuman and myself yesterday morning, and I am keenly aware of a dimension of uncertainty that was present in Giraiazal's anticipations. Yes, trouble is unavoidable; yes, there will be bloodshed--but there is a possibility that we might reduce the trouble and the bloodshed to a tolerable minimum by judicious action, whereas a stubborn refusal to act would surely make matters far worse than they need to be. Why else would we have been allowed to hear the warnings that the Lord Vizier has issued to us? It seems to me--as it must surely seem to Giraiazal--that we have a responsibility to do what we can, else Damozel Fate might be far less generous with her warnings in future. Is that a fair summary of the situation, Giraiazal?"

"I suppose it is," Giraiazal conceded.

"Good," said Viragan. "It appears that my old friend Orlu is suspicious of me now--but he may still be well-disposed towards you, Lord Vizier, because of the effort you put into the work of saving her from her dreadful disease. Under other circumstances, the Lord Chancellor would be the logical choice as an ambassador, but he is the king's uncle and might be suspected of having cunning motives of his own. You, Giraiazal are clearly impartial, and you are a diviner of genius. In this instance, you are the one who must go to Orlu's camp and do your utmost to reduce the damage that his army might inflict on Scleracina. Do you not agree?"

Giraiazal understood that he could not refuse the regent's instruction. If Viragan wanted him to act as a go-between as well as an instrument of propaganda, then he must do it, and make what provision he could to save himself from being murdered in the process. "I will, of course, be only too glad to do everything in my power to smooth this unfortunate dispute," he said, "but in all honesty, and having consulted all my oracles as carefully as I can, I cannot promise that any news I bring back will be good."

"You underestimate yourself, Master Magician," Viragan said, oozing generosity. "Triasymon will surely agree with my judgment that you are a man of unusual intelligence and quality. If anyone can sort this misunderstanding out, it is you. Shall I order a carriage, a coachman and an escort?"

Giraiazal could see only one way in which he could make room for his own cleverness to operate in this affair. "No, Your Highness," he said. "I think it might be better if I went alone. I can ride." Nearly a thousand days had passed since he had last sat astride a horse, but this was obviously a mission best undertaken without attendants who would report back every word he said to Viragan.

"Are you certain?" Viragan said. "You would be far safer in a carriage, given that you are so poorly." It was obvious from the way he spoke, however, that this was one point on which he was prepared to compromise; the idea of Giraiazal riding alone to the enemy camp obviously amused him.

"Quite certain, Your Highness," Giraiazal said. "I shall set out as soon as I have gathered the equipment for my journey."

"That is good," Viragan said, seemingly very satisfied with the results of his merciless mission. "The matter is very urgent."

Brian Stableford

Prophecy is an art best reserved to reclusive scholars, practised as a secret vocation. Those so-called eclectic magicians who think of divination as a natural extension of the practical craft of healing run the risk of profound philosophical confusions. The prophet who seeks to establish an ideal long-term relationship with Damozel Fate will do well to adopt as his first and firmest commandment an unbreakable resolution to refrain from any interference in her business. The unavoidable price of gaining greater insight into the unwinding pattern of inevitability is an adamant determination to be silent about the insight in question, and any prophet who aspires to significant success must be prepared to take no action whatsoever in respect of the revelations vouchsafed to him.

This is, I admit, a difficult commandment to obey. The temptations inviting a prophet to reveal or act upon what he knows are considerable, and they increase in direct proportion to the prophet's competence. The wisest prophet of all, according to this argument, is the one who will not even commit his wisdom to parchment, lest his anticipations should be scanned by curious eyes--in which case, I freely admit, anyone who read these words would be bound to doubt my claim to be the greatest prophet who has ever existed.

Fortunately, because I am the last prophet as well as the best, there is not the slightest risk that any of my contemporaries will ever read this document. A sceptic might suggest, in consequence of that observation, that there is little point in my taking the trouble to record the fruits of my awesome wisdom--but I have my reasons, which you might learn, and might even understand, if you are ever able, and willing, to read my manuscript to the end.

The Revelations of Suomynona, the Last Prophet

233

Brian Stableford

The stables contained in the palace of Clarassour had a great many mounts to choose from, and Giraiazal was content to take the advice of a groom as to which one was most likely to get him to the north side of the island in reasonable time without spilling him on the road.

The magician was not an accomplished horseman, but he had learned in infancy to climb into a saddle and sit still while being conveyed at a steady trot, and he had become accustomed to such transport in his student days. He was grateful to find, when he set off on his mission, that the knack was not entirely lost to him--although he anticipated that he would be very sore when he eventually climbed down again, and had therefore taken the trouble to take a generous flask of opium with him, as well as a water-bottle. He was correct in this anticipation, as he usually was in all his anticipations, but in spite of his precautions the journey took a great deal longer than he would have liked, and had to be completed in no less than five stages.

Under other circumstances, Giraiazal might have been interested to see something of the interior of Scleracina, but he was in no mood to take note of the various differences in vegetation and architecture that distinguished the nation from the other islands on which he had lived. The roads were much less busy than those on Yura, and were by no means so richly lined with houses and inns, but Scleracina and Yura were both gently-contoured and almost entirely deforested, so they seemed essentially similar by contrast with the magician's birthplace, Natalarch, whose hills were much more irregular and considerably less hospitable to agriculture.

Had Scleracina's fields been planted with more determination and skill they would doubtless have been much richer than they were, but the island's fishing fleets and tradesmen had always been more crucial to its fortunes. Much of the land across which Giraiazal rode was lightly planted, and many crops were engaged in a ceaseless struggle with weeds that more energetic cultivators would have pulled up. Harvesters were busy everywhere, but not because their plantations were ready; the farmers and their labourers were trying to take up what they could and race to market before their produce could be requisitioned by soldiers on the march.

Nobody paid overmuch attention to Giraiazal once he was beyond the outskirts of the capital, because no one outside Clarassour recognised him. He had taken care to dress in very plain clothes, displaying neither livery nor insignia, with his protective charms and amulets carefully stowed inside his shirt and such magical apparatus as he had thought it worthwhile to bring secreted in his saddlebags with his food and water. He had intended to present the image of a steward or an artisan of modest means, but he had buckled on a short sword in order to deter any casual

234

vagabond who might think him worth robbing for the sake of his luggage and horse.

No one questioned the magician's right to be on the road, or his wisdom in heading for Harstpoint, although he passed few other travellers headed in the same direction--most of those who were rallying to Orlu's cause were using more discreet routes. He was not challenged until he actually arrived at the perimeter of the rebels' encampment, which he did not long before midnight.

When he told the sentries his name and the nature of his business they allowed him to pass, and even provided an escort to take him directly to their leader's tent. He arrived there in a state of barely-suppressed trepidation, but Orlu--who had both Akabar and Cardelier in close attendance--did not seem displeased, or overly surprised, to see him. Cardelier shook his head sorrowfully as he met the magician's eye, but said nothing.

The merchant prince immediately ordered that his visitor should be given bread and fresh-cooked meat to eat, and honeyed wine to drink. Although Orlu did not share the meal he kept his guest company in quaffing the wine, and set a brisk pace in so doing. The meat was a little too red, and its fibres caught between Giraiazal's slowly rotting teeth, but he was hungry enough, and well-enough anaesthetized, not to care. When Giraiazal had finished eating, Orlu sent Akabar and Cardelier about their business so that he and the magician could talk privately.

"I have it on good authority that you succeeded in preserving my daughter's life in spite of my own failure to locate the source of her disease," Orlu said. "I am grateful to you for that. I'm less grateful for the declaration that was uttered in your name yesterday, but I understand how it came about, just as I understand how it came about that you now come to me as Viragan's ambassador. I shall not harm you--you may depend on that."

Giraiazal was prepared to believe that promise, because he was confident that Orlu's first impulse would be to try to use him, just as Viragan had. "Alas, I did not realise that your daughter was still in danger," Giraiazal said, partly because it seemed like safe conversational ground, and partly because it was a point he wanted to emphasize.

"Nor did I anticipate that she would be in any further danger, if only the disease could be cured," Orlu admitted, readily enough. "I did not realise how much danger I was in myself, when I went in search of that cure. Did Cardelier tell you what had happened to me when you spoke to him in Clarassour?"

"No, Your Highness."

"Forget the Highness--I'm a mere rebel now, it seems. My water-barrels had been spiked--not with a violent poison that would reveal itself as soon as the tainted casks were tapped, but with something slow-acting and stupefying. Then we were holed beneath the waterline, whether from within or without I never ascertained. We were lucky enough to make a landfall before the ship went down--had we taken to the boats thereafter we'd have made easy pickings for a pirate fleet that began quartering the region. Not Viragan's ships, of course--he was too sly for that--but old enemies who had found a new freedom to operate since Yura's collapse. We fought them on the island where we'd been cast ashore, but we couldn't have held out for long if they'd been entirely serious. Fortunately, they didn't take to the insects and the rats any more than we did, and they had the choice of going home and leaving us to rot.

"The isle where we were cast away was a foul place, without much shelter, and anything we built was torn apart soon enough by storms. The birds were lazy enough to provide us with some easy meat, but there were too many of us to be economically fed. We'd stripped the isle bare of nuts and edible beans within a tenday, and we had no nets or rods to help us fish, so we had to settle for small fry stranded by the tide. If we'd thought we'd be stranded there forever we'd likely have turned our minds to the prospect of playing the cannibal, but I knew that my captains would come after me, and I calculated that even if they didn't run into the particular scum who had followed us ashore they'd find others like them who had heard rumour of what had occurred. I knew it was a waiting game--but it was a very tedious wait, and I lost half my men to sickness before relief arrived. After that...well, I needed to know how many ships I could gather, and how many men I could count on. I wasn't among friends, no matter where I went to ground.

"I never did reach Kalasperanza, so I never had the chance to look for the cure for which I went in search--but I've been told that you nursed my daughter through her illness regardless, and restored her to health. I thank you for that with all my heart, and I beg you to tell me the truth of what went wrong thereafter. It's said that she was foully murdered, but no one seems to know for sure who did it. Do you?"

"The exact circumstances of Queen Calia's death remain shrouded in mystery," Giraiazal told him, after making some show of swallowing a fragment of food that he had been patiently excavating from a crack between his teeth. He was fearful of relaxing his guard too much. "You are expecting me to say that it was Viragan, and perhaps it was, though not necessarily in person. He is a clever man with a whisper. He has half-persuaded the credulous crowd that Urbishek's coral statue has come to life, possessed by a demon, but he may have persuaded Lysariel of something else entirely. At any rate, Lysariel killed his brother and called him murderer."

"To put it bluntly, then," Orlu said, "either you do not know the truth or you are afraid to tell me what it is."

"I have tried to use my powers to solve the puzzle," Giraiazal said, carefully, "but astrology and cartomancy are more useful for looking into the future than uncovering the secrets of the past. I cannot say for sure whether your daughter was murdered or not--or, if so, by whom." He took a deep sip from his flask in order to suppress a headache and oil his tongue. "Lysariel's cry cannot be taken as evidence that Manazzoryn really was guilty of Calia's murder. Lysariel's senses had been deranged for some time; he fell prey to strange delusions long before Calia recovered from her illness. I might have cured him, had I been given the chance, but I could not get near him. It is possible that Viragan only pretended to have lost him, and then sent him to kill his brother, having filled his muddled head with lies, but I cannot pretend to know what happened. Viragan's schemes have already gone awry twice, when Calia did not die from the spider-bite and you survived his trap. He is not as clever as he supposes, and may know less than he pretends."

That made Orlu thoughtful. "I can believe that," he conceded. "Is it possible, do you think, that the coral statue really is animate? Might it be the hidden player in the game?"

Giraiazal did not know how superstitious Orlu was--but that was not the only factor he had to bear in mind when framing his answer. He was trying to dislodge another stubborn piece of meat with the tip of his tongue, but it was too tightly gripped between his teeth. "I cannot say that it is impossible," he admitted, when he finally gave up the struggle. "We live in a world where few boundaries can be set to possibility. I dare not declare that the statue could not have walked away, nor that it could not have been responsible for Lysariel's apparent liberation from Viragan's custody. If even the tiniest fraction of the wisdom of lore and legend is true, stranger things have certainly happened. But I will say this: if there is some intelligence animating the coral statue, it is not the soul of your daughter Calia, Calia was alive and well when Lysariel became convinced that the statue was alive, and if it did walk away it did so before Calia fell to her death. If this creature is indeed a hidden player in our drama, it is playing its own game. It is not your ally."

Orlu looked long and hard at the magician. "Well," he said, "I suppose Cardelier is right. You do have the semblance of an honest man trapped in a dishonest vocation."

"I wish I could agree with you," Giraiazal answered, "but that is not what I believe or feel. My profession is as honest as it is permitted by circumstance to be. So am I. I wish we were both much better than we are."

Orlu smiled at that, albeit grimly.

"Well," he said, "we must agree to differ on that point. Be reassured, though. I shall not expect you to take my side openly until I win the war, even though I do not believe that you are Viragan's passive instrument. You examined the statue, did you not, even though the sculptor did not want you to come near it? Did it seem to you to be alive?"

Giraiazal sighed. "It did seem to me that the statue had changed its position very slightly when I last saw it," he admitted, "and I cannot account for the light that burns unsteadily inside it--but even if the coral is alive, that does not mean that the image can move as if it were a living human being."

Orlu nodded his huge head, while pensively tugging at his beard with his right hand. "If the statue was stolen," he said, eventually "where is it likely to be?"

"I have no idea," Giraiazal confessed. "All diviners have some skill in the art of sortilege, but in this instance my powers have proven inadequate. The supreme effort required to cure your daughter seems to have exhausted me. If the image was taken from the island by ship, you might be in a better position to find it than I am--but if it is still on the island, the first place I would want to look for it is Viragan's house. He did seem genuinely surprised when he heard that it was no longer in Lysariel's apartment, but he is a clever man and might have been pretending. If he does not have it, I cannot hazard a guess as to who might."

"That does seem the most likely hiding-place," Orlu agreed, although his manner was very off-hand. Giraiazal wondered whether Orlu might have another suspect in mind, but before he could ask, the pirate had shot another question to him. "Was the sculptor really guilty of sorcery, do you think?" Orlu wanted to know.

"If intention is guilt, Your Highness, it would be hard to find a man in Scleracina who is innocent. Everyone tries to use magic when desire outstrips reason--even men who do not really believe that it will work. As to whether his sorcery was effective...that depends what he was trying to achieve. It did not save his life."

Orlu nodded his head again, and took a deep draught from a cup that he had just refilled, as if to drown the darker component of the memory. "I suspected for a while that you might have had a hand in my misfortunes, "he told the magician, "and I might suspect you still if I had not had such firm assurances that you nursed my daughter back to health in spite of the curse that had been laid on her. I suspected Yura too, even though the apparatus of its oppression had collapsed--and the world has too little time left for the rebuilding of such complex instruments. I have tried to suspect this Urbishek, and even the coral image, no matter how absurd such suspicions seemed. I did not want to blame Viragan, you see. I wanted him to be the man he seemed to be: a friend and collaborator, satisfied to share good fortune with others. But he is not that kind of man, is he?"

"No," said Giraiazal. "He is not."

"He is the kind of man who would rather risk the ruination of all than settle for less than absolute dominion," Orlu went on, as if he still did not want to believe it. "Whenever he makes a concession, it is because he intends to recover what he has conceded and much more besides, by means of violence. I thought that he was content to let my daughter be the queen, but he was not. He wanted her to be the queen, so that she might be removed, leaving his own daughter without a potential rival. He wanted Lysariel to be king, so that he might be obliterated, and his brother with him. He is a man who would far rather stab a rival in the back than meet him face to face, and is prepared to go to considerable trouble to do so. I am not like that--I am the kind of man that he has only pretended to be. Do you believe that, Giraiazal?"

"Yes, I do," Giraiazal said, glad that he could say so honestly, although he would have said it dishonestly had he needed to.

"I hear that Viragan has confined the king again," Orlu said, with the air of a man returning to more practical matters. "He is keeping him under a stronger guard than before--presumably to deter another rescue attempt?"

"That is so," Giraiazal confirmed.

Orlu was looking at the magician very steadily now, measuring him with a stern gaze. "I am not the kind of man that Viragan is," he said, softly. "But I am the kind of man who will not tolerate treason. I am the kind of man who does not like to be cheated, or slyly attacked. I will see justice done in Scleracina, and a rightful king upon its throne or I will die trying." In spite of the wine he had drunk--and Giraiazal suspected that Orlu had been drinking for some while before his arrival--the pirate prince pronounced his words very sharply, with meticulous precision. Giraiazal waited for Orlu to continue, certain that he had more to say.

"The two people who stood between Viragan and the regency have died with unreasonable alacrity, have they not?" Orlu eventually went on. "One slain by an unknown hand, and the other by a madman who had been in Viragan's custody until he was mysteriously set free. I am not the only man betrayed by Viragan--he is a traitor to the entire realm. But I will not ask you to make any public declaration to that effect, or even to tell him that I said so when you return to Clarassour, lest he should blame the messenger for the message. What I want you to tell him is this: that I will meet him, man to man, in any place of his choosing and at any time of his choosing--and that if he does not care to choose, I shall make my own arrangements. You were sent here to persuade me to go away, or to undermine my authority over my captains, but you cannot do either of those things. I cannot be persuaded to go away, and my captains cannot be persuaded to abandon me, no matter what the stars may say, or any other of your oracles. Unlike Viragan, I do not think you are a liar or a charlatan, and if you were to tell me that I really am fated to lose this war, I would believe you--but that is not the reason why I have not asked you the question. The truth is that even if the universe is set against me, I intend to fight--but my fight is with Viragan, not with Scleracina. If he wants peace, as I do, then we may all have peace--provided that he will fight me man to man. Only persuade him to do that, and you will have succeeded in your diplomatic mission. There is no need for war, if

239

Viragan does not want war, but there must be a settlement between the two of us. Will you tell him that?"

"I will," Giraiazal promised, "but I do not think he will agree to your terms."

"Nor do I," Orlu confessed. "But I shall do my very best to make myself clear, and I shall be grateful for any help you can give me. I do not want a war; I am a man of business, who values a comfortable life above all else--all the more so since there is so little time left for the cultivation of comforts--but I am not afraid of war. I am the father of a daughter who has been foully murdered, and I am in honour bound to seek vengeance. All I want is to meet my enemy, face to face. I shall let that be known, to everyone who cares to listen."

"Viragan will call you a madman," Giraiazal said, quietly. "He will say that he is not your enemy, and that you too have been cursed by the coral bride. When he comes after you, he will come with an army."

"I know that," Orlu said. "But if I can have my way, I will. If Damozel Fate is kind, I shall have my confrontation. All I want is to face Viragan in a fair fight. If I am fated to lose that contest, so be it. If I win, though, I shall have need of your wisdom, your intelligence and your art, and you may be sure of my friendship. I trust you, Giraiazal, because you lifted the curse that was put upon my daughter, even though the outcome of your struggle was to force the one who cursed her to substitute brute force for skill, with the same end-result. If you had not done that, I would not know, even now, who my enemy is. I trust you now to understand that my enemy is your enemy, and to deal with me as one honest man with another."

Giraiazal knew that all of this was seduction and manipulation--that Orlu hoped to make use of him just as Viragan had made use of him. But what could he say? What could any man say in response to a speech like that?

"You shall have all the support that I can give you from within our enemy's camp, my lord," the magician promised, judiciously. "If I can persuade Viragan to meet you man-to-man I shall do it--and if I cannot persuade him, I will do whatever I can to ensure that you get your chance regardless of his wishes. But in the meantime, I shall have to pretend as cleverly as I possibly can that I am taking his side."

"And that," said Orlu, "is what Cardelier means when he says that you are an honest man trapped in a ludicrously dishonest vocation."

10

Wherever and whatever our most distant cousins are now, we may be sure that they have long since forsaken the emotion and mortality which shaped the lives of primal humans--but they must have given these disabilities back to us deliberately, either for reasons of aesthetic propriety or fond nostalgia.

My reasons for believing this are entirely logical, and based upon what I consider to be reliable evidence, but I admit that I do feel a certain warm contentment in being spared the dreadful suspicion that we are nothing but discarded relics: the mortal residue of that which was cast aside by other and better humankinds, carelessly eliminated from their wondrous Epic and condemned to die with the bloody and senescent sun. Even if I harboured that suspicion, however--and I am addressing myself now to a hypothetical reader who presumably does--there is one consolation I could still retain. Even if the worst possible interpretation of our predicament were accepted, there would still be one thing of which we could be legitimately glad, and proud.

No matter how many or how few humankinds have preceded us, we are the first and the only ones to be truly free.

We, and we alone, know that the world has no future beyond the span of our petty and ridiculous lives, because we know that our children--or, at best, our children's children--will be consumed by the final death-throes of our parent star. Of all the generations of all the humankinds that ever were, ours is therefore the first to be free of any obligation to make provision for the future.

The Revelations of Suomynona, the Last Prophet

"I have had a very bad time, Master Magician," Orlu said. The wine he had quaffed had made him garrulous, driving him to continue the conference even though he had said what he needed to say.

"Yes, Your Highness," Giraiazal said. "I understand that."

"Stupefaction, shipwreck, storms, starvation...." Orlu went on. "and then, to survive all that only to discover that my beloved daughter the fledgling queen is dead, having first been ruined by the poison whose cure I tried to find, then cruelly felled by an assassin's hand. Her husband the king is imprisoned as a madman....and my adversary Viragan is regent, swollen with pride at everything he has accomplished. Have your oracles told you, Giraiazal, that Manazzoryn's unborn child is destined to sit for a long time upon the throne?"

"They have assured me of it, my lord" Giraiazal murmured, relaxing because the serious work appeared to have been done and because the prodigious amounts of opium he had quaffed had rendered him dangerously calm. "Zintrah's son will be king, and will enjoy a longer and happier reign than his father." He realised as soon as the words were out of his mouth that he had said more than he intended, but for a few moments Orlu only looked perplexed. Then the implication of what Giraiazal had said finally sank in.

"His father?" the merchant prince echoed, incredulously. "Are you saying that the child is Lysariel's, and not Manazzoryn's?"

"I believe so," Giraiazal admitted, knowing that he had no way to retract the implication, "but I cannot be absolutely certain. Every oracle at my disposal speaks forcefully of the regal future awaiting the son of Lysariel--but it is not impossible that Lysariel has another son, somewhere on this peninsula. Then again, perhaps the son anticipated by the oracles is yet to be sired."

"But you have cared for Zintrah as you have cared for Calia. You must know more than your oracles have told you."

"I know that Zintrah helped us seduce Lysariel away from his coral fetish when his delusions were bad," Giraiazal said, carefully. "I know that Zintrah spent a good deal of time at her father's house when Lysariel was first taken there. And I cannot help but wonder whether Lysariel was so ready to believe the worst of Manazzoryn because his own conscience was troubling him."

As Orlu considered the import of these revelations his eyes grew dark and his features set like stone; his intoxication was shifting into a bleaker phase. "So the only thing of which anyone can be perfectly certain," he said, "is that the child is the grandson of Viragan."

"That was always certain," Giraiazal agreed.

"Would it have amused my friend, do you think, to have contrived matters in such a way that even though my Calia was married to the king, it would be his own daughter who got his child?"

Giraiazal said nothing in immediate answer to that, although silence was as affirmative as any words he might have spoken. After a pause, he said: "Viragan could not have known that Lysariel would be so badly affected by Calia's illness. He could not have anticipated the opportunity of which Zintrah took advantage. If Lysariel had stayed by Calia's bedside, as a good husband would have done....if he had not had the image to put in her place...."

"I take your point," Orlu said, coldly. "Viragan is a clever man; he makes opportunities, and he takes opportunities, as the situation requires. He was always an expert haggler. You will forgive me, Master Magician, if I beg leave to hope, in spite of all your oracles, that Zintrah's child might be a girl."

"Certainly," the magician said.

"But you do believe that it will be a boy, and that he is fated to live long and prosper?"

"He will reign for a long time, if the oracles can be trusted," Giraiazal confirmed, still choosing his words carefully, "but that implies nothing as to Viragan's future, or yours. What I have foreseen is that Scleracina's season of of troubles is hardly begun, let alone concluded."

"The island will soon be racked by fighting, then by hunger and disease," Orlu said. "You see, I can play the prophet too. But I have an advantage in that regard. I could see to it that those predictions come true, if I wished. I only wish that I could see to it that they did not--but that prerogative, alas, is Viragan's. Are you perfectly certain that a son of Lysariel will emerge from this season of troubles to preside over its aftermath?"

"As certain as I can be," Giraiazal said, stubbornly.

"Well then, "Orlu said, darkly, "if that is the promise of Damozel Fate and the presumption of prophetic wisdom, it only remains to men of my humble kind to bow to the inevitability. You and I must do whatever we can to ensure that this future king is advised by good and honourable men, and not by villains."

"I will know more," Giraiazal said, "When I know the day and hour of the child's birth."

"I dare say you will," Orlu told him. "It may be that you shall know more than you suppose, even before that day arrives. You will sleep, I dare say, before you ride back to Clarassour? You look as if you need to. "

"If I can," Giraiazal answered, his anxiety referring to his saddle-sores rather than to the twinges of conscience, "and if I may."

"You shall have the best bed in the camp," Orlu promised. "While you rest, I shall instruct Captain Akabar to write a letter to my dear friend and fellow merchant prince, to explain why I have made my camp here, and to invite him to the meeting of which I spoke earlier. He is less likely to be angry with you, I think, if you carry a written message rather than having to voice my conditions yourself."

"You are very thoughtful, my lord," Giraiazal assured him

"I am more thoughtful now than I have ever been before," Orlu told him, "and I owe that to you. Sleep soundly, my friend."

Perhaps it was his skill as a morpheomorphist, or the effect of the wine, but Giraiazal did sleep soundly. He also slept for a much longer time than he had anticipated--and that was most certainly due to the stress of his unaccustomed exertions of the previous day. If he was troubled by bad dreams they fled the reach of his memory as soon as he awoke.

Orlu had obviously been up and about for hours, if he had slept at all; he was remarkably unkempt when he came to see Giraiazal. Even so, he greeted the magician heartily, gave him a good breakfast and ordered that his saddle and luggage should be fitted to his horse.

"Are you well enough to do this, Giraiazal?" he asked.

"I feel much better today than I did yesterday," the magician assured him. I am a little sore, but the fresh air has done me good, and sleep has completed its work."

When Giraiazal had climbed on to the horse he had borrowed from the palace stables, Orlu gave him a sealed letter to carry to Viragan. "I dare say we might avoid war, if Viragan could bring himself to act honourably," the pirate told Giraiazal, as he bade him farewell, "but I cannot believe that he will. You have foreseen troubles, and troubles there will doubtless be. It need not be the kind of conflict that sets family against family, town against town and businessman against businessman, if Viragan will only see reason, but he has never been a reasonable man." The bright morning light did not seem to have infected the merchant warrior with optimism; the shadow in his dark and careworn eyes was black and bleak, and his stance was one of resignation.

Giraiazal agreed with Orlu's judgment that Viragan would never agree to meet him in an honest duel, and not merely because Viragan was slightly the smaller of the two; he too feared the worst. His aches and pains were redoubled as soon as his mount set off, and his mood grew worse as he crossed the island from north to south. He soon realised, moreover, that events had moved on while he slept.

The very first inn at which the magician paused to rest his horse and take a little refreshment was all abuzz with the news that a troop of a hundred men had attacked Viragan's house during the night, killing thirteen of the regent's servants. It was only by a freak of chance, apparently, that Viragan had made good his own escape before the house was put to the torch. The attackers had suffered even heavier casualties, leaving no less than thirty dead men behind when they made their retreat--but they had got what they came for. They had seized Lysariel before withdrawing into the last fugitive shadows of the dying night.

Giraiazal was unable to enjoy his meal, and rushed through it. He ordered a new horse to replace the one Orlu had provided, and rode to Clarassour at a canter so violent that he was almost thrown every time it was necessary to turn a corner or halt at a crossing. When he arrived at the palace, it was to find that Viragan had already issued a proclamation from the palace gate, declaring that Orlu was a traitor and an outlaw who must be hunted down with all expedition and put to death.

Giraiazal had no alternative but to hand over the sealed letter he bore, although he felt a distinct thrill of anxiety as he watched the regent break the seal and hand the text to Sharuman. The moments that passed while the captain whispered the message into his master's ear, while even the Lord Chancellor tried in vain to make out what was being said, were uncomfortably long; the magician had to steel himself to meet the prince's angry gaze thereafter.

"Do you know what is written here, peacemaker?" Viragan demanded.

"Not exactly, Your Highness," Giraiazal hastened to say. "I only know that as he gave it into my hands, Orlu told me that he believed that war might be averted and your differences settled."

"He lied," Viragan said, tersely. "What did you say to him, by way of making peace?"

"I told him that we had all been hurt by tragedy," Giraiazal said, making every effort to feign sincerity. "I told him that we all stood in need of healing. I told him that the fate of the realm, and Manazzoryn's unborn child, hung in the balance, and that it would require two brave, strong and generous men working in unison to save the situation. I also told him that my oracles were unanimous in declaring that he could not win, and that the only hope that he and his captains had of living any longer and finding any kind contentment was entirely dependent on their leaving Scleracina, separately or together, and never returning. I was very eloquent, Your Highness, and I am sure that my words were widely overheard. I did not imagine...."

"No," Viragan broke in. "you did not imagine that he would send his men a-raiding while you slept in his tent, or that he would take your promises and threats so lightly. You're a fool, Master Magician, like all your kind. You try so hard to see what is written in the stars that you are blind to the obvious. But I'm partly to blame, for thinking that Orlu might be persuaded to see sense, and waiting patiently for your return when I ought to have been making sure of my own defences."

"Is there no possibility of putting an end to this conflict?" Triasymon asked.

"See for yourself," said Viragan, snatching the letter from Sharuman's hands and thrusting it into the Lord Chancellor's hand--but Triasymon had never learned to read either. Viragan took it back again and gave it to Giraiazal.

"He calls me usurper," Viragan said, furiously, as Giraiazal's eyes scanned the parchment. "He calls me murderer, thief and traitor. He accuses me of killing the queen, of telling Lysariel falsely that Manazzoryn was to blame, of stealing the statue of his daughter and putting false rumours about to represent it as some vengeful demon brought to lie by black magic. Lies, every word of it! All lies! And he demands what he calls *satisfaction*, insisting that I meet him in a trial by ordeal to prove my innocence."

It was an accurate account of what Orlu's scribe had written; Giraiazal had no difficulty imagining the tone in which Orlu had dictated the missive to Akabar. Viragan's indignation was equally palpable, and so seemingly transparent that Giraiazal could almost have believed that the regent meant every word he said. He wondered whether it might not have been better, after all, had Orlu let him deliver a message orally, and he could not bring himself to be grateful for Orlu's kindness in sparing him the sight of what had actually been written on the parchment.

"What can we do?" Triasymon asked. "What can we do to prevent this catastrophe?"

"Nothing," Viragan said, succinctly. "The catastrophe is already upon us. We did not want a war, but we have one. Now, there is only one thing to be done, and that is to win the war. Every man in Scleracina who is charged with the responsibility of maintaining arms and armour must put on the royal colours, and report for duty to his appointed commander. Anyone who does not report before nightfall must be reckoned a traitor. We must send envoys out to every village, every hamlet, every fisherman's cot. We must gather as many men as possible under our command, and make the most of our undoubted advantage in numbers. How many men does Orlu have with him, Master Magician?"

Giraiazal had not counted, or even taken the trouble to make a good estimate, but it did not seem to be a good time to confess ignorance. "Eight hundred and eighty," he said, having decided that a round number might sound like a guess, or a careless approximation. He wondered whether it might be worth raising the question of whether Viragan ought to consider the possibility of demonstrating his innocence of the charges levelled against him in a formal trial by ordeal, given the assurance of all available oracles that he was sure to prevail.

"He must still have a hundred or more loyal servants in Clarassour," said Viragan, "even discounting those who were killed last night. We must send men to arrest the ones who are known to us, although the greater number will be skulking along the hedgerows by now. He will have men in every other port, no matter how small, but so have I—and I command the loyalty of everyone whose first and only allegiance is to the throne. We can overwhelm him, if we are quick enough. We can smash his army before its ranks are properly formed, if we are as swift as we are decisive."

"But..." Triasymon began—and then bit his tongue. Even Triasymon could see that the regent was in no mood to hear objections. The Lord Chancellor stood quietly aside while Viragan sent forth his orders in a stream, screaming at regular intervals for more men to carry them. It was not until the regent had finished giving out urgent instructions that he looked at Giraiazal with a more equable expression.

"You look terrible, Master Magician," Viragan observed.

"I need rest, Your Highness, and medication," Giraiazal said. "If I might be permitted to retire?"

"Go to your bed, then! And when you next consult the stars, make sure that they utter definite prophecies of Orlu's death and my success."

"I shall do my very best, Your Highness," Giraiazal promised, and crept away. He managed to climb the staircase to his room without calling for assistance, but it seemed a hollow victory by the time he reached the top.

Had every man supposedly obliged to keep arms for Scleracina's defence actually done so, Viragan could have mustered an army several thousand strong within a day, but the island had been subject to Yura for far too long. Few of its citizens had any weapons in store, and most of those who did keep weapons had long since lost the habit of keeping them in good repair. As things were, the trickle of men reporting for duty to Viragan's hastily-commissioned recruiting sergeants never seemed likely to become a flood.

Even as the regent was hurling forth his instructions, moreover, the rumour was flying through the streets of Clarassour that Orlu had made a new pledge of allegiance to King Lysariel, who was mad no longer, and who would take personal command of the forces massing in the north, thus making them the legitimate army of Scleracina.

Giraiazal, who was no longer content to rely on Burrel as a mouthpiece for gossip, did not remain long in his bed, nor even in his rooms. He began to move about the palace as discreetly as possible, taking the utmost care to study the continued progress of the new whispering campaign. He had no difficulty doing so, despite the insulation provided by the palace walls.

The magician was glad to discover that the rumour had also gone far and wide that Orlu had challenged Viragan to a duel, so that their differences might be settled without any other bloodshed, but that Viragan had refused the challenge.

Giraiazal guessed that both the rumours of Lysariel's recovery and Orlu's challenge would grow as they flew--especially the first, which lent itself more readily to further embroidery. He was correct, although he was a trifle anxious when Burrel, jealous of the competition he now faced, took care to report insouciantly that Giraiazal's own name was now being widely mentioned in connection with the sorceries that had brought disaster to the island.

Ordinary grief occasioned by the king's loss of his beloved Calia, it was now said, had been exacerbated and perverted, first by the malignity of the seductive statue and then by the effects of a magnum of wine given to Lysariel as a wedding-present by his vizier, who had been under the mistaken impression that it had come from ancient Yethlyreom. Speculators differed, according to Burrel, as to whether or not another wine had been substituted for the intended gift by an agent of Yura bent on revenge for Scleracina's secession from the empire. At any rate, the intoxicating effects of the addictive liquor had been further amplified by the consequence of its withdrawal, which had plunged the king into such abyssal depths of confusion and anguish that he had slain his own brother. Time had allowed him to recover his former equilibrium, however, and he now understood exactly what had been done to him...and by whom.

Giraiazal suspected that Orlu was too sharp a player to lay out all his cards at once, and that there would be more and worse to come. It appeared, however, that this first propagandistic salvo was more than sufficient to instil doubt into the minds of many of the yeomen who were bound to answer a summons to the defence of the realm. Some of those who put on the royal colours in readiness to report to the palace to receive orders from the regent's men must have gone inland instead, in search of King Lysariel and his general Orlu. A far greater number must have hesitated, keeping their options open while awaiting further developments--with the result that Viragan's army did not grow nearly as rapidly as he had hoped or anticipated.

Every new day brought a new raft of rumours, some of them so carefully crafted that even Giraiazal was lost in admiration of their craftiness. It was said that the great artist Urbishek had not been a sorcerer at all, but had been deluded into thinking the luminous coral would be the ideal fabric for a statue, as had the unfortunate Lysariel. It was suggested that the mischievous spirit that had possessed the statue had actually been imported into it by the man who had condemned Urbishek as a magician and had extracted a false confession from him by torture: Viragan. As for the murder of Calia, if it had indeed been a murder at all--Giraiazal was deeply impressed by the cunning modesty of the claim--rumour now said that no one could possibly take seriously the claim that Manazzoryn had been responsible. Only one person had gained by the tragic death of Scleracina's queen, and that had been the man who now ruled as regent in the name of his unborn grandson: Viragan.

Under ordinary circumstances, slanders of this kind would never have been voiced within the palace--but this was a time of war, and official opposition only gave them greater currency. This second broadside of hearsay undoubtedly sent more men-at-arms to gather about Lysariel's standard, but it seemed to have an even greater effect on those who had already reported for duty to Viragan's commanders, who began to desert in considerable numbers, thinking that the impending war now seemed far too finely balanced for their liking.

In the meantime, news of the challenge that Orlu had issued to his erstwhile friend, offering to settle all matters outstanding between them in a duel, continued to spread and to attract a great deal of sympathetic attention.

Brian Stableford

Part Four

Brian Stableford

The Revenge of the Coral Bride

1

There is nothing like a war for increasing the demand for a prophet's warnings. In times of peace, people are inclined to take the future for granted; although they know perfectly well that disaster may strike at any time, like lighting from a cloudless sky, they find it difficult to be direly anxious when all seems to be well. As soon as their neighbourhood and nation are immersed in conflict, however, they become obsessed with the calculus of fate and chance. Experience suggests that for every man violently dispatched in the course of a war half a hundred perish from hunger and disease in the war's aftermath, but it is the violence of battle that excites the imagination and focuses attention on the question that drives more men to oracles than any other, thirsty for intelligence: *shall I be safe?*

Alas, there is no time less profitable for the consultation of the stars and the dealing of cards than the days surrounding the outbreak of a war. No matter how dutiful the Motile Entities may be in dancing a reflection of events to come, they are limited in their expression. When events move swiftly, when countless individuals are faced with urgent choices, when the best-laid schemes unravel and the most fervent desires become confused, the very stars are dazzled. No matter how many trumps a deck of cards may possess, nor how ingeniously they may be laid out by the seeker after inspiration, the stories they suggest have too much narrative order in them, and too much vulgar normality, to express the arbitrariness and sheer insanity of war.

The Revelations of Suomynona, the Last Prophet

Giraiazal had not lied when he assured Captain Cardelier that he did not consider himself to be an honest man in pursuit of a dishonest vocation, but he had not told the whole truth. Like every other diviner, he was conscious of the extent of his own improvisations--and, like every other diviner, he feared that every other diviner might be less dependent on such artifice than he was. His real attitude, although he would never have confessed it, was more nearly the opposite of Cardelier's: that he was a dishonest man doing the best he could to protect the honour of an honest profession.

War brought self-doubts bubbling to the surface of the magician's consciousness that might otherwise have been repressed. As the demand for his testimony increased by leaps and bounds he began to admonish himself privately with fierce accusations--that he was careless in his observations, inept in his calculations, uncreative in his interpretations and unadventurous in his prescriptions--even though he knew that the only rational manner in which to meet the hectic demand for his services was to improvise and invent.

What he had to do, according to all the relevant calculations of necessity, was to provide his clients with a measure of reassurance and a measure of hope, without actually making any firm predictions as to the possibility of their survival. The chief difficulty in flowing this policy was linguistic, in that he had to couch exactly the same advice in dozens, if not hundreds, of different phraseological formulas.

Fortunately, the man most likely to be resentful of evasions, platitudes and meagre manifestations of doubt was far too busy to plague his Grand Vizier with demands for enlightenment. Viragan was already well enough aware that if he were to triumph over his enemy he must act swiftly, before Orlu could amass an army capable of storming the city, and before his own incompletely-gathered forces suffered any further depletion. Four days after Giraiazal's return, therefore, Viragan marched out of Clarassour with a force of eleven hundred men, five hundred horses and three hundred wagons, intending to meet Orlu on the nearest convenient battlefield. Before he left he gave Triasymon and Giraiazal extremely stern instructions to see that Zintrah was well cared for.

Zintrah was not as fearful as she might have been, because her father had assured her that all would be well and she had grown used to accepting his assurances, Even so, the circumstances in which she found herself were very stressful. Giraiazal had to give her potions to help her sleep on more than one occasion, although he was careful to make them innocuous lest they affect her unborn child. He often had to sit with her during the strength-sapping hours of midday and the ominously deep hours of midnight darkness. In the meantime, it was left to Triasymon to receive the dispatches that Viragan sent back, have them read to him, and execute the instructions contained therein.

It was as well, Giraiazal thought, that Viragan had set up a council of his most experienced captains to see to the defence of the city, because that did not seem to be the sort of task for which the Lord Chancellor's own education and experience had prepared him. On the fourth day after Viragan's departure, however, Triasymon dutifully came to Zintrah's apartment to summarize all the news he had received for the benefit of the queen-in-all-but-name and her faithful physician.

"There has been no battle yet," Triasymon told them. "Orlu has chosen to retreat before Viragan's advance. For the time being, he seems intent on keeping his little army on the move, thus requiring Viragan's army to pursue him. Wherever he goes, Orlu requisitions the food his followers require from the local landholders, then burns all the remaining supplies. His strategy, for the present, is to force Viragan's men to follow in his wake and to ensure that while they do so they will become hungry and frustrated."

"And what will my father do to counter that strategy?" Zintrah asked.

"He has not confided his strategies to me," was Triasymon's answer.

"Of course he has not put them in writing," Zintrah retorted, impatiently. "There is always a risk that dispatches sent from a moving force to its base will be intercepted and read. But the captains he left here must know, even if you do not, what the logical counter-move must be."

"I assume, Your Highness, that he will attempt a pincer movement," Giraiazal put in, soothingly. "He will calculate the direction in which Orlu's army will move, and send a portion of his own forces to occupy some high coign of vantage or narrow bottleneck, from which they may mount a delaying action. If that advance-guard can hold the ground for as little as half a day, Viragan's main contingent will be able to close the gap, thus trapping Orlu's forces between two fronts."

"But if he divides his company," Zintrah pointed out, "his numerical advantage will count for less."

"That is true, Your Highness," Giraiazal conceded. "The strategy carries a certain risk. If Orlu discovers what Viragan has done--assuming, for the moment, that Viragan has done what I have suggested--he will not engage the advance-guard at all. As soon as he discovers their position he will probably reverse the direction of his own march and fall upon Viragan's depleted force before they can arrange themselves to their own best advantage. But Viragan will anticipate exactly such a move, so he will have given instructions to his advance-guard that if they see the enemy turn, instead of coming forward to engage them, they should make all haste to fall upon them from the rear, thus completing the pincer movement on a different field. On the other hand, Orlu, having anticipated this manoeuvre...."

"Enough!" Zintrah cried. "Who will win, Giraiazal? Just tell me that."

"All the indications favour Viragan, at present," Giraiazal replied, honestly enough. "Orlu is but recently returned to the island, and his organization has been considerably depleted while he was away. Viragan has not been regent long enough to generate fervent rebellious sentiment; although his army has suffered desertions and he has had to make certain

255

that Clarassour can be defended, he ought to be able to make up those losses quite easily--and Orlu will not endear himself to the islanders by stealing the bulk of their stores and destroying the remainder. Viragan ought to be victorious in the end, unless some unexpected disaster overtakes his forces."

Once they had quit Zintrah's apartment, however, the news that Triasymon shared with Giraiazal was not as straightforward.

"There are rumours circulating," the chancellor told the vizier, "not merely in the port but in the palace, which say that the child in Zintrah's womb is not Manazzoryn's but Lysariel's."

"Are there indeed?" Giraiazal murmured, feigning amazement. "I cannot imagine where labourers and kitchen-servants might come by an idea like that--but we are at war now, and there is such a profusion of rumours in circulation that no sensible person will be prepared to credit any of them."

"But this is a very awkward rumour," Triasymon said, fretfully. "There was confusion enough in the minds of Scleracina's liege-men already. The notion that Manazzoryn's wife might have betrayed him, with his brother the king, is bringing in a rich harvest of uncertainty. The assurances you gave to Her Highness just now are simply not reliable-- especially since you did not see fit to remind her that Orlu has Lysariel with him, who is still the king. We do not know how many of Viragan's men are likely to fall away or switch sides as their long march goes on. His notional advantage is melting away with every day that passes, and Orlu is leading him a merry dance. If the armies do not meet soon, the hunter many become the hunted." The Lord Chancellor did not seem entirely convinced that this would be a bad thing, but he had better sense than to say so, even to Giraiazal. Triasymon also had more sense than to confess his awareness of other rumours that called his own loyalties into question, on the grounds that his only surviving nephew was now in the rebel camp, just as Giraiazal knew better than to observe that had the rumours been believable, Triasymon ought indeed to have switched sides.

"Our duty is to maintain calm in the palace," Giraiazal told the fretful Chancellor, in a hushed whisper. "Whichever force returns to Clarassour victorious, you and I ought to be ready to welcome them. Whoever wins this silly war, life must go on...at least for a little while. Perhaps Lysariel is sane and perhaps he is not. Perhaps Viragan will win the forthcoming battle, and perhaps he will not. Whatever the outcome might be, we ought to be ready. Be patient, Lord Chancellor, even if you cannot be calm. And above all else, be careful."

More dispatches arrived on the eve of the following day to say that the two armies had come into conflict, but that no resolution of their differences had yet been attained.

"What does that mean?" Zintrah demanded, when the information was relayed to her.

"It means that there will be another battle tomorrow, Your Highness," Giraiazal told her, deciding for once to be blunt.

"What does it really mean?" Triasymon asked, when he and the magician had left her quarters again.

"It means that the two sides have now tested one another's resolve," Giraiazal told him. "If both commanders are satisfied, there will be a real battle tomorrow. If neither one is satisfied, they will make another half-hearted attempt to engage and then fall back. If only one is satisfied...."

"You are supposed to be a prophet," Triasymon reminded him. "What will actually occur?"

Giraiazal shrugged his shoulders. "The stars and common sense are both inclined to favour the supposition that few men on either side of this sort of conflict have much stomach for real fighting," he said. "Both sides must have gone into today's skirmish looking for an excuse to withdraw-- but that withdrawal can only be temporary while their ultimate commanders are determined to fight. The officers will force the infantrymen to engage the enemy again--and again and again, if necessary--until they accept that there is no way out of the impasse but victory. When the mood of the fighting-men changes, they will throw caution to the winds and substitute bloodlust. That may happen tomorrow, or the next day, or the next--but eventually, it will happen. Then there will be a real battle, and a real tragedy. As to who will win...I doubt that the Motile Entities and the major arcana have come to a firm decision, as yet."

The magician was as confident of this analysis as any prediction he had ever offered; remarkably, it turned out to be quite mistaken. On the third day thereafter the dispatches told a very different story, and the riders delegated to carry them had tales of their own. Even Triasymon could understand the gist of it, although Giraiazal took far greater care to piece the evidence together so that he could form a proper estimate of what had occurred. This time, he did not attempt to display his cleverness by offering his conclusions to Zintrah or her uncle-in-law.

What had happened, the magician deduced, was that the common soldiers on both sides had calculated the logic of their situation in much the same way that he had. They had realised that no matter how reluctant they and their designated enemies might be to spill one another's blood, their officers would eventually leave them no option, forcing them back into the field until fear made them furious. Having made this estimate, they had gone into the running battle's third day with the tacit intention of leaving those whose fight it actually was to engage one another directly, as Orlu had so often, and so loudly, demanded.

Giraiazal knew that it could not have been easy for the men in the ranks to contrive a situation in which Orlu and Viragan actually came face-to-face. He guessed that they could not have done so without a measure of co-operation from the princes' captains--but it seemed that even the ex-pirates' closest and most practised henchmen had grown used to conflicts that were far less evenly balanced, and whose profitability was far more easily discernible. The problem with making an army of men who were used to fighting for reasons of business rather than reasons of politics, he supposed, was that their minds were apt to remain focused on loot rather than glory when their loyalty was put to the ultimate test.

Thus it was, Giraiazal deduced, that when Orlu and Viragan had been persuaded to come within a blade's reach of one another, the supporters who ought to have been surrounding and protecting them had not only fallen into a sudden disarray, but had actually paused in their own combats to await the outcome of the contest of the generals. Such things must have happened a thousand or a million times before, Giraiazal realised, but those left to tell the tales had always reinterpreted them in terms of the heroism of the few rather than the discretion of the many.

For fully half an hour, Giraiazal was avidly informed, the two merchant princes--who were so very nearly equals in skill and experience--had traded blow for blow. He knew that storytellers are overfond of such finely-balanced conflicts, and are prone to underestimate the cumulative effect that cuts and bruises have on human flesh, but in this case he was persuaded to set scepticism aside. The onlookers were violent men, who understood that only the rarest fights last more than half a dozen thrusts, and that even those are apt to end with both combatants falling exhausted to the ground, so they must have been honestly astonished to see that this particular fight really did involve men of uncommon determination, skill and stubbornness.

Orlu and Viragan had kept on hacking away at one another with their swords long after their arms should have grown too tired to lift a reed, and they had kept on intercepting one another's blows with their shields and their mailed forearms long after their flesh should have wasted into a mass of bloody pulp. By the end of the half-hour, the pauses between their thrusts had extended to two minutes and more, but both men were still standing, and neither was inclined to call a truce. Their officers were ready to swear that they might have continued for half an hour more, had Orlu not slipped in the broad pool of slowly-leaked blood that had formed about his feet, so heavily that he lay supine on the floor with his arms outstretched, unable to lift so much as a hand.

It had taken Viragan another two minutes to take up a position standing over his enemy, feet astride his abdomen, but once he was there it had required only a little extra effort to run the stricken man through.

Because Viragan had aimed for the softer target of the belly rather than risk blunting his weapon on Orlu's ribs, the beaten man had had time enough to curse his slayer very loudly and with some elaboration before the victor turned away. The envoys sent to relay the news had memorized the stream of curses very competently, and had no difficulty in improvising whenever a gap crept in. Giraiazal could not be sure whether they were being honest or merely flattering when they reported that Viragan had mocked his opponent by telling him that his doom had been foretold by Giraiazal the Great, and that Orlu had acknowledged his folly before adding a few more curses of an especially bloodcurdling nature.

Fortunately, the envoys reported, the observers of the duel had all been very well aware of the fact that a dead man's curses have little or no effect, unless he happens to be a powerful magician, so Orlu's former followers had instantly thrown down their weapons and proclaimed their loyalty to Prince Viragan the Mighty, and to Queen Zintrah's unborn child. If any were troubled by the necessity of swearing such an oath they kept their doubts to themselves.

Although very near to collapse himself, the envoys reported, Viragan still had voice enough to welcome these new followers, and charity enough--although Giraiazal interpreted it as prudence--to order no immediate reprisal for their temporary dereliction of duty. He had, however, commanded that King Lysariel should be brought to him immediately. Alas, this had proved to be impractical. Although Lysariel had been seen in Orlu's close company immediately before the commencement of the duel, he had evidently left the field some time before its end. There was no sign of him.

Triasymon, as might be expected, received this news with mixed feelings. "Poor boy," he said to Zintrah and Giraiazal. "The madness must have come upon him again, if it had ever really let him go."

"Poor boy," echoed Zintrah, but said no more.

"At least he is alive," Triasymon said. "That, for me, is the best part of this whole sad story."

Giraiazal, on the other hand, could only see the final item of news as bad. While Lysariel remained alive but unaccounted for, the rumours that Orlu had put into circulation and enforced with his dying curses could not be conclusively laid to rest. Indeed, they would continue to thrive on the mystery of the king's whereabouts and the uncertainty as to his state of mind.

Viragan's cavalrymen began filtering back into the port soon after nightfall, but his infantry lagged far behind and Viragan was apparently in no state to ride.

It was not until the following noonday, therefore, that the cart in which the Prince Regent was lying pulled up outside the palace. By that time, however Viragan was sufficiently well-rested to get down unaided and to walk proudly up the steps to the great oaken door, buoyed up by the enthusiastic cheers of the crowd that had gathered in the courtyard. His daughter was there to meet him, as were his loyal Lord Chancellor and Grand Vizier.

"You have won a great victory for truth and justice, Your Highness," Giraiazal proclaimed, raising his voice so that the assembled multitude might hear it very clearly. "Everything has come about exactly as I foresaw it!"

"My victory might have been foretold by the stars," Viragan assured him, unable to speak quite as loudly as he might have wished, "But it still required winning. I hope that you will not claim all the credit for yourself, my friend." He was obviously in a good mood in spite of the battering he had suffered

"Are you terribly hurt, father?" Zintrah asked, anxiously.

"Sore rather than hurt," was the merchant prince's reply. "Nothing that one of your pain-killing potions won't soothe, Master Magician--as you doubtless foresaw."

Giraiazal had indeed anticipated this particular need, and he produced the necessary flask of opium with a flourish, carefully displaying it to the crowd before handing it to his master. Viragan recklessly--and perhaps unwisely--drank its contents down in a single draught before lurching through the doorway.

It was a moment of triumph for everyone who cared to claim a share of it, and a moment to savour--but Giraiazal did not linger long among the intoxicated, even when Viragan fell into a sleep so deep that he obviously would not be waking up the same day.

The magician knew that Viragan's returning army must have left behind a legacy of bitter resentment, which would extend throughout the farmlands of the nation's interior. Although the campaign had been relatively brief, Scleracina was a relatively small island; there could hardly be a single landholder whose barns had not been robbed and fired, or a single husbandman whose herds and flocks had not been scattered and slaughtered. Although much of the pillage had been conducted by Orlu's men, Orlu's men were now Viragan's men, and Viragan's victory had established him as the only person from whom recompense might be sought. In the wake of the returning army, therefore, there would follow a host of the partially-dispossessed in search of compensation that would not be easily forthcoming.

As civil wars went, Scleracina's had been a trivial affair, but Giraiazal understood that it would nevertheless have a dire effect on the island's marketplaces, and hence on the island's morale. The death of Orlu had put an end to overt conflict, but not to covert confusion--and too many mysteries still remained unsolved.

Where was Lysariel? Was he sane or insane? Would he ever return-- and what might he do thereafter?

All of these questions were, of course, forthrightly put to Giraiazal by Viragan as soon as the overdose of opium had worn off--by which time he had been fending off similar enquiries from Triasymon and Zintrah long enough to make them very impatient.

Giraiazal had made every possible effort to find the answers in the sky and on his tabletop, but he had found the skies unclear and the trumps confused. He had been forced to draw on all his reserves of inspiration and imagination to make himself certain of anything at all--and what he discovered in his possession, in the end, was an inchoate mass of decidedly ominous data.

"The stars and the cards are agreed that some of us will see him again," Giraiazal eventually reported to all three of his most urgent enquirers, endeavouring to be scrupulously accurate now that the end of the emergency no longer licensed blatant propaganda, but also scrupulously discreet. "I am sure that we shall see him once more--at least once, but perhaps only once, and briefly. He is saner now than he was, but the thread of his life is nearer to breaking. Damozel Fate seems determined that he has one last thing to do, and I think that his determination to do it will not easily be thwarted."

"What thing is that?" Viragan demanded.

"He has not yet formed a precise plan of action," Giraiazal told the regent, warily, "but it concerns his heir...I mean Zintrah's unborn child."

"Have we anything to fear from him?" Zintrah wanted to know.

"I cannot believe that he would harm you, Highness" Giraiazal promised. "As for the rest of us, I cannot be absolutely sure."

"And what of the curse of the coral bride?" Triasymon asked. "Is that concluded now? Shall we ever see her again?"

"The mystery of her whereabouts will eventually be solved," Giraiazal said, "and the statue will one day be broken--but I cannot tell exactly when or how that will happen."

"But there will be an end to her malign interference in our plans?" Viragan said. "You can assure me of that, at least."

"Oh yes," said Giraiazal. "When the statue is broken, there will be no further sorcerous interference in the affairs of Scleracina."

Brian Stableford

The etymological origins of the word "herbasacralism" are, like those of every other word in current usage, utterly lost in the mists of antiquity. This does not, of course, prevent herbasacralists from arguing about the precise significance of the word and its subsidiary parts. While the first syllable undoubtedly refers to the vegetable nature of the remedies employed in this branch of practical magic and the suffix "-ism" is a commonplace, there is considerable disagreement regarding the middle element of the description. Some practitioners hold that it is a meaningless extension intended to remystify and redignify the vulgar term "herbalism"; those at an opposite extreme hold that it is a contraction of a combination of terms that would have made the label inconveniently long if they had been retained in full. Most scholars of the latter variety agree in presuming that "ral" is a contraction of "real" but disagree as to the correct expansion of the remainder, a majority favouring the view that "sac" is a contraction of "search" while the minority opinion prefers the thesis that "asac" is a diminution of "association". Other practitioners opine that "sacral" must be seen as a unit, but disagree as to whether the term should be considered synonymous with "sacred" or in reference to that part of the lower back or spine known as the sacrum.

The Revelations of Suomynona, the Last Prophet

What Giraiazal told Viragan, Triasymon and Zintrah was true, not merely in the sense that it was his actual opinion honestly derived, but also--as it eventually transpired--in the sense that his modest talents as a diviner had, for once, not let him down. Indeed, all that he had divined, including the information he had cautiously kept to himself, turned out to be

263

reliable. He understood, though, that while Viragan was recovering from the after-effects of his epic battle and Zintrah was nearing the day when her child would be born, neither of them would be grateful for the information that that their time of troubles was not yet concluded, and would result in further fatalities.

Although the civil war had been quickly settled, the scars it left upon the land were not easily healed. The shortages in Clarassour's marketplace grew worse as the ravaged fields of Scleracina produced their poorest yields in many years. The herds and flocks had been badly depleted, but the survivors grew thin nevertheless for want of fodder, and a murrain broke out among the cattle which spread from herd to herd with grim implacability. All this would not have been disastrous, but the fishing fleets which had long been the island's principal bulwark against famine found that its neighbouring waters had become suddenly and unaccountably barren--and this turned the catastrophe into a crisis.

The gloom induced by this slowly-evolving situation was somewhat alleviated by the gradual approach of the day when Zintrah's child was due to be born. Giraiazal was more certain than ever that the infant would be a boy; the signs were clear. He was certain, too, that the boy was the heir to the throne whose long reign had been foreshadowed even in advance of his conception--which was, of course, as firm a proof as any prophet could ever derive that he was Lysariel's son and not Manazzoryn's.

The magician was naturally inclined to leave this last conclusion unmentioned, or at least unemphasized, but good news was in such short supply that he permitted himself more latitude than usual in issuing loud guarantees that the boy would be healthy, and that his reign over Scleracina would be extensive. Despite the rumours about the child's parentage that were still in circulation, and the fact that Scleracina still had a living but mysteriously absent king, the citizens of Clarassour were virtually unanimous in considering the impending advent to be an occasion worthy of celebration. Any feasting would inevitably be muted by the dearth of provender, but preparations were made in a brave and generous spirit.

Zintrah's labour was long and very arduous, and Giraiazal's talents as a herbasacralist and morpheomorphist were stretched to the full while it lasted. Common opiates administered in doses that he considered safe proved insufficient to ease her distress, and she begged for more with increasing frequency and desperation. When the magician told her that he dared not give her more opium for fear of harming the unborn child she begged her servants to fetch the phial of mandrake pollen that he had given her as a wedding-present, but he forbade them to bring it.

"This is not the right time," he told her, sternly. "Mandrake pollen is as dangerous to a foetus as an excess of opium, if not more so. I have made the most careful examination of the stars, and I have shuffled and dealt my cards with great skill. Their testimony is clear: you will come through this ordeal well enough, and your son will be healthy. The precious pollen must be saved for another day."

"I wish you had never given it to me, you old fool," she railed. "Much good your wedding-gifts did my husband and his brother! Even Calia might have done better to die swiftly, rather than allowing your damnable preservative to prolong her agony! What use are all your plants and potions if you cannot even help me to deliver my child in peace?"

Giraiazal forgave her readily enough for these insults, because he had seen women in labour before, and knew that they often spoke intemperately even to their husbands. Had Zintrah's husband been in attendance, there was every likelihood that she would have turned against him too, perhaps even to the extent of telling him that the child was not his. Fortunately, the only other male attendant upon the birth-process was her father Viragan, and Zintrah had respect enough for him not to be too excessive in her accusations.

Viragan was a hard man, although he had not yet fully recovered from the injuries inflicted during his epic duel with Orlu. Indeed, one of the reasons why Giraiazal's stock of opium had run low was the unexpected demand placed on his supply by Viragan. Giraiazal saw something new in the regent during the long vigil he kept beside his daughter's bedside; the former pirate was unusually quiet, and not a little distressed, but he understood the necessities of the situation as well as Giraiazal, and when Zintrah cried out for a potion to drown her pain he only begged her to be patient, and assured her that all would be well. He gave no explicit indication, other than a few dark looks, that Giraiazal would suffer if the promises of the stars and the trumps were not fulfilled, but he seemed genuinely grateful as well as glad when they eventually proved reliable.

Zintrah completed her labour with a little of her natural fortitude still in hand, and she gave birth to a robust and clamorous boy. Her Highness remained confined to her bed for the next four days, but the infant suckled well and she recovered her strength by slow degrees, while never failing to supply his. Viragan and Giraiazal came very frequently to her room, in order that they might share in her joy and continue to assure her that all was as well as could be expected beyond the walls of her confinement.

They spoke the truth; despite the lack of provisions, the celebrations brought a new mood to Clarassour and the hinterlands alike. Every man, woman and child on the island, no matter how dire their individual circumstances might be, found a sign of hope in the birth of a future king whose reign was guaranteed not to be short by Damozel Fate herself.

The child was named Hatarus.

On the fourth night after the birth, everything seemed so calm that, with only two or three exceptions, the whole palace slept content--

including, it appeared, the guards who had been set to watch the gate and the sentries patrolling the corridors. One of the exceptions was Giraiazal, and even he was not awake because he could not sleep. He was not in the least restless, but he was worried, because he had seen signs in the sky that something was to happen that night: not something terrible, but something unusual. He did not see the guards sleeping outside the gate, nor did he realise that the sentries were not on the prowl as he made his own pensive way through the corridors, but he inferred that they must have been derelict in their duty when he caught sight on an intruder stealing through the shadows, and recognised him as Lysariel.

Giraiazal swiftly suppressed his first instinct, which was to cry out and raise the alarm. He was intensely curious to know what Lysariel's present state of mind might be. For this reason, he shrank back into the shadows himself, and followed the king on tiptoe all the way to Zintrah's room.

Although Lysariel carefully left the door ajar, Giraiazal could not see what was happening inside, so he had to imagine the expression that came into Zintrah's eyes when she opened them, awakened either by a slight sound or a premonition, to find Lysariel standing over the crib that lay alongside her bed. There was light enough for her to see him, even though Giraiazal could not, for there was a candle burning in the room.

For a moment or two, Giraiazal imagined, the mother of the newborn would hardly have dared to breathe. She must have studied the face of the displaced monarch with great concentration, and even greater anxiety, searching for signs of madness. She must have remembered what Giraiazal had said about seeing Lysariel one more time, and perhaps she also remembered his judgment that she would be in no danger from him.

Lysariel, the magician supposed, would be content to look down at the child. What else could he be doing for the several minutes that elapsed while Giraiazal waited, impatiently, for an informative sound to compensate for his lack of sight?

Eventually, the sound came

"Is he mine?" said Lysariel's voice, softly. "Is he truly mine?"

Zintrah hesitated for a moment, but in the end she replied. "Yes," she said, "he is yours. I was a little too successful in distracting you from your coral bride, was I not?"

"It was the one moment of real comfort I had during my madness," Lysariel told her. "Had it not been for the wine of Yethlyreom that Giraiazal provided, I think I might have died. Had it not been for your kindness, I think I might have wished that I had." There was no sign of madness in his voice that Giraiazal could detect.

"I loved Manazzoryn," Zintrah said. "I truly did."

"So did I," said Lysariel, still speaking very softly. "With all my heart."

"You should not have hurt him," Zintrah said.

"No, I should not have hurt him. I was...not myself."

"You called him murderer."

"Did I?" Lysariel's voice carried no conspicuous burden of astonishment, but Giraiazal wished that he could see the boy's face. He was sure that if he had only been able to see the face, he would have been able to judge the honesty or dishonesty of the question.

"Manazzoryn did not kill Calia," Zintrah told him. "Whoever told you that he did was a liar."

"A liar," Lysariel's voice repeated, like an echo.

"Where is the coral image, Lysariel?" Zintrah's voice had softened now, perhaps because the fear occasioned by seeing him at the crib had evaporated--or because she realised that she had an opportunity here to solve the mysteries that even Giraiazal could not unravel.

"Where indeed?" Lysariel countered. "Where is my wife when I need her most? Where is the mother of my legitimate heir?"

"This is your heir, Lysariel," Zintrah said--and as she spoke the king's name, Giraiazal nearly jumped out of his skin, because a hand had fallen upon his shoulder. A second hand made haste to clamp itself upon the magician's face and close his mouth, but the swift pressure was not quite adequate to prevent the escape of a reflexive yelp. It was not a loud sound, but Lysariel and Zintrah must have heard it, given the quiet of the night. They fell silent, while Giraiazal tried to relax himself. He knew, of course, who it was that had seized him; the roughness of the hands and the odour of the other's sweat identified him as Viragan.

The door that Lysariel had left ajar swung open. Giraiazal's wish was granted: he could see Lysariel's face now, no more than half-shadowed from the candlelight in the corridor and the nightlamp in Zintrah's room.

"Prince Viragan," Lysariel said, colourlessly, "and my faithful Grand Vizier. Do come in."

Viragan released the magician, and shoved him forward. Lysariel stepped aside as Giraiazal stumbled past him. Viragan followed, closing the door behind him.

Zintrah was startled by the entrance of the newcomers, but Lysariel seemed almost to have expected the interruption.

"So, Master Magician," Viragan said, wryly, "you were right. We are, indeed, privileged to see Lysariel again. *Once more* were your exact words, I believe."

"At least once, Your Highness," the astrologer said, wishing that he could remember exactly how he had phrased his prophecy and hoping that he had followed is normal cautious instinct. "I think I said *at least once, and briefly*. There is nothing here to warrant alarm, sire. I have heard every word that was spoken. Lysariel has no intention of hurting anyone."

"That is true," Lysariel said, mildly. "I have no quarrel with you, Prince Viragan. You were right to restrain me while I was mad; I only wish you had done so more efficiently. My first release was no liberation; all that was set loose was devilry and dolour. My second release brought me even more misery and woe. I shall leave now, if you wish, and will gladly give you my promise before I go that you will never see me again--but I had to see my son before I went. Will you tell me his name?"

"His name is Hatarus," said Zintrah, when Viragan hesitated.

"You are very generous, King Lysariel," Viragan eventually said, adopting a silky tone and manner. "I must confess, though, that I am reluctant to accept your offer while my curiosity remains unsatisfied. So many unsolved puzzles have accumulated, on which even the mighty prophet Giraiazal has been unable to shed much light. Who was it that broke the lock when you were first released from captivity?"

Lysariel met Viragan's stare quite steadily, and Giraiazal was convinced that he caught a gleam of amusement in the younger man's eye.

"It was Calia," the king declared.

"And was it Calia who told you that Manazzoryn was a murderer?"

"I suppose that it must have been, if it was anyone."

It did not seem to Giraiazal that Lysariel was uncertain in his own mind, nor that the king was resentful of Viragan's questions. Some kind of game was being played--but to what end? Was Lysariel a player, or merely a pawn? If he was a pawn, whose pawn was he, to the extent that he had not been Viragan's?

"And it must also, therefore, have been Calia who took you away from the field where I slew Orlu?" Viragan continued.

"I suppose it must."

"And do you suppose that it is Calia, too, who has given you shelter and protection since that day?" Viragan must have known that Lysariel would not betray the name of the person who had done that, if it had not been his coral bride, but he obviously felt obliged to obtain some sort of answer.

Lysariel smiled wanly. "Yes, I suppose it has been," he said, still manoeuvring cautiously, concealing the end of his strategy. "She loved me dearly, you know, and love like that can endure long after death. I loved her too, and I understand how love like mine could endure in the same way.

"But Calia is dead," said Viragan. "Calia was dead before you were first released from imprisonment."

"My wife is alive in my mind," Lysariel told him. "She has always been alive, and always beautiful, in my mind."

It occurred to Giraiazal then that Viragan had asked the wrong question, and that Viragan had been asking himself the wrong questions for quite some time. But Viragan had not paused before asking another, which he obviously considered a clever one: "But if she is not dead," Viragan said, "how could Manazzoryn be a murderer?"

268

Lysariel hesitated for several seconds before answering that inquiry. He turned his face away from the flickering nightlight, so that his eyes were shielded from its light. "I remember now," he said, his voice expressing mild surprise. "I remember what she told me. She said that if Manazzoryn had not tried to take her by force, so causing her to fall, she could not now be quite so angrily and quite so enviously alive. It is because she was murdered that my beloved will outlive us all."

Whatever Viragan had expected, it was not the accusation that Lysariel had uttered so casually. He shook his head in bewilderment. Giraiazal judged that Viragan knew perfectly well that Manazzoryn had not killed Calia--and must, therefore, know who had. He also judged that Viragan had not the slightest idea why Lysariel had said what he had said, or whether he really believed it.

"Calia *is* dead, Your Majesty," the magician said, trying to make his voice soft and soothing but not quite succeeding. "You would not believe it at the time, but you were not yourself then. Now that you are recovered, or nearly so, I beg you to take my word for it. When the living become the restless dead, their natures are much changed. Whatever the coral image is, Lysariel, she is not your wife, let alone your beloved. Whatever demon it is that inhabits the statue--or seems to--is a pretender and a liar; it has no claim on you."

Lysariel turned to meet the magician's gaze. "Or seems to," he echoed. "You do not know, do you, Giraiazal? You do not know whether my wife is animate or not. You do not know whether she is a phantom of my imagination or a living thing. But I know, Giraiazal. *I know.*"

"I know that you know, Lysariel," Giraiazal countered. "But I do not believe that everything you think you know is the truth. I believe that you have collaborated in your own delusion, to hide the real reason for your assault on Manazzoryn even from yourself. Someone has been pouring poisonous whispers into your ear, and I believe...."

"He is still mad," Viragan interrupted, swiftly, although he had entirely mistaken what Giraiazal was about to say. "He is calm, but he is mad."

Giraiazal had no doubt that Viragan believed it, but he was not prepared to dismiss the matter so easily. He felt sure that a morpheomorphist of his abilities could make the king understand what had actually happened to him. But Lysariel had already shrugged his shoulders, uncaringly.

"Perhaps I am mad, Prince Viragan," the youth said. "I will admit, if you wish, that I am a little too unsteady in the head to debate definitions with a philosopher. In Giraiazal's sceptical eyes, and yours, my wife may seem to be dead, but she is most certainly alive in my eyes, and in my heart...and I am not the only one who knows it. It does not matter what you believe. Whatever state she is in, it does not make her demands less clamorous, nor her wrath less furious."

269

"But you are free of her now, are you not?" Giraiazal was quick to say. "She is gone, and you are free?"

"Is that what you think?" Lysariel said. "I have certainly lost sight of her, for the moment--but she has not lost sight of me, and she never will. You may imprison me again, if you wish, but you cannot keep me. When she has need of me, Calia will reclaim me. I am hers, now and forever, no matter what. But I wanted to see my son, and she let me come. I wanted to see my son, and she gave me my eyes. I wanted to see my son, and she gave me my thoughts, my flesh, my cleverness. Could I be here if it were not for her kindness? Wherever I go, I am hers."

"She cannot hurt you while you are here," Giraiazal said--but it was the wrong thing to say.

"She has not the slightest need or desire to hurt me," Lysariel answered. "She would never hurt me. She is my wife, after all. She is angry, but not with me. She is envious, but not of me. She is my queen, my lover, my soul. But I needed to see my son, and she answered my need. Perhaps I shall never see her again, but that is for her to determine. Perhaps I was foolish to come here, but a man has his pride--and I am a man, as well as a king--and a man must show a certain zeal in the demonstration of his pride, even when he is unremittingly sane and sober. The boy is my son, when all else is said and done."

"It is because he is your son, Lysariel," said Viragan, his voice sounding unexpectedly heavy, as if it had suddenly been weighed down by sadness and sympathy, "and because you are a man as well as a king, that you must go away now, and never return." But the merchant prince was standing between Lysariel and the door, and Giraiazal understood that what he meant by "go away" was that Lysariel must be killed.

Lysariel knew that too; he had been warned by the kindly captor who had given him permission to come. He stepped backwards instead of forwards, and turned towards the curtained window that lit the room by day. It was glazed, but the glass was mounted in a frame that could be swung upon a hinge to let air in. "I know," the king said, without specifying what it was that he knew. "You will not see me again, I promise you." So saying, he leapt at the curtain and disappeared behind it. Giraiazal heard the catch click, and the frame creak upon its hinge, but nothing else.

Zintrah's room was on an upper floor, and the window was set three manheights from the courtyard below--but when Giraiazal and Viragan had wrestled the curtain aside in order to look out at the torchlit court, there was no one to be seen.

Lysariel had vanished.

Etymological disagreements regarding the exact significance of the term "herbasacralism" might be deemed trivial, were it not for the fact that they imply different theoretical bases for the treatment of physical injuries. Both contractionist theories imply a process of empirical analysis by means of which treatments were associated with diseases on purely rational grounds--as, perhaps, does the interpretastion of "sacral" as a reference to the lower back. The suggestion that "sacral" might be synonymous with "sacred", on the other hand, suggests a fundamentally mystical or intuitive series of associations. Practitioners inevitably differ on which of these theoretical bases is preferable, and their preference is highly likely to determine, or at least to influence, their etymological interpretations.

My judgment--which is, as usual, authoritative--is that these disputes are entirely irrelevant to the real issue, which is the question of how it came to be the case that potions brewed from various vegetable residues are effective at all. The notion that any kind of empirical process was involved is ludicrous, because it would imply an incredible pattern of coincidence between possible human ailments and naturally occurring remedies. The notion that medicines identified by any kind of mystical or intuitive process could be effective in any other way than invocation of a placebo effect would be equally ludicrous, were it not for lingering doubts as to whether any contemporary medicines have real effects other than analgesia and euphoria.

The Revelations of Suomynona, the Last Prophet

Viragan continued looking out into the empty night for a full minute, while Giraiazal stepped back into the room and looked into the cot, where

Hatarus was sleeping peacefully. Then the merchant prince shrugged his shoulders, in a cautiously purposeful fashion, as if he were pulling himself together. He turned round, but he did not look directly at Giraiazal or his daughter. "How very annoying," he murmured. "I shall have to scold my men with the utmost severity, and instruct them to redouble their efforts in scouring the city and the island. On the other hand, I must accept the possibility that it will do no good. If Lysariel could get all the way to my daughter's bedroom without attracting attention....well, we ought to hope that he had done what he came to do and will now let us be, ought we not, Master Magician?" As he added the final few words his gaze moved again, recovering its piercing quality as it settled on Giraiazal.

"He did not seem to wish us any harm," Giraiazal pointed out.

"Is that what you think?" Viragan seemed far from convinced. "I formed a very different impression. I would have preferred it had he launched himself upon me as he launched himself upon Manazzoryn, intent on doing his work with blades and brute strength."

"Perhaps we ought to take him at his word," Giraiazal suggested. "Perhaps he really did come to see his son."

"Perhaps he did," Viragan acknowledged, although his voice was still dubious. "A romantic gesture: he had to see his son once, before retiring forever from public life. You did predict that, did you not, Master Magician? You promised that we would see him once more--but was it once only or once at least? No matter--you cannot promise me now that he will not return, can you?"

"I wish I could, Your Highness," Giraiazal answered, diplomatically. "This meeting was fated, of that I always felt sure. I have seen no definite evidence of any further return--but I cannot promise that none will yet appear in the pattern that my dexterous mistress is busy weaving."

"And the time of troubles of which you have spoken so often?"

"The time of troubles is not yet concluded," Giraiazal admitted. He took care to sound far less confident of that conclusion than he actually was.

"He is no longer quite as mad as he was," whispered Zintrah, addressing herself to the empty air rather than to Giraiazal or her father. "He knows what he is doing now--and what he has already done. Oh, Lysariel! Oh, Calia!"

Giraiazal was still trying to meet Viragan's eyes, and was surprised to see a brief glimmer there that might have been sympathy--but it was gone in an instant. "You may be right, Your Highness," Giraiazal said, thinking to deflect uncomfortable attention away from himself. "Perhaps he is no longer quite as mad as he was, and perhaps he understands what he has done. Perhaps he has a purpose now that he did not have before. We can only hope that it may work to his advantage."

Viragan shook his head. "I have men to scold," he said. "And I must set them all to work, much harder than before. He has escaped me twice, and I shall not let it happen a third time." He walked out of the room with a very determined stride, although he was still limping. Giraiazal knew that the determination overlay a deep-seated unease; for all his cunning and common sense, Viragan was a superstitious man, his mind more than willing to accommodate the possibility that Damozel Fate harboured malign intentions towards him. And for all his hardheadedness in matters of business, Viragan was not incapable of feeling guilt. He had killed his rival in a fight as fair as any that was likely to be seen in Scleracina before the world's end, but the sequence of events that had concluded in that fight had been rotten with disguised malevolence, sly assassinations and subtle curses.

Giraiazal turned back to Zintrah. "All will be well, Your Highness," he told her. "Whatever becomes of Prince Viragan, and whatever my mistress has in store for me, Hatarus will grow strong and live long. He will inherit the kingdom that is his due, and he will rule it as long as it survives. Whatever time is left before the end of the world, he will have the very best of it. There is no one in the world more fortunate than he."

"But what of Lysariel?" Zintrah said, tearfully. "What of my beloved? Shall I see him again, Giraiazal? Shall my son see his father again?"

"I do not know," Giraiazal answered, truthfully. "I have seen no such meeting fated, but the future is full of nuances and shadows. I do not know."

The magician returned to his tower knowing that he had been consistent, having given the same advice to Viragan and Zintrah. Two days later, though, he had cause to regret that he had been so indecisive in his predictions. His understandable--perhaps even laudable--desire to leave Zintrah with a measure of hope had lost him an opportunity to enhance his reputation in Viragan's eyes. What he had seen and felt had been more reliable than he had dared to believe; he, Viragan and Zintrah had indeed seen Lysariel alive once more, and once only, before the king's body--still recognisable in spite of the hideous mutilations to which it had been subjected--was washed up on the northern shore of Scleracina, not far from the grotto from which divers had harvested coral for the manufacture of Urbishek's statue.

Even before the body had been transported to Clarassour the rumours had arrived, declaring that the king had been tortured and murdered by his coral courtesan. The rumours were unequivocal as to the motive for the crime, which was said to be jealousy, but they were perversely unclear as to the precise origin of the monster's jealous rage. Some said that Lysariel had refused to be her consort in a kingdom beneath the sea because it would have required him to be remade in coral himself. Some alleged that he had been caught by the jealous creature, weeping salt tears for his human wife. Some expressed the opinion that he had decided to abdicate his throne in favour of his brother's son, thus proving to the coral succubus that her own child would never sit upon the throne of Scleracina.

Triasymon was the only person who bothered to ask Giraiazal for an expert judgment on the matter. The neglect of others might have seemed suspicious, were it not for Viragan's habitual scepticism and Zintrah's timorousness, but Giraiazal knew better than to wonder why anyone might avoid consulting him about matters already decided. He did wonder, however, why Triasymon had taken the trouble to come to his rooms to ask questions; the Lord Chancellor obviously felt that this was not a matter for the council-chamber or for some discreet covert on the ground floor.

"I do not know for sure, my lord," Giraiazal confessed, when he was asked whether the coral bride really had killed Lysariel, and--if so--why. "I doubt it, but the coral image seems to be immune to all my enquiries. She has no horoscope, and the cards are blind to her actions and motives alike. It is possible that she has no effective existence outside Lysariel's mind, but I dare not rule out the possibility."

"Dare you take it for granted that if the coral image really is animate, it is also guilty of the crimes with which it has been charged?" Triasymon asked, revealing a greater complexity of thought than he had ever seemed likely to achieve.

The Lord Chancellor's tenacity startled Giraiazal as much as his subtlety; the magician had grown used to thinking of Triasymon as a man whose only wisdom consisted of contentment with his own inaction.

"Who else do you suspect?" the magician asked, interested to discover whether Triasymon might have conceived and cultivated the same suspicion as himself.

Alas, Triasymon only said: "I can only think of one possible alternative." After a long pause for thought, however, he went on. "Perhaps I should have told you that I saw Lysariel two nights ago."

Giraiazal immediately remembered that Triasymon had also been present when he had prophesied that they would all see Lysariel at least once more. He also felt a slight flicker of guilt, because the Lord Chancellor was not the only one who had kept quiet about his encounter. All he said, however, was: "Did you, my lord?"

"Briefly," Triasymon confirmed. "He seemed to be in a great hurry to leave the palace grounds. I begged him to stay, but he said that he did not dare. He said that he remembered having killed Manazzoryn, but that he had been deluded into believing that Manazzoryn had tried to rape Calia and that she had fallen from a window in the struggle. He said that he no longer believed that to be true."

Giraiazal deduced from this that while he had found a certain suggestive enlightenment in Lysariel's words, Lysariel had found a parallel inspiration in Viragan's. "Did he, perchance, say who it was that had persuaded him, or venture any hypothesis as to who really killed Calia?"

"No," said Triasymon. "He did not. But he did say that no harm would come to him, if only he could return to his wife. He said that if only she would consent to receive him in her arms, all would be well--not merely for him, but for everyone."

"A large claim," Giraiazal observed, in a neutral tone. *Or a suicide note*, he added, silently.

"He seemed to feel that he was in grave danger," Triasymon amplified, "but not from the coral image."

Giraiazal was not about to be cajoled into making unwise accusations himself. "From whom, then?" he said, feigning bewilderment.

"From Viragan," Triasymon said, only a little reluctantly. Giraiazal did not know whether to be glad or sorry that the Lord Chancellor had jumped to the all-too-obvious conclusion.

"Viragan's men were certainly searching for the king," Giraiazal confirmed. "They sought to confine him for his own safety, as they had done twice before."

"He had escaped twice before," the Lord Chancellor pointed out. "I do not know how he did it on the first occasion, but I do know that when he was liberated by Orlu's agents he took no part in the fighting. Even so, he was with Orlu's army until the final confrontation, and I cannot help but wonder whether Viragan's heart had hardened against him in consequence, and whether the prince's agents were given orders not to take him alive."

"Have you asked Prince Viragan whether he ordered that Lysariel should not be taken alive?" Giraiazal asked, knowing perfectly well that Triasymon had not.

"I thought it best to consult you first," Triasymon said.

"You were wise to do so," the magician confirmed. "My expert opinion, offered without the slightest hesitation, is that you should not voice these suspicions again--not here, and certainly not where anyone else might overhear them."

Triasymon looked at Giraiazal long and hard then, digesting the implications of this statement as best he could. "Very well," he said, finally. "Perhaps we should talk about something else. So far as I can recall, the only person who ever saw the coral statue move is you. Lysariel certainly insisted that his wife was alive and very well while he was locked in his apartment with the statue, but he was very much deluded then. No one has seen the statue since it disappeared from the apartment--no one, at least, who has lived to tell the tale. Even you have felt free to voice the suspicion, more than once, that it might have been carried way by a gang of thieves. It seems to me, after much careful thought, that the statue has become a very convenient scapegoat. Lysariel was mad, so the statue must have been to blame. Lysariel escaped, so the statue must have been to blame. Lysariel killed Manazzoryn, so the statue must have been to blame. Lysariel is murdered, so the statue must be to blame. But there is not a single witness to support any of these conclusions, with the possible exception of you, Master Magician. You are the only person who had the opportunity to inspect the statue closely after it was removed to Lysariel's new apartments."

Giraiazal realised, belatedly, that he might not be the only party to the conversation who had not been entirely honest in voicing his suspicions. It had not occurred to him that Triasymon might suspect *him*.

"Can you really think that I might have stolen the statue?" Giraiazal asked, mildly. "Do you think that I spread the rumour that it had come to life in order to conceal my theft?

"Did you?" Triasymon asked.

"No, I did not," Giraiazal assured him. "But I think I might have guessed...."

"So have I," Triasymon interrupted him. "When I considered the matter carefully, I concluded that you had merely been misled, just as Lysariel was misled--and just as Orlu was misled. You played your part in that business too, of course, but you were just a dupe."

"You are not very polite, Lord Chancellor," the magician observed, referring to the interruption rather than the observation that he had been duped. It had been on the tip of the magician's tongue to tell Triasymon the name of the person who really had stolen the coral bride, and why-- assuming that he had divined it correctly--but now he decided to keep his own counsel for a while longer.

"If I am less than polite, Master Magician, it is because I am so very confused," Triasymon replied. "I have lost two nephews, who were like sons to me. I saw one slain by the other, and now I have seen the corpse of the second washed up by the sea, vilely disfigured. I loved them both, and I know that they loved one another before Viragan's captain came thundering at my door with his double-headed axe. I would like to know how this happened."

"We are all victims of Damozel Fate's whim," Giraiazal told him, his voice taking on a cruel edge. "We are all bound to Lady Death. No matter how great or small we are, nor how extravagantly our apparent fortunes might shift, we are inhabitants of a dying world. We are the lost, the forsaken, the damned. We struggle to make the best of whatever time we have, but there is folly in everything we do, everything we are. What is it that you want, Triasymon? Vengeance? Understanding? Hope?"

"I want you to assure me that the coral image is not alive and never has been. I want you to assure me that its curse is not to blame for the long sequence of misfortunes that began with Queen Calia's mysterious illness."

"You would do better, my friend, to believe that it really is alive," Giraiazal told him, bleakly. "It is in your best interests to believe that it is really to blame--*entirely* to blame--for everything that has happened to your nephews. As you have said yourself, it is a very convenient scapegoat. You and I, and all men like us, should be glad of that convenience."

"I am not like you, Giraiazal," Triasymon said, dully.

"Then you should try harder to become more like me," Giraiazal replied. "The practice will do you nothing but good. It requires no magic to believe the impossible--it only requires a healthy credulity. If you want assurances, I can assure you that the coral bride is at the very centre of this whole affair. I am certain now that Lysariel is not the only one who believes that she is alive, after her own fashion, nor the only one prepared to act on her behalf in the quest for vengeance. Animated or not, her curse has real power, and you had best make sure that you do not fall victim to it."

"Thank you for your advice," Triasymon said, coldly, as he rose from his seat. "I really wish that I could take it." But he paused as he reached the door, and turned back to Giraiazal.

"If a coral image of my wife had told me that my brother had tried to rape my actual wife, but had only succeeded in causing her to fall to her death," the Lord Chancellor said, "I would refuse to believe it, because coral is only coral, no matter how cleverly it might be cursed. But if a man came to me and said: *I saw this happen with my own eyes*, I might be swayed. I would like to think that I would not, but I might--provided, that is, I had reason to think that my brother had a motive for acting as he was accused of acting, and a reason to feel guilty about the provision of that motive. I believe you know as well as I do that it must have happened that way."

"A magician," Giraiazal told him, "believes only what is written in the stars or depicted in the cards. Even then, a magician is duty-bound to question his beliefs. No matter what he knows, or does not know, a magician is bound by his duty and his art to ask what effect it may have to say what he believes or to reveal what he knows. Every man, whether he knows it or not, and whether he is educated or not, ought to be a magician at least to that extent."

"They were my children," Triasymon said. "I could not have loved them more if they were my own sons."

"I do not doubt that," Giraiazal said, although he suspected that Triasymon's plaint was a lie born of shame, as so many lies are. "But you can do them no good by being foolish. You have a grandnephew who will be a king, and who will reign as long as any king can in a world that is sick and dying. You might serve as his loyal Lord Chancellor, and I as his faithful Grand Vizier, if only Damozel Fate has reason to smile upon us."

"Reason?" Triasymon said, before he closed the door behind him. "Is Fate possessed of *reason*?"

Giraiazal knew that he reply would not be audible, so he did not trouble to raise his voice. "Of course not," he murmured. "She is completely mad. But how can we expect anything from her but malignity, unless we humour her as best we can?"

If contemporary medicines derived from plants do have real effects in combating injury and illness, the only conclusion a rational commentator could reach in searching for an explanation of the fact is that one or more of the ancestral humankinds must have decided to arrange matters thus. The physicians of some long-departed race must have found it convenient to mass-produce treatments by recruiting plants as agents of manufacture, modifying their seeds in such a way as to ascertain that the leaves, roots or reproductive organs of the mature plant would be rich in curative compounds. These compounds must be mere biochemical by-products so far as the plant is concerned--and could not, therefore, have arisen naturally--but may prove invaluable to human users.

This thesis may seem implausible, in that it gives rise to the corollary supposition that thousands of plant species, which nowadays grow wild, were once deliberately cultivated, having been strategically modified as crops. The implausibility of this thesis is, however, an illusion generated by the inability of the ultimate humankind to maintain more than a few dozen crop species, all but a few of which are food-producers. If there is any truth at all in the legends we retain of the accomplishments of our predecessors in the Great Epic, there must have been a time--an unimaginably long time, in fact--when every single organism cohabiting the Earth with the relevant humankinds was an artifact intended to serve some human purpose. What we think of as wilderness is, therefore, merely a phase in the long decay of an order whose perfection lies far beyond our meagre capacity for aesthetic appreciation.

In settling on this conclusion we must, of course, avoid extrapolating it to an absurd extreme. It would be ridiculous to suppose that the curative plants growing all around us were left behind by their makers in order to serve that purpose. Even if we are something more than mere detritus--as I believe we are--the arguments supporting that contention cannot be extrapolated to take in every living thing that survives alongside us. We should be duly grateful for the fact that we find so many useful medicines conveniently packaged, but we should not let that gratitude lead us to a mistaken impression of what we are and why we are here.

The Revelations of Suomynona, the Last Prophet

The funeral of King Lysariel was a lavish affair. The royal household and the citizens of Clarassour gave free rein to their mourning, glad to be in possession once again of unambiguous emotions. While the king had been mad no one had cared to think much about him, but now that he was dead it was easy to miss him and to weep for what might have been had his reign not been cut so tragically short.

As soon as Lysariel was safely buried, Giraiazal retired to his turret. He intended, as always, to busy himself with new observations of the movements of the stars and new calculations as to their significance, although he had a subsidiary motive too. He was ill again, and did not like to be too far from a chamber-pot for any length of time. Although he had dosed himself very carefully with potions that would normally have been effective, his guts seemed seriously inclined to rebellion. He had been forced by the corollary aches and pains to increase his regular intake of opium even further.

Triasymon's visit had unsettled Giraiazal more than he would have thought possible, and he now wanted to make every effort possible to justify his suspicion as to who had stolen the coral bride from Lysariel's room, and to discover exactly what kinds of lightning might descend from the dark clouds of uncertainty that were still gathered over the island's future. In spite of his discomforts, therefore, he pressed on with his work as hard as he could.

He was startled by what the telescope revealed. While determining the current positions of the Motile Entities he discovered no less than three nebulae that had previously been invisible, and two new comets. The magician had never known such a profusion of novelties, and strongly suspected that there was no record of any such multiple occurrence in the surviving annals of astrology. He cursed the heavens for their astonishing inconstancy, although he knew well enough that he ought to have have remained serene. After all, if the approaching end of the world could not be expected to bring forth an unusual profusion of unprecedented omens, what could? He was ashamed of the swelling resentment which bade him ask, with bitter complaint, how Damozel Fate could be anything other than a fickle mistress when the writing she inscribed on the walls of the universe was so soon scribbled over by graffiti--but he made what efforts he could to suppress that resentment, in order that he might set about making new calculations.

Alas, when he attempted to draw precise and detailed accounts of the future of Scleracina, Giraiazal's equations soon filled up with intractable unknowns, and threatened more than once to lead his reasoning into mocking paradox. He gave up in frustration, and turned to his cards instead, more in desperation than in hope.

When he laid out the fortunes of Triasymon and Zintrah he found the Vampire Queen in both of them, keeping close company with such ominous partners as the Hanged Man and the Sullied Virgin, but he could not free his numbed mind of clouding doubts when he attempted to translate vision into prediction.

Giraiazal was as certain as ever that the Vampire Queen was the symbol of the coral bride, but he still could not tell whether she was Lady Death's handmaiden, or Damozel Fate's jest, or merely the hapless instrument of a cruel and secret obsession.

The display he laid out for Hatarus was, as usual, bereft of imminent threats, but it was also empty of any detailed insight into the constitution of the future king's court.

As the comets' tails began to unfurl in the three days that followed, like those of displaying doves, the contagion that had already taken hold in the palace crept out of the sewers of the port into the narrow streets, and a new epidemic of disease extended its dread hand to clutch the stomachs and lungs of old and young alike. It was not the Platinum Death, and the great majority of those who suffered it recovered their health within a tenday, but it was a sore inconvenience to the commerce of the city, which had only just begun to show signs of recovery from the effects of the civil war. When disease is added to hunger the complaints of the afflicted are more than doubled, and superstitious fears are easily agitated.

The whispered rumours that ran around the streets of Clarassour, before casually intruding themselves into the hottest kitchens and draughtiest corners of the palace, were adamant that the coral bride's curse was now about to reach its dreadful culmination. The rumours also spoke of a vengeance yet to be exacted--but on whom, and for what crime, no one was certain.

Giraiazal knew that of all the dire things he had foreseen before Lysariel was crowned, Zintrah's crisis alone remained to come and go. The magician had been patient before, because his sights had always been set on the next step in a continuing sequence, but now he grew anxious. His inability to penetrate the murk of unsettled possibility that lay beyond Zintrah's time of trial distressed him considerably.

Even common sense declared that with Lysariel and Manazzoryn dead and Hatarus' good fortune apparently secure, the future ought to be becoming more predictable, not less. It was unbecoming as well as frustrating for a magician of Giraiazal's abilities to be obliged to take the view, familiar to ordinary folk, that time alone would tell him what would happen tomorrow and the day after, let alone what part he would be privileged to play during the long and relatively calm reign of Hatarus, son of Lysariel.

Giraiazal hated the necessity of being impatient with the slowness and secrecy of the steadfast hours--while the debilitating effects of his illness grew gradually worse--but impatient he had nevertheless to be. He hated even more the necessity of being astonished when he was summoned to the council-chamber by a man-at-arms babbling about a challenge and a duel, but that too was necessity. He made what haste he could, but by the time he arrived there was nothing he could do to prevent the next phase of the unfolding tragedy.

Triasymon had not taken his advice. The Lord Chancellor had accused Prince Viragan, before a crowd of witnesses, first of having murdered the queen, and then of having lied to King Lysariel about the circumstances of her death, while Lysariel--having been cleverly drugged or insidiously ensorcelled--was in a state of heightened suggestibility. Triasymon had also accused Prince Viragan of having secreted the spiders that had caused Queen Calia's illness within the fruit placed in the sculptor's studio, and of having murdered King Lysariel.

Prince Viragan would probably have killed Triasymon before he was half way through this litany of complaint had the chancellor not claimed the privilege of issuing a formal challenge, which was due to him since he had been elevated to his proper position in the island's aristocracy. As things stood, the regent had had no alternative but to wait, and then to point out that he had already been subject to one trial by ordeal in respect of these charges, and had proved them all to be lies.

Technically speaking, Giraiazal thought, Prince Viragan was correct in that assertion--but, given the confused circumstances in which his duel with Orlu had come about, there was bound to be some doubt as to whether it really counted as a trial by ordeal. Triasymon's challenge, by contrast was quite unambiguous, although it seemed to Giraiazal that the ploy was bound to be self-defeating, given that Viragan's victory--which would supposedly demonstrate his innocence of every charge laid against him--was surely inevitable.

Viragan, having had the privilege of the choice of weapons and armour, had elected to trust his sword and to dispense with all artificial protection. Given that the pirate prince had been exceedingly well-trained in swordsmanship, that he was a full handspan taller than his opponent-- with a correspondingly greater reach--and that he had made a full recovery from the injuries inflicted during his duel with Orlu, it seemed unlikely that the contest would extend for a more than a minute before Triasymon was fatally skewered, unless Viragan desired that it should.

Giraiazal knew that it might be unwise even to speak to the Lord Chancellor in such circumstances as these, let alone to whisper in his ear, but he could not resist going to him and saying in a hushed voice: "Are you completely mad, sire?"

"It seems that madness runs in the family," was Triasymon's riposte-- which confirmed, so far as Giraiazal was concerned, the hypothesis that Triasymon's challenge was merely a convenient means of committing suicide.

Giraiazal knew that it could do no good, but he felt obliged to whisper: "You are making a terrible mistake, my lord. Viragan did not kill either of your nephews."

Triasymon looked at him very sharply, but he only shook his head. "He planned to kill them from the very beginning," he said. "It was always his intention."

"Yes, it was," Giraiazal admitted. "But the fact remains that he did not do it, and is sorely confused by the fact. Ever since the coral bride was removed from Lysariel's room, his plan has taken on a life of its own, and it is driving him to distraction. If you had only let things lie...."

"What?" said Triasymon, as Giraiazal trailed off. "What if I had let things lie? Would the coral bride have delivered her own punishment? Would she have killed Viragan as she killed my nephews?"

Strangely enough, given that he was not merely a great prophet but one who had lately become obsessed with penetrating the stubborn curtain of mystery with which Damozel Fate had veiled her plans, Giraiazal had never asked himself that question. What *did* the coral bride have in store for Viragan?

"It's too late," Triasymon said, succinctly. "There's no going back. Best scurry away, Master Magician, lest you be damned by association. My mind is not to be changed, no matter how you plead."

Giraiazal understood that Triasymon had raised his voice in order to exonerate the magician from any suspicion of complicity in what he was about to do. It was an act of pure kindness. There was nothing more for the magician to do but withdraw, and that he immediately did.

"Well," Giraiazal muttered under his breath, as he retreated to a corner of the room, while the other councillors used upturned tables and chairs turned backwards to form an approximate square, "I suppose the removal of one more piece from the board might help to simplify future possibilities, although it is hard to imagine that one of my troublesome comets will condescend to flicker out when the poor fool dies."

Viragan was too wise a man to be overconfident about any contest of arms, even against such a raw opponent as Triasymon, but he was also wise enough to know that a formal trial by ordeal had to be treated as an item of theatre. There was a sense in which he had only to win, but there was also a sense in which an extravagant manner of winning might testify to the utter absurdity of the charges laid against him. Giraiazal was by no means surprised, therefore, when the prince decided to make a speech before taking his stance.

"I fear, my lord, that you are the victim of a delusion as terrible as the one that claimed our king," Viragan said. "I want you and everyone else here to know that I do not hold you responsible for the lies you have spoken. I understand that the coral succubus has you in her power, just as she formerly held your nephew in thrall. She is the source of these appalling calumnies, and I am sorry for the necessity she has imposed upon me, which requires me to kill a man I would far rather have counted a friend. I shall take no pleasure in the infliction of your death, and will do what I can to ensure that it is merciful. I only wish that I had the opportunity to face the true author of this tragedy as I now face you: openly, in honest combat."

"If I am wrong," Triasymon replied, "then you may well have that pleasure to come. If I am right, of course, you never shall."

Viragan frowned when he heard that. Giraiazal realised that the prince had been so concerned with the formulation of his own fine words that he had not anticipated any such reply. Giraiazal could not blame the regent, for he would not have thought Triasymon capable of playing so neatly and so economically with the niceties of paradox.

"Scleracina is privileged to have the services of a great magician," Viragan said, improvising as best he could. "Giraiazal the Herbasacralist has been busy of late helping to fight the epidemic ravaging the city, which is doubtless also the work of the coral sorceress, but he also has a reputation as a master of anathematization. When this petty affair is done, I shall command him to lay the most powerful curse of which he is capable against the coral monster, to ensure that it will make no further trouble within or against this realm. My only desire is to keep us all safe from harm, and I will do everything within my power to ascertain that yours is the last blood to be shed at this vampire's whim."

The expression in Viragan's eyes as he looked at Giraiazal was difficult to read, but the magician knew that he was not being admonished or punished; this was merely a matter of convenience.

"I shall gladly do as I am bid, Your Highness," Giraiazal replied. "Anathematization is an exhausting process, which costs a magician dear, but you are absolutely right. This monster has done too much damage; it must be stopped."

Triasymon was not finished yet. "It is as easy for a magician to cast spells against imaginary demons as it is for a master swordsman to murder a novice," he said. "Custom declares that the winner of this fight is to be held innocent of all charges, but we have come too near to the end of the world to preserve our trust in custom. This is a time without precedent, when precedent has lost its power. On this occasion, death is the only testament of certainty. Know that as I die, I shall curse you with all my heart. I have no more power to do so than Giraiazal has power to curse the monster of your imagination, but I do it anyway."

"Pure madness," Viragan observed. "I pity you, my friend, and cannot bear to delay your release any longer." So saying, he placed himself at the ready, with his sword--a heavy sabre--extended horizontally before him.

Triasymon had been provided with an identical weapon, but he had not strength enough to hold it steady while the appointed referee counted down to the commencement of the battle.

When the count ended the chancellor lunged forward with all possible urgency, but the thrust was badly directed as well as slow. Viragan turned it aside with his own blade, but refrained from making the obvious riposte. Indeed, the prince stepped back a pace or two, deliberately allowing his opponent to recover.

Triasymon lunged again, just as furiously.

Viragan turned the attacking blade away, just as easily.

Triasymon attempted a horizontal sweep, which Viragan blocked with a vertical blade. It was Triasymon that stumbled as the impact jarred him. Again Viragan gave him time to recover, and time to thrust again. This time, Viragan's parry was more forceful, and Triasymon was jarred again, but the Lord Chancellor knew enough to cling hard to the handle of his weapon, and was not dispossessed of it.

Again Triasymon lunged forward, his desperation plain for everyone to see. No one present had watched the fight between Viragan and Orlu, but everyone had heard it described, minutely and without too much exaggeration, if not quite blow for blow. Everyone had heard how evenly balanced that fight had been, how taxing it had been for both combatants, and how it had been settled as much by luck as skill. This one was bound to seem its polar opposite; no one watching could believe for an instant that Triasymon would ever lay his blade upon Viragan's flesh, or doubt that Viragan could strike a mortal blow at will.

In spite of what he had said, however, Viragan was in no hurry. Several distinct accusations had been hurled at him, and his intention was to make it obvious that no matter how many slanders were aimed at his person, he could turn them all aside with ease.

Triasymon cut at Viragan's feet, and missed. Then he improvised a move that no fencing-master would ever have endorsed, attempting to roll his body forward and thrust upwards as he completed the somersault. It would have been amazing had the ploy succeeded, and it certainly took his opponent by surprise, but all Viragan had to do was to kick Triasymon aside and send him sprawling--and that was exactly what he did. Then the prince waited patiently for his adversary to pick himself up, still clinging to his sword.

Any more would have been excessive, uncomfortably reminiscent of a many-clawed cat toying with a helpless mouse. Triasymon's next thrust came within a hairsbreadth of cutting through the cloth of Viragan's ruffled shirt, but that was because Viragan had allowed it to endanger him. This time, having deftly turned the blade aside, he rammed the point of his own weapon into the soft flesh beneath Triasymon's breastbone, and then crouched down in order to drive the metal upwards. The thrust was fatal, and immediately so. Triasymon's last breath escaped in a moan rather than a scream.

Viragan placed his foot on the fallen man's chest and drew his weapon out, releasing a gout of arterial blood that drenched both his boots. The stink that rose from the body seemed to fill the council-chamber, but Viragan gave no sign that he had sensed it.

"Work on your anathema, Master Magician," was all he said before striding out of the room. "I want it pronounced in the plaza, before the sun begins to set, and I want every word of it to be clearly heard and understood. Sharuman will help you if you need a scribe. Make an end of this tragedy, I beg you."

"I do not need Captain Sharuman's help, Your Highness," Giraiazal said, meekly. "I need no scribe to help me memorise an anathema. You are absolutely right, of course. It is certainly time for an end to be put to this affair, no matter what the effort might cost."

If the lore of legend can be trusted, there were a few among the primal humans who could not see the obligations they had, and were direly reckless of the future of their own kind, but that recklessness had a definite and inevitable effect. Those primal humans who could not see, or decided to ignore, their responsibility to the millions of millions of millions of human beings yet to come had to be reckoned *evil.* Their fellows had no alternative but to consider them treasonous adversaries in the human Epic: dismal creatures so vile and villainous that we cannot possibly imagine how repulsive their contemporaries found them.

There are no such villains in our world, for the recklessness of the doomed is without consequence. The idea of evil has lost its meaning. We are free to do exactly as we wish, for an equal judgment has already been passed upon us all, and the universal sentence of annihilation can neither be appealed nor set aside.

This is the truth, and there is no doubting it: *we are free.* If we refuse to live as if we were free, we are just as much as fault as those of our remotest ancestors who refused to recognise their manifest obligations to the future of the manifold humankinds, and thus claimed a freedom to which they were in no wise entitled.

The Revelations of Suomynona, the Last Prophet

Giraiazal pronounced his anathema with all the force and theatricality he could muster, calling down the wrath of every demon whose name he knew upon the head of the coral succubus. He had prepared himself for the performance by dosing himself with a powerful stimulant as well as the now-customary pain-killers, and he was extremely light-headed, but he knew that symptoms that might be taken for intoxication in a common

287

man could easily pass for supernatural inspiration in a magician, so he was satisfied with the manner of his delivery. He had grave doubts about the effectiveness of the curse he had launched, given that he did not know the monster's true name, or even whether it had one, but he had not expressed those doubts to Viragan or anyone else.

When Giraiazal had concluded his oration he made a great show of his collapse, although he really was exhausted. Viragan was quick to order four of his men to make a stretcher and carry the magician back to his tower--but they had to let him down at the foot of the staircase winding up to his turret because the spiral was too tight to accommodate the stretcher. One of them stayed with him as he made the ascent and saw him to his bed, even helping him to don his nightshirt, but the man retired very promptly thereafter, having the normal superstitious fear of a magician's den. Burrel and Mergin promised that they would take good care of him until he was well again, but it was obvious to Giraiazal that they had grave doubts as to the prospect of his recovery.

Giraiazal was glad to lie down for a day or two, for he had indeed been very busy dispensing medicines to the sick, sending forth agents to purchase more ingredients, and pursuing his own divinatory researches. Knowing that he would not be expected to show himself for some time, he dosed himself very liberally with a rich mixture of medicines, hoping that sleep and the synergistic effect of the various restorative compounds would restore his strength. He soon lost track of time, and of the sequence of events. He seemed to wake up again and again, but was never entirely sure that he was not dreaming that he was awake. He was often aware of Burrel or Mergin fussing around him, trying to make him drink water, a solution of opium, skilly or broth. He could not collect his thoughts, but he became preoccupied with the idea that if only he could exert his powers as a morpheomorphist to the full he might ensure his own cure. Alas, he could not focus his mind on any such task, and only added to his anxieties.

He had no idea how long he had been in this state when Mergin shook him awake far more urgently than she had ever done before.

"I don't want any food!" he protested, when he was capable of speech. "I only want to be left alone."

"So you shall be, Master Magician," said a voice that was certainly not Mergin's or Burrel's. "When you have done one last thing for me. Get out, and don't come back!"

Giraiazal forced himself to sit up, and blinked furiously to clear his eyes. He could not see very clearly when he had done so, but that was because the night was very dark and the candlelight very faint. Even so, he recognised the shadow that was looming over the bed. He realised that the last instruction had been issued to his servants, who had obediently left the room.

"Prince Viragan?" he said.

"Yes," the regent said. "I summoned you, but your servants said that you could not come--so I have come to you."

"If you need a potion," Giraiazal muttered, "I'll need Burrel to make it up. I can barely stand."

"There's no need to stand," the regent told him. "I don't need a potion. I need you to tell me something."

That brought the magician sharply to his senses, because he immediately jumped to the conclusion that Viragan wanted to know who had persuaded Lysariel to kill Manazzoryn, and why, and who had then killed Lysariel, and why. If the pirate prince had already deduced the answer, and merely wanted confirmation, it would be safe enough to confirm the conclusion--but if the frustrated schemer was still lost in the labyrinth of his confusions, even pointing out the obvious might be a terrible risk. "What do you want to know?" Giraiazal asked, fearfully.

"I want to know whether you really do have the power to shape a man's dreams, and by that means to armour him against distress," Viragan said. "No tricks, mind, like the one you played on Meronicos. I am speaking of the true art that you employed on Calia. It *was* true art, was it not? You really did shape her dreams, and gave her the ability thereby to cure herself? You have helped my daughter too, by the same means. It is something that might work on anyone, is it not?"

Giraiazal tried to calm the frantic beating of his heart, and used the back of his hand to wipe cold sweat from his brow. "Yes, Your Highness," he said, eventually. "I can shape a man's dreams as easily as a woman's. I helped Calia, and I helped Zintrah--and I would have helped Meronicos, if he had not been so utterly determined to distrust me."

"Are you strong enough to do such work?" Viragan asked, in a voice whose calculated harshness could not quite conceal a note of plaintiveness.

"I think so, Your Highness," Giraiazal said. "But your daughter might have to come to me, if her dreams are the ones you want me to shape. I have already established a bridge of sorts between her dreams and mine, but I will need to see her and place my hands on her head."

"No," said Viragan, as Giraiazal had known he would, "it is not my daughter's dreams that I need you to shape. It is my own."

"Ah!" said Giraiazal, softly. He understood--or thought he understood--how Viragan had arrived at his present state of mind. As he had told Triasymon, the regent had been thrown into a state of profound confusion since the coral bride had disappeared from Lysariel's room. His first thought must have been that the statue had been stolen by an enemy, who intended to thwart his plans--but that was not what had happened. Viragan had intended to contrive Manazzoryn's death, and Manazzoryn was dead. Viragan had intended to contrive Lysariel's death, and Lysariel was dead. Viragan had twice captured Lysariel and put him safely away, and twice Lysariel had been released. The second time, admittedly, the culprit was known--and Orlu, at least, had died by Viragan's own hand, if not quite in the way intended--but when Lysariel ought to have been seized a third time he had been spirited away.

In a way, Viragan might have found these mysteries easier to deal with had they been translated into enemy action, but they had not. Indeed, they had so far served only to advance his plans. It was as if, having been formed, his plans had taken on a life of their own, reducing him from author to mere instrument--perhaps forcing him to wonder whether he might have been a mere instrument from the very beginning, and whether he might at any moment become disposable, his usefulness ended. Had he been able to take a distanced view of the matter, he would almost certainly have seen what was happening, and how, and why--but he could not distance himself. He had always been a sceptic, ready to dismiss all magic as charlantry, but that had been an easy pose to maintain while he was in control of his own destiny, when the things that he required to be done happened only because he did them. Now that the connection between his intentions and their fulfilment had become mysterious and obscure he was ripe for conversion to credulity--so ripe, in fact, that he had all-but-completed his own conversion.

Giraiazal got up from his bed, unsteadily. Viragan put out a hand to help him--and then, without being asked, guided the magician to a chair by the cluttered table. Then, again without being asked, Viragan began clearing a corner of the table so that he and Giraiazal could sit facing one another across the right angle.

"I want you to help me renew my strength of mind," Viragan said, when they were both ready. "I want you to help me as you helped Calia: to shape my dreams to give me armour against...."

"Against what, Your Highness?" Giraiazal said, softly. "I cannot help you if you will not tell me."

The pirate hesitated before answering, his pale eyes catching the glimmer of the candle-flame like polished opals. "Against the curse of the coral bride," he said, finally. "Alive or not, she has some kind of power--and whatever your anathema may have accomplished, I can still feel her close behind me, as if she were forever peering over my shoulder. Whenever I go to sleep there is a dark presence in my dreams, always close at hand but always shadowed. Whenever I turn to see who it is, it is transformed into something harmless, something familiar, something useful--but it is only a matter of time before it reaches out to touch me, to hurt me, to destroy me. I know that you cannot exorcise the demon unless you know its name, but I also know that you can help me to endure its attentions, to protect myself against its malice. I know that you can add your dream-force to mine, as you added it to Calia's and saved her life. I know that you can shape my dreams in such a way that I can see the face of the shadow which is haunting me, and face it as I faced Orlu and Triasymon, and defend myself in the only way I know. You say that

Meronicos died because he would not trust you--well, Giraiazal, I understand very well how he felt and how he thought, but I am a more flexible man by far than the Idol of Yura. I can trust you, Giraiazal, if I only have reason enough, and I have reason enough tonight. Only swear to me that you will do for me what you did for Calia, and I will let you into my dreams. I will let you into my dreams as willingly as she did--more willingly even than my daughter, let alone Meronicos the Malcontent."

"I know your dreams, Prince Viragan," Giraiazal said, quietly. "But I need you to be honest with me, if I am to give you the help you need. I know that you did not persuade Lysariel to kill his brother, nor did you kill Lysariel. But you did try to poison Calia, did you not? And when I saved her, you seized the opportunity to throw her from that window, with your own hands."

"Yes," said Viragan. "Yes, I did. That is how I tested your power, Giraiazal. That is how I know that whatever tricks you play, you are a true morpheomorphist. Orlu escaped my traps by a fluke, but Calia was saved. Everything has gone awry since I threw her from that window, but that is not your fault, Giraiazal. You did what you were bound to do, and I have no complaint against you. You do not like me, I know. To the best of my knowledge, there are only two people in all the world who do. But I know what a pride you take in your work, Giraiazal. I know how much pride you would have taken in saving the Emperor of Yura, and how much pride you might take from saving me. I trust you, Giraiazal, because I know how strongly you crave opportunities to demonstrate your power. Well, I offer you one now that you certainly cannot refuse--and I think you know how valuable my gratitude will be."

Giraiazal swallowed a phantom lump that had arisen from abyssal depths to clog his throat. "I will do my best, Your Highness," he promised. So saying, he reached out to place both his hands of Viragan's head, and Viragan leaned forward to meet him.

"Before I return to my bed," Giraiazal murmured, "I shall make myself a potion: not a sleeping-draught, but a potion to stimulate the vision of the soul. By increasing the clarity of my own dreams, I shall attempt to lend you the power to see the web of causation that surrounds you. Take your sword to bed with you, my lord. Rest your fingers upon its hilt, so that it will be in your hand when you dream. Once you can see the web clearly, you will know where it needs to be cut. As soon as you touch the web, its spinner will emerge from the shadows, anxious to secure you with new and stronger threads, but you will have your sword."

"But what of the coral bride, Master Morpheomorphist?" the pirate whispered. "Shall I be able to kill the phantom queen with my sword?"

"Her curse is not what you think it is, my lord," Giraiazal said. "Queen Calia is dead and the statue cannot move. Her voice is not her own, and may not be able to sustain itself now that Lysariel is dead. My intelligence is your intelligence now, and my dream-vision is yours. When you sleep, you will see what you need to see, and when you next wake up you will remember what you have dreamed. It may be that what you have seen will require interpretation, but when I have told you what your dream meant, you will know the truth."

Giraiazal meant what he said. He knew that the truth would become manifest eventually, and that he would be a fool to continue hiding what he knew while he had a chance to ingratiate himself with Viragan. He also knew that he had to present the truth as something he had derived by magic, not as something so obvious that it could have been deduced by any man whose mind was unclouded. While Viragan remained regent and Giraiazal was his trusted Grand Vizier, both would surely be safe--and the greater the dependence the magician could cultivate in his patient, the greater would be his fraction of the power they shared.

When Viragan left the magician's apartment, therefore, he was satisfied with the result of his quest--but not as satisfied as Giraiazal.

The magician was as good as his word. As soon as the door had closed behind his visitor he set about gathering ingredients to make a potion. He left his opiates untouched, and his euphorics too, seeking out jars and phials containing tinctures and powders that would stimulate his inner eye. He dissolved the resulting compound in alcohol, and drank it down. Then he returned to his bed. He did not suppose for a moment that he would have any difficulty falling asleep, in spite of the fact that he had taken no opium. He was extremely tired.

He had not snuffed out the candle on the table, but he observed through half-closed lids that its flame had sputtered out as the wick fell into a pool of soft wax. He was glad of the darkness, because it seemed to him to be a canvas that his inner vision would soon begin to decorate, and brightly--but as he let his eyes close he heard a noise like a footstep, and started in alarm.

"Who's there?" he demanded. His ears told him that the intruder was by the foot of the bed, moving sideways through the room--but after he had spoken, the feet shifted their direction, and the invader came around the bed to its left side, moving towards the pillow from which his head had lifted slightly.

"Who is it?" Giraiazal asked, for a second time, when the footfalls ceased. "Burrel? Mergin?" He knew that Viragan had sent Burrel and Mergin away, and that he had not heard the door open since the pirate prince had left--but how in that case, could anyone have come into the room?

Giraiazal rarely had occasion to strike a light using a match or a tinder-box, but he always kept several such devices on his bedside table, ready to hand. He groped for a match now, but his fingers fell upon an empty surface. Someone--probably Mergin, who had a tidy mind--had removed his stock.

The footfalls ceased as the mysterious intruder became still.

It seemed to the magician that the intruder must be only just out of reach, but he dared not lean over the edge of the bed in order to extend the compass of his arm. He had the uncomfortable feeling that his uninvited guest was looking down at him with eyes that were quite untroubled by the darkness.

"Who dares steal from a magician?" he said, when he was unable to bear the silence any longer.

"Why, anyone at all," said a murmurous, seemingly-female voice, "provided that he knows the limitations of a sick and exhausted man."

Giraiazal thought that he recognised the voice, but knew that the appearance had to be deceptive.

"Queen Calia is dead," he said, weakly. "You are a mere mimic, whoever you are."

"Am I?" the voice replied.

Giraiazal sat up in bed then, and smoothed the folds of his nightshirt. "Strike a light!" he said. "You have my matches. Strike one, and show me your face!"

"That is not necessary," the voice assured him.

The first thing that pierced the darkness was the glare of two yellow eyes. That would have be intimidating enough, but the internal illumination which set their stare ablaze spread by slow degrees to the remainder of a face: Queen Calia's face.

"It is a mask!" Giraiazal protested--but the light illuminating the face came from within, and was far too steady to be a candle-flame set behind a translucent mask. Nor did the gradual spread of the illumination stop when it had limned the features of the face. It descended to show a pair of shoulders, and then the gentle curve of a breast.

"You are an illusion!" was Giraiazal's next attempt to avoid the unacceptable conclusion. "This is not even my dream, but poor Prince Viragan's. He thinks himself the victim of your curse, and nothing I could say to him could have stopped him seeing you when he and I feel asleep. But I know what--and who--you really are."

"Are you certain of that?" the apparition asked.

"I am," Giraiazal said, boldly, "and Prince Viragan has wisely come to me for help. You cannot torment me as you might have tormented him. I know you. I know what you really are, and what hopeful force has made you seem animate. I do not fear you. I am not mad, as poor Lysariel was. I would have cured him of his folly, with the aid of the wine of Yethlyreom, had I not been opposed--but I know now who fed his madness, and was glad to share it."

"Perhaps you do," said the coral bride, "and perhaps not--but you shall hear what I have to say in either case. You are a great magician, are you not? Can you doubt that the words of a phantom have oracular authority, however they might be produced?"

"You are not a phantom," Giraiazal said, firmly. "You are a shared illusion: a figment of a dream."

"And that makes me an oracle, does it not?" the coral bride persisted, glowing ever more fervently. "You will unravel my meaning in the morning, will you not? So you are bound to heed what I say, and do as I ask are you not?

"I suppose you are an oracle of sorts," Giraiazal conceded, having been forced to admit to himself that the apparition had a point, and was at least polite enough to acknowledge his ability as a morpheomorphist. "Why should I doubt it? But Queen Calia is dead, and you are a mere simulacrum: a demon come to inhabit a dream. You must beware, lest I use my magic to cast you out."

The radiant figure, fully illumined now, stared down upon him implacably. "Is that really what you want, Giraiazal?" the creature asked. "Have you really no ambition but to see me gone?"

"Why should I not?" he countered. "You may be an oracle of sorts, but you cannot tell me my future. What use are you to me?"

"I could tell your fortune," the image said, "which is more than you can do for yourself. But that is not why I have come. I want you to bear witness, Lord Vizier. I want you to come with me to fetch my husband's lover, and accompany her to a place of reckoning. My history has been much confused in the telling, perhaps irrevocably, and I should like its climax to be clear."

"If clarity is what you desire," Giraiazal retorted, "perhaps you should not have come into my room like a stealthy thief, hiding yourself in shadow and confusion. If you wanted to be clear, you might have presented yourself in bright daylight, in the plaza before the palace gate."

"I might have come openly and deliberately along the shore, as my husband once did," the coral bride conceded, "but he was the king, for whom men were obliged to make way. Against me they would have put up barricades, setting some of them afire; they would have showered me with spears and arrows; they might even have taken sledgehammers and axes to my bright limbs. Perhaps they could not have destroyed me, for I am neither soft nor brittle now, but they might have prevented me from reaching my goal. I might have been forced to kill a dozen, or a hundred, merely to ensure that others would not dare to step into my path--and when I reached the palace gate, I would have found it barred against me and heavily defended. This way was easier. Will you come with me now, Master Magician--or will you try your curses first, to satisfy yourself that you are impotent?"

"I am very ill and very tired," Giraiazal admitted. "I have already done what I could to hurt you, but it seems that your demonic allies are more powerful than my own." He got up from the bed and stretched his aching limbs. "May I put on my best shirt and robe?" he asked.

"Certainly," said the coral bride. "It would not be fitting for the mother of the king to blush at your appearance."

Giraiazal took off his nightshirt and changed his underwear before dressing himself in his official costume. The interval gave him an opportunity to think, and weigh his options. This was Viragan's dream, and Viragan would doubtless make his appearance soon enough, but Giraiazal had sworn to help the prince in every way he could. It was not surprising that the coral bride intended to take him to see Zintrah, because Zintrah had always had a key role in Viragan's plans, and hence in Viragan's dreams, but what dangers and opportunities might such a meeting involve? Given that the coral bride's curse had manifested itself in Viragan's dream--by no means unexpectedly--as an animate statue, how should he formulate a plan to destroy the statue, or at least to force it to show itself as it really was? It seemed perfectly understandable that the animate statue intended to seek a reckoning with Zintrah, and perfectly understandable that she wanted witnesses, but how might Giraiazal transform that reckoning to his own advantage, and demonstrate that he was a very able witness indeed?

Until he knew more about what the dream-bride intended, it was impossible to judge what might and ought to be done--but one thought that did occur to Giraiazal was that witnesses were no use to anyone unless they survived to say what they had witnessed.

The light that had flared within the image became muted again before it followed the magician from his room--but the eyes remained visible, their stare always accusing, and the sound of the creature's footfalls remained more distinct than those of Giraiazal's slippered feet.

The magician led the way down the stairs and through the corridors to the room where Zintrah was sleeping alongside the infant Hatarus. He and his follower passed through three archways at which sentries were posted, and found two more guards camped outside Zintrah's apartment, but all the men-at-arms were deeply asleep, as if their drinking-water had been dosed with opium.

Zintrah had not taken any kind of sleeping-draught. She started awake as soon as her bedroom door creaked on its hinges. Her night-lamp was burning, only a little muted, and she recognised Giraiazal immediately, even though she could not see at first who--or what--was behind him.

"What do you want, Master Magician?" she demanded.

Giraiazal did not answer. It was enough to take half a step aside, in order to discover whether the coral image of Queen Calia was visible to Zintrah as well as to him. Half of him hoped that it would, half that it would not--and there was an extra, arithmetically nonsensical, part of him which dared to wonder whether even he was really present, really visible, and really material.

Zintrah squinted and blinked, and then rubbed her eyes with her knuckles. There was more fear in her actions than disbelief. Giraiazal guessed that she had never quite dared to believe that the image was only a statue. "You and she are in league," she whispered, eventually. "I suspected it all along. Your anathema was a fake. You planned it all from beginning to end. Sorcerer!"

Giraiazal could not help feeling deeply offended by these unjust accusations. He had thought that Zintrah, in spite of the rough and rather contemptuous treatment she had afforded him of late, knew that he was as firmly on her side as he had been on Calia's. "No, Your Highness," he murmured. "I planned nothing. Like you, I have been an innocent and helpless victim in all of this."

Zintrah's expression, eerily shadowed by the low-set night-lamp, suggested that she was not convinced of her own innocence, let alone of his.

"Come, sister," said the coral bride. "Bring the child."

"You shall not harm him," Zintrah said to the statue, anxiety for her child making her suddenly brave. "I will not permit it."

"I would not harm a hair on his head," the creature replied, in a voice that had become strangely soft. "He is the child of my beloved, Lysariel, and should have been mine. Nor is it you that I have come to kill, traitress that you are. I need you to bear witness. Come."

Zintrah remained where she was, but she turned her head to search for help or inspiration.

"Giraiazal?" she said, anxiously. "If you are not with her, you must stop her. Bind her with magic and bid her be still."

"I have tried that," the magician said, bitterly. "I have cursed her with all the force that I could muster, but she simply will not go away. Either she is a demon, far more powerful than those I may command....or she is naught but a fragment of a nightmare. If so, the same is true of you, and even of me--but I have to ask you not to be afraid, for your father's sake. We must help him in this, for he needs us both, and he has had the grace to admit it."

Zintrah could not understand or be satisfied with that, but he had not expected her to. "Do something!" she commanded. "You must be able to do *something!* What kind of wizard are you?

The statue turned its own head to follow the direction of Zintrah's furious gaze. "What kind of wizard are you, Giraiazal?" asked Calia's stolen voice. "What have you ever done to protect those in your charge, save to watch and wait and capitulate with the instructions of your vile mistress? What Earthly use are you in defying the vicious dictates of Damozel Fate?"

"I have provided such wards against misfortune as I could!" Giraiazal objected, badly stung by the injustice of these taunts. "I have used my powers as a physician and a seer as well as any man could. As for my mistress, Damozel Fate, she is hardly mine to command or defy. I am her plaything, as are we all, and am not at fault because her game is winding to its close. If you will only face me honestly, and let me curse you by your true name, I might show you exactly what a magician can do." His irritation ebbed away while he spoke, but he felt no conspicuous relief.

"You know my true name," the statue said. "I am Calia, and was Calia long before the day my other self was born, let alone killed."

"Calia?" Zintrah repeated, complainingly. "How could you be Calia before Calia was born? How could you be anything before you were carved?"

"If nothing were settled before it occurred," the coral bride informed her, "the future would be unknowable even to the meagre extent that our Master Magician can divine it. Causes have always preceded events, and there are seeds of identity in human beings before they or their mothers or their mothers' mothers are ever conceived. All this is a mere unfolding, an efflorescence of the twilight, slowly opening to catch the final rays of the doomed sun. While there is light, there ought to be seers. While Fate is a Damozel, she requires admirers and suitors as well as victims. Come with me, sister, and see what I must do."

Fine words, Giraiazal thought. *But I do know your true name, and it is not Calia.*

Reluctantly, Zintrah got up from her bed, clutching Hatarus to her breast as she rose to her feet. She handed the child to Giraiazal while she dressed herself, but she took her son back as soon as she had put her slippers on.

Giraiazal wondered whether Zintrah, like him, had reasoned that if she were being asked to serve as a witness then she would not be murdered before she gave testimony as to what she had seen. He would have been better pleased, of course, if Viragan's daughter and Manazzoryn's bride had risen so boldly because she had remembered that she still had his wedding-gift to aid and protect her--but he could not quite bring himself to believe that.

"If you really were an aspect of Queen Calia," Giraiazal said, "animated by a common soul, then you would know how hard I laboured to save your life when you were bitten by the spider. You would know, too, that Zintrah laboured alongside me, lovingly and unselfishly."

"I thank you for your labour, Giraiazal," the coral bride said. "But I cannot thank Zintrah for hers."

"Why?" Giraiazal objected. "Because she seduced Lysariel? I thought that it was Lysariel you could not forgive, when you found out that he had seduced her. That was why you turned on him, was it not? Because he trusted you so well that he finally let slip that Hatarus was his son-- although I am not the only one who could have told you that long ago, had you only cared to enquire into the matter. And have you not punished Zintrah enough by contriving the death of her husband? It was you-- was it not?--who lied to him, saying that you had seen Manazzoryn attempt to rape Calia, and cause her to fall--even though you knew all along that Viragan had murdered her."

"What?" said Zintrah, before the coral bride could make any response. "You are a liar, Giraiazal! My father would never do such a thing, any more than Manazzoryn would! Calia's death was an accident!" The performance was unconvincing. She did not believe what she was saying, although she obviously wanted to.

Giraiazal sighed. "Never mind," he said. "It will be over soon. I now her true name--and Viragan will know it too, when he wakes."

"You know my true name, Giraiazal," the beautiful illusion admitted, "but not my true nature." So saying, she took a stride forward, and then another, reaching out as if to take Zintrah into a fond and sisterly embrace.

Zintrah shrank away, but there was no avenue of escape open to her. In the end, she had to allow the arms of coral to enfold her, and suffer their tender embrace. When she was released again, quite unharmed, she did not seem at all relieved.

"Come," said the statue. "Your father is waiting."

6

It is true, as anyone who cares to look around may see, that the vast majority of those who populate the dying Earth show not the slightest inclination to rejoice in their freedom. They remain enslaved--despite that they are by no means *contentedly* enslaved--to the impulses innate within their flesh and their society. They toil in the fields and upon the surface of the sea to bring in harvests of grain and fish; they labour in manufactories to produce goods, and tools for the further production of goods; they harbour deep affection for their homes and their spouses and their children while they nurse bitter grudges against those who have offended or opposed them; day after day they nurse the hope that the next day might be better than the one preceding it.

In a world which had a future, all this would qualify as ordinary human life, for the essence of all life is reproduction and the essence of human life is progressive, keenly-motivated endeavour; in our world, however, it can only qualify as absurdity.

The people of the world have all heard the prophecies that tell them the sun is about to die. They cannot deny what they have heard, yet still the greater number undertake to live as if there were a future; still the greater number undertake to live as if duty were all; still the greater number refuse to recognise the futility of everything they do and everything they are. We may choose to see this folly as tragedy, or we may choose to see it as comedy, but we are bound to see it as one thing or the other--which is to say that we are bound to see it as art.

The Revelations of Suomynona, the Last Prophet

It seemed that Viragan was indeed waiting, although he did not seem to know exactly what it was he was waiting for. He was alone in the smaller room adjacent to the council-chamber, standing before the makeshift throne, on the spot where Lysariel had slain Manazzoryn. He was fully dressed and fully armed, although he had followed his usual habit in being economical with his armour. His sword was unsheathed, although he was weighing it in his hand almost as though he had never used it before, and had forgotten how best to exploit its power.

It seemed that he did not become aware for some time that he was no longer alone, although he was already speaking to himself when Giraiazal opened the door.

"So this is how it ends," he whispered, his gaze fixed on the gleaming blade of his sword, which reflected candle-light into his feverish eyes. "I win the game. I win the prize. I become what I am. And I am ill. I am ill, and I am dying. I have dispensed illnesses, and poisons. I have made illness my servant, to strike where I desire, and now it turns on me. It does my bidding, and shows me my victory, and then it turns, like a serpent taken by the tail. I know the signs. I cannot read, but I can feel. I know what is written in my living flesh. It is the same spider, the same venom. My flesh will grow brittle, and abscesses will swell within, although the cracks in my hardened skin will not be wide enough to let out the pus. The soft tissues beneath the tumours will be rent instead, and the horrid fluids discharged into my gut. I wish I had the amulet, even though it probably has no virtue left in it. I wish I had the girdle too, even though it is probably no more than a mere tangle of threads. That fool who thinks himself a magician can no more cure me than he can cure himself. I am lost. I have won, but I am lost. Everything I wanted is mine, but my hand did not win it, and I am reduced to waiting. My destiny has grown wings and taken flight without me, and left me helpless. There is nothing I can see, nothing I can hold. It is out of my grasp and out of my reach. The world is ending, and there is nothing left to any man but what he can seize in his own hands, and make with his own skill. That I had, and that I have lost. The magician cannot save me now."

"You must save yourself, Your Highness," Giraiazal said, "but I am with you, and your daughter too. You have our strength as well as your own. You came to me for help, and I am here."

Viragan started. The sword moved, catching the candlelight as it did so, two points of light glistening on the blade like the huge moist eyes of an owl in search of prey.

"Father?" said Zintrah. "Help me, father! Calia has returned from the grave, and I need your protection."

Viragan looked around then, to see who had intruded upon his soliloquy. There was no recognition in his eyes. He did not seem to recognise his daughter, nor his grandson, nor his friend Giraiazal.

Perhaps we are not here, Giraiazal thought. *Perhaps he is alone with the coral bride. Perhaps she needs no witnesses after all.*

Zintrah stepped forward, with Hatarus in her arms. Giraiazal followed her. The light of recognition dawned at last in Viragan's eyes-- although, like Zintrah before him, Viragan did not see at first that there was anyone behind them. The coral bride was as slender and slight as her model, and she remained at a standstill. It was not until the magician and the mother of the king drew slightly apart that Viragan's quizzical expression darkened into frank alarm, before turning into an alloy of astonishment and wrath.

There was a long silence while the merchant prince looked from one newcomer to another, and weighed the situation as carefully as he had been weighing his sword.

"I felt the moment coming," the regent murmured, in the end. "Although I am no diviner, I knew that I had an appointment with Fate. I remember now, Master Magician I had underestimated you--I only hope that I realised that in time. I did not believe that you could hide the statue where I could not find it--but it was you all along. I suppose that I ought to have reconsidered when I saw you perform your make-believe exorcism. I knew that you were not cursing her. It was all a sham--but it seemed to serve my purpose, so I let it pass. Now, the curse has fallen on me. You are exceedingly ungrateful, are you not, Giraiazal? I have done everything for you that I could, and now I am cursed for my trouble."

"You are mistaken, my lord," Giraiazal said, quietly. "You came to my room, asking for my help. I promised to shape your dream, and here I am. We are allies now, my lord--allies at last. You must not allow yourself to be confused. You must try to see your adversary clearly. You have my magic to aid you, if only you can focus your thoughts and use your sword."

Viragan looked at the weapon he held as if he still could not remember how to use it. "You let me down, Giraiazal," he said. "You cursed the demon, but it would not go. You let me down, and I am not a forgiving man."

"One cannot exorcise a demon if one does not know its name," Giraiazal told him,"and even if one knows its name, still it must be confronted face to face. Nor are you the only one who is unforgiving....although I think your adversary could have forgiven you anything, if only you had not killed Calia. You should have shared your plans more openly, Your Highness. You should have told those closest to you what you intended."

"Yes, father," Zintrah said. "You should have told me. You should not have killed my sister."

"She was *not* your sister," Viragan snarled. "She was Orlu's chit--just a meaningless detail, a pawn for sacrifice. Who could ever have imagined that she would return from hell a fury, filling her carven image with uncanny life? Well, it seems that I must confront the monster whether I know her true name or not. If you could only exorcise her now, Giraiazal, even I might learn to forgive. I know how to be grateful, when I have cause." It was probably a lie, Giraiazal realised. The magician wondered whether he still had a choice--but he had told the truth when he had told Viragan that his adversary was as unforgiving as he, if not more so, since Calia had fallen to her death.

"The magician cannot exorcise me," the coral bride said. "He guessed my true name long before you came to him for help and found him too weak to be unforgiving--but he cannot drive me away, no manner what he does, for I am no common demon."

"This is your dream, Prince Viragan," Giraiazal was quick to say. "You are the one who can drive the monster away, or slay it, if you can only see it for what it really is."

"Tell me, then," said the merchant prince, capitulating with the logic of the situation.

Giraiazal opened his mouth and began to form a name, but suddenly found that his head was spinning and his stomach nauseous. He tried to speak, but could not do it. *But I am only a figment of a dream* he protested, silently. *How can I be ill, or poisoned?* He felt that his flesh was becoming hard and brittle, and that abscesses were swelling in his tissues, straining against the pressure of his awful solidity.

Meanwhile, the coral statue began to glow with an inner fire that put forth heat as well as light; the magician had to stagger back, shielding his eyes. He heard Zintrah whimper with anxiety as she too stepped back, leaving Viragan and the coral bride to stare at one another.

"You are not Calia," Viragan said, coldly. "I killed Calia. I had to kill her twice over, thanks to the magician's meddling, but I did kill her. I threw her from the window, since she would not consent to die from the spider's bite. You might have been hewn from magical coral, which became capable of animation once it was lifted from water into air, but you are only coral. You are not Calia."

"I *am* Calia," the image replied. "I was Calia before the world was born, and I will be Calia long after the world has ended. Love is a supernatural force, after all; it can defy logic and work miracles. True lovers are not separate individuals; they are one and indivisible. I thought, for a while, that Lysariel was also Calia, also bound to her by fate and folly, but he was a living lie. He betrayed her--and that was worse than killing her. As for Manazzoryn--he despoiled her. It *was* a kind of rape, no matter how it was accomplished. I could live with Lysariel, because I knew that Calia loved him, but I could not let Lysariel live with Manazzoryn. And when I knew what Lysariel had done, I could not let him live with himself. I am Calia, you see. She is dead, but I am alive. She will always be alive, so long as I am alive, and in my eyes she is eternal. That is what love means."

Viragan was staring into the glowing amber eyes, as if he were seeing them for the first time.

"*Sharuman?*" he said, as though it were incredible. "Is that really you?"

Giraiazal had sighed as soon as he heard the name pronounced. *Am I not the greatest morpheomorphist in the world?* he congratulated himself, privately. *Am I not the saviour of empires, the maker of kingdoms? Am I not...?* He stopped then, because he realised that the dream was not yet over--and had, in fact, only just attained its point of crisis.

"You must have known that they were doomed," Viragan whispered, incredulously. "You must have understood. You were the only one who ever understood. You were my right arm. You were the only one I ever trusted. *I would have given you my daughter!*"

"It was not *your* daughter I wanted," said Captain Sharuman, who stood where the coral bride had stood, with his double-headed axe in his hands. "It was not *your* daughter I loved."

"You never breathed a word," Viragan said--but it was more an accusation than an expression of wonderment. "You should have told me!"

"It was you," said Sharuman, softly, "who should have told me. Was I not your right hand? Was I not the only one you trusted?" Was I not the one who should have been *told?* His voice had risen as he spoke, until the last sentence was almost a scream.

"Traitor!" howled Viragan.

"Murderer!" Sharuman howled, in return. The whole palace shook with the violence of their anger. Indeed, it seemed to Giraiazal that the whole world trembled. He realised that he had not given sufficient consideration to the effect it would have on Viragan to discover that his closest lieutenant had been following his own strange agenda for some little while. Nor, for that matter, had he given sufficient consideration to the question of exactly whose dream this was, and how many dreamers might be party to it.

"You betrayed me," Viragan said, incredulously, "for some worthless little trinket of a girl. *You* betrayed *me*, for love of Orlu's daughter. Why, you only saw the girl half a dozen times before we brought her to the palace, and never exchanged a word with her. Are you mad, to think that I could forgive you this?"

Suddenly, it was the coral bride who was standing before Viragan, not Captain Sharuman--but she was still holding the double-headed axe.

"That will not save you," Viragan said, waspishly. "I know you now. I should have known you long ago. Who else could have removed the statue? Who else could have spirited Lysariel away from my house, and from the battlefield where I slew Orlu? Who else could have commanded the loyalty of *my* men, sufficiently to throw me into such dire confusion that I began to believe in miracles? I even began to believe in that ridiculous little magician, because he seemed so much more plausible than the idea that you could betray me *for love*."

Giraiazal wanted to cry out then, to warn Viragan that he must trust his morpheomorphist, or his dream could turn back into a nightmare--but Giraiazal was still too sick to speak, his flesh having become so hard and so brittle that he might have been a tree of coral straining against a storm-tossed wave. He wanted to cry out because he was afraid, terrified that he might lose a second opportunity to prove exactly how great a wizard he was. He wanted to howl at Viragan in anger, to insist that Viragan must not treat him as Meronicos had, must not throw away his last chance to demonstrate that he was a great healer, a great wizard, a great man, and a great prophet--but he was helpless, a mere minion of someone else's dream

Viragan lifted his sword, and the coral blade lifted her axe. Viragan had plenty of time to choose his position and his stance, for the animate statue seemed to be in no hurry at all to engage him.

Giraiazal wondered what would happen if Viragan contrived to land a blow. The coral bride was neither brittle nor soft, but she was material, and the sword was heavy and sharp. Even if she were neither shattered nor cloven in two, the impact must disturb her and cause her injury. If nothing else, the force of the blow would send her spinning across the room; Viragan was a very strong man. The magician knew, however, that Viragan's sword was not such a fearsome instrument as the double-headed axe wielded by the coral bride. If *she* were to land a blow....

So slowly did the coral bride come to the conflict that Viragan found time for a contemptuous sideways glance at Giraiazal. The magician tried to meet it squarely, and tried to signal with his eyes that which he could not say aloud--but his unglowing eyes were as mute as his paralysed voice. He told himself, desperately, that he had not failed. He had not, admittedly, contrived to prevent the murder of Calia or the maddening of Lysariel, but he had put up a good fight against incalculable odds. In order to contrive the death of Manazzoryn the protection he had provided had had to be cunningly removed. Viragan had sought to use him a dozen times, and Giraiazal had consented to be used, but all the while he had been a thorn in the prince's side: a thorn that the prince had never dared to tackle directly. Like the Emperor of Yura before him, Prince Viragan of Scleracina had been forced to come crawling to Giraiazal of Natalarch, begging for his help....but Prince Viragan, like the Emperor of Yura before him, was too weak and stupid to trust the only man in the world who was able to help him.

Fool! Giraiazal would have shouted, if he could. In the absence of his cry, the room was silent; Viragan and the coral bride were still measuring one another, still wondering where and when to strike.

The silence was broken by the cry of Hatarus, who had finally awakened from his innocent sleep.

"Demon!" Viragan shouted raising his sword above his head and bounding forward.

That seemed to Giraiazal a perfectly ridiculous thing to say and do. Viragan knew, now, that his adversary was not a demon, but only a friend seduced by love. The regent knew, too, that no swordsman should ever raise his weapon above his head as if it were a sledgehammer, no matter what kind of opponent he had to face.

As the sword's blade fell upon her from above, the coral bride raised her own hands high and blocked the sword with the haft of her axe, deflecting it sideways. Then, as Viragan stumbled, she whirled her own weapon around and launched a horizontal sweep that struck the regent's head clean off his shoulders.

Giraiazal could hardy believe it, even in a dream.

The coral image spread her arms wide, as if to luxuriate in the fountain of blood that gushed from the neck of her headless victim. The statue's radiant form was extravagantly spattered with red. The blood seemed impossibly brilliant as it began immediately to boil.

The coral bride looked from side to side, as if to make sure that the witnesses she had summoned were paying proper attention.

Hatarus was still howling. Zintrah was moving in a carefully considered arc, coming towards towards the throne so that she might set her son upon it. Having done that, she positioned herself squarely in front of the wailing infant, hiding the boy from the statue's furious sight.

"He is the king of Scleracina," said Zintrah, defiantly. "He is the rightful king, destined as such for a thousand generations. He will doubtless be the last to sit upon the throne, but it is his and he will have it."

"He is the rightful king," the coral bride agreed. "Long may he reign, if the sun will only condescend to light his way." Then she turned to Giraiazal. "Do you know my name?" she asked, menacingly.

Giraiazal contrived a gasp, by way of indicating that he could not speak.

"I am Calia," the statue said. "You cannot command me, much less exorcise me, but my work is done. I suppose I ought to go now, of my own free will." Giraiazal was only mildly astonished, because he knew that the coral bride was, indeed, capable of acting freely. Viragan had let him down; his morpheomorphic art would certainly have succeeded had the merchant prince only been capable of trusting him, but Viragan had ben a rough seaman at heart, and a piratical one at that; his dreams had never been the dreams of an authentic aristocrat.

"Farewell, dearest of sisters!" the coral bride said, blithely. "Farewell, unhappiest of magicians!" As the statue made as if to perform a deep but mocking bow, it was suddenly struck rigid. Its forward momentum caused it to teeter, and then to tumble. It fell very slowly, but as soon as it hit the marble floor it shattered into a thousand tiny pieces, showering Zintrah and Giraiazal with stinging shards.

7

I am the world's last prophet. I make this statement confidently, because the end is now so near that there is no time for others to be born who might yet acquire the wisdom I have stored and nurtured. Mine is the last word, and if any of my fellows cannot hear and heed it they are deaf to sanity.

That last word, as I have said before, and still insist, is *freedom*.

What we do now is without consequence. What we do now has already been punished, with the utmost severity, by the march of time. Among all the humans that have ever lived, among all the manifold humankinds, we alone have the privilege of personal creativity.

I do not mean by "the privilege of personal creativity" merely that we have the opportunity to play with the detritus of a million lost civilizations whose mechanical means were infinitely greater than ours, and the legacy of a million visitations by alien entities of every degree and kind of strangeness, although of course we do. Such things are handicaps and restraints more often than they are means, and even those who are vain enough to term themselves magicians have no more at their disposal than a few tiny fragments of dubious knowledge and a few trivial tricks of unreliable expertise. What I mean by "the privilege of personal creativity" is a matter of ends, not means.

No matter what a man of our era seeks to become, the means he musters will be slight and treacherous, but he is free to deploy them as he may desire, to any imaginable end--provided only that it is immediate--or no end at all.

Morality is extinct; it perished with the certain knowledge of the imminent extinction of the sun.

There are no more heroes, because there is no more progress for heroes to foster. There are no more villains, because there are no more prospects to be blighted.

In this world, uniquely, all stories are *pure*, possessed of no other quality but meaning, however carefully or recklessly that meaning may be embodied in manner and style. Our tales, unlike those produced in every other culture that preceded ours, have no morals.

That, I confidently believe, is why we are here: to produce tales without morals. No other explanation makes sense.

The Revelations of Suomynona, the Last Prophet

When Giraiazal awoke, blinking his eyes against the ruddy light of dawn, he was not surprised to discover Captain Sharuman sitting beside his bed.

"Why, Captain," he croaked, glad to find that he could speak at all, "I have had the strangest dream."

"Have you, Master Magician?" Sharuman asked, coldly.

"I dreamed that the coral bride came to my room, and led me downstairs. I dreamed that she killed Prince Viragan with an axe, and then exploded into a thousand pieces."

"That was not a dream, Master Magician," Sharuman told him. "That was exactly what happened. *Exactly* what happened. You really saw what you thought that you had only dreamed. I can prove it to you."

"How?" Giraiazal asked.

Captain Sharuman picked something up from the floor beside the bed. Giraiazal recognised his slippers--but they were stained with blood.

"There are bloody footprints leading all the way from the throne-room to this attic," Sharuman told him. "You were there when Prince Viragan was murdered. So was Zintrah. You saw it done; his blood bathed your feet. You saw what happened. The coral bride killed him--but then your anathema took effect. The coral bride was destroyed; her curse has run its course."

"Zintrah..." Giraiazal began--but Sharuman had not finished.

"Zintrah saw it all," the captain said. "When she woke this morning, she too thought that it had been a dream, but it was not. It was real. She understood that, when I had explained it to her. Her slippers were bloody too, you see. That was the proof she needed. You will have to go to her, of course, if you are well enough; she needs your help, and I know that you can help her, as you helped her sister. If I did not know that...if I were not grateful for that...but you know what you saw, do you not? You know that Viragan really was murdered by the coral bride."

"Yes," said Giraiazal, meekly. "It was not a dream. I really did see it. Viragan is dead--and you, I suppose, will be regent."

"That is too much responsibility for one man," Sharuman told him. "A fool might be so ambitious, but a wise man knows his limitations. I shall invite my friend Captain Akabar to assist me. He is a good man, and a steady one."

"Not the kind to fall in love, at any rate," Giraiazal murmured.

"Don't speak of things you don't understand, Master Magician," Sharuman said, in a low voice. "Stick to what you know. You are not devoid of imagination, but there are things you do not understand. Prince Viragan was right, of course--I only saw her half a dozen times, while Viragan and Orlu were setting their rivalry aside and striking their bargain. It was enough. Perhaps he was right, too, when he said that I should have told him--but what could I say? What could I say, to a man like that? He should have told me what her intended, but he did not. I stood by and watched her married to Lysariel, because I thought it was what she wanted, and what she deserved. I thought he loved her just as I did--and when he went mad with grief, I was convinced of it. That was why I let him kill Manazzoryn for her--and why I brought him back to her, when I had her image safely hidden away."

Sharuman paused momentarily, as if overcome by a sudden flood of emotion, but he recovered his voice soon enough. "I brought him back...after all, I owed him something...but I didn't know...I couldn't imagine...until he told me that he had been to see his son. *His* son! I had intended him to kill Viragan, too...but after that, I knew that I would have to do it myself. I'm glad I did...except, of course, that I didn't. *She* did. She was entitled to curse him, after all. It was her vengeance. I *can* trust you, Giraiazal, can I not? You did see what really happened, didn't you? You saw Queen Calia strike her murderer dead, and then consent to the disintegration of her coral image, so that her soul might return to the world beyond the world."

"Yes," said Giraiazal. "I know what I saw. You can depend on me to tell the truth." He knew as he said it, though, that the relationship was not reciprocal. Like Viragan before him, Sharuman could trust Giraiazal--but Giraiazal would never be able to trust Sharuman.

"I shall tell the council what you have just told me," Sharuman assured him. "You had best go to Zintrah, if you are well enough--I fear that she is falling ill, and I would not like to think of poor Hatarus being left alone in the world. He is the king, after all."

Giraiazal put on a pair of boots, leaving his blood-stained slippers where Sharuman had set them down. As he descended the stair he carefully avoided stepping on the red footprints that led to his door. As he went through the corridors to Zintrah's room he found a second set of footprints, but servants were already busy scrubbing them away. The sentries in the corridors were all wide awake, and he passed several who were in the process of answering questions put by their officers. Every one of them was protesting loudly that he had never been asleep, even though the discovery of Viragan's decapitated body, surrounded by the smithereens of the coral bride, had already given the lie to any such assertion. The soldiers and the servants looked around as Giraiazal passed by, but he could not read the expressions on their faces.

Zintrah was in the grip of a high fever, continually racked with terrible spasms. Giraiazal sent one of her ladies-in-waiting to find Burrel and Mergin, so that they could make up a potion according to his instruction. By the time they arrived, his throat had become very hoarse, and he felt very ill himself, but he was able to whisper his instructions. When the potion was delivered, he divided it in two, giving half to Viragan's daughter and drinking the rest himself.

Although Giraiazal's fever was not as fierce as Zintrah's, nor his fits as severe, it was obvious even to the servants that the two of them had been seized by the same affliction, and when the symptoms made further progress the disease was recognised as the one which had caused so much suffering to Queen Calia. Their skin grew hard over the entire extent of their bodies, and their flesh became gradually vitreous. They were in agony, but neither had sufficient power of voice to scream; they could only whisper. Their eyes stood out from their heads as they strove to give vent to their anguish.

Giraiazal was carried back to his own apartment, and immediately set Burrel and Mergin to the work of brewing more potions. He drank their concoctions down as fast as they could produce them, but he was never convinced that they had followed his recipes correctly. Burrel told him that Sharuman had sent Zintrah the amulet that Queen Calia had worn during the worst phases of her illness, but that it seemed to have lost its virtue. Burrel also told him that Zintrah had commanded her servants to fetch the phial of mandrake pollen that the magician had given her for a wedding present. As soon as it was given to her she had opened it and breathed the contents in. Her pain had abated, although not immediately, and she had begun to recover her strength--for which she sent him her profuse thanks. Giraiazal envied Zintrah this relief, and cursed himself roundly for not having kept the mandrake pollen for his own use--but he quickly repented of this bitterness, reminding himself that a physician's first duty was to his patients, and that the ethics of his calling demanded altruism in matters of attitude as well as conduct.

For three long days Giraiazal conserved the dutiful hope that he might have succeeded in saving Zintrah as he had succeeded in saving Calia, even if he had sacrificed himself in so doing, but the further news his servants brought him was bad. At the very moment when Zintrah had become convinced that Giraiazal's magic had saved her from the evil that had threatened to devour her--to the extent that she was ready to come to see him, so that she might serve as his nurse exactly as she had once served as Calia's--she suffered a relapse. Thereafter, she grew steadily worse again while the magician's condition improved a little.

This abrupt reversal of fortune threw Zintrah in such utter despair that she was moved to send a letter to the magician. Had she been able to write it herself its contents might have remained secret, but because she had to dictate it to a scribe they were common knowledge throughout the palace before the day was out.

We are being punished, Zintrah informed the magician. *The coral witch has condemned us to death for what we did.* Even as she was lying at death's threshold, Zintrah had diplomacy enough not to spell out exactly what she meant by "what we did", but the effect of this delicacy was worse than anything she might have specified, because it left speculation to run riot.

Giraiazal was careful to dictate his own reply instead of writing it himself, although it would have had to be read aloud to its recipient in any case. *We are not deserving of any punishment,* Giraiazal wrote in reply. *We have been innocent bystanders throughout this unhappy course of events. Everything that you and I have done, we have done believing that it was for the best--or, at least, that it would do no harm. There is no justice in the afflictions that Damozel Fate has inflicted upon us, and you must not believe that there is. You deserve to live, and you need to live, for the sake of your child. I have given you the benefit of such magic as I have; now you must summon up the last of your strength. You are a queen now; you have the power of command.*

Zintrah sent her sincere thanks by way of reply, and praised the magician for his loyalty and his honesty, but she had not the strength of mind to stop at that, and caused Giraiazal to lament that he had not given Manazzoryn's wedding-present to Zintrah and kept hers for himself. *You have done everything you could,* Zintrah instructed her scribe to write, *but I am my father's daughter, as I always was. His sins are mine now. I am heir to his destiny. All I need now is medicine to dull my pain while I die.*

Giraiazal knew that if his apprentices gave Zintrah as much medicine as she desired, the opiates themselves would kill her--but in the face of her continued distress he could not order them to desist. Burrel assured him that she did not suffer overmuch during the three further days that she lingered.

Giraiazal was so dispirited by now that did not expect to survive for very long after Zintrah died--but despair did not have the same effect on him as it had had on Viragan's daughter. His disease continued to harass his flesh and mind alike, but he grew no weaker. His skin erupted in boils, and his belly swelled up with cysts, and he wept black blood, but he did not die.

When opiates failed to kill him, as they had failed to relieve his agony--perhaps because his body had become inured to their effects by long and generous exposure--Giraiazal lamented yet again that he had not contrived to obtain a much greater supply of the mandrake pollen he had given Zintrah, and cursed himself again for that failure. He wished fervently that in the absence of any such relief he might simply cut his

Brian Stableford

own throat, but he found when he made the attempt that he could not do that either--and when he begged Burrel to do it for him, Burrel steadfastly refused to make himself a murderer.

"The world will end soon enough, master," the boy said, disproving yet again the dubious axiom that there is wisdom in innocence.

Giraiazal was generous enough to curse himself rather than his servant for this failure, although he might have acted differently had he still had the slightest confidence in his ability to make his curses work. Perhaps, even at the end, he underestimated himself. The magician's body became a battleground; first it was tattered and torn, and then it was seared and scorched--but the battle was too evenly balanced to be won, and its forces were dispirited, as if by bitter doubt born of malicious rumour.

Giraiazal often wished that he had sufficient power of fantasy to escape into delirium, but he had ever been a scholarly man, excessively determined to know and live within the truth. He remained conscious of his suffering and conscious of its source--and he cursed himself again and again, thinking all the while that his curses were impotent, for the unwise choice that had appointed Damozel Fate his fickle and faithless mistress.

When his fevers finally abated, Giraiazal was able to take enough nourishment to restore his strength by slow degrees--but the restoration of his senses was only partial. He found, to his horror, that he was no longer completely in control of his voice or his limbs. When he opened his mouth to speak, gibberish sometimes poured forth instead of the words he intended to pronounce, and when he attempted to exert his authority upon the flow, its incoherence was as likely to increase as to decrease. Worse still, his arms and feet began to strike out of their own accord, arbitrarily and violently.

The magician's newly-appointed apprentices, at a loss to know what to do with him, informed Prince Sharuman and Prince Akabar that he had become violently mad, and could no longer be trusted not to injure those who toiled to help him. Prince Sharuman kindly sent his own recently-appointed Grand Vizier, the former Captain Cardelier, to examine the magician and to report what ought to be done with him.

Cardelier arrived with two soldiers, who were instructed to bind the magician to his bed in order to make sure that his convulsions could do no harm, but then he sent the soldiers away, and Giraiazal's apprentices with them.

"I know that you cannot talk sense, old friend," Cardelier said, "but I hope that you can still let me know that you understand me. Can you blink your eyes twice to signal that you can?"

Giraiazal made every effort to contradict the assertion that he could not talk sense, but his voice was in a rebellious mood. Eventually, he gave up the struggle and contrived, though not without difficulty, to blink his eyes twice.

312

"Good," Cardelier said. "You know, I think, that I always liked you, and once tried to help you when I thought you might be in danger. You may, therefore, be assured that I have not the slightest wish to do you harm. Were I still a pirate captain, I would make every effort to spare you any further distress--but I am a Grand Vizier now, and although I do not pretend to be a diviner or a physician, I am an honest man trapped in a dishonest profession.

"It is my sad duty to inform you, old friend, that you have become something of a liability to the new administration of our proud and tiny nation. This is not because you have gone mad, of course, or because you strike out helplessly against your faithful servants when they try to feed you. It is an accident of circumstance entirely unrelated to your own misfortunes. I shall not bore you with matters of political detail, and I am sure you understand the broader outlines of our situation--continued food shortages, endemic disease, quarrels generated by grudges formed during the civil war, and so on. The simple fact is, old friend, that it would be convenient if we could find a scapegoat who could bear some of the burden of these misfortunes on our behalf, and you would have been convenient even if the late queen mother had not been so obliging as to provide written evidence of your involvement with the demonic depredations of the coral bride. I know that you worked against her as best you could, but the fact that your anathema did not take effect until she had murdered Prince Viragan and spread the plague throughout the city is now interpreted by the common folk as clear evidence of your complicity in her vile work. If Urbishek were still alive we would be only too happy to burn him, but that option expired some time ago.

"I want you to know that I really do feel bad about this. So does my master Prince Sharuman, who was very grateful to you for the honest account you gave of his predecessor's sad but timely demise. If it is any comfort to you, the shards of the statue that were scattered around the headless body and steeped in Prince Viragan's arterial blood are fetching phenomenal prices in all the marketplaces of Ambriocyatha--five or ten times as much as they would obtain if they did not have such a wonderful story attached to them. You really have done a great deal of good for the kingdom of Scleracina, and its people are grateful for the whim of the late Emperor of Yura that brought you--and me, of course--to their humble shore. I wish that there were some other way that you could continue your good work, but necessity is a hard taskmaster, and you will be far more useful now as a condemned traitor than a mere disease-ridden madman.

"There is, however, some good news to ameliorate the bad, which I have carefully saved for the last so as not to have to leave you on a sour note. Justice requires that sorcerers be burnt alive in the plaza, but Prince Sharuman and Prince Akabar are agreed that in your particular case--and given that they have a reputation for generosity to maintain--it would not be inappropriate to show mercy. Prince Sharuman has therefore decreed

313

that a narrow cage of iron should be built to confine you, to whose bars your wrists and ankles are to be bound in order to prevent your convulsions from causing you undue harm. The cage is to be hung from the arm of a mainmast bedded in the stones of the plaza, which will be lowered twice between midnight and noon and twice between noon and midnight so that you may be fed and watered.

"Your new abode will not be a comfortable one, especially in the full glare of noon, but the long nights will give you abundant opportunity to study the stars and make your mental calculations regarding the exact day on which the world will end, and any other matters that happen to catch your fancy. As a scholar, you will doubtless find your captivity less onerous than a common man would. I will do my very best to ensure that you are well fed, but I fear that I cannot provide you with any kind of companionship, because it would reflect badly on me were I to be seen talking to a condemned sorcerer. I'm a foreigner here, you see, and I have to be careful, as I'm sure you understand. If you could possibly contrive to blink your eyes twice more to signify that you have understood me, I would be very grateful to you, for I'm a busy man and would not like to think that I had been wasting my time."

Had he been able to do so, Giraiazal would have maintained a very steady stare, but he lacked the necessary self-control. Almost by reflex, he blinked--and then, without undue delay, blinked again.

The Grand Vizier smiled. "I knew you would understand," he said. "I am glad that you accept our gift in the spirit in which it is offered.

All the revelations of all the prophets of the past--no matter whether those prophets were true or false, their revelations accurate or mistaken--were inscribed in a record whose title was *Futurity.* These, and these alone, are the Revelations of the Last Prophet, who has nothing left to him but truth, and no possibility of being mistaken; they are inscribed in a record whose title is *Futility.* I have no need to regret that; I should, instead, be proud of it--and I am.

There is nothing more to add to this particular argument but detail and decoration, although I have a great deal yet to say about other matters--including, of course, my own purpose in compiling these secret explanations of the way of the world.

The Revelations of Suomynona, the Last Prophet

Giraiazal was placed within his cage before nightfall, and it was hoisted up to its appointed position, above the crowds that passed ceaselessly back and forth through the plaza in front of the palace gates,

Although he fully remained conscious of his awful plight, Giraiazal's mind became, for a while, a mere passenger in a body that would not have obeyed him if his limbs had not been so carefully immobilized. The harder he tried to exert his will upon them, the more unruly his formerly-private bodily functions became. Fortunately, his apprentices, untrained and unpractised as they were, were able to prepare potions that gave him a little relief from the worst effects of his imprisonment, and Cardelier fulfilled his promise to make sure that the magician was well fed. With this assistance, and the fresh air to which he was now constantly exposed, his condition began to improve by slow degrees.

Brian Stableford

Giraiazal understood--and would have understood even if Cardelier had not taken the trouble to tell him--that Prince Sharuman and Prince Akabar did not think of him as an enemy, and bore him no ill-will. The two pirates were as honest and good-hearted as any two pirates were likely to be, having been educated by men like Orlu and Viragan. They knew that the former Grand Vizier had done what he could to save Queen Calia from the effects of the spider bite, to save King Lysariel from the grip of his madness, and to save the realm from all the misfortunes that had afflicted it. Indeed, when Sharuman came out of the palace--as he sometimes did--to stare up at Giraiazal imprisoned in his cage, while playing absent-mindedly with his double-headed battle-axe, the magician sometimes believed that he could detect clear signs of honest regret that such a good source of prophetic skill and practical advice was going to waste.

It was possible, Giraiazal thought, that the real reason why the recently-elevated Prince Regent had ordered that everything possible was to be done to keep him alive was not to prolong his misery, but to keep him in reserve, in case circumstances might one day permit his release and rehabilitation. Giraiazal could appreciate the logic of such a policy, although he had to admit, when his insanity abated sufficiently to allow him that much presence of mind, that the eventuality could not be considered likely. He did wonder occasionally, when he was capable of wondering, whether Sharuman might have poisoned him because he was in possession of a secret that the regent wanted to keep, but that did not seem likely either. It would not have mattered in the least whether he had trumpeted it abroad that it was Sharuman, not the coral bride, who had beheaded Viragan, because no one would have believed him. The people of Scleracina were ignorant and foolish, but one thing they were wise enough to know for sure was that King Lysariel's coral bride had been animated by the spirit of his dead queen, and had entered into an unholy contract with the exiled Yuran sorcerer Giraiazal to curse the island with many misfortunes.

As his recovery continued Giraiazal was able to reassure himself with increasing frequency that he was utterly undeserving of his condition. He was able to remind himself that he had always done his best to make the best possible use of his skills and gifts, no matter what anyone might think. Alas, he obtained no solace from the relative clarity of his conscience. He knew, after all, that the world had done nothing to deserve its senescence and helplessness, but that it was doomed regardless--and that he, as a trivial parasite upon the world's bounty, was hardly in a position to expect a kinder destiny.

How much better things must have been when the Earth was in its prime, he thought, on one occasion when he found himself firmly in the grip of stubborn reason. *How happy magicians, prophets and their clients must have been in the days when the future seemed endless, when justice*

316

had scope to work, when intelligence could be confident that its best-laid schemes might extend successfully for thousands of lifetimes! What virtues must men have owned in ages when virtue could bear rewards! What joy must have swelled in human hearts as the knowledge took hold that every good deed might bear fruit in perpetuity, while every evil circumstance was reparable! But how can I complain, when I know well enough that one thing Damozel Fate could never leave to choice is the matter of birth. Yes, I would have chosen to be born a million or a thousand million years ago, and so would every man who has the misfortune still to be alive; that is exactly why we are refused the opportunity. Like every other man who has ever walked the surface of the planet, I must make the most of what I have, and if I have had less than the meanest creature of the better humankinds, still I have had more than the meanest of the worst. If I cannot be saved from the ignominy in which I find myself, then I must find what compensation I can in the hope that I might live to see the sun's death with my own mad eyes.

When he recovered the ability to speak clearly again--although it was never more than occasional--Giraiazal was tempted to shout at the crowds that passed below him, protesting his innocence of the charges laid against him and issuing charges of his own against Prince Sharuman. He set that temptation aside, though, not because he was afraid of being taken out of his cage and burnt for slander, but because it would have been undignified. He decided that he would rather keep silent than give the world the benefit of his recovered coherency, although he continued to mumble incoherently when his control lapsed, as it frequently did.

During his intervals of lucidity, Giraiazal made every effort to take advantage of the opportunities pointed out to him by his old friend Captain Cardelier, to make observations of the stars and to continue his work as an astrologer. Without clients, he could not be a practising astrologer, but he could still be a theoretician and a philosopher, and he finally began to take an interest in the fundamental issues about which the astrologers of Yura had disputed so fiercely. He was able to devote a great deal of time and thought, not merely to the corresponding roles of the white star, its red companions and the Motile Entities in reflecting human designs and desires, but also to the contentious matter of whether that influence ought to be reckoned coincidental or teleological.

Eventually, Giraiazal came to believe that he had solved this ages-old conundrum, and took some satisfaction from the thought that his unjust imprisonment had deprived the world of that crucial insight into its own nature. He could of course, have communicated his discovery to Burrel or Mergin when they came to feed him, or even to Prince Sharuman, when the regent took time out from the responsibilities of his office to stroll along the waterfront, but he maintained his policy of keeping silent whenever he had sufficient control of himself to speak clearly. He told himself that Burrel, for all the flair he was showing as an apprentice herbasacralist, had not the breadth of mind to become an eclectic magician. As for Sharuman...well, he was always so utterly lost in thought when he walked by himself that it did not require a morpheomorphist of genius to deduce that he was, at heart, a dreamer: a man who preferred illusion to reality; a connoisseur of remorse and regret. A man like that, Giraiazal decided, was even less fitted to receive a vital truth than a jumped-up kitchen servant who fancied himself a magician.

Giraiazal lived thus, in his high-set and awkwardly narrow cage, for hundreds of days. He was as carefully tended as circumstances would permit by his dutiful apprentices--who soon grew used to calling themselves magicians, and representing themselves as magicians, although they never had more than an elementary understanding of the healing properties of common plants.

As they gained in cunning, though, Burrel and Mergin began to spread the rumour that Giraiazal the Caged was actually an oracle of sorts, within whose seemingly nonsensical babbling great truths and prophecies were contained. The meaning of these pronouncements, they insisted, could be discerned--albeit dimly--by those who had the knack of it.

Eventually, the ingenious apprentices began to boast that there was not another oracle like the caged magician in the entire world, and never would be. Although their reputation as diviners grew by virtue of this invention, Giraiazal's heirs were not particularly grateful to their erstwhile master, and as their own sense of self-importance grew they began to treat him with increasing contempt and cruelty.

Giraiazal forgave them readily enough for this neglect, judging that they would have done more to please him if they had only been confident that they would be rewarded in consequence. Sometimes, even though they had no idea that he was in any condition to profit by it, they still spoke to him lucidly and at length, telling him their hopes and fears as well as bringing him all the latest palace gossip. The fact that they did so with a certain malice and mockery in their tone did not detract overmuch from the value of the information.

So seemingly successful was Giraiazal the Caged as an oracle, in spite of all the difficulties attendant upon his consultation, that the boy king Hatarus came unscathed through all the conspiracies and plots that surrounded his throne while various would-be merchant princes vied for the privilege of displacing Sharuman and Akabar. Sharuman and Akabar thrived too, and when Akabar was, eventually, poisoned by an unknown enemy, Sharuman continued his heroic work alone...and more days passed, in tens and hundreds, while Giraizal and the world waited, more or less patiently, for extinction.

By the time that King Hatarus was no longer content to be called a boy, preferring instead to style himself Hatarus the Great, Emperor of the Scleracinian Reach, Prince Sharuman was also dead, struck down by yet another plague. Cardelier had been another victim of the same epidemic; his position as Grand Vizier had been taken by the magician Burrel, even though Burrel had been suspected of practising sorcery ever since his former mistress, Mergin, had been burned in the plaza as a witch. The babbling of Giraiazal the Oracle had faded to a mere whisper by then, and its reputation as a wellspring of prophecy had begun to decline, but Hatarus continued to pay for the oracle's keep regardless, on the grounds that no emperor could sensibly count himself great unless he had a conspicuous fount of prophecy at his beck and call.

Had he only had proper possession of his facial muscles and his common sense, the ancient Giraiazal might have dared to laugh at the thought of a king who was sufficiently vainglorious to count himself a great emperor, even though he had nothing over which to rule but a small, desolate and plague-ridden island whose population was numbered in the thousands, and nothing to pass on to his descendants but the certainty that their realm and their world were already lost and damned. Even as he was, the patient oracle sometimes imagined that he could hear the distant laughter of his dainty mistress, Damozel Fate--who would doubtless continue to laugh, he presumed, when the treacherous sun had swallowed up the last relics of the ultimate humankind.

Brian Stableford

Printed in the United Kingdom
by Lightning Source UK Ltd.
104011UKS00002B/46-51